T0283160

recommended for all library collections. This is epic fantasy adventure at its best."

—Booklist (starred review)

"Fast and fun and filled with crazy magic. I can't wait to see what Christopher Buehlman does next."

—Brent Weeks, New York Times bestselling author of the
Lightbringer series

"Chock-full of wry wit, foul language, and characters who arrive on the page with savage, sordid pasts hot on their heels. Often humorous, occasionally horrifying, and sometimes incredibly poignant, I love every single page of this book. Every sentence, even. It's that good."

—Nicholas Eames, author of Kings of the Wyld

"Packed full of magic, mayhem, and mischief, Buehlman's world and characters are artfully rendered."

—Publishers Weekly

"Equal parts fairy tale, D&D adventure, and acid trip. Buehlman has successfully blended the essences of these elements into something at once familiar and fresh. I look forward to returning to this evocative and f*cked-up world!"

—Jonathan French, author of The Grey Bastards

"The Blacktongue Thief is a master class in voice and thoughtful world design, with a wonderful cast and a protagonist who grabs you instantly. Fans of Lynch's The Lies of Locke Lamora will love this one."

—Django Wexler, author of The Thousand Names

"The Blacktongue Thief is the printed version of a song a bard would perform in a rustic tavern long ago. Yes, it has the rhythm of music deep in its bones . . . but what really makes it feel like bard song is its way of continuously drawing you back in by continually upping the peril the hero finds himself in, so that you buy the singer another beer in order to find out what happens next. When it looks like the audience might wander off, the bard tosses in a kraken, giant, or brawl to pull the crowd back in."

—*Locus*

"Dark, gritty, lightning-fast, intelligent, irreverent . . . I loved it."
—Anna Smith Spark, author of *The Court of Broken Knives*

"Masterfully woven, joyfully mischievous, but also tragic and so heartfelt. Fans of Nicholas Eames and Joe Abercrombie will love *The Blacktongue Thief.*"
—Brian Naslund, author of *Blood of an Exile*

"Those with longer memories might also be reminded of the great Jack Vance, with his unique blend of invention and humor: a very welcome revival."
—*The Wall Street Journal*

"Buehlman's prose floats nimbly from grisly to lyrical and back again, evoking a damaged world that's by turns bleak and starkly beautiful. A fantastical road trip with a hard-boiled sensibility, complete with shape-shifting assassins, murderous kraken, and some delightfully gruesome magic."
—A. K. Larkwood, author of *The Unspoken Name*

"Nobody combines the lyrical and visceral quite like Christopher Buehlman. *The Blacktongue Thief* is fantasy of distinction—in its wit, its hard magic, its chiseled detail. Prepare to be transported."
—Andrew Pyper, author of *The Demonologist* and *The Homecoming*

"Simply put, Buehlman's latest novel is a raucous laugh followed by a punch in the gut—it's brilliantly wild and full of heart. If you're looking for an entertaining fantasy tale that slyly delves into deeper topics, try this one."

—*The Nerd Daily*

"Instantly immersive, with wit as sharp as a thief's blade and the most frightening take on goblins I've ever read."

—David Dalglish, author of the Shadowdance series

"*The Blacktongue Thief* is fated to steal a lot of readers' hearts with its charm, humor, intensity, and unrelenting fun."

—*Novel Notions*

Also by Christopher Buehlman

The Blacktongue Thief

Those Across the River
Between Two Fires
The Necromancer's House
The Lesser Dead
The Suicide Motor Club

THE
Daughters' War

Christopher Buehlman

TOR

TOR PUBLISHING GROUP

NEW YORK

THE DAUGHTERS' WAR

Maps by Tim Paul

A Tor Book
Published by Tom Doherty Associates / Tor Publishing Group
120 Broadway
New York, NY 10271

www.torpublishinggroup.com

Tor® is a registered trademark of Macmillan Publishing Group, LLC.

ISBN 978-1-250-88767-2 (hardcover)
ISBN 978-1-250-88768-9 (ebook)

Our books may be purchased in bulk for promotional, educational, or business use. Please contact your local bookseller or the Macmillan Corporate and Premium Sales Department at 1–800-221-7945, extension 5442, or by email at MacmillanSpecialMarkets@macmillan.com.

First Edition: 2024

Printed in the United States of America

0 9 8 7 6 5 4 3 2 1

For
Elizabeth
the best goddaughterrr ever

———— • ————

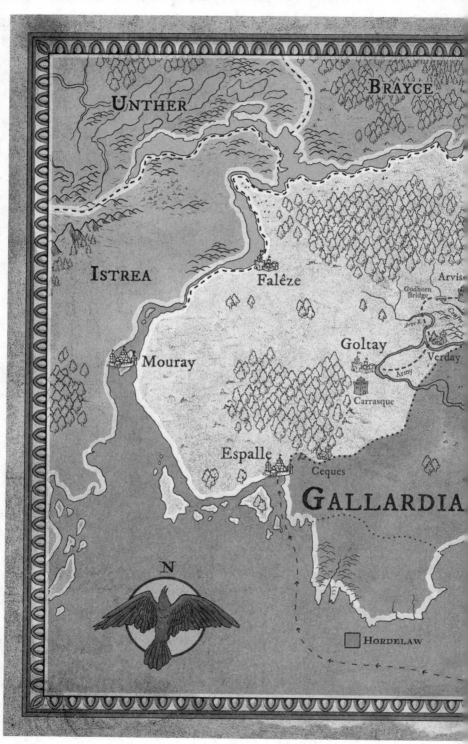

ISPANTHIA

Cestia

Cassene Sea

Liróç

Trepair

Gaspe

Durain

Carfour

Aperain

Cheraune

Zeray

Gallōt

Orfay

Thediers Warborder

Sabouille

Western Army of Ispanthia's path

Hot Sea

Map by Tim Paul

BOOK

1

—— · ——

Espalle

1

I saw my first goblin the same day I saw my first shipwreck.

I was under sail, on my way to war.

On my way to fall in love with death, and with a queen.

On my way to lose all of my friends, and two of my brothers.

I would see a great city fall in blood and fire, betrayed by a false god.

Later, I would be commanded to die on a high stone bridge, but I would fail in this.

The rest of the First Lanza of His Majesty's Corvid Knights would not fail.

This is not a happy story, but it is a true one.

I have no time for lies, or for liars.

The name of the ship I sailed on was the *Rain Queen's Dagger*, and it was a troopmule, packed with goblin-meat, which meant new soldiers like me. It leaked and rolled about during storms, and there was a smell you could not help but wrinkle your nose at. I tried never to wrinkle my nose because this was a haughty way to look, and it reminded me of my father's first wife, Imelda, who is not my mother.

There had been a battle.

The sea was rough and littered with masts and beams and with sailcloth. Here and there firejelly burned below the waves as though small suns tried to shine in the deep. Here and there the body of a man or a dam, or clumps of them, or goblins, floated.

I had seen goblins dead before, we all had. They do not rot, they just shrink and dry and harden. Flies want nothing to do with them, and only birds with great hunger will peck at them. Sharks will eat them, of course, but a shark will eat a wooden oar, I have seen this. Because they do not rot, everyone was bringing home dead goblins from the last two wars. They were popular exhibits in circuses. We have used many dead goblins in training, especially to make the war corvids hate them.

And they hate them much.

But on this day, I saw my first one living.

It clung to an island of wreckage that was sinking.

One thing I can say for goblins, they look as awful as they are. They look like they want to eat the meat from your thighs, and they do. Kynd are not always so easy to read—many of us hide cruel natures behind fair faces, or have our kindnesses overlooked because our flesh is twisted.

Goblins are honest killers.

And they are fucked-ugly.

This one looked to be perhaps four feet tall, on the larger side for them; it was a sailor, so it wore a simple hemp jerkin and leggings of kyndwool, or human hair, from the manfarms. I did not know what any of that was at the time. Its tough flesh was pink and gray, and this one was too far away for me to see its teeth, though I knew these were triangular and sharp enough for shaving; nor could I see its tongue, which was shelled. These articulated tongues help them make the buzzes and rasps that serve them for consonants.

This biter was badly injured and trapped, its larger arm caught between two sections of a ship's hull. And it was not alone. A kynd woman clung to the same wreckage that was grinding the biter's arm to meat. Her hair was bound in a mariner's braid, her leather pants puffed at the thighs after the naval fashion, and she came into sight as the wreckage slowly spun. She was injured, too, her linen shirt red at one side, but she did not care about her injury.

She was watching the goblin.

"Help her," a woman yelled at our ship's captain. The captain was a whitehair of sixty years with a pipe full of fastleaf and a shapeless red hat; he was like an old sailor from a joke. The dam who shouted had the look of a knight, finely dressed in fine armor, and, if she did not step away from the railing on this rough sea, would soon make a fine ornament on the seabed.

"Turn this fucked thing and save her!" she said again, pointing. The captain shook his head and puffed, letting smoke out with his words. "We cannot linger. If it was a biter juggernaut that wrecked this ship, as I have heard rumor there's one in these waters, we'll be the next ones they pound to kindling."

The knightly dam saw that the captain was right and said no more about it. Three archers near the ship's rear, however, began loosing arrows at the goblin. The first shafts missed, thanks to the distance, the motion of the troopmule, and also the spin of the wreckage the sailor and goblin clung to. At last, one arrow struck the biter in its hip, and it rasped like they do, not a sound for forgetting. The shipwrecked woman crawled over to it now. She nearly slipped off the wreckage but caught herself. It tried to bite at her but had neither speed nor strength. She held it down by its neck. She ripped the arrow from its hip and plunged this into its eye, then she stirred the arrow to be sure.

I gasped.

I knew the violence of the sword-yard well—the chipped tooth, the bloodied head, the broken finger. I was also familiar with the blood-business of a country estate—the hanging of pigs and deer, the putting down of sick livestock, the whipping of thieves, and the hanging of poachers and deserters. But this of the arrow and the eye, and the scrambling of the goblin's brain in its skull, was so sudden and brutal that I was struck with fright.

This was no academy sparring match I went to; this was no bout of footboxing.

We were sailing for a killing field.

The soldiers on our ship cheered, and those on the ship next to us. We were many troopmules, I do not know the number, but too few warships, and only small ones. We had lost our best escort, a royal dreadnought called the *Brawling Bear,* when it hit a goblin seatrap and had to put in for repairs.

Only with the cheering did the woman realize we were near. To her great credit, she did not beg to be saved. Instead, she waved at us, her hand dark with the creature's greenish blood.

The kynd on the ships cheered again, some saying "Gods bless you!" or "Mithrenor keep you." One of the few young men on these ships filled with women yelled "Marry me!"

"I will!" she yelled back, though weakly.

A third cheer rose up, greater than the first, because we could all see that she was a woman of spirit and a good Ispanthian.

And then the little island of ruined wood and rope bobbed up once and sank below the surface of the water with great finality, taking the sailor and the goblin down with it.

The cheer died.

Everyone went silent.

I had now seen a goblin and a human die in this war, and within moments of each other; I have since thought how apt this was.

Our two species are wed in death.

2

From time to time during this long voyage, I would scan the faces on the deck of the nearest troopmule, looking for my brother, Amiel, so we might wave at one another. I took comfort from this, and I think he took even more. He is no warrior, and this voyage to occupied Gallardia scared him even more than it scared the other green youths, prisoners, and oldsters he shipped with.

I saw him soon after the business with the goblin and the dam. He wore a good velvet doublet, dove gray and silver, and his ceremonial sword. He had failed the military proofs but, as a duke's son, was expected to serve in some way. He would be a supernumerary, which means something extra. He would be attached to a wizard, and he would do the tasks his temporary master required.

This was not just any wizard, some starter of small fires or weaver of illusions; one for making love philters, or tattoos that might or might not protect one from minor curses. Fulvir was perhaps the most powerful magicker in the Crownlands, and almost certainly the strongest one openly fighting for us in this war. The goblins would know him, and fear him, and want him dead. My little brother may not have been a fighter, but he was going to war all the same, and I hated it.

I looked more closely at Amiel.

What was he wearing in his hair?

White natal-day ribbons!

I suppose it was the fourth of Highgrass after all.

"Some fucked eighteenth birthday," I said.

"Whose?" the captain said. "Yours?"

"Well, certainly not yours," I said back to him, and he laughed in that mad way of fastleaf chewers.

I was not eighteen, though.

I had just turned twenty.

Amiel stood near the prow of his ship, the *Lady of Groves,* and he scribbled in a writing tablet he was having pains to keep dry in the ocean spray—the seas were still quite rough. I had seen him throwing up for the first days out from Ispanthia, and I had been seasick, too, but only the first day. It is best to be abovedecks for that kind of thing. Today, though, he seemed to be in good form. I worried about him, how could I not?

He was my Chichún.

Well, ours.

We all called him Chickpea because he was the only one of the Duke of Braga's four children to be born bald. The rest of us had come into the world with thin black hair that soon fell out and grew back thick. But he was mine. I remember struggling to carry him when he was two and I was only four, telling everyone that Chichún was my baby now.

That is the last time I remember wanting one.

Amiel was not just writing, though—he was shouting a poem at the dolphins jumping in the ship's wake. It was a good poem, about Mithrenor, the god of the sea. Amiel's long hair was blowing in the wind, making him look quite the romantic figure.

Whose badly fucked idea was it to put such a boy in a war?

And why with the wizard?

I knew that Fulvir, called Fulvir Lightningbinder, had helped to create the war corvids now in the hold below my feet—for this bone-mixing magic, he was also called Fulvir the Father of Abominations. He was rumored to be mad, though those of his country of Molrova all seemed half-mad, with their language of lies. Why must my Amiel be posted with such a man? He could have served our brother Pol, who was a general. It would not have been as good for him to go with our eldest brother, Migaéd, because Migaéd . . . had difficulties.

I had enlisted in an experimental unit, the First Lanza of His Majesty's Corvid Knights, and we were going to find out how

good our birds were at killing goblins. Though we did our best
to train it out of them, they had already shown they were good
at killing us. Obviously my birds had not yet murdered me, but
I had seen a dam killed by her raven—a quick death, it must be
said, but difficult to watch if you have not embraced the mysteries
of the Bride.

Now I saw a couple of speardams on the *Lady of Groves* laughing unkindly, watching Amiel at his poetry-shouting. They began
to swagger toward the prow of the ship. Clearly they intended
mischief, and it seemed to me that women of their age who had
not been mustered before must be prisoners.

Knowing how to whistle loudly can be useful, it is something
I taught myself to do as a girl. I whistled, and many on that ship
looked at me, the bravas with the spears included. I now rolled
up my left sleeve to show them the tattoo of the sword wrapped
in three flowers. We were perhaps too far away for them to see it
clearly, but they knew what it was. They might not have been able
to count the flowers, but they recognized the symbol and understood that I had spent some years studying Calar Bajat under a
high master of sword. I looked at the speardams in a way to show
them I would remember them. Amiel saw me now and waved. I
lowered my sleeve and waved back. He then blew me an extrav-
agant kiss, which I returned, though more discreetly. I am not
given to fabulous gestures, just what is needed.

The bravas found a better direction to walk in.

Later I would try to remember the poem he shouted at dolphins, but I could not.

"Who is the pup?" Inocenta asked.

You will hear much about Inocenta, she was my best friend, if
siblings do not count. Shorter than me, though I am not tall, but
stout, and strong of arm and leg. Her ginger hair was what most
remembered about her, it is an uncommon color in Ispanthia. I

should say, her hair was what you remembered if you never fought her at practice. If you had, you would remember that she moved her axe so fast you had to watch her shoulders to see where it might go, and still you would be wrong; and even if you put your shield in the right place, she'd hit it so hard she'd numb your shield arm to the collarbone. And then of course her next blows came, as fast as clapping. Still, I mostly beat her, though less often than I beat the others. That was in training, though. I would not have wanted to fight her for blood. There was something of the animal about Inocenta.

"That is my brother," I said.

"Amiel."

"Yes."

"Had to be."

"Why?"

"Because the other one is a general, and that boy is no more a general than my tits."

"I have three brothers. And you have no tits, you cut them off."

"I will cut yours off, too."

"Maybe if you were faster."

"I will remind you that you said that when you are picking up your tits. Is your other brother a general too?"

He was a sixt-general. This was not a general who commanded armies, but one who wore a fine suit of armor with no dents in it. This was a general of bordellos and sitting for portraits.

"Not a proper one."

"What is he, then?"

I considered what to say about Migaéd.

"A luckless gambler," I said.

Someone on a forward troopmule shouted, "Land, land!"

We were approaching the shores of Gallardia.

Inocenta looked at the horizon we sailed toward.

She said, "So are we all."

3

Before we went ashore, our birds would need feeding.

They became mean when hungry.

As I opened the hatch, and started down the steps into the gloom, the smell hit me. It was not just the smell of eighty-eight raven-like birds the size of stags, we were all used to that. It was not just the smell of their waste, which was made worse by the warmth and lack of fresh air. No, the worst of it was their food, rotting in barrels. After weeks at sea, the pieces of goats and sheep and dogs, of fruits and moldy hard biscuit, and of fish caught in the ship's nets, had ripened into a stew that devils of any hell would be ashamed to serve the damned. But these huge cousins of crows and rooks were carrion birds at heart, and they had stomachs like anvils. They preferred fresh meat, of course, and would puff their feathers at the smell of organ meat, which was the best for them—but they were hungry, and they wanted the foulness in the barrels.

And I would need to watch my hands while feeding them.

"*Nourid*," one said, in the flat, rough voice they use.

Food.

Now several others echoed this. One even said "Galva," and that was my handsome boy, Bellu, who I think was the strongest of all of them, though I am not unbiased. Dalgatha, my skinny girl, added "dom Braga, Galva dom Braga," because she was the smartest and could learn long names. I wondered sometimes if my father, Roderigu Elegius dom Braga, the duke of that rich province, crippled in the first goblin war, would be offended to hear our name come out of a mouth about to consume filth. Perhaps less offended than he would be to see his daughter shoveling it.

I wheeled the first barrel out, took up the shovel.

All the dams in my lanza had worked with these war corvids for nearly a year, bonding to our pairs, but also trading sometimes so the death of a raven knight would not mean her birds had to be put down. We took turns feeding so they knew each of us was at least useful. To our own birds, we were something like a parent, teacher, and comrade in arms all rolled together. Or so I liked to think that is how my pair, Bellu and Dalgatha, saw me.

Certainly Bellu.

"Galva is a bitch," said Richu, Inocenta's wicked male. She taught him that, I heard her do it. Though the sting is lessened because I have heard Richu say "Inocenta is a bitch" as well. Sometimes swords cut their owner. The word Richu says most is "Ow," not because he has been hurt, but because he has made humans say that so often he imitates it. He likes to cause small hurts. Of course, war corvids' sharp, hardened beaks can pierce chain mail if they try, or tear the muscle whole from your arm—grab, twist, and pull. Birds who attacked their mistresses in earnest were put down, they all knew it, and so the ones who had survived were the ones who did not truly hurt us. But Richu would pinch you through leather or chain, where he would bruise and hurt, but not maim. And you would say "Ow," and he would say it back, like the *jilnaedu* cruel idiot he was. The bird's full name was Censerichu, because he was given to fart evilly and much, like a censer-boy swinging incense smoke, though this incense could be sold at no market.

Soon it was sunset, and I stayed on deck instead of going below to drink and play Catch the Lady with the others of the lanza. Though I like this card game better than Towers, which makes kynd into devils. Much blood is spilled over Towers, I have seen this. Nobody dies playing Catch the Lady, which is not for money, at least not among people of quality.

Also on deck was our commander, Nouva.

"The sunset is beautiful," she said, inviting me to speak with her. We were not to start conversation about trivial matters with those of higher rank, but could speak freely if they did. She had extended me a courtesy. And what she said was right. The sky sat purple over a sea, finally calm, that lay like metal, or like mother-of-pearl. Clouds here and there. I am not a poet, like Amiel, but it is enough to say this sky deserved his words, not mine.

"Very beautiful," I agreed.

Nouva was beautiful, too, in her way. Not like a maiden in a flowered crown, not romantically, but in the way that the right tool is pleasing to the eye. Her dark brown skin and blue-black hair spoke of Ispanthia's mountains, where the blood of the old Keshite empire ran strong. She looked like a wooden thing, with her sharp cheekbones and noble blade of a nose. My family had some of these features, but our skin was fairer, diluted. Our eyes ran to common blue rather than the imperial golden brown.

Nouva had ten years more than I and had fought in the Threshers' War. A goblin had bitten her left thumb off, but she could still hold a shield, and command came easily to her. Her birds were Gannet and Whistle. Gannet was a bit too gentle for this work. Whistle was not gentle, and neither was Nouva. She had never married, or, to say it more properly, she had married the sword and shield. I wondered if I might follow such a path. I would rather this than to be packed off to some foreign prince's bed to wail in childbirth a half dozen times, and, if I survived that, to oversee cooks and stewards and to overlook infidelities, and poor manners, and to be loved less than a hunting dog.

Nouva Livias Monçera was the *lanzamachur,* or spearboss. Not that many of us used spears, but a lanza is also a unit. Forgive me if I tell you too much of military matters, I will try not to. But some points seem to require clarification. If I say a *lanza,* I can mean an actual spear, or a unit of fifty to one hundred soldiers. If I say a *daguera,* I can mean a dagger, or one of those in command under the lanzamachur. Inocenta was the first daguera, next in command after Nouva. I was second daguera, though I had no experience of combat. I had been offered lanzamachur owing to my birth, but if I were interested in rank, I would not have volunteered for this unit. It was right that one who has seen combat should command. I joined this terrible experiment, against my father's wishes, to forget I am the Duke of Braga's daughter, not to use it for advantage.

I wanted to put the skills I had learned to test, and to service.

I was going to Gallardia to kill goblins, because they had killed our horses.

Our family was rich in horses before the goblin-brewed plague we call the Stumbles, as if it were something funny, came and took all of them. Well, almost all of them.

"I have heard your brother Pol has been made third-in-command of the entire Western Army now that Jabat has been slain."

"I have a letter from him that says the same."

The battle of Orfay had been lost a month before, and lost badly. My brother knew more about it than most—he wrote to me about it. I received the letter just before I took ship. Here it is.

Dearest Galvicha,

How excited I am to see you again after so many years, though of course one could wish for happier circumstances. I know that our several duties will prevent us spending as much time together as we would like, but I will do all I can to make you welcome in my tent when our schedules allow. If there is any way I may be useful to you or our little Chickpea, please send word to me via any military runner you see, or with a member of the Runners Guild if that is all you can find, and reverse the charge.

Your flotilla is expected at the port town of Espalle, which we have recently recaptured. It was not in goblin hands long, but long enough, so brace yourself for what you might see there. You will see that it was a pretty town once, and still is in places, but Our Friends are a murderous scourge who ruin all they touch, Sath burn them all to ashes.

I have news.

Owing to the lamentable death of General Jabat, a very brave man who served with Father in the Knights' War, in the fine old days of cavalry, when we used to beat the biters to every battlefield and ride them under hoof, I have been jumped up from quarut-general to terce-general, with a like expansion of my responsibilities. This is not something I have desired, but there is a feeling on the part of the king and his Council of Pillars that younger blood and fresh ideas are needed. I feel neither young nor fresh with the weight of the defeat at Orfay upon me. I feel both guilt and relief that the forces under my command arrived too late, or I should be dead like Jabat and Prima-General dom Lubezan, first commander of the western armies. Lubezan is to be replaced by a terce-general who has won a series of victories in the east, a woman of merit rather than blood whom everyone calls the Pragmatist.

I hope she can turn things around here.

If I may be blunt, we are losing.

Orfay was the worst defeat since the Threshers' War.

I will step in here to say that the second goblin war, called the Threshers' War, sticks hard in my memory, though I was too young to see it.

It was mostly fought in Gallardia, as is this war, but of course it also spilled into Unther, Ispanthia, and other countries of the Crownlands, which you call Manreach. My father, being who he was, was always among the first to learn of our kynd warriors' defeats, and these were many.

I remember the yellow surcoats of the Runners Guild boys who came to the gatehouse of the estate when I was a girl. How they carried a message to my father, taking only a quick gulp of water before they ran to where he was. You can tell the urgency of a message by how the runners drink on a hot day, after a long run, and whether they stop to cool down and dry off.

These did not, and it was the first time I had seen that.

It was not the last.

I remember asking my Holtish governess, Nunu, about it all. The war was already on, we had already sent our first men, and even children knew this. But because the first war, called the Knights' War, had gone so well, everyone thought this one would, too. It was not yet called the Threshers' War, because we were not yet down to sending farmers with flails to fall like wheat.

Like many children, I had dreams about goblins.

Of course, I still do.

They are just more informed.

"Would you be afraid to meet a goblin, Nunu?" I asked that day of the first runners, early on.

"I shall never meet a goblin," my governess said, "and neither shall you."

"How do you know?"

"Because goblins do not come to Ispanthia. And especially not to Braga."

"What if they do?"

"In that case they will be making a terrible mistake, because your father will kill them."

"He cannot kill them, can he? He walks with two canes now because of goblins."

"He will send his men to kill them, then."

"Like other men are killing them in Gallardia?"

"Just so."

To return to the letter, here is what Pol says of Orfay:

First, our armies heard the sound of the carnyx, a strange horn they blow to cause fear in us. I have heard the sound from afar, and sometimes I hear it again in nightmares.

One wizard of theirs sent sigils aloft into the sky that sickened our soldiers to look upon. He could not work direct harm upon our armies, mailed and plated as they are in steel, which damps magic, but he worked far from the battle, and sent the sigil high. By the time word went round to look down, not up, fully a third of our heavy infantry was vomiting in their helms and barely strong enough to stand. Then they hit our lines with ghalls, frightful creatures of human stock they bred up underground for size and strength. Pale as codbellies and half-blind, eight feet tall and crazed with mycological brews—among these godsmilk, their wretched pleasure-drug, which yellows the whites of the eyes and enslaves the mind. Imagine these quarter-ton behemoths, oblivious to pain, armored heel to crown, swinging great mauls and two-handed swords neither you nor I could lift, let alone wield, crashing into our vanguard just as our lads and dams were heaving up their oats and found their legs made of grass. Once our lines were in tatters, in came their palisades, chariots pushed by war boars, rolling with their shin-high blades, ridden by biters shooting crossbows or gigging with spears. I hear you have been training to face these. We have some hope that your corvids might prove effective in flanking them, or leaping them.

Sath the All-Seeing knows we can use some advantage.

Another battle is coming. The great city of Goltay is threatened, and if it falls, the killing will be worse even than on the plains of Orfay. The Western Army will march to prevent its fall, or to take it back. This contest may well decide the course of the war, and whether Gallardia will be liberated, or Ispanthia enslaved beside it.

I will not shy from telling you I wish you had not come.

Your rank allows you certain privileges, the king knows the blood of the great houses must survive. I am quite sure that, as the duke's only marriageable daughter, a match

can be made, and a good one, even after the impression you
made on King Conmarr's boy when he came to court you
three summers ago.

To interrupt the letter once more, I will say that this Durwain, third son of King Conmarr of Holt, called on me at the High Sword Academy of Calar Bajat between lessons. He insisted, with my father's blessing, that I meet with him. He proposed a meal by the river nearby. I received him politely enough. My fellow students made much of his visit, of course, Holtish princes being something rare in Ispanthia. I enjoyed the musicians he brought along, and his conversation, at least at first. The quail was good. The apple cider was not bad, nor the apple brandy, though I prefer wine, and the cold in Holt kills all grapes but those too sour for pleasure. He told me my Holtish was excellent. I told him that if that were true, I had my Holtish governess, Nunu, to thank. I complimented his mint-green doublet, which was silk, and quite fine if one cares for such things. When he dismissed the musicians, I told him I should return to my dormitory. He insisted I remain, so I did, with reluctance. When he took advantage of my inexperience and attempted to lay hands on me, it was clear to me that he had spent more time studying seductions than grappling, and he had more ribbons than muscle. To his credit, I will say that the spot he chose by the river was very fine. I still have an image of him bent over its waters, drooling blood from his broken nose, next to a cracked cider bottle and a very pretty willow tree. I also remember cattails, and delphinium. I walked home unmarked except for a small cut on my knee from his tooth, which I later heard that he lost.

My father made apologies to the king of Holt, saying it was unfortunate that the prince had slipped and hurt himself—that he should have been warned how treacherous the bank of that river could be. King Conmarr replied that the boy needed to learn how to tell dry ground from slick, and to proceed, or not, according to terrain.

Durwain died near the beginning of this third war, killed in an ambush. Another thirty of his guard were cut down trying to save his body from being taken.

They were not successful.

To continue Pol's letter:

Little sister, this is the worst place I have ever been, and I tell you this not to scare you, because I think you do not scare easily; but to let you know honestly and without ornament what awaits you. The biters regard us as animals, and, when they take us, show us nothing of the small mercies kynd allow one another in war. They do not ransom us back to our families, they do not treat our wounds. You will hear no accounts of life in their prisons, for these are rather livestock stalls, and no one returns from them. The cities lost in the Threshers' War that were not destroyed are under Hordelaw, which is to say that they are left to govern themselves, but forbidden weapons and armor, even metal tools. These cities are required to tithe of their own populations, giving over one in nine to the manfarms, with preference to those who have not produced children. Also, at sexual maturity, every citizen receives the Hordelaw cut, and an outer tendon of the dominant thigh is severed. Kynd with this injury will heal enough to walk, and to work, and to farm, but they will never run swiftly or jump well. They will tire at marching, and have pains to keep their balance under duress. So, you see? Under Hordelaw, we are kept as docile as cattle, but left to feed ourselves, and to breed. Whatever towns fail to meet the biters' requirements are butchered at once.

There is much discussion in the high command about why the goblins are pushing so hard this time. Some think a disease of the seed has spread in the manfarms, and that the biters seek fresh bloodlines. Others say their seers have told the Imperatrix and her council of generals that the Horde's military advantages are temporary—that kynd will soon make some advancement in arms or magicks, and that Gallardia should be broken and occupied and Ispanthia bled dry while they still master us in the field.

I like this latter theory and hope it is so.

Of course, Ispanthia and the other Far Banners are fighting to keep the parts of Gallardia which are still free out of their grasp. Small pleasures may be found even in such a place, and I have found more than my share. This was a beautiful country, perhaps even more so than Ispanthia, if I may utter such heresy—but where the war has touched it, it is death, and ruin, and sickness, and among those who survive there lingers such a palpable despair that it might settle into one's joints and unravel one's resolve.

But that is what the gods are for, is it not?

To lift us when we are broken, and to stanch us when we bleed faith.

There is vital work to do, and, with Sath's light and warmth in our hearts, we might yet prevail and drive the Horde back at least to the borders settled by the last treaty, if not out of Gallardia entirely. Sath is a great enemy to goblins, his light burning at the edges of their darkness, sure to drive them away even as the sun, after a long night, takes back its due. Some say the Vaults of Mysteries kept by Sath's temples house pieces of the sun itself, burning in glory only the priests can stand to see. I heard a song about how Sath will one day decide we have suffered enough, and teach his priests to forge these pieces of sun into weapons of blinding light. Could this be what the goblin seers fear?

I do not know how much more Gallardia can suffer.

Perhaps it bears the heaviest burden because it honors so many other gods before Sath.

Perhaps this is why Ispanthia prevailed in the Knights' War, and why it suffered less in the Threshers'—we honor other gods, of course, especially in the country, but in civilized places, at least, such as our esteemed capital of Seveda, and in the rich lands of Braga overseen by our father, Sath sits at the head of the table.

I believe that, with the Bright One's help, we can win. We must. What else, retire to Ispanthia and wait for them to come home to us? They will, if we do not stop them here. They will try to cross the Blue Mountains before winter and put Ispanthian towns under Hordelaw, first in the north, and then everywhere.

I see the need to muster women, and the old, and those of gentler natures.

But I would rather fight unburdened by worry for you, and for Chichún.

Find me, little sister.

I will serve you as I can.

> *Yours in all respect,*
> *Pol dom Braga*

But I showed you the letter because Nouva, my commander, had asked me about my brother's promotion. Let us return to the deck of the *Rain Queen's Dagger* that last evening before we made landfall, during a sunset of particular beauty.

"I met him, you know," Nouva said, of Pol.

"Yes?"

"In Seveda. Very kind. Reminds me of Gannet."

I laughed at this, because I saw it, too. Nouva's corvid Gannet, like my older brother Pol, was large and strong, but not always quick enough to defend himself when others squabbled for advantage. Still, I thought, how could Pol do else but rise? He was so competent and strong. He was fair and truthful, and I thought surely such traits would be enough.

How little I knew of the world.

Nouva and I spoke for a time, as night birds cried, and as unknown things moved in the water, and until the sky had become a blue hardly brighter than the black sea. She retired below, with the hard, wild dams under her command, and left me to the wind and stars. There is no night sky like that at sea, though they say the same of the desert, and I had not seen a desert.

Here were the Eyes of Nerêne, two stars the color of amethyst peeking over the western horizon. They would rise high, summer being their season. Nerêne was the most popular of several goddesses whose province was love, so of course she was Gallard.

Gallardia was a country of art and food and sculpture. Every court worth its crowned heads had a Gallard chef, or portrait painter, or dancing master. No soil was so fertile or black, except perhaps in Unther. No wine was so good, except perhaps some of Ispanthia, which I honestly believe to be the best. But, again, I know that I might be biased. I like wines best that are too dark to see through, and so dry they almost burn to drink, and such qualities are the gift of drier, hotter, browner Ispanthia and its chalky soil.

Gallard wines are lighter, and sweeter, though a few in the south of Gallardia rival those of my country. Gallard wines, according to their songs, are made to be drunk from the bodies of one's lovers. Nerêne's temples are found in every worthy town. They do not have a native god of war, or of death, but borrowed theirs from us, and from Unther, and the Gunnish Islands.

Of course the goblins went to soft, pretty Gallardia.

And now we were coming, too.

4

We sailed into Espalle, a town of medium size with a calm, deep harbor. Its brightly painted houses and manors had been built up gentle hills that embraced the bay in the shape of a crescent. On both the east and west sides of town, the cliffs of Espalle stood white against the blue sky and darker sea. On Crab Island, to the east, the lighthouse still stood, though its lantern had been put out and would warn no more ships off the rocks known as the Widow's Teeth. These rocks stood on the other side of the eastern cliffs, visible to us though not the town proper. On the western cliffs, we saw the fortress I later learned was called the Drum, but this drum had been beaten hard; its north wall had collapsed, tunneled under by the sappers of the goblin Horde, its limestone charred from where its hoardings had been burned. Farther west, I saw the amphitheater, which dated back to Keshite times, and also strange, giant faces.

These faces had been directly carved into the cliffsides, their features simple and with overlarge eyes. These were the works of ancient tribes, I guessed, before the Kesh came north with roads for their elephants, and with math, and science, and perspective in art. A soldier of my lanza stood near, as though she knew I wondered about the figures. This was Alisenne, whose father had been a Gallard of the Runners Guild, and famed in his youth for winning races. I outranked Alisenne, so I said, "Do you know who they are?"

"The Fishers of Espalle. Old gods. They stare at the sea and charm fish into nets."

Seagulls and terns cried, wheeling in the sky over the cliffs.

"I suppose the biters had not been here long enough to clear the nests," Alisenne said. "Goblins hate birds. One of the only things they seem to fear."

She had some experience and had volunteered for this lanza. She was the best of us with a bow, and half Gallard besides, so she would be of use for both foraging and translating.

Inocenta smiled. She had a wicked smile.

"Yes. I shall be glad to introduce them to our children."

Belowdecks, several corvids cawed loudly, as if they knew we spoke of them.

We docked roughly, with much bumping against the pier.

Taking the birds ashore was difficult.

Once we marched down the ramp, we formed up in the Plaza of Anchors, in the shadow of gibbets where executed criminals swung. Also in the plaza, many injured were waiting transport home. We were bothered by all manner of beggars, whores, and even children trying to sell us charms made from goblin's teeth or woven from their colorless hair. Nouva handled and then broke the nose of a pennycock who kept getting in her way, and after this we were left alone. I still remember her wiping his makeup off her knuckles, which Inocenta found hilarious, and I wondered if he were covering some skin condition to have put it on so thick. Nouva smelled of his perfumes after, too, which also amused Inocenta greatly.

We walked on the sides of the corvid column and kept the great black birds in the middle, four abreast, though we had to break up awkwardly when we came to narrower streets.

Forty-eight of us, eighty-eight of them.

Most of us had two birds, but some had only one.

We had started at fifty and one hundred, but some birds had fallen sick, or needed to be put down—during our long training at Galimbur, one dam had been maimed and another killed, both by their corvids.

Of course, the people of the town, those who had come back from hiding, wanted to see the corvids. They were fine to look upon individually, but when they were formed up and moving in a column, the best word for them was *magnificent.* If I close my eyes I can still picture them with their tar-black feathers giving off blue highlights and their great curved beaks and the breastplates they had learned to tolerate—even Inocenta's Richu allowed her to strap him in. The breastplates shone that day in the strong sunlight. The spurs we had fixed to their heels shone as well, ten-inch blades they could kick an ox to ribbons with, I have seen this. One difference between these giant war corvids and the ordinary ravens our magickers raised them up from was in the way they walked. Crows and ravens are awkward on the ground, waddling like old men, or hopping. Some blood of the great running birds of Axa had been mixed into these corvids, so they did not waddle.

They strode.

As with goblins, they looked exactly like the killers they were.

Sometimes those who were ignorant of the corvids asked if we rode them. Even if it were possible, I do not think they would suffer this indignity. Their bones were too light for this, though they were also too heavy to fly. They could make great leaps, however, using their wings.

If a bigger corvid is hatched someday, I would not want to ride it.

They are not horses.

They are not dogs.

They are *corviscus,* and there is nothing else like them.

Nobody cheered as we walked by.

Many begged, but we had no food on our persons; it was all at the wagon, with the regular army, who had already passed.

This third war was starting its third year.

The Gallards had suffered in ways I could not then imagine. Everyone was used to the sight of soldiers coming home broken, burned, subtracted of legs and fingers, blinded, or mindwrecked by the biters' endless variety of poisons.

But I was not used to seeing maimed and hopeless children.

I was not used to hunger so extreme.

But hunger was not their only malady.

All the Espalleers seemed unwell in some way or other. They limped from the Hordelaw cut or they looked old, even the small boys and small girls, or their hair was thin from grief and illness.

I have only a little Gallardian, but, as Gallard and Spanth are cousin tongues, I understand more than I speak, so not all of what was said as we passed escaped me. I saw a little *gailu* with a large, skull-hugging pink scar where half his hair should have been, and thought *scalped.*

The half-scalped boy asked his mother why we had no banners.

"These are not for parades," she said of us, and she was right. I thought I heard some small hope in her voice, seeing the birds. I wondered how many times that coal had been lit, and put out. Espalle had a good port, had seen more than one army get off ships and march through town. And still it fell.

What good would less than one hundred corvids do, or half that number of dams, and most of us green as grass? The army seemed to wonder this, too. There were those who thought of our birds as a new weapon of great promise; and yet there were still enough men of earlier days in positions of command to scorn something so new, and in an all-female unit. Even among female officers, there were those of the city who doubted the magic that made these birds, and also those of the country who hated it as witchcraft.

But these of Gallardia were too desperate to care what laws of the gods or of nature had been broken to make these birds. And, seeing our *corviscus,* they could not question their power.

One far-too-skinny little girl stole her hand out of her mother's grasp and came toward Bellu, meaning to pet the corvid's beak. I held the tether hard, pulled Bellu's beak away, just as the mother picked the girl up, despite her protests. The little one said something like, "No, Mama, they are here to save us, they are our friends!"

Bellu *was* friendly, as corvids go, but the girl's pale arm was sized like the goblin limbs these birds had been taught to shear and mangle, and I could not say what was going through Bellu's mind as he turned his golden eye at the child, his eyelid blinking once, twice, again.

But he had not lunged after her, and that was enough.

"Good Bellu, my handsome boy."

Dalgatha tugged at her tether now.

"You too," I said. "Skinny is a good girl too."

Though it tasted like dirt in my mouth to call her Skinny after seeing the survivors of Espalle.

I kept an eye out for Amiel as I marched.

I hoped this magus he had been assigned to would be lenient with him, would let him come find me. Nobody had told me to keep him safe, but I had given myself this task. I had sworn it to Sath, and had bargained with him, telling him to take me rather than Amiel if one of us must die, and to let us die together if both must. But Sath is a silent god, at least to me, and I had no sign if the deal I proposed had been accepted. I would think of it, then look to the sky, hoping to see a hawk or falcon, which are his avatars. Once I thought I saw a large hawk, but it was a buzzard. I hoped that was chance, and not the sign. I hoped Sath did not know how scared I was to die, but of course he must have known. Perhaps that was why I had not seen the falcon assuring me I could protect my Chichún.

Espalle's buildings had suffered nearly as much as its people.

Goblins hate symmetry, so they wreck it where they can. If they can pull off the corner of a building without too much trouble,

they do so. Here and there, once-fine buildings sagged and gaped
where they had been damaged in this way. If a door stood exactly
in the center of a façade, goblins would make a door-sized hole
near it to destroy the balance. I had heard this, but now I saw it
with my eyes. Here was a pretty wooden arch with a notch cut
up high to spoil its lines. There was a plane tree felled to break
the circle of a round fountain. And everywhere, litter. The litter
of the strong, vined trellises that once covered the alleys. Broken
arrows, crossbow quarrels, broken ladders, dead livestock, dead
goblins. The dead of the town, though these were already being
cleared, or at least staged to be cleared.

It was in the courtyard of a once-elegant but now cornerless
and half-burned inn that I saw my brother.

Not the poet, Amiel.

Not the general, Pol.

I saw Migaéd dom Braga, holding a bottle of wine at half past
middlehour, squinting with a frown at a hand of cards.

He was playing Towers.

Migaéd was, if I am honest, a very handsome man, though in
the way that a person of experience will see through. His beauty
was like fine paint on a building shot with termites. You know
the sort. Always in debt, however much money he was born to,
and in this case it was a fabulous amount. Always abusing the
trust of some lover who anyone can see is too good for him. Your
dog will not like him, and dogs are to be listened to in these matters. I know, I speak ill of family against my own rule. But one
may speak truthfully of family to others who are also family, and
I have not much left.

You will have to do.

I did not yet know my eldest brother the way I would come to.

I still loved him at this time, and my heart gladdened at the
sight of him.

I waved, but he did not see me.

I noticed the banner of his regiment, which said *The Scarlet*

Company of Sword and Horse, the letters in gold, as was the figure of a horse rearing, and a sword. Not so different from the family crest of dom Braga, which is a crowned horse rearing over a skeleton. This unit was assembled by our father, just for Migaéd, and for the sons of lesser nobles than the illustrious duke. Never mind that there *were* no horses, or at least too few, and all of these were mares, and too old for service.

I now whistled that loud whistle I told you I have.

Next to Migaéd, whose armor was very fine, a fleshy man also in good armor and with his huge mustache obviously and dishonorably dyed, looked up from his cards at me, then widened his eyes at the sight of the birds. All of these wealthy, soft-looking men looked. The women serving them looked as well, and these dams were clearly Espalleers and probably whoring themselves. It is to be expected in such dark times, and they should not be blamed. Rather, it seems to me that these men might have given them silver for pity's sake rather than exploiting them, especially with their own deaths so near. With death, we were taught, would come the revelation of what the gods truly wanted from us. I doubt even the worst of them want us to make lamed widows and fresh orphans dirty their knees for coins.

Migaéd looked up now, sleepily, and I waved again as we marched by.

He squinted at me and got to his feet, though still leaning on one of the barrels that served them for tables.

"Galvicha?" he said, using my "small name" as both he and the second brother, Pol, would do, despite my twenty years.

"Yes!" I said. "I shall find you when I have liberty!"

"Wait," he said, while his eyes picked out Nouva at the head of our formation. "Lanzamachur, I am Sixt-General Migaéd dom Braga, and I would speak with my sister. Halt this unit."

"Halt," Nouva said, then clenched her teeth. Migaéd was not the first to abuse his honorary rank. Sixt-generals had irregular commands, usually of small importance, and they were almost always the less able children of powerful lords. Sixt-generals could order people about and had their own retinues. They dressed in fine clothes, and even received medals, usually unearned. This was a good way to keep the drunks, gamblers, and hotheads of great families from mischief without dishonoring their households. Everyone in the Western Army knew which son of dom Braga had iron in his blood, and it was not this one.

And yet, this one, too, had to be obeyed.

I could feel the eyes of my fellow soldiers on my neck like a second ration of the sun's heat. Migaéd strolled over to me, taking his time about it. He stopped ten paces short, wary of the birds. Bellu puffed his hood feathers in interest—perhaps he knew this smallish man who smelled of wine and whores was related to his mistress.

"Come to me, Daguera," he said, using my rank. Then he said, "Daguera dom Braga," and laughed for no reason, or perhaps because the rank was so much lower than the name.

Even while I felt shame to see Migaéd waste the time of my lanza and my commander, I became drunk with nostalgia when he came close and I smelled his blend of oils with its hint of musk and cedar. Suddenly I was four years old again and he had me up on his neck, playing my stallion. I was eight, just about to start my sword lessons, and he was on break from his training, shaking my hand mock-solemnly and telling me what a good soldier I would be. He brought me flowers from the field once, on Lammas Day, and called me Queen of the Harvest, to cheer me when I was in bed with a fever. Even then I knew the scratch of his carelessly shaven cheek against mine was unlike that of Pol, or Father, when the duke suffered a daughter's embrace. I could always smell drink on Migaéd's breath, but as a girl I did not know all the evils drink brought. I knew only that when he spoke to me he made me feel grown-up, and special, and worthy of being listened to.

These are not small things to any child.

"Sister," he said.

"Brother," I said, and offered a nod. When my eyes returned to him, they begged him to be brief.

"As you see, my men and I have found a jolly, shaded inn, well out of the heat, and a barrel or two of the Gallard grape. It has been so long since I have seen you! You look quite the fierce young dam-at-arms, don't you? Join us for a spot of lunch, and a round or two of Towers!"

I opened my mouth to speak, but no sound came out.

Nouva spoke.

"Sixt-General, with respect, the daguera is needed. We go to secure our quarters and settle our birds. She will have liberty this evening."

Migaéd did not like to be thwarted. No one does, but it is worth learning how to keep it from one's face. My brother's face showed contempt before he put a smile back on.

"Well, I shall hardly be standing upright by evening, shall I?" he said, giving his wine goblet a shake.

Grandfather's springwood shield slid from the stump against which Migaéd had leaned it and fell onto the ground, its steel boss in the shape of a blowing storm-man pressed into the dirt. I started at the sight of it. I had not seen it for many years, but it had been a friend of my early childhood, for it hung in our great hall. Though I got only a small glimpse of it now, I believe this glimpse was important, a sort of wink from the gods. The shield has a large part to play in this story, and will suffer the bite of spears, and quarrels, and bear a bloody handprint.

It has thunder in its wood and lightning in its metal.

It was made for Corlu dom Braga, my father's father, a man who it was said would break his back before his word. He had been loved in Braga for his honesty more than the king in Seveda for his gold and titles.

"Seriously, Lanzamachur, I can send a couple of lads along to do whatever Daguera dom Braguera—ha!—is required for . . ." And here he looked at Bellu and Dalgatha, who had both cocked their heads at him. ". . . unless it has to do with these beasts, and surely you have enough dams here to see to *them*."

I could see he was on the verge of making his request a formal command.

I said, too low for anyone but him to hear, "Please, brother."

His eyes met mine. They were comely eyes by their shape, but burdened with drink, the whites shot through with small red veins. His eyes searched mine for a moment, and he saw at last that I was in earnest.

"Sath's hot arsehole," he said, "I can see you dams are all business, and much to your credit. You have passed my test, sister Daga-laga-braga. Go now and serve the king, may he live a thousand years, and his mustache ten years more."

The fat man with the disgracefully dyed mustache laughed a loud *ha* at this. Clearly he wore his mustachios long, black, and worked into horns because that is how our sovereign, Kalith, wore them.

I mouthed *Thank you*, then said, "I will find you this evening, Sixt-General dom Braga."

"Do," he said, then seemed to forget where he was, then to remember. He smiled at me and staggered back to his game. Nouva ordered us forward, and I marched, touching Bellu just for the comfort of his feathers under my hand.

I knew that one dam of our lanza, Vega Charnat, was looking at me with resentment. It was how she looked at everything that was not a beer or a fight. I turned and found her eyes, small in her large slab of head. She had her helmet off, as most of us did, so I could see her flat boxer's ears, which had been hammered to gristle on the streets of Galimbur, Ispanthia's second-largest city after Seveda. Galimbur is a rough city, a fortress city full of soldiers and blacksmiths and leatherworkers, and all the best hand-fighters come from there.

Vega hated me for having two birds—one of hers had died.

She hated me for beating her at the sword.

She hated me for coming from wealth, and for having power-ful brothers.

She believed she could pound me to sleep with her big, hammy fists, if only she could find a gap between being punished for striking one who outranked her, and being challenged to a for-mal duel, where she knew I would kill her with my *spadín*.

Things had not yet reached that point, but I did not see how to avoid conflict with her. I wanted this not because I feared to be punched, though of course I did not wish to be.

I simply did not care.

It is tiring to deal with someone who has made an enemy of you when you do not think of them at all.

But, of course, this is often why they hate you.

5

We were quartered at Espalle's old horse market, which had many stalls for our birds. Even after so many years without horses, the town had not torn down the market with its many stables. To do so would have been to accept that horses were gone forever because the few remaining mares were too old to be bred, even if a living stallion could be found. Only mares who had been with foal when the equine plague struck survived, and not all of those.

Espalle's sentimental feeling was not uncommon; in every city in the Crownlands one still found stables, hitching posts, and watering troughs—though of course these troughs also served oxen, donkeys, and other beasts. I was not yet born when the Stumbles first struck, spreading down from the northern, Holtish town of Pigdenay. An animal stricken with the disease would begin to stagger and trip and lose balance. It was better to put the beast down then, because the end of the disease was painful, as its brain swelled in its skull and it went mad. The plague took some time to do its work. Horses that had been hidden away caught it years later, and some in the universities believe this is because it harbors in us, in kynd, though it does us no harm.

I have a memory that may be a dream, but I think it truly happened. I was a small child, perhaps four, and I saw three of my father's horses in a field at dusk. Two of them swayed on their feet, as if they listened to some music only they could hear. The third stood well away from them, frightened of them. The third horse was named Idala, or Star. She had been foaling when the illness came to Braga and so was proof against it. Her foal died. She was an ordinary horse, meant for riding rather than war, but by the simple fact of her survival she became a thing of great value.

Idala was a great friend to me when I was a girl, and I will speak more of her.

Once our birds were fed from their shrinking store of food, we settled them in their horse-stalls and set a couple of dams to watch them and try to keep them out of mischief. We set up tents in the auction hall, which now had no roof, though it did have a large bronze statue of a rearing horse, which the goblins had toppled, but not destroyed. We set this up against a wall, and many of us kissed the legs of the beautiful statue.

The next question was how to bathe.

Fresh water was scarce in the city because the goblins would drop the scraped, pink bones of their victims in our wells. They shat in the wells also. They would do these things near the coast, at least, because, unlike us, they can drink seawater. Alisenne found out from survivors that the bathhouse of Espalle had been used by the biters as a slaughterhouse and was now unclean. Even if this were not the case, it would have been too small to serve the entire western Ispanthian army. One thing Spanths of all stations share is a desire to be clean. If you want to offend a Spanth, stand near us with your ripe armpits or crotch, or your greasy, uncombed hair. If one is on campaign, or aboard ship, this is forgivable; but in a decent town, for one who has resources, it is in very poor taste.

The Holtish are the worst for this.

At the end of the afternoon, we walked to the sea and stripped down, and bathed with little pieces of soap our cook, Bernuz, had made for us with potash, sheepfat, and sea-buckthorn oil. There was much trash in the water, and at one point it was necessary to push a dead man away with a stick. When he floated back, Inocenta scolded him, and told him their relationship was over and he should leave her alone. I have always thought 'Centa was a beautiful dam, but never more than when she made me laugh.

After we dressed, we shared around some wine on the beach

and sang songs. It was a beautiful day, despite the death and wreckage around us. Few gifts serve a soldier as well as finding beauty in ugly places, and humor in the lap of fear.

Most of us were now at liberty. I did not wish to leave, but I told my brother Migaéd I would see him, and it is important to do what you say you will.

"He has passed out," the fat man with the bad mustache told me when I went back to the inn.

I had trouble remembering where the inn was because the streets of Espalle are tight and winding, and all I could remember was that the sign showed a wolf or a dog or a badly drawn cat and three stars. So asking for the name of the inn was no good. Later I followed the sound of drunken laughter, and at last found the Scarlet Company of Sword and Horse, still with no horse to speak of, though many of these bravos brayed like asses. I doubted very many of them were of use in a fight, though they had under their command a number of common soldiers of Braga, and a few foreign sell-swords. I made note of one man wearing ring and leather armor, a hard-looking Galt who lingered near the officers but did not overindulge. From his bare feet and his spear I thought him to be a Coldfoot guard—these are known to hire out as mercenaries.

The fat man introduced himself as Bolsu dom Gatán, so I told him my name as well, though he already knew. I could not help noticing how fine his armor was—nearly as good as Migaéd's—with an engraving on the breastplate by an artist of quality; two boars standing on their hind legs faced each other as if they were going to fight, with fearsome tusks and mad eyes. I had the thought that a boar was an unfortunate symbol for a family that ran to fat, then I thought this was uncharitable. Then I noticed that the collar of his shirt, which sat like small wings above his gorget, had been lightly stained, as though by ink, and then I realized that the dye from his mustache must have run down his neck.

I bit my cheek hard to keep a solemn look on my face.

"May I see him?" I said.

"I do not suppose there would be any impropriety in letting the sister view the body," he said, or some such university words, and called for Pedru, my brother's servant. Pedru was a boy with an honest face, and I liked him at once.

I was shown into a room that smelled of warm bodies and wine, and where an olive oil lantern smoked in the weak light coming through the window. A woman of no more years than I had, and perhaps fewer, was just dressing, and at first she did not look me in the face. I thought at the time it was shame, and it may have been, but also she will not have known I was Migaéd's sister and with my plain armor and *spadín* I was dressed for killing.

Before I looked away from her half-nakedness, I saw the angry pink frown of the Hordelaw scar just above her knee. I tried to put a less hard look on my face, but I doubt I did it well. I do not do that well.

I saw my grandfather's shield again, closer now. It was called the Mouth of the Storm, and it was beautiful, with its light-colored springwood blushing pink, and with its fine metal, though now in need of a polish. This was the closest I had seen the shield since it hung above the hearth in the great hall of our manor in Braga. I remember loving the metal boss in the form of a man of clouds blowing, his mouth in a small o, his brow furrowed. As with many things from childhood, it now looked smaller than I remember—when I was a girl, it seemed big enough to make a roof for a playhouse, or a small boat. When I left to study the mysteries of Calar Bajat, I was homesick. I often dreamed of home, and sometimes of the shield. More than once I dreamed that monsters were trying to get into the manor, and I had to get that shield and my grandfather's lance. But the things always came in through the hearth, and by the time I got to the great hall, they were between me and the shield. I would wake just before they ate me, my heart racing, wondering why I was in a dormitory instead of my bedroom.

Sometimes I had good dreams about it, as well. My favorite was that tiny pear trees were growing out of the wood, with pears no larger than peppercorns. But if I took one, it would grow until it filled my palm, and I would eat it. Springwood is nearly extinct now, as you know. It was harvested faster than it could grow back because the wood continues to live after it is cut, so it will repair itself if it gets sunshine, and water. Also, it is very strong and flexible, and nearly impossible to burn. When it is charred, however, though it loses its ability to heal itself, it becomes even harder, and lighter, and sometimes charred springwood is used instead of live for ships. Though more often it is left living. Most of the trees became ships for the navy, but some became armor, and some became shields.

Migaéd should have been caring for it better than this, leaving it lying about in need of a brush and oil.

The woman had finished dressing now, and made for the door without speaking, but what was there to say?

My first thought was that she was what soldiers call a *sop,* good only for absorbing seed, cleaning messes, and wiping the shit of babies. It is possible to call someone a bitch and still have respect for them. To call a dam a sop is to invite violence. Unless of course they truly are one, in which case it is to invite tears.

But then I felt badly for thinking this of her. I did not know her or what she had been through in this horror of goblins and foreign armies, besides having been lamed and whoring herself for food or coin or drink. She looked back over her shoulder as she limped into the garden, probably for Migaéd, but I caught her eye and gave her a nod. She let a sad smile touch her lips. In that moment I thought hers was the face of all Gallardia, and I wished I could touch her hand or her arm in fellowship.

But it was too late, and she was gone.

My brother lay on his stomach, one cheek of his buttocks exposed. I covered this with a sheet, then shook his shoulder. He groaned but did not wake. It was then that I noticed vomit on the floor, and decided not to wake him, telling myself it would embarrass him if he knew I saw him in this state.

But the truth is that it embarrassed me.

I looked at the shield again and saw the reflection of the lamp's little flame in its metal, and this pleased me.

I left Migaéd's room and passed back through the courtyard, ignoring the calls of his bravos for me to join them for a drink or a round of Towers. The sun was nearly down, so it must have been late, this being summer.

In the courtyard, I passed a man squatting over a latrine ditch to shit.

"Feeding the goblins," he said, and I thought it was just a vulgar joke until I passed the far end of the ditch and noticed goblins down there, arranged so their open mouths could be shat and pissed into.

At the time I thought this display was in poor taste, but, having some experience of goblins since then, I have changed my mind.

How ugly and dangerous they looked, even in a midden.

How sharp their teeth were.

6

"Galva," someone said, and I knew who.

"Amiel!"

This was only a block from the Inn of the Badly Drawn Beast and Three Stars—my youngest brother must have been on his way to see my eldest also. I grabbed him to me tight and held him long, both of us laughing for joy. I released him, said, "Let me look at you!," and held him a bit too tight at the shoulders, not to be mean but maybe because I was afraid he might disappear.

"Why is no one feeding you?" I said. "And where is Munno?"

"Munno fell overboard during that awful storm," he said, his smile vanishing. "He could not stand to be belowdecks anymore." This was the servant Father sent with Amiel to help him get settled with the wizard *he* was to serve. Munno was then supposed to find a ship back to Ispanthia. The storm was not for forgetting—it had sent our ships up one side of a wave and down the other, and at least one girl had sworn her life to Mithrenor if he would just stop beating the sea with his whip.

"That is sad news," I said, and it was. Munno was a simple man who liked peas more than meat, and who shared his small quarters with a three-legged goat named Burcatu, or Bouncy. He had been sent because he spoke some Gallard, and because he had military experience, though he was already getting old by the time I left home for Galimbur. He was faithful, however, and that is no small thing in a manservant—Munno would have gladly stepped in front of a knife to save any of the duke's children.

Especially this sweet, mild boy who never meant harm.

"Come," I said to Amiel, "let us see if we can find a bottle of wine in this town."

"I am supposed to see Migaéd just now. Come with me?"

"No, I have already been. The heir of dom Braga is . . . indisposed."

Amiel's face sank.

He knew well enough what *indisposed* meant.

It was not an easy matter to find an open inn or tavern in the sad streets of Espalle, with its wrecked buildings and its downed trellises. A word about the trellises, because they are a thing particular to southern Gallardia. These Gallards have an eye for making practical things also beautiful, and such were the sturdy wooden *treiaçes* that ran from roof to roof providing shade from the strong sun here. It was said that kynd with good legs could run from one end of Espalle to the other without using the ground, and that many a beautiful dam had been serenaded by musicians strolling above and passing cut flowers down through holes worked into the design. It was the geometry of these designs that had offended the biters, who, as I have said, are sickened and angered by straight lines, regular patterns, and much of our music. Thus some *treiaçes* were still intact in the town of Espalle, but many had been brought down and these now littered the cobbled streets, along with the grape leaves and ivy that often twined through them. Over the days we camped in town, however, much of this was gathered by the army for firewood.

It was on a street of tanners that we found a guesthouse with candles lit outside to invite custom. Amiel and I pressed into the crowded space, and I was aware that Ispanthian soldiers were not so many here as Espalleers, with their unwashed hair and feet. Yet I could forgive them this owing to the great tragedy their town had suffered. We found no table inside, but, once we had paid much for small cups of wine measured practically to the drop, and also sour and with gravel in it, we sat against a wall in the courtyard out back, using a dry-rotted crate as a table. The smell of urine once used by the tannery was strong.

"You look good, Chichún," I said to him, and I meant it. He was skinny, but his eyes shone, and he looked fit in the way of

a runner. Also, his black doublet with many small copper buttons suited him, as did his wool stockings the color of rust. He
looked well put-together, but not a walking invitation to robbery.
He wore his long hair down, with one small scholar's braid in it,
as university students wore it in Seveda. This struck a pang in
me. He should be there now, studying poetry, but the king had
forbidden the university to accept healthy young students. Only
the infirm could now enroll, and, though Amiel had failed his
arming trials, he was still shipped off to war. This seemed wasteful to me, and it was not the only complaint I had against King
Kalith the Usurper even before I came to know the woman who
should have inherited our throne.

"Thank you," Amiel said, "so do you," though this was only
courtesy. I knew my face showed how tired I was—I do not sleep
well on a ship—and that my hair had been cut to bangs in front,
the rest chopped to collar length with no attempt at art.

"How was your first day in Gallardia?" I said. "Have you found
your magus?"

"Yes. He found me and brought me to a small farm he has commandeered just west of town, where he keeps mixlings, mostly
bull-men and failed corvids. His name is Fulvir Lightningbinder,
though of course his real name is something unpronounceable
and Molrovan. His accent is quite thick. He *sounds* like he comes
from a place of snow and ice and lying for the sport of it. Molrovans are hard to understand at first, with their art of polite
untruths, saying 'The day is quite cool' when it's clearly blazing
hot, or 'It pleases me when you drop your bags loudly while I am
reading.' But there are rules to it as well. They speak plainly about
vital things, and only lie when the actual truth is obvious. One
day in and I am getting the habit. But I did not find him at first. I
wandered the docks for some time asking after him, and I was a
bit overwhelmed. Did you see the gibbets?"

"How could I not?"

"One sign said 'Godsmilk takers,' and I had to ask what that meant. Do you know?"

"Yes."

One of the first sights as we came to land was a scaffold where many dead hung, I mentioned this before when I was speaking of how hard it was to get the birds ashore. The closest bodies on display had been boiled alive up to the breast, their skin falling off them, their yellow eyes staring. I say yellow, because these had been found to have taken godsmilk, a goblin drug brewed from their endless underground libraries of mushrooms. There is nothing so addictive, and no quicker way for them to make a traitor. The drug makes you dream with great pleasure, it is said, and you crave these dreams so fiercely you become enslaved. The first taste is supposed to wedge the door open, but by the second taste, the taker cannot be trusted again. Luckily, there are tokens of its use, chief among these, the whites of the eyes go yellow because it harms the liver. Those who have it forced upon them by biters are put to the sword. Those who take it willingly are boiled.

"I felt sorry for them."

"They had only themselves to blame."

"I wish I had your moral clarity."

I did not know what to say to this, so I grunted, which made him laugh one quiet *ha,* which in turn made me smile. To love someone well is to know their small noises, and to hear home in them. This is not a small thing on foreign soil.

"The wounded were hard to see as well. Their injuries . . ."

I had seen the same bunch he saw, crowded together, most keeping as well as they could to what little shade there was. Some lay with their wounds exposed to sunlight, hoping Sath would heal them. Barber-surgeons with butchers' aprons stiff from blood and from sweat prowled the departing wounded for silver as shamelessly as whores offered themselves to those coming in. Flykeep boys with jars full of white wrigglers would dab rotten wounds with maggots for copper. Seagulls cried overhead, and I gave them little thought until I saw something I did not know they did.

"What?"

"Sorry, I got lost. Something I saw."

"Tell me."

I smiled and shook my head. I did not want to tell him about the barber-surgeon cutting off a wrecked foot and pitching it onto the pier, where seagulls fought over it. Or the big soldier with one eye covered with a blood-crusted bandage who limped over with an axe. I thought she meant to harm the birds, but she chopped the foot up and said, "You are in the army now, gulls. You have to share."

One flew off with a big toe.

Those who were on their way from the war laughed.

Those of us just coming to it stared.

There is something to be learned from this.

Then the soldier with the axe sat, slumped over, and went into a tremor, moving her head and all her limbs helplessly. Others went to try to help her, but her earless, noseless friend waved them off, saying, "She does this now."

Amiel broke the silence by saying, "I almost got a girlfriend. At the docks."

I blinked and came back to myself, understanding his words and then saying, "This is not difficult to do."

"No, she was not a . . . woman who sells herself."

I raised my eyebrows at him.

I was only aware of one who might ever have been called his girlfriend, a second cousin of ours named Aura, who was famous for her thick, curly hair. I did not know what was between them, but it was more than nothing. Though Amiel was smart, the smartest of the four of us, he could be fucked-foolish when love moved him. A knight's squire, older than him, bigger than him, had spoken ill of Aura in front of Amiel, calling her a poet's sop. Amiel challenged that boy to duel him with slakeswords. Very formally, in a letter. This was one summer I was home from studies, and I knew enough of swords and of Amiel's poor use of them that I feared for him, and thought to take on his challenge, though he never would have suffered this.

Of course, Father stepped in, saying by no means should boys so young fight with sharp steel, but that a wrestling bout might serve better. Father thought this would teach Amiel a lesson without doing him real harm, for even to box a boy as strong as the squire might have been dangerous for little Amiel. So wrestle they did, and Amiel was folded, thrown, spun, slapped about with the squire's open hand, and actually made to eat dirt. Father thought seeing Amiel defeated might cause Aura to move her affections to a stronger boy, but he had not expected the squire to humiliate him so. Aura was so moved by the sight of the poet suffering for her that they became even closer. I remember them catching frogs together at the marsh that summer, and watching her lay her head in his lap while he read to her. And Amiel, having been so rewarded for his act of chivalry, only grew more foolish.

As for the squire, if he learned the wrong lesson from his victory, it was short-lived. Bandits set upon him one day, and these took no coin from him. Rather, they spun him, folded him, threw him, slapped him about with their open hands, and made him eat so much dirt that it was said he shat a farm after.

I was told this by one of Father's rougher men-at-arms, who had a black eye and dirt under his fingernails when he told me.

The squire never spoke ill of Aura dom Altea again.

And I do not think Amiel found love after her again, despite his many fine qualities, and for this I am sorry.

"I am intrigued," I said. "Tell me of this new girlfriend of the Plaza of Anchors."

He smiled that bright smile of his.

He loved telling tales.

"She had a bandage where her arm should be. But she wore her helmet at a rakish tilt and walked with a swagger. I liked her for that. She saw me looking at her, and said, 'Get on the boat with us, boy. Come on, I will keep you warm and take you home to your mum. You are too young for this slaughter-yard.' I protested that I had eighteen summers. 'Ooooooooh,' she said, as if impressed, and then she said, 'Well, you won't have nineteen.' And then she turned from me as if I had never been there. You know, I started telling you about it because it seemed funny. But now I feel cold because I think she may have been right."

He became sad, so I squeezed his arm until he looked at me.

"Ay," I said, "that is not how it is going to be."

"Why not?"

"Because I say so."

"Is that how it works?" he said.

"Yes."

"And why is that?"

And then we both said at once "Because I say so!" and we laughed hard.

It was good.

7

My curfew was the eleventh hour and Amiel had to get back to his strange wizard, so we parted ways after having one more cup of wine each. Mine seemed, if possible, even smaller than the first, but I was glad to have any at all, things being what they were.

In the morning the lanza fed its birds, and then we exercised them four at a time. This was a matter of putting them through their commands, all of which could be given by voice or by hand. *Attack, Fall back, To me,* and *Turn* are what you think. *Fetch* could mean to grab a weapon from the field—these birds are very good at finding dropped items—or it could mean to pull a goblin out of a small space. At least, so we had trained them. These birds would be the first war corvids to see action, a gift, as I have said, from the very Fulvir Lightningbinder Amiel now served.

Shiver was a command we especially hoped would work, as it caused the beasts to raise their wings and move them very fast, as a shield against arrows and bolts. It worked well enough with blunted ones, free of venom. And the birds had been bred to resist the goblin toxins we knew about, and the few that had been dosed back in Ispanthia had indeed survived, all but one. I did not know what effect *Shiver* would have on goblins that saw it, but these beasts stalking forward with their heads down and their wings in a blur is not something I would like to face. These blessed engines of the Bride had been created to kill Our Foe, and we had every reason to believe they would do this well.

Gallard children had lined up on a brick wall to watch us, and I could see Nouva thought about chasing them off. But she let them stay. I also thought the children were far enough away for safety, and this needed to be so—if one of the corvids decided they were goblins, there would be blood. But these children were made hopeful at the sight of these monsters, monsters that were on their side for once. Here were five children who would go home and tell others that Spanth war corvids had come to Gallardia, and they had never seen anything so fierce.

This was not without value.

Some hopes are worth risk.

After the birds were exercised and secured, it was our turn. Some of us would play goblin, fighting in wedges of three with short wooden gisarmes—a sort of spear with one backward-facing hook, the preferred weapon of the biters. The goblin-dams were to fight low and dirty, hooking legs, one hooking a shield sideways while the others drove up at the chin. Two might tie up a sword-arm while the third hooked the kynd's heel toward the sky and sent the dam on her backside. Nouva, Inocenta, and the others who had faced them before taught us how they fight—or at least how they fought last time.

The biters adapted as quickly as we did, and we could take nothing for granted.

Their poisons had not been so fast or efficient in the Knights' War.

They had no godsmilk in the Threshers'.

And yet, these women had survived the massacres of the Threshers' War, and that was because goblins *could* be killed, and outfought, even without horses.

Kynd in these days had better armor, better tactics.

And now corvids.

I had seen the veterans watch the birds tear through dead goblins in their armor like scythes through wheat. I would not say they were confident—rather, I would say they were like the boys on the wall.

They dared to hope.

As for the techniques we were currently training with, I could repeat the corrections of the Threshers' War veterans in my sleep.

"No, Galva, keep your guard lower. No, Galva, don't put your face so close to hers, she will bite. No, Galva, do not try to sweep them with your leg, they will spur you and never let go." This is another thing about them—Our Foe have a hook on their smaller arm instead of a tenth finger, on the forearm, and they are very good at sinking that into you and hanging, anchoring you so their hivemates can gut you or bite you.

Of course, after nearly two years in the army, adjusting the ten years I had studied killing kynd under a private tutor and then at the academy of Calar Bajat, I was praised sometimes as well.

"*Good*, Galva, you would have had its arm off! *Yes,* use the shield to batter, it is heavy enough to break their legs."

"Horned god of fuck, she nearly broke mine," I remember that a goblin-playing dam named Olicat said before limping off.

"All right, good work," Nouva said, clapping twice. "Take the better half of an hour. Get water, a lot of it, and sit out of the sun."

She did not have to tell us that last. Even Ispanthians from Coscabrais or Veista Pulcanta in the south were suffering in this day's heat. I filled my wooden mug with greasy water from the trough and sat in the warm shadow of the wall where the kids still chattered.

"Ay, ay!" one said down to me. "You Spant?"

Gallards do not have a "th" sound.

"I am."

"You kill goblin?"

I did not know if he meant had I killed some, or would I, so I assumed the latter.

"I will kill many. What is your name?"

"Name? Me?"

"Yes you," I laughed at the shy, shirtless little monkey, leaning out to see him better, though this put me back in the sun's eye. "Who else?"

He was silhouetted now, the sun sharp unto blinding behind him.

"Sambard," he said. Then shrugged, saying, "Sami."

"An honor to meet you, Sambard. Sami. I am Galva, though when I was your size they called me Galvicha."

"Gal*veecha*," he sang. "You are knight?" he said, pointing at my shield and wooden sword.

"Yes," I said.

"Dam Galvicha," he said mock-seriously, then broke a smile like swallows in flight. He had much charm, this one. He would make a handsome man, if he lived, with his skin the color of olives and his hair wild and black, and with the light in his eyes, if he could keep that. Now he tossed a piece of smooth, amber-colored glass into my lap and the awed sound the other children made told me this was precious to him. I looked up into the sun to see him again, squinting, and I wished my money-pouch was closer so I could toss him a piece of silver. I had no doubt his family could use it. There would not be time for me to fetch it before I was summoned back to duty, but I decided to keep my eyes open for this one.

"*Mertasse*, Sire Sambard," I said, also solemnly, and he giggled, and put his hand over his mouth. Now someone out of sight called him away, another child rather than a mother, I thought.

He and the others slipped from the wall faster and more silently than cats.

Of course they were quick and stealthy, they would not be alive otherwise. Every Gallard in this town, from the smallest child to the most stooped grandmother, was a survivor, and each of them deserved respect. They had all seen too much. I have not said yet how the dead smelled in their houses, or in the woods, or how the flies buzzed in these hot, reeking places, sometimes suddenly and furiously in the woods and then there would be a stink and picked bones, and teeth smiling in a spoiled cheek. Or a wing would beat in the brush and then a buzzard would fly in their heavy, guilty way, leaving the wreck of someone's father or wife or sister behind until you left and the buzzard might return. I had seen priests and healers carrying quartered human parts out of an Allgod church the biters had used as a butcher's mess, trying to keep stray dogs away while they sorted which pieces belonged together on the street-cobbles. Some of the town had cried during this evil business, but most just wore the mask that one's face becomes after too many outrages. Many of these bones taken from the fouled church had been small. I had not yet had time to think on that, but this child brought it back to me. Tiny leg-bones. A small shoe with buttons. I felt tears try to break from my eyes. Instead of fighting them back, I looked up again where the boy had just been, just for an instant, and let Sath in his blue cloak sting my eyes. I turned my face from the fighting yard so I might not be seen and let myself cry hard. I thanked Sath for the gift of this funny little monkey to remind me what was at stake in these courtyard games.

This may have been the last time I felt Sath had given something, rather than just taking.

I would not worship him much longer.

But I still have Sambard's piece of colored glass, as you see, and you will have an easier time taking my last golden valor from me than this unasked-for token of a small boy's warmth in a place that should have already killed that in him.

It was soon after sparring that a messenger came wearing the livery of my brother Pol, terce-general, and the second son of the Duke of Braga.

"What business did that lass have with you?" Nouva asked.

"My brother would like me to attend a service with him tomorrow at the temple of Sath in honor of the new commander of the Western Army."

She considered this, creasing her handsome, dark brow. Turning her smart, golden-brown eyes up to me.

"Of course you will go."

"It was an invitation, not a command," I said.

"An invitation from a terce-general *is* a command. Your presence feeding and training with us for one day weighs far less than your words in a high commander's ear, especially when we are running out of food for these beasts. The quartermaster delivered three days' worth, and we won't see him again for five. Go. I have written down the birds' daily needs, see if you can get your brother interested. If not in their ability to fight, then at least in reducing the odds of an accident. You know how they get when hungry. And you know the old boys further down the chain from Pol dom Braga would like an excuse to kill our birds and pitch fifty mouthy dams back into the shield wall."

So I went.

8

The temple of Sath in Espalle was large and built with skill, a good place for the consecration of a new supreme commander of the Western Army.

The old off-white stone had been too strong for the biters to pull down, so they had tarred one corner black to break its lines to the eye. To the rear of the main building was the Vault of Mysteries, which was as good as its name. It was without windows and hung with doors of solid bronze, and only the elect of Sath—his priests and those they blessed with their key—were allowed to enter. No one outside their order spoke of what was stored within, or what went on there. Wonders and gold? Carnal rites? A pile of old tan men walking about naked with tinted sun spectacles on? Or perhaps, as Pol had written, pieces of the sun itself, too bright and hot for those not ordained to withstand. Those who knew did not say, and no small number of kynd entered the priesthood just to know the secrets of the order. Yes, the goblins had forced their way into the Vault, but perhaps those hot pieces of sun had driven them out again. In any case, the army had respected Sath's holies enough to leave it to the priests. Now the Vault was secure once more and the lay folk did not learn its secrets.

The fragile and beautiful glasshouse in front of the main temple had been spared because Our Foe used its focused heat to dry their many varieties of mushrooms, and, it was said, to torture captives they wanted information from. I wondered if they knew we tortured our own in there.

We went in.

I stood with my brother in the nave, close to the altar and glass-house. We had little time to speak before the ceremony began. He only said, "Galvicha! You look like a proper killer. You will be my close-guard! But shhh, the rite is about to start, we will speak after."

I felt honored he had me at his right side. And, though it does me little credit, I was young and it pleased me to have him call me a killer. He meant it kindly. He meant most things kindly. He was born a very different man than Migaéd, for as much as they shared a womb one year apart.

To describe him, so that you might see him in your mind's eye as I do, Pol was handsome in a plain way, less likely to turn the eye for his face than for his form. He was built tall and broad through the shoulders. His hair was running thin at the top, which was new to me. He had briefly gone to the same sword academy where I studied, before my time of course, but he had only lasted three months.

Migaéd was jealous of both of us in this—the eldest son of dom Braga had wanted to attend, but one is only ever *invited* to study the deepest mysteries of Calar Bajat. When his younger brother Pol was invited, Migaéd wrote the academy a letter asking if there had been some mistake.

He received a short reply.

Thank you for your interest.

There has been no mistake.

As it turned out, Pol was not suited for the highest level of *spadín* technique, though my instructor, Yorbez, had said he lacked nothing of speed or strength. This was why he had been invited to the academy in the first place. But, as Pol discovered, not all who are offered instruction will receive the sword tattoo.

"Fah, he was thick through the arms and could really batter, the Bride knows, but he was impatient and hot, the sort that can be goaded into overreach or undone with footwork. He never learned to be the arrow relaxing into flight rather than the tense bow at full draw. He will do better with a poleaxe, splitting the little pricks like firewood. I would not like to fight him with a polearm in those hands. Are we sure his father wasn't a woods-man, or, to speak as friends, a great horny black bear?"

I remembered Yorbez's words about the black bear as I looked upon Pol's beard, short and neat and oiled, but black as night except for . . . was it so? A gray. Now two. He was young for his rank, quite young, but he was no longer a boy. His eyes seemed heavy and sad, which I do not remember of him from my girl-hood.

Ten years is a long time between siblings, though.

A small lifetime.

The morning sun shone in the glasshouse, its facets sending colored light back through the nave as a crystal or a diamond will—if you have not seen one of these temples, I do not have the words for it, except to say that it takes light and makes a sort of song from it.

A *censerichu* passed close to us, swinging his censer so we breathed smoke of cedar and lavender. Each season has its in-cense: myrrh in the spring, bergamot in the fall, sage in the gloaming. In the winter, pine. When the trade routes to the south were open, wealthy churches like ours in Braga, and perhaps this one, would be burning ylang-ylang in the summer; but I was to find out from my fellow soldiers that lavender and cedar were the summer scent in most churches—the more expensive herb only grew in far Axa, or in parts of Old Kesh now under Hordelaw. As a duke's daughter, it had not occurred to me that the gods would smell differently to the poor.

Now the censer-boys stood on either side of the priest. He was an older man who wore spectacles of green glass that let him look long at the sun without blindness. The three *gailus* sang the helion, making long tuneful sounds that might have been small words, but were not. The sounds, somewhere between singing and chanting, were meant to touch some part of the listener that was beyond the reach of death. It was said the helion could heal, though I knew of no one whose wounds had closed or whose cancer had shrunk away because a priest moaned pretty sounds at them.

It *was* pretty, though, I had to allow.

The effect on Pol was obvious. It was clear to me that he was still devout. Some part of me envied him that and thought myself insufficient. A better kynd than myself would have felt some connection with the god whose home we stood in, but I was more interested in looking at the others present. There were not many, and, aside from guards, all of very high rank. One saw steel and leather, but also velvet, silk, and gold. This rite would be the new commander's introduction to her high officers; she would address the gathered army on the morrow.

Surveying the crowd, I was struck again by Pol's height. He towered above most of those present. It was then that I realized just how many in this temple were women.

I looked for Migaéd, but did not see him—as I have said, sixt-generals are for wearing fine clothes, not for true command, and are often excused from the greater honors as they are not needed. He will have been invited, but may not have managed to keep himself sober enough for a public event. Or maybe the thought just bored him. In any event, he did not witness the Pragmatist's ceremony.

I recognized Segunth-General Samera dom Vinescu, ranked just above Pol and thus second-in-command after the one who would be anointed here. I admired her armor, which was of plate on the breast and scales fashioned to look like fish scales below. All of it was richly trimmed, but also battered. Here was a dam who said "Follow me," not "Go ahead of me." I noticed she did not make the Gesture of the Caught Sun when the others did, and this made sense later. Her god was Mithrenor, not Sath. I caught Pol looking at her more than once, and put this down to her beauty, which was considerable, and not harmed by her nose, which had clearly been broken more than once. But when she turned her head to look at Pol as well, seeming already to know where he stood, it occurred to me that something was between them.

This was not my business, I would put it from my mind.

Now the priest raised the *ferula solar,* a staff topped by a golden disc with many silver points of sunburst, diamonds among these to make it glitter. He was so tanned he appeared Keshite or Axaene, but this is normal for the priests of Sath. They lie nude in the sun by pools and turn themselves like rabbits on the spit so they are colored evenly. It is said by vulgar persons that they even kneel prone to let the sun shine where it should remain dark. Also, the acolytes and younger or more fit priests wear only the gold-trimmed white dhoti, a traditional garment going back to Old Kesh, similar to the ones we wear at Calar Bajat practice. Ours are red, though, we bleed too much for white. Old and fleshy priests are allowed to wear robes, though these are few because their practice involves running, swimming, and other exercise that keeps one lean and hard. Sath is a vain god who made us in his image so he could look upon his own beauty, and he expects us to preserve it.

Especially the men.

There are no priestesses to Sath, nor nuns. Sath's church is one of the few things men have kept only for themselves through the Goblin Wars, despite the lack of men—the last king, a great friend of this church, exempted those in Sath's service from going under arms. You can imagine how fierce the competition became to wear the white and gold. You will forgive me if I point out that our present king, Kalith the Usurper, made himself head of the church, at least in name, and for this reason was excused—by his own edict—the honor of risking death in this fucked and gruesome war.

Forgive me, it still makes me angry.

The helion was over.

The priest lowered the Icon of the Blessed Sun.

He said some uninteresting things, and then gestured with

pomp at the glasshouse, where a woman now stood. She wore only a white robe, which clung to her with sweat. Her arms were raised straight above her head, palms in, in the Gesture of Receiving. She had perhaps forty-five years, her brown hair cut short and starting to gray. She looked fit to swing a sword, but it was also clear that she spent more time in the map-tent than at drills. It was not until she opened her eyes that I found her remarkable, though she did not do this for some time. She was receiving the Hardship of Sath's Kiss, the light of the sun focused on her through the lensed facets of the glasshouse. The sweat was said to purge one of weakness, as the heat was said to overcome any who were not fit for whatever trial or honor brought them to this place. I could tell she was a woman of strong will—many of those whom I had seen receive the Hardship trembled, or swayed, or moved their lips in quiet pleading.

This dam stood like stone as the white light blazed on her face.

I liked her for this.

The priest spoke on and on. This blessed general would have victory, Sath would arm her against our foe, and so on. How could we, reflecting the god's beauty like a million pieces from a shattered gazing-glass, do aught but win, for these reasons, and those, and something-or-other as well. Priests of Sath like to hear themselves talk nearly as much as they like to look at their reflections.

But now he said her name.

"Prima-General Peya Dolón Milat, come to your soldiers that they may know their new commander."

A door opened in the glasshouse. An acolyte took the woman's arm and led her blind from that place of great heat and light. She was dried, and she was dressed behind a held cloth. She still did not open her eyes when handed a mug of cool beer. She drank it down, and her generals and their guards and scribes and body servants cheered for her. Beer was Sath's drink, with its barley and wheat and hops plants drinking sunlight and turning it into something like gold.

The gods of wine were darker.

It was now that our new commander opened her eyes, and even from some distance they reminded me of those of a carrion eagle, that great bird of southern Ispanthia that would drive vultures and jackals from kills and sometimes took dogs or small children.

These were hard eyes, that had seen the carnage in the east.

Patient eyes.

Eyes that saw how many in that church were already dead and did not yet know it.

9

I will always remember the walk from the temple of Sath back to the villa Pol had taken over. It was strange to see soldiers, some older than him, stand straight and salute as we passed. This man, who had grown up in the same house I had, who had also stood in the deep shadows of the library or great room and listened to the clip-clop of the crippled duke's two canes, was now just as important as our father, at least in the eyes of soldiers. One dam on the street of Espalle, weary from carrying her poleaxe and pack, straightened and saluted as he passed. This was repeated with archers, badgers, knights, even a little boy with a drum on his hip and eyes too old for his face. Any of these might die because certain words came out of my brother's mouth, or because they did not. I knew then that I would never want great military rank, or to be responsible for anyone but myself and those at my right and left in the field.

I have not changed in this opinion, though I have not always been able to shape my own fate.

In the hills above town, I could see that the vineyards had been crowded with tents, and above the streets here I saw the bare arms and legs of dams who had been billeted in the hot upstairs of houses as they tried to get some air. I do not know how many had lived in Espalle before the goblins, but our army was many times that number, and the smell and noise of soldiers dominated every space. The streets were mostly cobbled, so few latrines could be dug. Waste was thrown out windows, and man and dam alike passed urine on the street. To this day, if I catch a whiff of piss, I think of that summer in Espalle.

The air was only a little better near the houses of the high command.

Pol's villa had once belonged to a wealthy family of Espalle, and it was very old, and very fine. One beautiful wall mosaic had been gouged up in places to break a geometric design. Another mosaic, with peacocks, and with the turbaned Keshite king Nayurbat the Good holding the axe-scepter with which he cut the chains of his slaves and made human bondage illegal in the empire, had no obvious center. Because it had no symmetry, the goblins had not bothered to destroy it. Still another, a floor mosaic with palm trees and a crescent moon, had been dashed with blood that had not been fully cleaned. This was no artistic comment, but only murder. Though I suppose it is not murder to slaughter a prey animal, and that is what we are to them.

"Why are you looking down, Galvicha?" Pol said, and raised my chin with a finger. "You are a dom Braga, the same as myself. We point our chins up."

"Until the fight starts," I said. Pointing your chin up is a good way to get your throat cut, or to be knocked asleep. You tuck your chin.

He knew what I meant, of course, and looked at me anew.

"Just so," he said, with a hint of a smile.

I did not tell him that I had my gaze down before because I was looking at the floor mosaic, and the blood. I was pleased to have earned his favor with my little pip of martial wisdom. I was such a fool. He brought me to the garden now, which still had citrus trees and many flowers, though it was crowded with several small tents. One section of the wall had been knocked down. Another section had been blackened as if by fire, and I did not at first notice the flat image of a cringing figure, not burned. A cart had been placed in front of the gruesome image to hide it, this spot where someone had been burned to death by fire magicks.

"Bring the pullet and fruit, please, and a little wine," the general told a young boy.

I was feasted then, the first of two times I would enjoy Pol's hospitality at this sad and beautiful villa. Chicken, and dates, and pears, and some hard sheep's cheese from Braga. I have never been one to care about fine food, but this was the best I had eaten in some time.

"What are you thinking about in that busy head of yours, Galvicha?" he said.

"Sorry," I said, "no thoughts worth words, Terce-General. Thank you for this."

"It is nothing," he said, though of course it was more than nothing—the weary dam with the polearm would have likely wept for a fresh date on cheese and a swallow of white wine from Unther.

"And none of that 'terce-general' business here, Galvicha. I am Pol when it is just us."

"As you wish, brother. Pol. I have a favor to ask," I said.

"Promotion? Done."

"*No!*" I said, too loudly. "No, thank you. I . . . the *corviscus*."

"Right! And how are they working out? Looks like you have all your limbs and digits."

"Yes. And if you would like me to keep them, these birds need more food. I have a list here of their daily . . ."

"You know, you really should let me send you home."

I stopped and took a bite. I chewed and swallowed. It is good not to speak quickly when vexed. I made my tone even when I spoke.

"Home? And what would I do there?"

"Why, you would manage the estate, of course. Father is not getting younger. And your mother . . ."

He softened his voice here because he was on treacherous ground. My mother, and Amiel's, was called Nera. She had been a dancer, of the dom Brecola, who had fallen into disgrace when her grandfather renounced the king and died for this. But her beauty and the fire of her spirit had caught the duke, and he not only bedded her, but married her. It is said they were happy for a year or two. But not all women are for children, and a great

sadness took Nera dom Braga upon my birth, and worsened after Amiel's. She was rarely seen out of bed, and had taken much
weight. Nunu raised me. It is fair to say that, though I grew up in
the same house with my mother, I did not know her. This makes
me sad. To hear of her skill dancing the old Keshite flower-dances,
which are greatly athletic, it is likely I owe much to her for my gift
at the sword. A painting of her in her youth hangs in the library,
and it is possible to fall in love with Nera dom Braga just from this
painting. But she no longer looked like her portrait. People of low
quality said my father should divorce her, but she was no trouble
to him. He was of an age to care more for warm brandy, books
about wars, and food that did not trouble his stomach than for
women.

And such needs as he had, I suspect Nunu saw to.

If it was so, I do not think of this as deceit.

Though my mother would not die in a physical sense until the
last months of this war, it seems to me that she had for some time
lived only as a ghost.

I thought it would be better not to say my next words to Pol,
but I said them anyway.

"Why do *you* not go home? You have a better head for figures
than I do."

He barked a little laugh.

"Me? How could I? I have responsibilities."

I took a long, slow sip.

"As do I."

"I have made oaths."

"As have I. Does my word weigh less than yours?"

He closed his eyes and breathed in, and he nodded once. When
he opened his eyes again it was if he were truly seeing me for the
first time that day, and not just as a parrot speaking the words of
her swordmaster.

"You have the right of it," he said. "A man or a dam must honor
their oaths, and you are not a child now."

I thought of the boy, Sami, with the sun behind him, and of the colored glass.

"There are no childhoods anymore."

"No," he said, "I suppose not. But I wish you had not made your muster-oath. I wish . . ."

He paused here long enough that it did not feel rude to interrupt him.

I lowered my voice to try to sound like Father and said, "Wish in one pot and throw silver in another. Then see which one they want at market."

He laughed, and said, sounding just like the Duke of Braga, "'Wish in one pot and shit in the other, but don't make a gift to me of either.' At least, so was the version I always heard."

"I almost never heard him swear."

"Ah," he said, and considered me again.

"Brother, about the birds . . ."

I told him about the corvids, how well trained they were, how dangerous to the enemy I believed they would be. I showed him the paper Nouva had prepared with their requirements.

"By the Firmament, that is a lot."

"It needn't be fresh."

"Do you think food has a chance to spoil around here, Galvicha? The belly of an army is hard to fill. We are in for a long and hungry march north."

"It seems to me, brother, that the army must commit to these birds if it really wants to see what they may do."

He nodded, looked at the paper again.

"And there are fifty of them?"

"No. There are fifty of us, almost. The birds are eighty-eight."

He whistled through his teeth.

"Eighty-eight times this," he said, holding up the paper, "is going to take some muscle. But let me see what I can do. I am new in my position, new to overseeing quite so much, and I have not got my hands on all the levers yet. Perhaps the new commander can help—among her other gifts, she is said to be a master of logistics."

"I am grateful, Pol," I said, and bowed without grace. It is hard to know what to do when close family is also great in rank.

"It is unfair that they eat us and we cannot eat them," Pol said. "It gives them a tremendous advantage in the field. Can you imagine if they were some kind of, I don't know, dangerous chicken? The battlefield speeches I could give. 'Come now, men and dams, we've a hard day ahead of us, but a glorious day. Fight for your king. Fight for your family's name. And fight for their very tender breast meat, and those delicious legs on them. Try not to damage those legs. Try to bonk them on the head.'"

He used to spoil his own jokes by laughing at them, but he did not laugh at this one, and neither did I. The idea of eating a goblin was so unappetizing that it overpowered the idea of the chicken. Though I did smile that one might be dangerous.

"One more thing," he said. "Take this."

He reached into his doublet and took out a small flask engraved with the image of a heart pierced by a thorn.

He handed this to me.

"Is it . . . ?"

"Yes," he said. "Bittermead."

It had been rumored that officers carried a poison that would kill them in a moment, and make their flesh a danger to goblins. It was also rumored that it did not work, only bringing death, and that it was a sort of pretty lie—one died painlessly thinking one's flesh would be spared the shame of being butchered and eaten.

"Have you got forty-seven more of them?"

"It is quite expensive, there is spellwork to it to make it steep the flesh so quickly. This is only for you, sister."

The expense of it told me it probably worked—if it was false, it would be cheap, and they would give it to soldiers of the line to make them less fearful.

"I do not want to be the only one in my lanza to have it."

"You sound like a Wostran Egalitarian."

"Forgive me, I do not know what that is."

"Did they only teach you sword in that school?"

"Sword is all I remembered."

"Take it," he said.

"No."

"Gods gathered, why not, Galva?"

"I will fight harder knowing I have no escape."

The next day the new commander of the Western Army was to speak.

It would be a day of events.

But before I speak of that day, I will tell you how I spent the night before, and many others besides. This has some bearing on the larger story, though it is not my habit to discuss private matters. I have mentioned Inocenta a great deal already, and you may have already begun to think that she was something more than a friend to me. This is true, though I will also say that she was not my lover, not in the way she might have been. I will even say, not in the way that she *should* have been, for it is possible to regret a thing not done as bitterly as any false step. No, in Ispanthia there is a path between mere warmth and fire, and Inocenta and I walked this path.

We were *irmanas apraceras,* sisters who embrace.

In older times, this was a way for wives left behind while their husbands were at war to ease their loneliness with one another, but now that most of the men had died, this same practice went into the field. When the campfires were doused, we had, for some months, been retiring to the same bedroll, there to enjoy one another's closeness. The touching was not so intimate as to bring release. It was for comfort, and shared warmth.

I think the restraint was more difficult for Inocenta than for me, not because I was some great beauty even before my scars, my broken nose, and other adjustments, but because she was already well initiated to pleasure. She spoke of many lovers, not to mention two children. These were staying in an *ucal,* or "hearth," in which those too old or unfit for arms, or those who had been crippled, combined households to care for the children of those away at war. Inocenta never told me the names of her children, saying she would introduce them properly to me should we all live, as if keeping their names against that day made it more likely to come. I begrudge no one their superstitions—we climb out of despair by whatever rungs we have at hand.

She did tell me, however, that her children's *ucal* was in rural Braga, and that in this one, fourteen children were seen to by an ancient couple, a one-armed young man who shouted in his sleep, a deaf woman, and a large Bragaene shepherd dog who herded the youngest about like ducklings. I thought more than once as we lay listening to each other breathe that perhaps we would be injured rather than killed and end up in such a place together. This was the closest I had been with anyone so far, except for a few fumblings I had permitted fellow students but quickly put a stop to, whether for shame or disinterest. This with Inocenta felt very right to me, though I could not see what was in it for her. It was a wonder to me that anyone would want to lie with me, as hard as a plank everywhere, all elbows and knees, with hipbones that could be made into axe-heads. Inocenta was softer, at least in the hips, though she was muscled like a bear underneath that softness.

And, of course, she had no breasts, having cut them off in the name of the Skinny Woman—she was an ardent follower of Dal-Gaata, the goddess of death, after whom my female bird, Dalgatha, "Skinny," was called. It was a happy accident that this goddess's name and our word for skinny were so close.

I suspected Inocenta was also a priestess, though the truth of this she kept even from me. I had asked her outright, and she had laughed and said, "You will have to come to altar to see who the Bride's beloved are."

At this time, I had not yet come.

Of course, I would.

But that is later.

Now I will tell you of the day the Pragmatist addressed her troops, and then of the coming of the juggernaut, and of a war of wizards.

10

The old amphitheater of Espalle was a wonder. It overlooked the sea, with five thousand seats carved from the stone of the cliff, rising out from a stage of beautiful pink flagstones. This of the stage was the same stone they had used to build the temple of Nerêne. Whoever spoke there spoke with the sea behind them. The shoreline was angled so one could not quite see the harbor, or hear the noise of ships, or the cries of those handling cargo. Of course, the main cargo now was more soldiers, and, one hoped, more food and wine and rope and shoes for those soldiers. Several more troopmules full of green recruits were putting in today, but the new prima-general's address would not wait longer.

Gulls and terns cried, some riding on drafts, seeming to hang in the sky above us almost still.

This is one of my favorite things to see.

We were crowded in tight, a great many more than five thousand soldiers present, and that still only a small part of our total number. Some of those in attendance, perhaps a hundred, were Gallards who had been attached to this army and would follow our orders until we made contact with a Gallardian unit of any strength. On the stage were only the high command—terce-generals and above, Pol included—and these stood at attention, waiting for the arrival of our new supreme commander. I sat in the middle with my fellow raven knights, as some called us, our corvids under watch at the horse market. Next to us were some engineers, and beyond them, big, fully-armored line soldiers leaning on their poleaxes, ignoring calls for them to sit so others might see. These looked like veterans. It would be good to fight next to such as these, they looked ready to trample and hack their way through anything at all.

Of course, at this point I had not yet seen a ghall.

I saw Fulvir for the first time now, at some distance. He was a smallish older man with a bald head and small ears. At this time he also had a beard, though the war would cost him this. I will say that one may speak against the wizard with reason, but that no single kynd was more helpful in that war, as you will hear.

On this day, he wore a Keshite kurta the color of mustard. I could see by the way people looked at him that many wished to speak to him, but none dared. Amiel was wearing a fur hat in the Molrovan style, and I thought it would vex him much when the heat of the day came. It was morning now, and still merely warm, though the breeze from the sea was pleasant.

I looked at my seagulls again, loved them for how little effort they spent, and how little they cared about us.

They were not at war.

They only had to fish and lay eggs and try not to be eaten.

They only had to be still and ride the rising air.

When I looked back down, I saw that Fulvir had begun to move. He was easy to see in his bright, fine kurta, and he walked toward the stage where the prima-general was now making her entrance. Drums beat, and a trumpet called, cutting through the talk of soldiers glad for a break from camp life, which is dull beyond words.

All eyes were on the woman in the center of the stage, who seemed to wear the sea behind her as a cloak. I had seen her before in the glasshouse of Sath's temple, wearing the robes of a supplicant. Now she stood armored, in a breastplate and gorget of dull color, and though I could not see small details at this distance, I would later see her more closely, and I can tell you that she was not bothered about having fine things carved on it save the scrapes of goblin spears or the grooves of their quarrels. Her chain mail gleamed dully, clean but not made for ornament. As for her eyes, they were hidden behind small spectacles, the kind the priests of Sath wear—the kind one can only get in Seveda, their glass slightly green against the sun, but not so dark as to prevent her reading a map by candlelight.

This was a woman who was said not to sleep.

I still remember everything I heard her say.

She was a serious woman, and while she lived no general was her equal.

Listen to her words:

"I am Commander Prima-General Peya Dolón Milat, but that is a great deal to say. Call me the Pragmatist, as does His Majesty, King Kalith. I have been gifted with this title because it is my habit to find the most effective way to accomplish tasks. When I am given a command, I follow it at any cost, and I expect the same from those under my baton, which means everyone now able to hear my voice, whether Spanth or Gallard. And you should *want* to follow the commands of someone who pulled the eastern campaign out of the shit, as I have done. Because *you are in the shit.* Your name will not pull you out of this shit, and neither will money. Luck may extract some of you, but your luck has been working so hard on your behalf already that it may soon die of exhaustion."

She paused here, and looked over her glasses, meeting the eyes of this one and that one. She had a way of looking at tedious persons that said, *I have met someone just like you before, and they had no better luck with me than you will.* She had a way of looking at serious dams and men that said, *I see you. I see what you bring here. We will do our best together.* I believe that those of courage and goodwill felt lifted up by her gaze, and that those who only looked after themselves felt accused and looked away.

In this pause, you could only hear the flapping of pennants in the wind.

Even the gulls had stopped crying.

"To be clear, I am not here to save you, at least not as individuals. Rather, I am here to save this army, or as much of it as I can. I doubt that will be a very large fraction. As an individual, your chances here are frankly terrible. In fact, I strongly suggest you stop thinking of yourselves as individuals. Think rather of yourself as a limb in the service not only of your country, but of Manreach. If your priority is the survival of the army and thus the survival of fellow kynd from here to the snow line, you may achieve your objective. Even in death. Even without your legs, or fingers, or tits, or cock. But if your principal hope is to get home alive and un-maimed, most of you are in for crushing disappointment."

My heart thrilled now.

Here was someone who told the truth.

I could follow such a woman into hell.

"Your enemies do not think of themselves as individuals, at least not when they are under arms. Goblins swarming become one big, ugly animal, united in purpose and incapable of betraying one another. Under my command, you will become a similar animal. Except you will be taller, stronger, and marginally less hideous to behold. Some of you, at least."

The army was eager to laugh, and they did so now.

She was winning us.

But she was not here to be liked, as she showed us with what came next.

"Now, it has come to my attention that in the chaos following the loss of your last commander, some tempers have flared, and the army has been beset by a plague of personal duels. As an Ispanthian, I know only too well how brightly the cheap jewelry of pride shines, and I have seen it wreck men of every station—and even a few women, from whom I had expected more. Though I have never personally felt driven to demand satisfaction of any fellow soldier, I know that is not true for many of you. So let me say now that I disapprove of duels generally, and in times of war, find them inexcusably selfish. Those of noble houses will remind me that your fathers have refused to cede the right to kill each other in the most stupid and wasteful possible displays, and I cannot argue this point, which His Majesty the King has enshrined in the Charter of Olives. But, in the interest of preserving at least minimal discipline, I have a new edict on the subject of personal affrays—those who insist on dueling will present themselves to me and will only proceed when you have received my express permission. Further, only one affair of honor shall be considered at any one time in the entire army, and no other request will be heard until the first has been settled."

Perhaps it was a trick of memory, but I believe even the pennants stopped blowing now. It seemed the gods themselves had at last found a dam who interested them, and they, too, were leaning forward to hear what she might say next.

"Is there anyone who now demands your right of high blood, and wishes to defend the honor of your house against one here present?"

This was such an obvious trap that I could not believe anyone at all would be stupid enough to raise a hand.

And yet I looked around in the stands to see, and, surely enough, some hands had gone up. *Fools!* I thought. *Have you got a thought in your heads? This will end badly for you.*

But then my breath caught in my throat.

"What is it?" Inocenta asked.

"I think I see my brother."

"What, the terce-general?"

"No, that is Pol, he is on stage," I said, then pointed. "There. The . . . the man with his hand up."

I had nearly said "idiot" but it is wrong to speak insults against blood, even when deserved.

But I thought at him, *Put your hand down, idiot!*

"By the Skinny Mother's hug, he's a bravo," Inocenta said.

"Is that bad?" I asked.

"Depends on what you mean by 'bad.' He is less likely to be killed by biters, but a jealous husband is another matter."

I felt I had to defend him in some small way.

"Perhaps he has cause."

Inocenta just grunted.

My heart dropped as I saw the Pragmatist point now, and it seemed she was pointing at my brother.

No, no, no, please, by the Bride, no!

By the Bride? Not Sath? I did not have time to examine this thought in the moment, but I think this was my first prayer to My Most Patient Mistress.

Migaéd had already put his hand down, and was now laughing with his fellows.

He had put his hand up as a joke.

I briefly imagined killing him myself.

"You. In the green," the prima-general said.

Migaéd was in scarlet.

I looked up to see another bravo, a Gallard by the look of him, in a fine doublet of sage green, raising his hand more urgently than Migaéd had, and standing almost directly behind him. The Pragmatist now asked this man his name and with whom he had a quarrel.

"It is with *me*," said an Ispanthian sword-dam, with a red sash around her lean hips. "I am Dama Isafrea dom Orván, a knight of Coscabrais, and I have stolen the affections of his wife, whom Sire Françan has been deceiving with numerous other women for some time."

"You are proud of this, you red-mouthed Sornian whore?" Sire Françan said. "You should be flogged and made to pull a shit-cart, not honored with a duel of sword and circle."

"Enough," the Pragmatist said, holding her baton above her head meaning *Attend me*. She continued. "Are you both then hot to defend your honor?"

They were.

"Very well. Come forward, please."

They went down through the gathered ranks in the amphi-theater to stand before their new commander-general, standing proudly and glaring at one another.

"I order both of you to remove your armor and smallclothes and stand before the company nude, each with your weapon of choice at hand."

"What!?" said Françan, his eyes comically wide.

The Coscabraisian looked no less shocked.

"Was I unclear?"

"But I protest," the Gallard said. "We are here to defend our honor, or at least I am, but . . ."

"If you speak out of turn again, sire, I will have you hanged for insubordination. Test me in this, I beg of you."

He did not.

"Now, call your squires and have them help you strip until there is not a thread upon you, or it will be the same."

Murmurs went through the ranks, but these died down as the man and woman called their seconds and stepped out of their armor and clothes. As this took time, the Pragmatist signaled to the pipes and drums to play a lively march.

When at last the two knights stood as their gods made them and had taken up arms before the quiet crowd, the commander-general raised her baton.

The music stopped.

The bravo and the knight looked at one another, then at their commander, then dropped into fighting stances. The Spanth stood in a low guard, her *spadín* forward in the posture of the greater horn, the dagger above, in motion, in the manner of the snake's head. The Gallard held his longsword in rooster guard, straight up, and put his left foot forward, ready to strike down with great force. Someone laughed, high up in the theater, and I thought it might be because of the bravo's body hair, which was much, especially in the lion's mane it made around his pink maleness.

The baton fell.

"Fight," the prima-general said.

The fighters circled without a blow.

This went on long, longer than martial caution might have explained, with only a few half-hearted feints exchanged.

"Well?" said the Pragmatist. "Did you not hear my command? I said fight, not dance."

"I . . . I have changed my mind," said Sire Françan, "and I am satisfied, if Dama Isafrea is."

The Pragmatist spoke before Dama Isafrea could.

"Well *I* am *not* satisfied. I commanded you to fight and you had damned well better."

The Spanth, understanding the gravity of her position, lunged hard at the legs of the Gallard, who thrust his ass and legs back barely in time, his manhood a-jiggle, and he slashed down at his attacker's head.

His blade was caught by her *spadín*.

She flicked his sword away and pressed, but he danced out of range.

Now he countered, driving with the point at her chest. She blocked this, cut a gash in his thigh, and received his pommel to her head in return. There was much blood, as it is with head wounds, so in a moment it looked as if she were wearing a red mask. Sire Françan was no less bloody, and he stepped back and nearly fell, the muscle of his leg ruined. They separated, and I think each was surprised to be so badly hurt.

"It is a different thing, fighting without armor," one engineer said to another.

"No shit," Inocenta said to her, making some around us laugh. The engineer looked hard at her. She stared back and said, "Would you like to go next?"

The other dam found somewhere else to rest her eyes.

The combatants looked at the prima-general, who waved her hand for them to continue.

They did. Seeing no way out of this but through the red door, they came hard at each other. It was a desperate thing to watch, having nothing to do with honor, as both were now simply fighting for life. Any technique that has not been drilled to the point of reflex goes out the window at these times, so that training, will, and luck decide which, if either, will survive.

Soon, they were both panting and bloody, lying on the stage, the Spanth's ear cut off, the bravo going "haa" with every breath out. He tried to get up and collapsed. His sword fell out of his hand.

The crowd murmured.

"Stop it," someone near the back yelled.

"Yes!" another said. "Stop it!"

"Silence," the Pragmatist said to the crowd. Then, to her own personal guard, but loud enough to be heard, she said, "Put Sire Françan's sword back in his hand, then move them closer together."

Three of her close-guards did this, arming the fallen Gallard, and dragging Dama Isafrea near him.

She was very pale, she had lost much blood.

"Fight," the Pragmatist said. "That is an order."

Neither one moved, both just tried to catch their breath.

The Pragmatist walked close to Dama Isafrea, then knelt to look her in the eye. What she said to her I do not know, but it caused the dying woman to act.

Dama Isafrea crawled with her knife to the bravo and killed him sloppily, cutting his throat as her head wound bled into his eyes so he could not see what she was doing, and she was too slick with blood for her wrists to be grabbed. This done, she crawled away from him and then curled up like a baby on the stage and lay still.

It was strange to see this with a peaceful blue sea behind them and the gulls still riding their warm breeze.

"Enough," said the Pragmatist. "We have a victor. Congratulations to Dama Isafrea dom . . . what was it?"

"Orván," her assistant told her.

"Yes, Orván. The honor of your illustrious house is upheld. Take her to the infirmary, please—I doubt she will live, but perhaps they can sew her ear back on for decorum's sake. And take this good Gallard away to the house of the dead."

Her soldiers did so.

Someone yelled something in the distance, but we did not at first know what.

"Now," said Commander Prima-General Peya Dolón Milat, "is there anyone else who would like to help the cause of the enemy by petitioning me to fight a duel?"

None in the old theater spoke, but the distant call came again, louder, so we could all hear what was said.

"Sail!"

Those around me began to gasp and I turned my attention from the carnage on the stage to the line of the horizon.

I gasped, too.

It had just become visible to us, as the fortress had blocked our view of the eastern horn of the harbor, and it had come from the east.

"A red sail!"

There, in the distance, a swatch of red had appeared, like the first stain coughed into the handkerchief of one who has a cancer in the lungs.

Bells in the town began to ring, in the tower of Haros, in the Allgod church, at the watchtowers, all took up the alarm.

It was unwise for a poorly defended town to ring bells of alarm at the approach of goblins by land, for they will often run at the town with speed, to stop any escaping.

Espalle was not poorly defended at this time.

But the threat was not approaching by land.

An enemy warship had come to the harbor of Espalle.

It had come from the east, chasing the last troopmules from Ispanthia.

I still see this goblin ship in my dreams, and it wakes me.

By the time my unit had formed up and marched to the Plaza of Anchors, the juggernaut had nearly made the harbor. It came around Crab Island with its burnt lighthouse and made for the troopmules now unloading at the dock. These had arrived perhaps an hour before, and had not seen the thing that was stalking them because it was hidden by spellwork. Now that the prey was cornered, however, the goblin mages let their spell slip and would spend their strength on destruction rather than concealment.

The seven troopmules each carried five hundred to one thousand soldiers, and were under escort by the dreadnought called the *Brawling Bear*, which I have mentioned before. It had hit a goblin seatrap and had been forced to seek a harbor where its springwood hull might repair itself. Three smaller fireships were also present, two of these Ispanthian and one Holtish. I do not think much of the Holtish as soldiers—except from their held lands of Galtia and Norholt, where the people are either criminals or soldiers of great valor—but the Holtish proper are good sailors, one can say nothing against their navy.

While the troopmules were docking, and thus vulnerable, the four warships fanned out at the mouth of the harbor in a defensive formation. Those who saw the whole engagement said that at the sight of the red sail, they had moved to meet it, the three fireships going one way, the dreadnought the other. But the wind had turned, and the fireships, which only used sail, could barely move no matter how they tried. The two Spanths were sprayed with liquid fire while they sat without wind, and they burned to the waterline. The *Bear* was a trireme, with three rows of oars, so it had done better, but not by much. It seemed the tide was against them, and this allowed the juggernaut to close and grapple. This happened before our arrival at the Plaza of Anchors, as it was no small matter to form up an amphitheater full of troops and move them through the narrow streets of a town. Even as we marched and jostled and waited for other units to go ahead of us, the Pragmatist had summoned Fulvir and other magickers and ordered them to prepare counterattacks, but these would come late to the fight.

We had already begun to hear the screams and crashes of naval combat before we came into the Plaza of Anchors. We could see the smoke from the two burnt Ispanthian fireships.

When we finally pushed our way into the plaza, our mouths fell open.

I had never seen a ship as large as the goblin juggernaut, nor as dreadful.

It was murdering the *Brawling Bear*.

There is no better way to say it; it was a killing, not a fight.

First, I will try to make you see the juggernaut before I tell you what it was doing to my brothers and sisters.

I counted four ranks of oars, though the counting was difficult because goblins hate straight lines. It stood high above the *Brawling Bear*, which I had thought the largest warship on the seas. The hull was gray-black, made of charred springwood, a tree that did not grow in the Hordelands—this must have been made from captured kynd ships. Even Molrova would not sell this precious material to goblins, or so I thought at the time. The sails were red, as I have said, though not regular in their arrangement, and the mainsail seemed to have a painting of some kind on it. Inocenta stood near me, looking through a field glass, saying, "By the Bride, oh the hateful devils, Lady help us." She handed me the glass so I might see as well, and I took it, though I was not sure I wanted to see.

I wish I had not.

The image on the mainsail was of a Keshite king or emperor, done in the style of a mosaic. He had brown skin and an off-white turban, and a pointed pink tongue stuck out to show its full length.

As I twisted the tube, adjusting the lens to see the image nearer, I found that the face on the sail was made of human hides. Pale northerners and lighter Ispanthians and Gallards composed the turban and the whites of the eyes. Keshite and southern Ispanthians had lost their skins to make up the warm browns. Those of Axaene blood formed the darker shadows and the pupils of the eyes. And when I thought my horror could not deepen, I saw that the hair of the portrait was actual black human hair, and that the gold trim of the turban had been given by blonds.

The sails were also patched here and there with human skins, the faces still on, as if tiny men and dams were falling around the giant central figure.

I will tell you one final thing about the face—a single tear made from blue colored glass and silver winked at the inner corner of one eye.

The message was clear enough.

Woe unto humankind.

My brother named this ship in his journal.

Look.

The ship that attacked the harbor of Espalle was called the Lament of Avraparthi, and it was one of only two juggernauts in the Horde fleet. If they had six of them, I think they would clear the oceans of kynd vessels, for we have nothing to stand against them. It was named for Avraparthi the Twelfth, the last emperor of the Kesh, who, two centuries after the cataclysm known as the Knock had brought the empire to its knees, signed a document ceding the lands of Old Kesh to the Horde. He did this in return for safe passage for himself, his court, and his large extended family to whatsoever nations in the Crownlands would have them. Many of these met bad ends in Ispanthia and Gallardia, but the emperor and his wives and sons went to Axa, the continent-nation in the east that

has little to do with the Crownlands. It is written that the
former emperor's family was treated respectfully, but that
he was exiled to a patch of rocks called Hotglass Island,
inhabited chiefly by reptiles, there to be an emperor to
lizards, since he was unfit to govern kynd.

It was a shame that the name had been so blighted by
this twelfth Avraparthi. The first to bear that name had
been a great general, the first to use elephants in war.
Avraparthi the Fourth had been called the Light on the
Water because he had built three universities. Avraparthi
the Mild, the ninth of his name, had been a beekeeper
and a poet, and had begun a seventy-year period of
peace with great advances in science and medicine. Now,
thanks to this emperor of lizards, the name was as dead
as the empire.

I moved the glass down and focused, seeing now the rows of
cages arranged on the sides of the ship. Naked kynd lay in these
in great agony, pink and peeling from Sath's kiss. Probably the
next to be eaten, one could not last long in such a place.

I lowered the farglass to the fabulous bronzework on the ship's
bow.

It was hideous as well as beautiful.

At the front, though just off-center, I saw a huge bronze goblin
face, with a mouth that opened as I watched, sucking in a brine of
bloody, greenish seawater and kynd sailors who had fallen over.
They were just too far away for their shouts to be heard. What I
could hear, though, was the sound of tortured metal being broken
down and formed again, for the moving bronze of the juggernaut
was not as the gears and cogs of clockwork machines—rather,
this solid bronze was manipulated by mages of great strength.
Extended into the water was a bronze arm, which scooped sailors
into the mouth. The goblin ship and the kynd ship both shuddered, just before I heard a distant crash. It seemed every voice

in the Plaza of Anchors cried "Ay!" at once. I moved the lens of the glass to see that the goblin had a second, much larger arm, that had been held up at a great height, holding a pick. The crash had been this arm descending, smashing through the decks of the smaller *Bear*. The arm rose again, one Spanth dam tumbling through the air like a child's doll. The arm now swiveled to change the angle of its strike, the sound of groaning metal coming to me once again a heartbeat later. Now the arm swung mostly from the side and down, knifing the *Bear* below the waterline, spilling more soldiers into the water with the force of its blows. The crowd around me gasped and sobbed. This was no ordinary ship being murdered by the goblins—the *Brawling Bear* was the pride of the Ispanthian fleet. There were only five ships so powerful in all our navy. The queen consort's brother, a naval officer, had been married on this ship with the bay covered in flower petals. This mighty dreadnought was, like the juggernaut, made of springwood, though of the rosy-white living kind, and could not burn.

But it could sink.

And with this spike driving holes into its hull belowdecks, it surely would. The goblin's smaller bronze arm scooped more struggling kynd from the water into the mouth, and its sharp, irregular teeth closed behind them like a gate.

I realized the farglass I was holding was not my own, and went to hand it back to Inocenta, but she now had a second one. Bellu nuzzled me and spread his wings, so I reached out to caress his beak. Then I did the same for Dalgatha so she would not be jealous, but she nipped at me because she knew I thought of her second. She is a smart bird.

I raised the glass again.

The Holtish fireship had filled its sails with wind and now circled the goblin and the dying *Bear* like a small dog, loosing firedarts of Axaene jelly from its several ballistas. It managed to burn some of one sail, and to kill a few biters on deck, but no more than this. Other darts flared against the hull, some of these burning the captives in the cages. These caused the charred springwood hull to smoke, but it never caught. I have been told that with normal wood, one such dart might turn a whole ship to a bright torch, but blackened springwood will not burn any more than the live sort. Years later, as you know, I would see such darts aimed at a ship I was on, and that is no joke. Burning is not a way I should like to meet the Exquisite One.

Though even this is something I would bear at her pleasure.

The name of this fireship was the *Sounding Bell*. Her captain was Dam Margalin Woodshire, a knight-maritime from the city of Lamnur. When she ran out of firedarts, she ordered her crew to ram the goblin, which did little more than break a few of its oars. The goblin ship turned and smashed its pick-arm to hold the smaller Holtish ship and swarmed her with goblin marines. We on the shore screamed and waved our weapons, and I cried at the bravery of this Margalin Woodshire, though I did not yet know her name.

It is good to remember those who stand.

As for those who flee, may their stolen years be many, and their dreams vivid. Captain Woodshire of Holt did not flee, and she went to the Beloved with honor, as did every soul on the *Sounding Bell*. Because she fought, four of the seven troopmules were able to unload soldiers before the killing thing came into the harbor.

But come it did, and it sank every ship we had there.

As it came close, the plaza was cleared lest the juggernaut spray us with fire while we gaped at it. We waited several streets away in case they sent soldiers into the town, but this never happened.

When the juggernaut had done its work, it sailed away.

But it did not get far.

I will leave it for Amiel to tell you of the battle of spellcraft that raged alongside that of wood, and bronze, and fire.

12

The only real challenge to the juggernaut was mounted by magickers, and the Pragmatist had sought out Fulvir Lightningbinder and two others for this purpose. The other two, a Gallard and an Ispanthian, were mages of a lesser order than Fulvir, and they were the first to attack. I did not see what happened to them, though I had a full account of it from those who did. I was serving Fulvir closely, and I will get to his business presently.

The Spanth witch stationed herself in an antlered bell tower at the temple of Haros. The Gallard mage took the top floor of a private house near the harbor. The Spanth sent fearsome lightning bolts at the decks and sails of the Lament of Avraparthi, and it is said she killed some twenty or more of those abovedecks, and badly tattered several sails. One of the goblin mages, however, summoned a water elemental from the greeny brine. I have never seen one, but the woman who told me about it said that it looked as if a running lizard made of water skipped along the surface of the bay, growing in size until it was larger than an ox, and that it launched itself at the tower of Haros even as the people on the streets screamed in terror. The Spanth magicker would not be going back to Coscabrais in glory, as it is said that she had bragged—her remains were found burst all over the inside of the tower, waterlogged and bloodless, countless gallons of seawater having entered her nose and mouth with great force. It is not known what the Gallard mage had attempted, nor what became of him. He was not found. Some say he fled, but, if he did, he took with him every stick of furniture that had been in the room he commandeered. Fulvir believes he was shoved into some other world, perhaps even whatever fell place the goblins themselves came from.

"At least he will have a nice bed to lie on when he gets there,"

Fulvir had laughed, though I saw nothing funny in it. This is normal with him.

The Pragmatist had known Fulvir was the most powerful card she had on the table, and she played him skillfully. I think even he was impressed with her, and he is impressed at nothing he does not himself accomplish.

"Do not make yourself a target," she instructed him at the start of the engagement, for she had commanded magickers in the east and knew something of the costs and rhythms of magical warfare. "I want the strongest harm you can bring to them without being taken yourself."

It is worth noting that the lesser magickers received no such instruction. They were sacrificed to make Fulvir's decisive blow more likely to land.

"I can think of several things I might do, but none of them are sure, and none of them are fast."

"Kill that thing without being killed. If you must choose between being quick and being sure, be sure."

"The goblin ship will do great harm in this time."

"It will do much more if it survives."

"The magic I am thinking of is of the highest order, and will not be without cost to the town. A terrible cost."

I will never forget what she said next.

"Gallardia has many towns. The biters have only two of those ships."

Fulvir turned to me and said, "Do you know the spot on the coast, a mile north, with the standing stones of the old tribes?"

"Yes," I said, for he had sent me near there to gather sorrel and thyme and other herbs before, which I thought he wanted for some spell, but they were just for cooking.

"Good," he said, "bring me there an infant, or three lambs, I do not care which. And please, come at a leisurely pace, we have all the time we want."

"Um. I do not know how I will . . ."

"Bring him," he said, pointing at one of his man-bulls, a huge horror named Billix.

So I took Billix with me and we commandeered three lambs from a nearby farm. Though, at four months old, these were almost sheep. I hoped they would serve.

"The king of Ispanthia will pay you," I said in my best Gallard, which is not perfect, and the elderly, coughing shepherd knew it was a lie, or at best wishful thinking, but he looked at seven-foot-tall Billix with his huge club and scale armor, and looked at his one crippled son and three daughters, one of whom was nursing a baby, and he struggled not to sob, shook his head, and let us. I did not offer to take the baby instead, not because I was afraid he would be offended, but because I was afraid he might agree. I believe it was no accident that this dwelling, on the way to the standing stones, had exactly one infant and exactly three lambs.

As Billix was too proud to lead an animal, he carried two over his shoulders, leaving me to pull one with a rope at something between a run and a walk. We got to the standing stones, and I looked toward the harbor, though because of the angle of the cliffs, I could see only smoke from the burning warships. This was the whole point of our remove. While lesser mages were sacrificed, wearing down the goblin magickers with their spectacular deaths, Fulvir could work his art in safety.

And a great and terrible art it was.

Billix stretched each lamb in turn over an altar-stone while I cut their throats, leaving a large pool of blood. Fulvir arranged several rocks at the western border of the blood sea, placed a piece of wood and a bronze coin in the blood, cut his own hand to bleed on these, then blew on the wood and coin. He then used his cut palm to push the blood, the twig, and the coin toward the rocks, saying nothing, which I found odd. Should he not have been muttering spellwork?

He swooned now, as if stricken by a wave of exhaustion.

"*Do you know a sad song?*" he said.

"*What Ispanthian do not?*" I said.

He smiled weakly, looking faint. Billix stepped in to hold him up.

"*Well,*" Fulvir said, fading. "*Please do not sing it as prettily as you can now. The spirits of this place will do no favors for music.*"

The saddest song I know is the Arvarescala, or "The Song of Arvaresca," told from the perspective of a man who was crippled in the Threshers' War, and whose wife was mustered to take his place. Arvaresca is a bleak Ispanthian province of rocks and shipwrecks and fishing villages, a place of beautiful cliffs, relentless wind, and fierce storms.

Arvaresca is made for despairing songs.

I sang its most famous one.

> If I had not fallen defeated
> And given my sword to your hand,
> If I had not fallen defeated
> And given my sword to your hand,
>
> Your bright eyes would still be shining,
> More fair than the moon on the sea.
> Your bright eyes would still be shining,
> More fair than the moon on the sea.
>
> Your hair would still fall on my shoulder;
> Instead, you cropped it all short.
> Your hair would still fall on my shoulder;
> Instead, you cropped it all short.
>
> Your daughter would still have a mother,
> Instead of a coin from the king.
> Your daughter would still have a mother,
> Instead of a coin from the king.

I have not enough legs for farming,
Nor fingers to romance the lute.
I have not enough legs for farming,
Nor fingers to romance the lute.

I beg for the bread on our table
And pull skinny fish from the sea.
I beg for the bread on our table
And pull skinny fish from the sea.

But I still have a voice to lament you
And I listen for yours in the wind
Yes I still have this voice to lament you,
Though yours has been lost in the wind.

By the time I finished the song, Billix had taken the now un-conscious form of Fulvir Lightning-Binder and walked the cliffside path back to the house and farm we were staying in with his me-nagerie of half humans and early attempts at war corvids. This is the strangest and most awful time, but it is also a time of wonder. I will remember these days for the rest of my life.

Forgive me, I must stop for a moment now.

13

The storm that came was the worst one to strike Espalle in memory. It started as a band of dark gray sky on the horizon that soon went black. The wind began then, flipping busted latticework and bits of trash through the streets, making plane trees creak and shop-signs flap on their hooks.

The corvids grew anxious in their stalls, and they snapped their beaks and croaked.

"Pet beak."

"Want food."

"Bad."

"Bad."

"Bad."

"Yes, it is bad," I told Dalgatha, hugging her head to me. I had gone into the corvids' stall to calm them, and many of the other birders did the same with theirs.

One thing I will never forget was the leaving of the rats.

Hundreds of them moved north, away from the harbor toward higher ground. I wanted us to follow the rats, but of course there was no question of moving the birds and their things with enough speed. We would have to take our chances here. We were not so very near the harbor.

When the rain came it fell hard sideways and got under the roof of the market and stung the skin. I bent between my two corvids, one arm around each of them, and tucked my face into Bellu's feathers, then into Dalgatha's, then back again. One of them clicked at me, perhaps Bellu, and I know they were both glad I was there. As I was glad to shelter with them and their familiar smell, which was even stronger when wet.

It was a very long night.

In the morning, our part of town was littered with new-fallen trees and branches, and there was water up to the ankles. Closer to the harbor, small houses had flooded, and tall ones had been torn down. With Nouva's permission, I went to see how things lay, and saw that one of the burned and ruined troopmules had washed up into the Plaza of Anchors, and lay there on its side like a huge whale, with many seagulls crying above it. A barefoot Gallard child carried a wet sack near me where I stood on a higher street. He left bloody footprints as he went. He was only one of many children who were climbing the unburnt bottom of the wreck, competing with the gulls to harvest barnacles.

Seagulls swarmed the town, for the dead were very many. Several houses of the rich with their pretty façades lining the water had been pulled into the sea entirely, stripped to the foundation. I watched from a higher street as the water began to flow back out of town, taking bodies and small boats and all manner of wreckage with it.

Early summer was not a season for storms here, many said, and dark magic was suspected.

Word began to spread of an Ispanthian boy who had taken three lambs from a shepherd north of town, a boy who had been seen with Fulvir, the Father of Abominations. Soon, a mob of angry Espalleers gathered, and they went to the house where the wizard stayed, and where my brother stayed as well.

Here is Amiel's telling of it:

I believe the people of Espalle meant to kill Fulvir.

Molrovans are little loved generally, since they sent no levies to the war this time, and they reserve their power to lord over their neighbors, stealing this or that stretch of land by bullying, using the threat of a war neither Wostra nor its other neighbors think they might win against such a large country that has spent little blood against the biters. The king of Molrova, who is by public record at least one hundred years old, but appears to be a robust man of fifty, claims the goblins are a problem only for the south, and even maintains trading colonies in the Hordelands. He permits the goblins to do the same in Molrova, though goblins do not well tolerate the cold and they make themselves ridiculous in furs and warm themselves in saunas.

That Fulvir himself has defied his goblin-friendly king and shown up to resist the invaders is a fact too nuanced for simple folk and their simple prejudice, especially when the wizard seems the most likely culprit in the matter of the freak storm that flooded Espalle, on top of her many other woes. No storm of this power had hit these shores since the Knock, and most storms came in the fall, not summer. The Molrovan arch-wizard's presence here was well-known, and the subject of much tongue-wagging. Would not a foreign mage of his fame and wealth have chests laden with gold, and silver, and undreamt-of wonders? This, more than any actual complaint, would prove the most tempting lure for the starved and impoverished Gallards. And so, a tattered, skinny crowd of maimed men and sick-looking women came to the wine estate where we made camp, bearing all manner of farm tools that doubled neatly as weapons.

They asked for him in Gallard, saying, "Where is Fulvir something-something? We are something-something and the storm something, and he must pay us." They were asking for money, which they would have taken, but it was clear to me this would end with bloodshed and a general sack of the premises no matter what sum I might have offered them to leave.

I knew that he was sleeping, that he would likely remain asleep for some time, muttering and seemingly terrified by whatever agencies visited him in dreams, perhaps demanding whatever he had promised in the place of standing stones. The spell he had worked was no small thing. To call a rain shower is beyond the power of many magickers. To call a storm that moves the sea? I do not think there are ten in all the Crownlands of Manreach who might accomplish that, and some of these would die of the effort.

"He sleeps," I said. "He is tired from the work he do."

I have not mastered past tense in Gallard.

This mob numbered perhaps eighty.

"Wake him," an old woman with a pair of shears said, snipping them viciously at a height and in a way that any man would understand.

I looked toward the large stone barn where the mixlings were kept, saw Billix, their foreman, looking from the darkness therein. At a word from me, he would bring his three fellow bull-men, and unleash the seven early models of corvids, each with defects of character or form that made them less fit than the ones being bred up now, but still lethal. Except for Ispra, who is a terrible coward, and would probably fret and caw well away from any action. Still, these were more than sufficient to deal with the threat these limping, Horde-cut Espalleers posed.

How might I turn them away without bloodshed?

Seeing to guests was one of my duties here. Fulvir agreed to take me on with the expectation I would deal with Spanths, and that the name dom Braga would carry weight with them; but these were illiterate Gallards, not Spanths, and the servants he had who spoke Gallard were part dog, with thick tongues and natures too servile or protective for nuance.

I cannot fight, but I understand nuance.

I wished I understood just a little more Gallard.

Several of them were going on now, and in a rapid, rural southern dialect that has nothing to do with the few formal lessons I had in school.

I looked again at Billix, who waggled his club in a questioning way.

A word about these bull-men Fulvir crafted—I must confess they make me uneasy.

Though they smile and grovel as they must, they like us no better than they like the goblins. And why should they like us? They are too much like men to be owned things. Fulvir's keeping of them, and his selling of them to this or that army, smacks of slavery, and nothing good comes of that.

Now this great monster was looking to me for command.

How had I come to a place of such authority so quickly?

Right, the last stewards had all died, and the apprentice Vlano, while bookishly talented in the art, was even more soft-spoken than I, and unfit to command the meekest songbird, let alone a mixling.

Zhebrava came around the house hopping and whistling.

She was three-quarters hare, only two feet tall, and served no purpose I could tell except as a pet—Fulvir was fond of dandling her ears while he smoked his pipe or read, which was most of what he did while not in the barn making abominations against the gods.

She was pointing toward the ocean, but the Espalleers did not care about that. They just saw yet another reason to smash the place up, hang this maker of freaks and flooder of towns, then see what he had in his chests. A lame man with thick arms and a flail limped purposefully toward Zhebrava, who cowered and moved away. I interposed myself, palms open, half squinting against the blow I expected to litter Fulvir's newly planted garden of nightshades with my brains.

The flail man wound up to do just that.

Several women readied short bows, the kind better suited for rabbits and birds than deer or kynd, but nothing I wanted flinging sharp and probably rusty barn arrows at me in any case.

I said "Please!" sounding like a nasal, terrified man-child, which I suppose I was, and the man lowered his flail and stepped back. Not because I had honked please, and in Ispanthian anyway because I was too scared to think, but because Billix was moving from the barn with two other man-bulls. The third held a chain that I knew would open the corvid enclosure. The door was already open a foot or so. I heard them cawing in excitement, sensing agitation and the nearness of violence. I saw a huge, black wing flapping eagerly, and knew that would be Gurgut, the largest of the misfits, who was too slow for war, but with a body the size of a large bull and a wingspan that could embrace a small hut.

Billix began to walk toward the mob with purpose.

If they were going to shoot him with arrows, now was the time, but they were afraid to draw this fight from forgiving potential into brutal reality.

Billix had nearly reached the looters.

"Billix, no," I said, remembering Fulvir told me these creatures were quick to anger and hard to stop once blood was shed.

Zhebrava, seeing she was not in immediate danger now, squealed and whistled, hopping up and down and pointing again toward the ocean. Her little arms and fingers were the most kyndish part of her.

Now Billix slowed and looked where the hare-girl pointed.

What he saw stopped him, and the other mixlings stopped as well. I looked.

Zhebrava was pointing at the rocks, at the bottom of the cliffs, on our side of those cliffs so the rocks were not visible from town.

A huge shape lay cracked amid the foam, trailing great red sails.

Dead goblins washed against the sharp rocks known as the Widow's Teeth, washed out a bit, then got pushed into them again.

The milky jade waters of the shallows had been polluted with the dark gray-green of goblin blood.

The mob now saw the purpose of the storm, and the heat and anger went out of them.

They marveled at the great wooden corpse heaving in the water.

The Lament of Avraparthi, murderer of the Brawling Bear, had in turn been killed.

14

Now that the last of our troops had come ashore—those who lived, at least—the army would soon leave Espalle and make for the great city of Goltay, which was in danger of falling. This city was the old capital of Gallardia, now famous as a center of culture and pleasure, though an earlier king had moved his court to Mouray, which had better walls.

Despite the danger of Goltay's fall, the destruction of the goblin juggernaut cheered those who saw it. Many of us went to look at the wreck more closely, and in so doing I found myself moved—not by the many dead goblins, who should all be cut to pieces and burned, down to the smallest hiveling, but by the sight of the ghalls.

Whether these pale, half-blind creatures who were two heads taller than tall men, and wider as well, were still kynd was a matter for scholars. You will remember that these creatures, which my brother had mentioned in his letter, come from humans captured years ago by goblins and bred underground for many generations. They tend to fat, but this fat hides muscle and strength that no kynd has. I knew they were used in battle, and more about this later, but I had never thought they might also serve on goblin ships. Who better to pull the massive oars that pushed the *Lament* through the water at such speed? Ghalls did not have much endurance, but they were kept in reserve for when a great rush of speed was desired. Now these ghalls floated facedown and white as fish-bellies in the water.

The dead who washed ashore were burned on a great pyre that very night, along with the hides pulled from parts of the wicked sail. A second pyre was lit in honor of Sath, and a night of jubilee was declared by the Pragmatist, who knew the importance of an army's morale.

Yes, Goltay would likely fall.

Yes, Espalle had been flooded and further wrecked.

But the second-greatest goblin ship ever built was no more. We were all to say that the attack of the Holtish ship captained by Dam Woodshire had cracked the juggernaut and left it vulnerable to the wizard's storm. But this is not how it looked to me, and I never said the lie. The Holtish captain should be honored for her bravery, but I believe it was Fulvir alone who destroyed the *Lament of Avraparthi*. The wizard was Molrovan, and could be cruel, but he served us well in this war, and he served me well after.

He deserves to be seen as he is, as do we all.

The entire company, save those watching the birds, had come to look at the wreck, and so had much of the army. The small, gravelly beach was mobbed. Inocenta stooped in the shallows to pick something up. A piece of wood, from the railing of the ship. A small brass lizard had been fixed to it. The goblins were fine sculptors, it seemed, for the lizard looked almost real. At the time I did not know its significance, but of course I now know this was to represent one of Avraparthi's subjects on Hotglass Island.

I think often of how cowardice diminishes one.

An emperor of men turned to an emperor of lizards.

The price to continue living is often too high, as the Bride teaches us, and many live to regret refusing the offer of a good death. Freedom from cowardice is Dal-Gaata's greatest gift, and one I pray she continues to provide.

Inocenta took the brass lizard off its wooden perch and kept it.

But she was only one of many looting the wreck that day.

"Lady knight, lady knight!" I heard a child's voice say, a voice I knew.

I took the amber glass from my pouch, placed this over my eye, and turned to look through it at the boy, Sambard.

As it was a night of jubilee, and my second-to-last day in Espalle, I was released from all duty not related to care of the birds. Many in the regular army had been ordered to help the people of the town clear rubble from the harbor, where the waters had drawn back, but our lanza was under orders from Nouva not to do so.

"If you are hurt by falling timber, who will mind your war corvids? The king did not train you two years to pull housebeams out of floodwaters like oxen. There are bodies enough for this work, save your strength for killing."

I did not agree with this, but I obeyed.

It is not without logic.

The boy Sami had invited me to a meal with his family, though he asked me to bring food if I could, for his sister to prepare. I promised to do so after I exercised Dalgatha and Bellu. While I worked with the birds, however, a messenger from my brother Pol came for me again, and she handed me this note:

Dearest Galvicha,
As the army will be leaving soon, and a night of jubilee has been declared, I am holding a dinner at my villa. I would be honored if you would attend. I have also invited Migi and Amiel. Would it not be lovely for the four of us to gather again? I cannot say when the last time was, but if it has been less than five years I will eat my boots. That is not what is on the menu, however. I think you will be pleased.
Come at the eighth hour of the day.

Yours,
Pol

I scratched out a note telling the young General dom Braga I would be there, and sent the girl off with it.

"Wait," I said, before she ran. "Do you know where I can get fresh meat?"

"Yes. Near town. But it is where the officers buy, it is not cheap."

"I should fear it if it were."

She laughed, and told me of a farm just out of town that still had mutton. I thought I could just get there and back before the third hour, when I was to dine with Sambard and his sister. I would not allow myself to be late for this meal with people who had suffered as they had. I would also try to be prompt with my brothers, but this second invitation seemed less urgent, somehow. The first meeting felt to have been arranged by divinity, and such roadsigns should not be ignored.

That is what I said to Inocenta, at least.

"Galva dom Braga, you do not know what it is to be desperate. Has it not occurred to you that they might be planning to garrote you for the coins in your purse?"

"I do not believe this."

"This child could be a Guild bait-boy, practiced at deceit."

"He is not a bait-boy."

"Will you bet your life on this?"

I thought about it.

"Yes."

"Then I am coming with you."

Sambard lived in a sort of tree house in the woods just north of town. He told me to go past the blooming lavender fields and to find the ruins of an old Keshite bridge. There are many such dry bridges in the south, in fields or woodlands that were once rivers—the old empire built things to last, and the Knock changed the flow of water in many places. It is beyond me to understand the scope of the Knock—even the catastrophe of the Goblin Wars must be dwarfed by that day and night of earthquakes, risings of the sea, and tearing of land that drowned cities, broke mountains, and toppled the greatest power ever to rule the lands of the kynd. Strange to think how almost the whole world had once been under the scepter of the emperor of Kesh, with his elephants and astronomy, and archers, and towers covered in beautiful reliefs. But these disasters of earth and sea had drowned their ports and buried their roads, and the Crownlands of Manreach won their freedom. And then the goblins had come, taking the great island of Old Kesh, so that all that remained to the Keshite king today was a small corner of the mainland, full of rocky hills and bandits.

How long had it been since Keshite armies trod these fields and roads?

Nine hundred years?

A thousand?

Gallardia was truly a beautiful land.

Birds of great variety called here, and flew in the trees through patches of sun. These woods were good to the people of Espalle. When the goblins came, some ran to the woods and climbed high, and some went down into the caves west of town, which are complex and deep. Those of the caves soon found that hiding from goblins underground is like hiding from a shark in water.

Always go up, away from them.

Always go toward light, and toward the cold.

Inocenta and I walked together, along with Alisenne, whom we invited because she knows the Gallard tongue. We were armored, and with *spadíns* on our belts and shields on our backs. Inocenta also had her axe, and Alisenne her bow. With Nouva's permission, we had also brought our six corvids with us. We fed them early, and gave them our own rations as well. It would be good to let them see that other people are friendly, if indeed they were, or to have them with us if they were not. Of course, with guests who had not been invited, one must bring extra. I had bought mutton enough for five, perhaps six, besides a bag of scraps and bones for the birds to have while we ate, and all of this had cost me deep in the purse. The loaves of bread Alisenne carried were not cheap, either, though the taste was not good and I believe some part of the flour was made from sawdust.

Inocenta carried the bag of mutton scraps, using her axe-handle to prod the birds when they got too interested in it. The worst bird for this was her own corvid, Richu, of whom I have spoken before.

Past the lichen-covered ruins of the bridge, the woods got thicker, and the shadows longer and deeper.

A light shone near my feet, moving back and forth, and I looked up.

Someone was catching the sun with a piece of mirror.

"Sami?" I said.

"Dam Galva!" the boy said, coming down the tree. Another boy and a small girl were with him, and I thought again of street cats, who are quicker and more cautious than barn cats.

Sami was unafraid of the birds, too much so, and I canted for the others to move them back when he came to embrace me.

I asked him, through Alisenne, if the small girl was his sister, and he shook his head no, pointing up at the tree. A pretty young woman of sixteen or so let down a rope ladder, smiling at us.

We tied the birds, and Inocenta threw them scraps. As they fought over them with much posturing and flapping of wings, we went up to the tree house to dine with these young survivors of Espalle.

The dwelling itself was clever in its design, with wattle-and-daub walls, and a thatched roof, also with a small clay oven and chimney. The openings that served as windows had been hung with found bits of glass in many colors, and these turned in the breeze, throwing light most agreeably. The sister, whose name was Larmette, had built almost everything. Their father had been a woodsman and carpenter, and she shared his gift, and had inherited his tools. The other children were orphans, too. I apologized for how little meat there was, but they laughed at me, saying this was more meat than they had seen at one time since before the war. They lived on squirrels and birds' eggs, and berries, and grubs from the undersides of trees, and, once the Ispanthian army came, from begging in town.

Larmette was a fine cook.

She had found garlic on abandoned farms, and a few blue carrots, and some snails. With the bread, which as I have said was not good, but filling, we each got enough. I shared a skin of wine around as well, though I had mixed this with water, as is better for children.

I made a gift to Larmette of a piece of cloth I had found in a market before I left Ispanthia. It was the kind of thing I might pull out when I wanted to see a bit of color. It had only been a trifle to me, with its design of birds and flowers in a pretty golden shade of yellow, and a rich blue, but she held it to her face and smelled it. She then wrapped it around her narrow waist as a sash, and said it was the prettiest thing she owned. Indeed, it stood out from her plain, soiled linen dress, and it brought out her eyes, which I only now noticed were a like blue to the fabric.

Her eyes were not dry.

Nor were mine.

Before we took our leave, we introduced the Espalleers to the birds.

"Will they really kill the goblins?" the small girl asked. She had been quiet as a stone all through dinner.

"I believe they will," I said, and, when Alisenne translated, she smiled her first smile since I met her and hugged my waist and for some time refused to let go. I felt badly because I had thought she might be simple, but it was just that she had seen too much. They all had, and I feared they would see more. I wanted very much to believe that our birds would kill the goblins, but I did not know. I felt stupid and weak, unable to tell these children anything useful or to save them from whatever horrors awaited them. What good outcome could they expect here?

I told Sami the army would leave soon.

"We know," he said.

"What will you do?" I asked.

Larmette looked much more like a woman than a girl when she said, "Follow it."

This troubled me.

The army was more dams than men now, but there were still enough men to make mischief, and not all dams are above the worst impulses of men.

This girl was too pretty to be near a war.

I gave her enough silver to make her eyes wide and said, "Yes, follow us. But only for safety. Not the other thing. If you need money, hire out your saw and make repairs—every army needs carpenters. You understand?"

Alisenne added her grave look to mine when she said it in Gallard.

Larmette nodded, but, I think, only to say that she understood.

We left and made our way back to Espalle.

Much would happen before we got there.

15

The first thing that tells you a goblin is near, if not a crossbow bolt in your guts, is its smell. There is no scent like it, and to have it in your nose again later will always take you back to the first time. I can only say that it is a wet smell, and strong enough to make the stomach tighten. I have seen people vomit when they first encounter it.

The birds became agitated not long after we passed the bridge again, and they began pointing their beaks in the direction of the tree line past the lavender field. Inocenta was the highest ranked, so she handcanted that we should go and see—this was how our birds acted when they caught the scent of the dead goblins we used to train them. I thought *perhaps these will be dead as well,* then felt ashamed of my cowardice for hoping it would be so. We put on our helmets, which we had been carrying for the heat, then shrugged our shields off and drew our swords. We fanned out so each of us had a bird at either side and just ahead, like three reverse Vs. This was our most common formation, and if ever I do not say how we were formed up in a fight, it was so. Birder behind, corvids just before. With their eyes on the sides of their heads, they could easily see us for hand commands, and had been trained to watch for them closely.

We walked with long strides, our shields in front just below our eyes, our chins tucked, *spadíns* down and to the side. The shields were of a loose kite shape, the lower point cut off, slightly rounded at the top, tapering down to offer some protection to the leg. Of course, the Calar Bajat shield is round, and I prefer a round shield to travel with, but these were good for war, as I soon found out.

I heard a snap from the trees,

Ta!

then a kind of whistle,

Thhhhwhew!

then

Ka-THAK!

The shield shuddered and I knew it had been struck. I cried out despite myself.

"Ay!"

Inocenta jabbed her thumb at the tree line, the signal to attack, then spread her hand, the signal for *shiver*.

The birds tucked their heads and ran, and we ran after them.

They also began to shiver their wings in fast beats above their heads.

I heard two more of the biters' crossbows,

TA-TA!

and I saw a blur high and to my right, and a bolt hit my helmet sideways, having been batted by Dalgatha's wing.

Almost there!

I was afraid, so afraid that all of my training seemed far away.

Their smell hit me, gods it was awful, and I saw movement in the branches.

There were only a few of them, I thought, and they were trying to run from our corvids.

I could not blame them.

To say our birds killed goblins that day is not strong enough.

They destroyed them.

They kicked with their metal spurs, they smashed with their wings, but most of all they gouged and sheared with their beaks. I was aware of a small limb flying—Bellu had simply bitten the arm from one and tossed it up against the bright sky, then batted that goblin to the side so he could go after another. I beat Inocenta to the injured one, who tried to shield its head from my blow with an arm that was no longer there, its other arm coming up with a small blade in it, its black, small eyes going white for an instant as a membrane blinked shut to protect them. I put my shoulder behind my shield and smashed into it, expecting to knock the creature down, but that is not what happened. Biters are strangely light, and there is something taut and springy about them. It simply moved back where a kynd would have fallen, and cut quickly at my face. I ducked to take the slash on my helmet, then stabbed up at its body, hard. My sword went through its hemp garment and into its plumbing, and it shuddered, closing itself around my sword and falling, the hook in its remaining arm tangling up in my chain mail.

I tried to free my arm, but I was caught.

It had died around my weapon and become an anchor.

Another one was coming at me with some kind of a club, but it was slower because of its huge, distended belly. I made ready with my shield, but it never reached me.

Dalgatha, my skinny, angry girl, leapt and bit its head off, and I was washed in its blood, which was lukewarm and thick, like oil, and with yet another kind of disgusting smell.

I tried again to free my sword, but now my hand was slick with blood, and I could not stop trembling.

Inocenta, shaking blood from her axe, came over and helped me.

"Calm down, be still," she said. "We finished them."

I stopped struggling.

My goblin's head flopped back, its eyes still white, those white membranes now locked as they always are when a biter dies. Its mouth opened, showing its awful, sharp, irregular teeth. To have this small, stinking corpse hanging from me with its teeth like a river-fish was too much. I heaved twice, but kept my food down.

Inocenta showed me where its arm-hook was caught in the links of my mail coat.

"Brace your boot against its face and yank out, hard."

I fought down my nausea and did as she said, but I was still stuck.

"Do I have to call you a sop?"

"Wh . . . What?" I said.

"*Harder, sop!*" Inocenta said.

I pushed off with my boot and yanked my arm back.

Its hook broke off and I was free.

"How . . . how many?"

"Eight."

"Are all of their soldiers this . . . fast, and hard to fight?"

"Soldiers?" Inocenta said. "My sister, these were sailors, weak from shipwreck. They have little armor, or none. And do you see the leggings, made from our woven hair? These are not their warriors."

I realized now that the second one, the fat, decapitated one who nearly struck me while I was hooked, had been holding an oar.

Just fucked-desperate sailors.

"Why is this one so fat?" I said, for one of them looked like a pregnant dam.

"You will not like it."

I seriously thought of leaving the matter there.

I should have.

"These were on their way to other survivors."

"And?"

"They gorge themselves and regurgitate for others to share," Alisenne said.

"Yes," Inocenta said. "Step on its belly and see."

"Please, no," Alisenne said.

"Go on," said Inocenta, "I bet eight pounds of thigh meat come out of its neck-hole, and a fucking hand for dessert."

I threw up.

After, I stood bent over and I made a sound between laughing and panting.

A mad sound.

Bellu came over to check on me, cocking his head and clicking.

I saw myself in his great black eye, my face a mask of their blood.

I saw the sun in his eye as well, weak behind clouds.

16

I was not injured in our combat with the three-and-a-half-foot-tall shipwreck survivors, nor were the other two dams. Our war corvids did most of our work for us. Richu had taken a bolt in his wing, but, as I may have said, they were bred to use their wings as weapons and shields, and they have little feeling there. The bolts these biters fired at us were neither poisoned nor of great weight, meant perhaps for taking game. One had lodged in my shield well below the boss, and might have tickled my thigh but for the tapered part.

The blade I had been attacked with was a simple meat knife.

I could not help feeling we had not yet been tested, and I was right in this.

Of course, skirmish or no skirmish, there was no question of missing dinner with my brothers.

A new bathhouse had opened in what had once been a laundry, the great stone vats now washing limbs instead of linens. These Gallards were desperate not only for Ispanthian protection, but for our coin. Spanths are famous, even mocked, for our cleanliness, so, in addition to butchering for us the last of their sheep and hogs, and pouring for us the last of their wine, and sending the last of their sons and daughters to fuck us, the Espalleers washed us. I did not wish to go into the sea again after what I had seen in it, so I was glad to soak in the steam and water, and to use the soap they sold us, which smelled of olive oil and lavender. My hands still trembled from time to time, but none of my fellow soldiers seemed to notice this, and they made much of us.

"Galva is blooded now!" Inocenta had said when we had arrived back at our camp, and there had been much cheering and some drinking.

It had been too much for me.

The bath was better.

Mostly.

There was some whoring there, as I could hear, and as I was soon to learn firsthand, but I wanted only quiet. And, foolish as it sounds from a soldier, I did not want to pay to be touched that way. Not then, at least. I believe it is true that some who sell their bodies are glad of it, but many more are in bondage. I would perhaps lie with a courtesan. But not a whore, or so I thought. I did not want anyone to pay in tears for my pleasure.

This was too much to explain when I was offered the penny-cock known as Rovain.

"Come on, Galvicha, we will pay for it."

"It is not a question of money."

"You killed your first goblin, you should celebrate."

"That is what I am trying to do," I said, closing my eyes and leaning my head back into the good, hot water so it stopped my ears.

When I rose up again, they were still there, my sister knights, meaning well—most of them, at least—but chafing me. They had the whore Rovain nude before me now, the faint tattoo of a rose on his cheek, his eyes closed.

"Is he not beautiful?"

"He is. Wait, by the gods, is he *blind*?" I said.

"Yes! It is why he did not go to war."

"Did he blind himself to slip the muster?"

"I think the Guild blinded him, but who cares? He is glad to fuck instead of fight. Smile, Rovain! No, *really* smile. How is the word in Gallard? Anyway, look at his . . ."

"I see it. Wait, what are those bumps? Is he sick?"

"They put small pearls under the skin. For our pleasure."

"All right, *that* is interesting. But it is not for me. Listen, if you wish to gift me something, pay him and let him go rest. And bring me wine."

"Fuck that," I heard a dam say, and I knew which one. Vega Charnat, the street boxer from Galimbur. "Fetch her wine if you will, she has the *dom* in her name after all, and thinks it her birthright. Maybe one of you will let her lick your squinny, we all know she prefers the saddle to the post."

I closed my eyes, then remembered the membrane on the goblin's eye, sick and white, and its many teeth in its pink and gray mouth, and its filthy, yellowish hook in my chain mail, and I shuddered.

"Oh, don't worry, Daguera. I won't give you a beating today. I will just take the pennycock and use him in your place."

You may be thinking that this was a gross violation of rank and protocol on Vega Charnat's part, and you would be correct, except for the Ispanthian tradition that rank and wealth are to be forgotten in the bathhouse. The bathhouse is a sort of secular temple to us, a leveler. It had its own god in Old Kesh, who passed their love of clean, hot water down to us, but in Ispanthia we leave even the gods outside.

I pushed the thought of the goblin down. He would be back, but for now I had to say something to this side of ham with the battered little ears. I could see Inocenta open her mouth to speak, but I gave her a small wave to show it was my affair.

"Yes, take him, Vega Charnat. But make sure you wash your saddle before you wave it at his post; it smells so much of donkeys, and of the road, you will make him wish his nose was blind as well."

Her eyes flared with wanting to punch me, but this would have been very poor form. The bathhouse was for speaking, not fists or swords. I might have offered her a duel before the coming of the Pragmatist, but it would not have happened here. Instead we stared at one another, locked in impasse. She could not hit me, I could not stab her, she could think of no worthy abuse to speak.

Rovain, no stranger to calming angry clients, now attached his mouth to Vega Charnat's breast. He took her by one hand, and used the other to feel the wall, walking backward, pulling her by tit and fingers toward the stone vat he entertained in.

"We will talk again, Daguera," she said, letting herself be led.

"Undoubtedly," I said, pinching the bridge of my nose and closing my eyes again.

My body jerked, remembering the feeling of my sword in the thing's guts, its hook trapping me there while another ran at me with its oar.

But then I made myself remember the pieces of colored glass that spun in the tree house, the smell of mutton and herbs.

And then I let myself remember the thing that made me happiest, and gave me the most peace.

An old brown mare on a brown hill.

My small hands on her hide, long ago.

I smiled, and slipped under the water.

17

The dinner at Pol's villa was a larger affair than the last one. There were many more people this time, and there was much activity, as servants were packing the house down even while officers and guests ate in the garden. Although it was getting dark at the eighth hour, as I was led through the house I could see that the mosaic stained by blood had been cleaned. The sweet-faced, turbaned king was still holding court in the main room, and once I got outside I saw that the shadow of the burned man or dam still marked the standing garden wall. Rubble from the wall that had been knocked down had been cleared. Some of the tents had been moved back to make room for a larger table, and we soon knew the reason for the fuss—the Pragmatist, supreme commander of the Western Army, had joined my brother. Segunth-General Samera dom Vinescu sat to her right. Guards stood behind each of these high generals, while other guests sat a bit farther off.

I had no fine clothes with me here, other than armor and the cleanest of my three shirts, so I was not sure if I was to stand or sit until Pol embraced me in welcome and gestured toward a backless chair.

"I heard you had some excitement today, Daguera Galva dom Braga."

"Uh, yes, Terce-General, I . . . Yes."

He explained to those gathered that I had killed my first foe today.

"May there be many more," the Pragmatist said to me, fixing me with that sharp gaze, and raising a glass to me with a small and precise gesture. I remembered the spectacle of the nude man and woman she forced to kill one another, the stains they left on the stone of the amphitheater.

A small glass with a bit of golden liquid in it was placed in my hand, and I smelled it.

Brandy.

I put it to my lips.

It was warm and good.

As if summoned by the smell of liquor, my brother Migaéd now arrived in the garden with two of his bravos of the Scarlet Company of Sword and Horse. Still I saw no horses. Migaéd dom Braga was announced, and walked to the table with care, as those will who know they are less sober than they should be.

He had his fine armor, and, on his back, the shield of our grandfather.

His eyes grew wide at the sight of me, and he smiled broadly.

"Galvicha!" he said, coming over to embrace me. "When did you get to Espalle?"

I did not tell him of his seeing me on the street, and even less of how I found him passed out when I called on him later. Drink stalks all of us in my household, but it seemed to have marked Migaéd, as a wolf marks a sick deer.

Amiel was announced soon after, and the four of us embraced. I would have rather this had been done in private, but whether I like it or not, dom Braga is a political house, so the sight of three sons, and one odd daughter, serving the king under arms is a powerful thing. It was clear to look at us that we were family. Yes, Amiel was the least athletic, as thin as a broom; Pol the tallest, broad-shouldered and commanding, but with his hair just starting to thin; Migaéd handsome and sly and ready to watch others work. And me? What did they see when they looked at me? Nothing, I guess. Nothing fit to marry off for advantage. Nothing fit for command or statesmanship, or even that most tedious duty, making conversation at dinner. A block of plain wood, ready for the chisel.

I was glad to see my brothers, but mostly I was eager for this to end so I could crawl in with Inocenta and simply be held with no words.

Though I would be lying if I said I was not interested to know what wine would be opened. Probably a wine from home, and they are the best in the world.

I was right, and soon my teeth were purple with the stain of the bragasc grape.

Of course, Migaéd's bravos spoke too much, and too loudly. My ears had become unaccustomed to the massed voices of men, lower and harder than those of dams, bullfrogs among crickets.

Worst was the round one, dom Gatán, with his mustache freshly dyed and the dye-stained collar freshly laundered, and the two boars on his armor looking more ready to fight than the man who wore them. He now told a vulgar story that was supposed to make Migaéd look generous and wise, but who that is wise lets a clown speak for him?

"And there we are, crossing the square with the hummingbird mosaic, what's it called?"

"Hummingbird Square," Migaéd said, timed just so, and got a laugh for it. He had a gift for making jokes out of nothing.

"Yes, but in Gallard?"

"Who cares?" Migaéd said, and got another braying laugh.

"Well, whatever it may be called, Migaéd espies a dogseller. You know, one of these fellows who conspires to lard his pantry by catching strays and selling them for meat."

I had seen this dogseller in the Square of Nectar, as Amiel says it was truly called, for once great vines of sweet yellow flowers grew there on lattices, and it was said you had to part the hummingbirds with your hand to move through them. The dogseller was a pathetic figure, with a floppy hat the color of rust—you could tell the hat had once been fine, but now he cast a lean shadow and dirt had mortared the creases of his neck.

Dom Gatán continued.

"No easy thing to catch these strays, once they get in a pack, as most of them are now, and most people like dogs too much to eat them, until they are starving, that is, and then they will eat the soles off your shoes. But once a poor dog is in a cage, permission has been given, has it not? You are not the one who declared 'this friendly fellow is for eating,' the dogseller is the one who did that. So he takes your money, pops a pooch on the head, stuffs him in a sack, and off you go."

Everyone at table looked bored with this man except the Pragmatist. She was looking at him in a different way, as if she was wondering what military use she could put this vainglorious, indulged man to. Bait, I think. I believe she was wondering if she could use this man as bait.

I now imagined the Pragmatist as dogseller, only with a cage full of kynd, and a goblin pointing at dom Gatán. She takes its money, pops Gatán on the head, pops him in a very large sack, and off it goes. I bit the inside of my cheek so not to laugh. As a girl, I did this more often than many knew.

"So Migaéd rides up to him . . ."

"Rides what?" the Pragmatist said.

"I beg your pardon, Prima-General?"

"What was he riding? You said he rode."

"Well, it is just a manner of speech."

"I see," she said, taking a small sip of her brandy. She had only one glass that night, so far as I know. "Please continue."

Dom Gatán took a large gulp of wine, for courage, it seemed to me. He would forget the display at the amphitheater no sooner than I would.

"Yes. Well. He walks up to the cur-catcher, and says, 'How can you sell these creatures for meat? Do you know how loyal they are? I will bet these fellows had names, and work that they did, before goblins killed their masters. And now you come and cage them, and make coin from their circumstances? For shame, man.' Of course the greedy little fellow starts chewing his hat, wondering if he is going to be flogged, and well he might have been, but our Sixt-General dom Braga is a merciful man, and he says, 'I will buy these dogs, every tail and snout. Here, take an owlet.' Which was more than fair for these curs, but the man protested that meat was dear in the city now, and he had a dozen of them, and they took him a week to catch. The cheek on the man! I thought surely Migi would strike him now. But still he would not, noble fellow. He placed the coin in the man's hand, gestured him off, and opened that cage. Freed the dogs. They were glad to be out of there, I can tell you, and one even took a . . . one even made waste before running. And the fellow had the nerve to sob into his hands."

I noticed again some looks between my brother Pol and Segunth-General dom Vinescu; very quick, very subtle, but they gave me again the feeling that these two were more than brother and sister in arms. I will tell you that this gave me some concern, as the segunth-general was married to the captain of her guard, a capable Calar Bajat swordsman who had studied at my school. As her guard, he stood behind her, so he could not see where her eyes went. Some would say that, as he was from a humble family and came to the academy on scholarship, he was lucky that a dom had wed him in a love match against her family's wishes, and at a very young age. But it seemed to me, if you marry for love only, what holds it together when love tires? It seemed to me, having observed my father the duke and his two wives, that love always tires, and that new passions arise. I thought, were it permitted between dams, that I could marry one such as Inocenta, for whom I had little heat but great respect and affection.

Of course the goddess of love and passion laughs when dismissed by those who have not yet felt her bite.

"We will meet soon, Galvicha," she might have said to me,

flashing her lavender eyes, "and you will be surprised how I come to you."

The Pragmatist left early, after eating modestly from the fine meal presented to us, but before she went she asked to see the shield Migaéd had leaned against a wall. As I have said, she missed little. He took the Mouth of the Storm up, displaying it to her with some pride.

She took from a pouch her small pair of spectacles, and looked at the engravings, the springwood, the boss with the storm-man blowing a wind.

"Exquisite," she said. "If I am not wrong, this was turned from the workshop of Master Jarnu Arnaz ej Lobunegru, you can see the small paw, the JL. Dating from perhaps 1170 Marked. He had a black tongue, did you know that? His mother was a Galt, and some say a witch. His best pieces were spellworked, though this sort of thing can fade. After a half century of life, does it still bewitch the minds of artists, as such items are said to do? Does it blow arrows and bolts away from you, as the relief suggests?"

"I have not been struck," Migaéd said.

You have not been a target, the Pragmatist's smile replied.

"I heard such a shield had been lost at cards in this army. Was that you?"

"You should have seen the hand I had, Prima-General. Happily, the shield returned to me."

"Well," she said, "better on a gambler's back than on a warrior's arm, I suppose." Did she look at me then? I think she did. "I doubt much harm will come to it from scolding dogsellers in a starving town."

Several mouths fell open.

She thanked Pol for his hospitality and left then.

Would that I had done the same.

18

---•---

I am in a delicate position now.

You know how I feel about speaking ill of family; Migaéd was still my brother, but there is no flattering way to tell the rest of the evening. And yet it is important to the story. Amiel wrote of it, I will let you read his words. It is a fair telling, and he is beyond the burdens of propriety. You may pass over the part where he speaks of me, it is not why I show you this:

The villa my brother, Pol, commandeered is a wonder of southern Gallardian architecture. The windows and doors are open to the breeze, which in better times must have smelled like flowers and the sea. That is not what Espalle smelled like last night. The goblin dead that washed up from the shipwreck were being cremated, and there is little worse than the smell of them burning. While it is not necessary to burn goblin dead to prevent disease, as they do not rot, the sight of them in all places like wicked dolls is off-putting, and the stare of their white, membraned eyes is thought to bring bad luck, or even foul magic.

Pol's serving lads, Edréz and Solmón (it is a good habit to learn and remember names), showed me to the garden, which, though the summer sun still lingered at the eighth hour, had been hung with so many candles that, as night came on, it outshone even the bright southern constellations which had been my only solace on the sea voyage here.

First I saw Pol, and we embraced, and I felt glad.

Then I saw Galva and my heart lit from within.

I do not know if it is because she is my full sister, or because she has always watched over me, at least those early years, and those holiday visits when she was home from the Academy of Sword, but I have always felt her to be something more than just a sister. Something between a sister and a best friend and a guardian spirit. She is more precious to me than cool water and a roof.

I was delighted when they sat me next to her.

There is nothing I would not do for Galva, who has ever been the best protector I have. It is as though some quality of a caretaker passed from my mindsick mother into Galvicha when Nera dom Braga abdicated her worldly concerns. Even just to be near my sister I feel safe, and respected, and that I am enough as I am. I know siblings must live their adult lives apart, but I would be content to be a close neighbor to her, and show her what I have written, and bring her black plums from my garden, as well as blueberry and mulberry—she has ever loved fruits of the blue or purple sort more than red or yellow. I would delight to see her teach sword forms to my children, to see if they might show some of Corlu dom Braga's metal since I have only ink and nectar in my blood. I would be kind to any husband of Galvicha's, even if he did not respect me, as soldiers often do not, so long as he was kind to her. And yet it is hard to picture Galva with a husband. Who could master her with the sword, and who that could not master her could master himself to be at peace with a stronger wife? As for myself, any spouse of mine will make Galva her friend and sister, or she will risk to lose my affection.

Migaéd is a more complex matter.

He started the evening drunk, and I believe Prima-General Peya Dolón Milat left early in part so she would not disgrace us by witnessing the further decline of the heir of dom Braga.

It was a mercy.

The departure of the Pragmatist caused others to take their leave, and many of the tables were cleared. The party became more of a family gathering at last, which is what I believe Pol wanted, though these hangers-on of the Scarlet Company buzzed about Migaéd like horseflies, laughing at his japes and talking too much.

He now produced a bottle of Gallard brandy called Faunsong,

and it was very, very dear. The eyes of those under his command
lit up, and they readied the little ceramic or wooden tipple-cups
they kept tied to their belts to receive his gift, should he offer, but he
had his eyes on me, and on Galva. The label of this bottle had been
hand-painted, not merely written on, and showed a faun peeking
at a nymph from behind a tree, the moon in crescent above them.
Even I had heard of this brandy.

"It was a gift from His Majesty, Luvain of Gallardia," Migaéd
said. "It came by the Runners Guild today."

Pol's eyebrows rose at this. He said, "Do you and His Majesty of
Gallardia often swap presents of this order?"

"It is a first," Migaéd said, "but hopefully not the last."

What was he up to? Was the king of Gallardia after something
from my father? Migaéd left the matter fogged in mystery and gestured for the larger serving lad, Solmón, to pull the cork. "Careful,"
he told Solmón, "that bottle is worth three of you, and your prettiest
sister."

At that, Galva, who had seemed ready to try this wonder, leaned
back in her seat. Pol took a glass of it. Migaéd saw his own glass
filled as well, but when he gestured for Solmón to pour for Galva,
she withheld her glass.

"What, Galvicha?" he said. "When will you ever get to try this
brandy again? They don't let it outside of Gallardia."

"It would be wasted on me," she said, "I don't know one brandy
from another."

"Oh, try it, sister," he said, in danger of looking a fool for having
a twenty-year-old refuse his generosity.

"Let those who love it have my share," she said, nodding at dom
Gatán, who was all but salivating at the scent of the divine stuff.

I misliked this man enough that I did something petty.

"I would try it," I said.

"There's the dom Braga spirit!" Migaéd said, standing shakily
and pulling the bottle from Solmón's hands, where the boy had
been drifting closer to the eager dom Gatán.

I will admit that in addition to being petty sometimes, I am also vulnerable to fine things, and this brandy was beyond anything I had ever tasted—at once warm and friendly, beautiful and old, a song and a breathless sprint.

"How is it?" Migaéd asked.

"Good," I said.

My mouth had more important work to do than speaking.

"How good?"

I put my finger up to gain a moment, then said, "Sublime. You built it up so, but then it beggared expectation."

"Will you write a poem about it?"

"Well," I said, "I should need a full glass before I could write a proper one."

"Ha!" said Migaéd, pleased. "Now there's wit for you. Take a lesson, Pol, lest our little brother sur . . ."

And here he belched whooshily.

". . . Surpass you in the king's favor."

Pol said, "I do not think Amiel cares about such things, do you, Chichún?"

"I cannot say I care nothing for the favor of a king. But I should rather earn it with verse or service than clever talk. Is His Majesty Kalith fond of poetry?"

"I have heard that he is," said Pol.

"What sort, do you know?"

Pol said, "He is rumored to be an enthusiast of . . . what's that school of poetry that describes the bittersweet, knife-edge remorse that comes to those who have done harm to the undeserving, some harm they cannot repay?"

Galva wrinkled her brow at this.

"The School of the Divine Pang," I said. "Its founder and most famous poet was the interrogator Imara dom . . ."

"Horseshit," Migaéd said, laughing.

Galva said, "The poems may or may not be horseshit, brother, but I would like to learn the poet's name."

"Imara dom Mirevu," I said, and gave Galva a thankful look.

"Her name does not matter," Migaéd said, his slur still mild but worsening. "Because she will never write anything as good as Amiel's verse."

I did not know it was possible to feel flattered and insulted at one time but, as I have said, my relationship with Migaéd is complicated.

"So, you did read the poems I sent you? I was sure you . . ."

"No," Migaéd said, "but I have them still. They are precious to me. And I know they are good because you are a dom Braga and could never write poor verse."

Pol laughed. "I am a dom Braga, and I have written acres of it."

"I mean, you do not trifle with this 'I stepped on a frog and now I'm sad' pukewater, do you?" Migaéd said, still focused on me.

"I do not favor the Divine Pang personally," I said, "but you are oversimplifying that school. There are many fine examples . . ."

"Tell us one of your poems," Migaéd said.

He had finished his brandy, and was now on a glass of wine one could have drowned a cat in.

"You want to hear a poem of mine?" I said, hoping I had misunderstood.

"Why not? Surely you have one committed to memory."

"You want to hear it right now?"

"No, when we are all marching in our different units. Yes, right now."

Now his gallery of sycophants joined in, one clapping, dom Gatán saying, "I would hear some verse. Yes! Yes!"

Now I made a very great mistake. I should have declined, given my brother's drunken exhortation and the little respect I had for his coterie. It would have been a simple matter to declare myself exhausted and take my leave for the evening, to go back and relieve the apprentice Vlano who was watching over the sleeping wizard. But I want too badly to please. So I recited a villanelle I had written for a girl who was as close to being my lover as anyone has come.

That she is my second cousin was perhaps all that kept things from going further, besides our youth, and my inexperience, I mean. I saw her again just before I shipped out for this place. She is married to a fat, legless knight who must be pushed in a wheeled chair; he has gifted her a baby so heavy it hurts her back to hold him.

Migaéd did not hear the poem, not much of it anyway.

Perhaps you have noticed that drunks do not have a long attention span.

Migaéd interrupted me once to tell me how much he loved my imagery, though I was only one verse in, and then stopped me again so he could have a piss.

"Please just give me a moment, won't you, Chichún? I am fit to burst with all this verse and brandy."

So saying, he half tripped over Grandfather's shield, which he had leaned against a tree, which bothered me tremendously. It seems a small thing, but this shield, besides being possibly magicked and certainly a family heirloom, was not for leaning against trees and drunkenly treading on while walking off to piss. Though I had never met him, I knew Grandfather had never treated it like that. Certainly Galva never would. The Mouth of the Storm had been given to the wrong dom Braga, and it made me angry.

Migaéd wandered off toward a cart, and began pissing on what looked like a sort of reverse shadow of a person against a blackened section of wall. It seemed the cart had been placed there to hide whatever it was.

The pissing was not brief.

"Why don't you finish the poem?" Pol said, seeming both mortified and unsurprised.

"No, wait for him, he will only be a moment," blurted dom Gatán. "It was polite of him to leave, so he could give you the attention your, you know, very structured and erudite poem deserves."

"I believe the boy should finish it now," Pol said, looking pointedly at dom Gatán, who seemed to suddenly remember he was in the presence of an actual combat general, not the merely ornamental one he drained wine barrels with, and found something in his little cup to look at.

It is a hard thing to realize, all at once, that a man you once respected and loved has become a burlesque.

I finished the poem.

"Bravu," said Pol. "I could not quill something that fine in a thousand years and fifty. You really should be at university teaching classes on that, not out here, in . . . this."

"It was truly beautiful," Galva said, and I could see she meant it. "If you let me walk you home, I will tell you what I loved about it."

In the distance, Migaéd was examining the burned-in artwork he had just pissed on. I believe he forgot where he was.

"Yes," I said.

"Wait just a moment, if you can," Pol said. "He will want to say goodbye."

"That is not necessary," Galva said, standing.

"Please," said Pol, and my sister hesitated for his sake.

Now Pol looked at the Sword and Horse men. "Best be going now, gentlemen. I will sort him out." The Bravos, only too glad to be released from their leader's embarrassing display now that there was no more food or drink to be had, mumbled a few goodnights and melted away without even waiting for the serving lads to see them out. Pol went to the wall, gathered Migaéd by the arm, and stood him up. I heard Migaéd say, "That was a person, was it not? On the wall? A burned person."

"Yes, I should think it was."

"I had a piss on him."

"So you did. Come on, brother, Galvicha and Chichún are leaving, and we don't know when we may see them again."

"Leaving?" I heard Migaéd say peevishly. "We are just getting started!"

"Gods gathered," Galva said under her breath as Pol stumble-walked the drunkenly offended Migaéd over to us.

"Now say good night and let us get you to bed," Pol said.

"We cannot say good night until we have sparred!" he said, and I was momentarily concerned that he meant me, then even more horrified to see that he meant Galva. Now he was fumbling with the slakesword on his belt, a thin, quick blade meant for duels without armor, and I think he actually wanted to try it against Galva's spadín, which is for butchery.

"Nonsense," Pol said, putting his hand on Migaéd's over the pommel of the slakesword. "You are too drunk to stand in a mild wind, let alone dance about with sharp steel."

"You are right," he said, gathering two sticks from a kindling pile. "We must have sparring swords. And we must have a contest. I have been offended, you know."

"What are you going on about?" Pol said.

"By her. Or by Father. It is rather unclear. But it all lies within this poisonous . . . missive . . . and I am offended."

At this, Migaéd produced a letter from a pouch and waved it about, before dropping it on the garden path, near an artful little statue of a squirrel I had not noticed.

Pol picked up the letter without opening it.

"Go to bed, Migi."

"You know, he wants me to give her Grandfather's shield?"

My heart cheered at this, for that was what I wanted as well.

"You did gamble it away," Pol reminded him.

"Well, I shall give it to her. After we spar. She can even use it in our match, to make things even."

He now walked purposefully toward the Mouth of the Storm where it leaned against its tree.

Galva said, "I have a shield already. Come on, Amiel."

Despite her words, I saw her eyes drawn to it.

In her heart, she knew the rightness of this shield going to her hand, but her pride was too great.

"Take it!" Migaéd said, pointing at it.

Pol now bent his head to read the letter, when it would have been better for him to mind our brother.

Galva said, still looking at the shield, "I could not trust the sincerity of the gift in your present state. And I will not spar you."

I should say here that once, after Father had gone to visit Galva near the end of her studies, he gathered the three boys together and said we should never spar her.

"Why not?" Migaéd had asked.

Father had considered his words carefully before saying, "One who has studied and thinks oneself capable might be undone to discover how much less one knows than one thinks."

Migaéd now tossed her a stick to duel with, but she sidestepped it.

He made a lunge at her thigh with his stick, and she stepped casually so it missed her by a cat's whisker, but miss it did.

She turned her back on him and walked toward the house to leave.

I moved to join her, but waited for Pol to finish the letter.

Now Migaéd took a few strides toward Galva and swatted her backside with the stick.

I never saw anyone move this fast before.

She turned, snatched the stick decisively from his hand, threw it in the air, then drew her sword and cut the falling stick in two pieces, one of these spinning off to hit Migaéd on the top of the head.

This all happened in two heartbeats.

In the third heartbeat she sheathed her sword.

Someone laughed, but Galva said, "You will never touch me disrespectfully again," with such weight that the laugh was stilled.

The blood went from Migaéd's face.

He said, "Fuck Father and fuck you. You are not getting that shield."

Her face reddened, as I had never seen it do before, and she shouted, "I never asked for it!"

Then she turned and walked away.

I had never heard her raise her voice in anger, not as an adult.

"She should not have to ask for it," I said, or think I said, though I may have whispered it. "It is hers."

I am ashamed not to have spoken it loudly.

I should have insisted.

Pol should have remembered his rank then, and ordered Migaéd to give our grandfather's shield to Galva. But he has always been strong in the face of the enemy, and weak before his family, especially Migaéd.

He looked at me hopelessly, apologetically, and tossed the letter to the ground.

I picked it up.

It was I who walked Galva home, and then I went off to my wizard's domain of unspeakable beasts, watching the half-moon shine on the sea.

I kept Father's letter to Migaéd, which I sometimes read to remind myself of my right to the Mouth of the Storm. I have guilt about it now and then. Our grandfather Corlu dom Braga had borne that shield in the Knights' War, on his warhorse, Punchel, trampling goblins into meal and splitting their skulls with his axe. It is said Punchel had been one of the finest warhorses in Braga, if not Ispanthia. Pol said that when he was little, the old man had been able to make him and Migaéd laugh by calling the horse "Punchy" in that gravelly way he had. He grew a crab in his brains, the doctors said. He was bedridden and speechless by the time I was a babe, only able to hold his fingers to my lips while I drooled on them. Or so I was told, I do not remember. He was gone before Amiel saw light. Funny that when I was older, everyone said I looked like him, in the color of the eyes and the way I cannot hide from my face whether I like or do not like someone.

I think I would have liked this man.

Here is Father's letter about the shield:

Migaéd, my son,
I have omitted the cheridu *from the head of this letter, trusting that the monies I have paid to the family of the Duke of*

Nemura will demonstrate my affection in the fashion most earnestly desired by you. Although the sum in question was well within my gift, it was not inconsequential, and there shall be no sequel, however "dear" I may declare you to be. If you find yourself tempted to wager at cards again, and I earnestly hope that you do not, please be sure that you bet no more than you carry. The officer's stipend I have secured for you should permit you to squander sufficient coin to ruin any three men-at-arms, so, if you cannot win gold at the officers' table, I suggest you lose silver with the infantry.

Touching matters of finance, please know that your lack of discipline with my treasury has made me question whether leaving its keys with you upon my death is indeed the best thing for this family. I have forgiven past follies, telling myself that you were young. I have forgiven the last one, telling myself that you are at least minimally brave, and that your presence on, or near, the field merits some understanding. But then, you are no longer so young, and your siblings are no less brave. You need not be reminded of the laurels with which Pol, though a year to the day your junior, has covered himself, and how quickly he has risen in rank. Even my daughter insists on serving in the most perilous fashion, having enlisted with an experimental corvid unit being tested against our foe; what's more, she does not piss our money away on games of chance. She would not even allow me to buy her a suit of armor, as I have done for you and for your brothers. That you offered your grandfather's springwood shield, the Mouth of the Storm, in payment of your debt has proven you unworthy to own it. My contacts tell me *Nemura* has returned the shield to you, which of course he was not obligated to do at any price; many men would have kept such a beautiful and useful article of war, and been well within their rights to do so. But know this: you are not that shield's owner, but its guardian. You will make gift of it to your sister. Pol has *enough fine things and will be more at the rear, if he knows what's good for him. Amiel is to serve a powerful magus I wish to bind to our family, also away from action.*

Give the Mouth of the Storm to Galvicha, for that is truly where she is going.

If you fail to honor my request in this, I will have the shield taken from you, and for good measure I will have you stripped of the fine suit of armor I had made for you in Galimbur—by an armorer with a three-year waiting list for his pieces, it must be said; I will ship it home to Braga and make it my heir. If it shows no more initiative than you, at least it has cost me only one fortune, and I can be sure the reflection I see in it is my own.

Your father for life,
Your creditor not one day more,
Duke Roderigu Elegius dom Braga,
Lord of Horse and Grove

Despite Father's wishes, I would not beg the shield from him, nor would I fight him for it.

Amiel had other ideas about the shield, though nothing would be done for some time.

His wizard was soon to wake from the sleep his calling of the storm had imposed on him, and to take his household quickly away.

The army was about to move out as well, heading for the same destination, though by different paths.

We were all headed for a great city the goblins were on the verge of taking, and we would save that city or seize it back and hold it.

Of course, you already know its name.

BOOK

2

Goltay

19

To move an army well is more difficult than to win a battle.

Many battles are lost before they are fought because soldiers are starving, or they have not slept, or they are so mad for water they cannot be kept in formation near a stream.

I will say that the Pragmatist moved her army well, as well as such a large beast could be moved.

The Western Army of the Illuminated Kingdom of Ispanthia was, to the best of my understanding, ninety thousand strong when we left Espalle, and we were one of three Ispanthian armies. There was also the Eastern Army, rumored to stand near fifty thousand, which kept closer to our border and which was working to stop the advance near Gaspe. The King's Army stood at perhaps ten thousand, and it never left Ispanthia and rarely left the capital. So the greatest part of the soldiers under arms for King Kalith at this time were under the command of Prima-General Peya Dolón Milat, the Pragmatist, now marching northeast for Goltay. We were to liberate and join with what was left of the Gallardian army commanded by King Luvain the First, which was now under siege at a stronghold near Goltay. We would also join with the armies called the Far Banners, or the Glorious League, and its troops from many countries. The Far Banners were also coming to lift the siege, and this became a race. As I have said, it is better to move an army well than swiftly, though a king in danger is reason to make exception.

It would take us weeks to get there, and, while sieges in human wars may last many months, the biters were unsurpassed at bringing down walls.

As you can see, the situation was fucked.

We had lost nearly two thousand with the sinking of the troop-mules, and, when we left Espalle, the once-lovely, rich harbor district was flattened and choked with mud, and the bay was so full of the dead that they could be smelled on the hot summer breeze in neighboring villages. Many crabs and eels who had come to feed on our dead were caught by local kynd, who could not afford to be choosy about the taking of food. It was the twelfth of High-grass when we left the town, with the sea behind it, and refugees at our heels.

Since many of these had been given the biters' cut last year, they walked with difficulty, and only the strongest could keep up. I knew Larmette had received this cut, but Sambard had not.

I expressly did not look for Sambard or Larmette among them.

I knew that if I saw them, I would be at risk to break the prima-general's newest decree—any who gave food to them would be flogged, and the tip of their nose cut off to identify them as a thief. This may not sound like such a great harm to you, with boatloads of the maimed and ruined coming home to beg, but in Ispanthia, to be a thief is a great dishonor. If someone cuts your nose without cause, and with the purpose of destroying your name, you are justified to kill them and to take their property.

I later found out that the Pragmatist had considered ordering us to drive off the camp followers to remove the temptation to feed them, but she did not for two reasons. First, she was concerned that these orders might not be followed, since many are good, and many who are not good enjoy whores. Second, she decided that if the followers dispersed, they were likely to end up in goblin bellies, so she allowed them to follow—as best they could—for the same reason you might take cattle from lands occupied by the enemy.

If we discovered so much food that it might be shared, the decree would be lifted, but we knew this for a fantasy. We would, for the next week or two, watch the refugees of Espalle starve and hear them plead, and eventually most of them melted away. It had seemed better to starve than to risk coming back under Horde-law, which the townsfolk assumed would be their fate without us, but once one actually begins to starve, it is a different thing.

Following this army in this summer of famine was like following locusts.

We ate everything, and shared not a crumb.

And the worst unit of the army, pound for pound, was the First Lanza of His Majesty's Corvid Knights. My brother had arranged more food for our birds, but, once we started on the march, their needs increased.

Of course they did—it is one thing to be on a ship, or in camp with one or two hours of exercise. It is something else entirely to march for fourteen hours a day. This is as true for kynd as it is for corvids, but, while we grumbled and tightened our belts, the corvids did not understand. If I had to choose a word for the way they seemed to feel about it, I would say *offended*.

These huge, deadly weapons were offended.

Of course something happened.

The bird's name was Melon, because that was her favorite food, when she could not get the liver of an ox, I mean. She escaped from her mistress and her pair-mate, Boxer, in the afternoon of our third day on the road, near a small village whose name I forget.

The bird had been crying "Food, food" all morning, but by middlehour had fallen into silence, or so her keeper, Olicat, said. For marching, the corvids are tethered together by a hemp rope through a metal eyelet on the breastplate. The hemp is tough, though the beaks on these birds can get through it, with effort. To tie them with chain, they would damage their beaks worrying at it—they are greatly bothered by chains near them.

A pair's knight holds them by a sort of leash, and carries a goad, which is a hooked baton about a foot long. It is not sharp enough to harm them, but causes some discomfort, and is the best way to show them to move one way and not the other. A tap

on the beak will also disrupt bad behavior, but, again, this must not
be too hard. It is necessary to have a patient hand, and to use this
sort of correction just enough to encourage them, but not so much
as to anger or threaten them. This is one reason, besides the great
shortage of men, that the bird knights have been women. Most men
want so much to control that they forget how to coax. You must
never let a corvid anger you—they sense such things, and men are
quicker to anger. They are also less concerned with the comfort of
others. This is fine for falconry, where a vulgar or idle nature may be
hidden behind the grace of noble and forgiving birds.

Corvids are noble, but they are not forgiving.

Melon had started jerking at her tether, which of course irri-
tated Boxer, who jerked back. I do not know if it was a weakness
of the rope, or the combined strength of both birds pulling at
once, but the tether broke, and Melon stepped away, spreading
her wings as if some part of her remembered that she should have
been able to fly had her blood not been tampered with to make
her a giant. Olicat tried to get the beast back, but Melon was just
too hungry, too tired of marching, too tired of listening. She kept
walking away now, more purposefully, as if she could not believe
her good luck. She looked back once. She loved her mistress—
they were bred to and would have been ungovernable without this
bond—but she left. Likely she thought she would find something
to eat and come back later.

When Nouva saw that Melon was not coming straight back
into line, she moved all of us out of column. The pikes and archers who had been behind us looked with interest to see what
was happening; we had spent so much time with these beasts that
it was easy to forget they were marvels to everyone else. Besides
that, the oldest dams of this bunch following us appeared to be
my age, the youngest boys with them perhaps fourteen. Even in
times of horror, the young are capable of wonder. I looked away
from these children, trying not to imagine their futures, but still
I saw them dead in the mud.

Melon turned her back and walked fast now, several of the birds saying "Bad" after her, but one saying "Go fast, go." Ordinary ravens, who were often either excited to see these monstrous cousins, or stunned into silence, cried in the trees as if encouraging Melon's escape. There were not many trees. This was farmland, and it had not yet been occupied by Our Friends.

Nouva looked at Inocenta, said, "Take your birds. Get her back if you can. If not, do what you have to."

Inocenta nodded at me, and we left.

We walked quickly, keeping our pairs tethered for the moment. We did not want to run, which might alarm the fugitive, nor could we let her pull farther away from us. She was coming up on a stone farmhouse that looked to be hundreds of years old. There were pens, but I saw no livestock. Just as I thought it might be abandoned, I saw a pile of freshly chopped wood stacked near a treestump, an axe in this. The door of the farmhouse opened, and a very pregnant woman stepped out, with a very old man beside her, holding a spear he did not look strong enough to stab butter with. I thought that the woman had probably chopped the wood. The old man knew we were Spanths, though, and asked in our language, "What are those things? Is the army near?"

He could not see the bird, which was approaching the house from the side.

"Get in and shut the door!" Inocenta yelled.

"I fought in the Knights' War, under the Far Banners, with the Count of Simonoy." This was a thing to be proud of, this Gallard had helped our country thirty years before as we were trying to help them now, but this was not the time.

"That is wonderful, thank you," Inocenta said. "Go inside."

"Arnaut," the woman said, pulling at his arm.

"Are there goblins near?"

"No, but something else is. Now *get the fuck inside!*"

At this moment the loose corvid cornered around the house,

and the old Gallard saw that it was coming toward him with purpose.

"Melon!" I shouted.

Arnaut put the young woman in the house before him—I credit him for this, people do not always do the right thing in hot moments—and he shut his door just before the bird leapt. It struck me that he put his hand on the small of her back to direct her, and in such a way that I later thought perhaps he *had* chopped the wood. I heard him draw the bolt. Melon landed where he had been standing.

"Melon, to me!" Inocenta said.

The bird put her beak at the bottom of the door and sniffed.

"*Nourid,*" she said.

Food.

We were almost to the house now, passing the axe and stump.

The flat head of the spear came out of the crack under the door, not fast enough to do harm, but Melon did not like it. She scratched at the door, leaving grooves. If she decided to kick, she would take it off its hinges.

I had my goad out, and Inocenta had a rope ready to put around Melon's beak. The bird cocked an eye at us and flapped her wings, then took off in a leap for the field of tall summercorn, which was pale brown and ready for harvest.

"Bad?" Dalgatha asked.

"Very bad," I said.

We broke into a run now—Melon could lose us in this field.

But the birds would be able to find her.

"Should we . . . ?" I started.

"No," Inocenta said.

I knew why she said no. If we set the birds after her, probably they would find her and hold her for us. We had trained them to discipline each other, to hold disobedience to us as the greatest wrong in their world.

But . . .

If one of them decided to side with Melon, the others might do so as well, and we would be down five birds, instead of one.

And perhaps two birders.

They could very well decide to kill us.

We did, in fact, lose sight of the bird.

Not for long, but long enough.

We heard the scream of an animal. *Scream* is the wrong word, but there is no good word for that sound. It was an ox. These Gallard farmers had hidden an ox in the summercorn stalks and Melon was killing it. We ran, but it was all over when we finally found the little clearing where the beast had been staked.

The ox was on its side, still breathing, looking at us wide-eyed with pain and terror as the war corvid poked her whole head into the animal's trunk, then came up slick and bloody, with a gobbet of liver in her mouth.

She looked very proud of herself.

She flapped her wings and blood painted the corn.

Blood dripped from the blades on her legs.

Inocenta dropped the loop of rope, slowly put her hand near her *spadín*.

I did the same.

I will never forget that sight of the bird, and the ox, and the corn painted with blood.

It was almost beautiful.

Now all four of our birds were asking, "Bad? Bad?"

"Bad," Inocenta said.

A drop of blood had hit her face, near the corner of her mouth, and it ran.

She slipped the tether off her birds.

When we returned, Olicat said, "Where is Melon?"

But she knew.

Our birds were bloody. Dalgatha was missing a tuft of feathers, and Richu had injured an eye. Bellu's beak had deep scratches in it from where he and Melon had locked up.

It had been brutal, but I had seen this once before, when the bird who had killed his mistress in Ispanthia was put down. It was best if corvids killed their own. We were to remain above this, like gods. It was good for them to fear us, but this must not be allowed to grow into hate.

"Where. Is. Melon?" Olicat said, with growing anger.

My heart broke for her. I did not think my birds would ever run off, but Olicat might have thought the same. I hated the fresh grooves on Bellu's beak from this fray—what would I do if I saw his handsome body torn apart, or if I were covered in Dalgatha's blood as she breathed her last?

Dalgatha knew I was upset, and turned her head, clicking at me.

I wanted to ruffle her crown feathers, but did not want to do this in front of my grieving sister in arms, so I stayed my hand.

"You will control yourself in front of these animals," Nouva said to Olicat. "You are the one who did not check your gear properly."

"I did check it, Lanzamachur," she said, trying and failing to keep the outrage from her voice.

"Was the rope frayed?"

"No, Lanzamachur."

"Then it was just bad luck. If you need a moment, step out of sight and get yourself together."

Olicat saluted, and walked away, toward the supply cart, behind which private conversations were had or shits were taken. One pissed anywhere, but even on campaign Ispanthians are mortified to shit in front of others if there is a way to be more polite. Vega Charnat handed Olicat a flask as she passed, and the smaller woman took it with wet eyes.

Of course Vega tried to give me a look, but I did not engage.

Nouva turned to me and Inocenta now, raised her eyebrows.

We told our commander what had happened.

The old farmer who had fought goblins in our country would want to be paid for his ox, which he had hidden from us. But his payment would be that all his corn and other animals would be taken by the Western Army of the Illuminated Kingdom of Ispanthia.

20

The next day the quartermaster's cart came to give us rations. Even with my brother's help, if he was still helping us, there was not enough. "About fucking time," Nouva said, wiping sweat out of her eyes with her sleeve and going to meet the quartermaster, three of us following behind.

"You know, he looks almost handsome sitting tall on his cart, with all that food," said Lena, a blond girl from the capital. With the sun on her hair it was hard not to think of the gold bits of the mosaic on the biters' sail.

"The food is handsome, but him?" Inocenta said. "You should poke it more often—your frustration is affecting your eyesight."

I felt my mouth warm to a smile at that. Inocenta said things I would never dream to say, and I loved her for it.

Inocenta spoke up again.

"If anybody wants to jump on that, I'd say do it now. He won't have sweet kisses after the bowl of shit Nouva's about to serve him."

If Nouva was paying attention, she did not say anything to us. She saved all her fire for the quartermaster.

"Where are the donkeys? Or sheep? I don't see any livestock for my birds, my friend, and I know you don't have enough butchered meat in that cart for eighty-eight corvids. Eighty-seven, I should say."

"Greetings to you too, Lanzamachur. And a fine afternoon it is!"

"It would look finer if I hadn't had to put a bird down for killing some old Gallard's ox yesterday. The silver in the shit-pile was that the ox fed the others, but not enough, not nearly enough. What do I need to do to get these monsters proper rations before they start eating *us*?"

While Nouva went on, the women and boys in the cart handed crates full of root vegetables and hard biscuits to me and the others. The rest of the company now formed a chain to move the provisions.

"Honestly?" the driver said. "Kill some goblins. Your unit is experimental and, for whatever reason, that puts it lower on the list than regular infantry or archers—I cannot get sheep, or donkeys, or even a half dozen barn cats for you unless you get reclassified."

"How the fuck am I supposed to do that while they've got us trailing along in the rear, in between the dregs of southern jails and children who can barely hold their pikes or draw their bows?"

"I am sorry that is your problem, but not so sorry that I am willing to make it mine. You cannot imagine how difficult it is getting a hundred thousand soldiers moved and fed in a country the biters have so thoroughly wrecked. I got my job despite my low birth and other gifts," and here he nodded at the blocky shoe that held his clubbed foot, "because I have a head for numbers and a knack for keeping records, both very un-Spanth-like traits, I need not remind you. If you want my advice, do not wait for orders to find and pick a fight with biters. Those orders will not come. Your unit is a jape to most men in command, and those women with gold on their chests are afraid to see you fight and then fail. Even if you succeed, there is a good chance men will say the birds did it all without you, or despite you, and give your corvids to men. If more men can be found. No, do something audacious, and seize the credit for yourselves. Until then, I should say *let* the birds eat the farmers' beasts. It is only because of us they *have* any beasts, or farms for that matter. Nobody wants to be in this fucked-tragic place, least of all me. Now do try to unsquint your eyes and see what a lovely day it is. You are missing your life."

I thought she would stab him.

But Nouva climbed up on the driver's step, grabbed the back

of the driver's head, and gave him a large kiss on the cheek. She then swatted his ox on the backside and sent the cart, which had already given all it had for the company, on its way.

It turns out I am not so good at reading what people will do outside of a fight.

But Nouva's swatting of the ox reminded me of something, which gave me an idea how to feed our children.

When we made camp that night, I got Nouva's permission to speak with my brother Pol. He was camped two miles ahead, and when at last I found his tent, he was not there. His boy Solmón told me he was meeting with other generals, and that he was not expected for some time. The boy knew who I was, though, and invited me to wait inside. There was no one else inside except the other servant, and I did not want them fussing over me, so I joined a group of soldiers sitting near enough a fire to have light from it, but not so near they took much heat. It was already a very warm night, worse than it had been in Espalle for want of a sea breeze. Two were playing Catch the Lady, and I wished I had brought my deck.

"Evening," one dam said to me in the broad way they speak in Veista Pulcanta. She was one of Pol's guards, a dark-brown-skinned woman with a poleaxe nearby and a mace on her belt. From the thickness of her arms, I would not want to hold a shield she was striking with that mace. Nor would I want to have to test her armor with a *spadín*, as it looked to be more plate than chain. If only we could afford to armor all soldiers so, the biters would break their teeth on us. This dam wore her armor like she was born in it.

I liked her at once.

"Evening," I said back to her. "Would you have a Lady's deck handy?"

"I am a Towers woman," she said, indicating a copper cup on her belt, the cup one placed wagers in.

"I would do as well to simply put my money in your cup."

"What fun would that be?" she said.

Now a skinny woman with her boots off—I guess she was drying them by the fire—plucked a guitar a few times. Then started to play fast, a *canta pulcanta*. She looked to be from the same volcanic shores as the guard, so it made sense. Now some began to clap in the way they will in the south of Ispanthia.

The guard sang.

> *You told me you were mine*
> *For all time, all time, all time,*
> *Yes you told me without lying*
> *You were mine all mine all mine*
> *Except that you were lying*
> *Just as fast as you could lie*
> *Lying lying lying lying lying lying*
> *And we did not have much time.*

At the "lying lying lying" part, everyone joined in, even me, and I am not for singing.

> *You told me we would marry*
> *You would marry marry me,*
> *Yes you told me without lying*
> *We would bed and then we'd wed*
> *Except that you were lying*
> *Lying lying lying lying lying lying*
> *Just as fast as you could lie*
> *And I wish that you were dead*
> *Ay!*

Now everyone began to cry "Ay!" and soon soldiers were taking to their feet to dance, stomping with their hands on their hips. This is not the sort of dance my governess tried to teach me, but one favored by those who work outside with callused hands. I put my hands on my hips and tried a few stomps, in time with the clapping and the crying out. I tried the clapping as well. I looked back at the broad-shouldered guard, who was smiling at me and nodding, pleased to see someone unfamiliar with this dancing try it anyway.

Now she moved closer and took one of my hands, which I allowed, and by the way she pressed my hand in hers, I knew I was to turn, so this I did. Turning and balance are no small part of my training, so I did this well, and people cheered. I was twenty years old, and not immune to good attention, so I began to do low turns, in a full squat, and then, when she let go my hand to give me more freedom, to leap while turning. The same move I would do with a *spadín* in hand to get so far under your blade you feared for your legs, and then rise to behead you. Only friendlier. The soldiers now cheered loud, and someone said "Calar Bajat!" and I winked at him, but kept dancing with my guard.

I was already dripping with sweat, and the gods knew when my next bath would be, but I did not care. Someone gave me wine, and I drank politely, then they gestured for me to have more, and I drank impolitely.

The guitarist, whom I had moved closer to, sang another three verses, and I danced and clapped with the others. This was becoming the best night I could remember since leaving school. Embers rose from the fire, then seemed to wink out in deference to the stars, which were many.

I saw the purple stars that were Nerêne's eyes, and I winked at them, too.

The guard seemed very beautiful to me, then.

She saw me thinking that, and moved to kiss me.

I turned my head, giving her my cheek in place of my lips, but smiled and did not move away from her. She kissed my cheek long and wetly and a thrill ran through me.

She said into my ear "Would you like to go to a field with me?" and I could smell the wine on her breath and the sweat of her gambeson under her armor. I saw her sweat like dew in her woolly hair and I wanted very much to go to this field with her.

But I had to see my brother.

Also I did not know if to do such a thing would hurt Inocenta. There had not yet been enough talking between us.

"I . . . I have a sister," I said, and she knew I meant an *irmana apracera*. As her light brown eyes looked at me, eyes it would be easy to fall into, I saw that she understood I was still bearing the burden of some innocence.

"Well," she said, easing back so I would not feel pushed, "if you decide you want something more than a sister, my name is Carlota, and I guard the general dom Braga."

I tried to catch my breath, and into her ear I whispered, "I will remember you have said this," then pulled away. I could see lanterns, knew my brother was coming. The music faded out, the guitarist now just strumming while a girl fed her wine. I used the cloth on my belt for wiping sweat, but it was already wet. Somebody passed me more wine and I nearly took it, then remembered Migaéd, and smiled and shook my head. As I left the fire, some clapped my arm or just touched me, as if for luck. Calar Bajat is much respected in Ispanthia, and I realized now my sleeve was open, and my tattoo showed.

I may have opened it on purpose.

I think now that I acted pridefully, that I was showing off. But I would forgive another twenty-year-old this, and so I forgive myself. This has been a hard skill to learn, the forgiving of self, and it is not always easy to know when it is good and when it is indulgent. But there is not so much time in life that we should spend it being sorry. It was a glorious hour or so, in a time of fear and horror, and I would not trade the memory of it for a feeling that I had behaved more properly.

Such things are good, in moderation.

Moderation, too, is good in moderation.

I did not become Carlota's lover, something I have regretted more than once, but I now believe things happened as they were meant to. Feeling desire for her awakened me just that little bit more, made me more ready for what was coming.

"Sister, you look a delightful wreck," Pol said, as he and his entourage strode out of the darkness.

"I . . . er . . . thank you," I said, and he embraced me.

I could see Carlota in the distance, wide-eyed with realizing she had tried to seduce a duke's daughter. I winked at her, and her face relaxed. She laughed and winked back.

"I need rest," Pol said, looking troubled, "and badly. But you would not have come to me with no reason. Did you get the extra food I had sent?"

"We did," I said.

"Is it not enough?"

"It is enough for camp, I think. It is not enough for marching."

He nodded. This made sense. He was about to offer to try to get us more, I think, but I did not want to add to his problems, which were many. I said, "I did not come to ask you to give us more food. I want permission for us to find it ourselves."

"So you want a writ."

"I do."

"Saying what, precisely?"

I told him.

21

Nouva held the document in her hands, looking at it in disbelief.

"He just *gave* you this?"

"He trusts me."

"Yes, but it is me he's authorizing to assume the privilege of his rank when I want to commandeer food."

"He said not to abuse it."

"This document was made for abuse."

"I trust you, Lanzamachur."

"Well, perhaps there will be a lesson in this for you, Daguera. Read it aloud to me so I can be sure I understand it."

"'By the let of His Majesty King Kalith the Second of the Illuminated Kingdom of Ispanthia, and by the hand of his agent, Terce-General Pol Finat dom Braga, undersigned below and with this seal as witness to his pleasure, Lanzamachur Nouva Livias Monçera of His Majesty's First Experimental Lanza of Raven Knights shall have all authority exercised by the terce-general aforementioned in matters touching the supply of food and fresh water for her command. The reader of this military writ is commanded to honor any request she may make touching on provision, and to supply her with such necessaries as her animals and kynd shall require to perform their duties to the King. Witnessed and signed this sixteenth day of Highgrass, 1224 Years Marked.'"

"Yes," Nouva said, "I believe that is clear."

"I believe so too, Lanzamachur."

"This is nepotism, is it not, dom Braga?"

"I cannot think of a clearer example of nepotism, as I understand it, Lanzamachur."

"Well. Good, then. Let us get these big, hungry fuckers fed."

What happened next is not one of the proudest moments of

my time under arms. For the next week of travel, we acted as
foragers, brigands, and tax agents, and we became among the
least loved units in the army. The writ covered all manner of mis-
deeds. We had gotten the access to food that the quartermaster
said we would need to distinguish ourselves to earn, but, in the
end, this was only a sort of loan. We would still have to prove
ourselves, but we had bought some time. And Nouva was not shy
about using her new power.

*You cannot take our cart and donkeys! How is the quint-general
to travel?*

Let him walk. Read the writ.

*These pigs are for the clerks, and for the musicians. What are
they supposed to eat?*

Let them fight goblins if they want meat. Read the writ.

I remember a farmer with a skin condition yelling in Gallard
while we took twenty geese from him.

Alisenne said something to him, I am guessing *Read the writ.*
Nouva held the writ before his pocked face, but the poor fellow
could not read Gallardian, so what was he going to make of Ispanthian military legalese? Nouva withdrew it before he could
touch it with his red, infectious-looking hands.

There was much more of this.

We were not training as much as we had been, what with
half of us raiding farms and overfed military units, but I saw a
change in the corvids. They became sweet again, at least those
who were sweet before they were starved and dragged across
Gallardia. Their feathers became shiny and healthy again, where
I had not noticed them growing dull because it had happened
slowly. I had noticed them getting thin, though, and within days
of the writ they looked fuller and stronger.

If the birds were friendly again, do you know who was not
friendly?

The rest of the fucked-angry army.

There was grumbling, both to our faces and behind our backs.

As time went on the military ranks of those heard to grumble increased. We had cover only so long as those ranks did not begin to approach Pol's.

Or until we did something noteworthy.

But, and this was strange to say, we were thwarted for some time because we lacked an enemy. The goblins knew the size of our forces, and for the time being they were not even raiding us. We may have been the only unit in the army whose commanders were sad not to find goblins. I oversimplify. I did not truly want to meet more of them, I was still nervous to think how much harder to fight their soldiers must be than their sailors, but I knew there was no way around them but through them.

And I did not want to wait any more.

In short, we needed to fight goblins before some unit we took food from fought us.

Gods help us, we got our wish, though only just.

The worst encounter with an Ispanthian unit happened before our first hard action with the enemy.

And you can probably guess what unit it was.

It was the new moon of Highgrass, seven days after our departure from Espalle, when we came to a village called Ceques, which I know was spelled with a *q-u-e-s* because I saw the sign for the town. Though to speak it, it rhymes with deck—you know these things, but Gallardian has always troubled me with its too-many letters. Ceques was far enough from the army that the official foragers had missed it. We moved fast with our cart and our birds, the donkeys pulling hard because they sensed the birds' hunger and had seen them eat donkey.

The country was hilly here, away from the sea, and there were many farms, though few with any food left. The people who lived here very long ago, before even the Kesh empire, had left many standing stones, and of these we saw a great variety. Some stood in spirals, some looked as if they were pieces in a game between giants. One group of them leaned so close together that traveling people had strung hides between them to make shelters, and these people were still here. This is how we found the village of Ceques, which the refugees were happy to direct us to for a little bread and copper, and for a splash of our wine, which was turning to vinegar in the heat.

Imagine how my heart froze when we came over the rise on the road to Ceques, and we saw the banner of the Scarlet Company of Sword and Horse. I wanted to say no, that we could not take from this group, but they were loading such a fat haul of pigs, chickens, melons, and summercorn into their carts that there was no question of leaving them alone simply because they were under the command of one daguera's brother.

This was going to be ugly.

I remember the wide face of dom Gatán sinking as we strode up to him. He sat astride a very burdened donkey, with a dirty-faced young woman or girl behind him on the animal. I could see that he was considering riding for Migaéd to warn him, but realizing that he could not outpace us on the poor animal, even if he dumped the girl, which I believe he considered.

"Ah, if it isn't the First Lanza of Buzzards come to pick us clean," he said. "No need to display your famous writ, Lanzamachur, it is well-known."

Nouva walked us past him without acknowledging him. She would not bother showing him the writ, he was not in command. Exactly what his rank was I did not know, except that he existed, like Migaéd, in that twilight place of privileged lordlings whose chief power was immunity from consequence. Most consequence, at least. They did not command armies in matters military, but neither could they be commanded, save by higher officers.

Like Pol.

And, by extension through the writ, Nouva.

Dom Gatán made sure to give me his eyes as I walked by, and I have never been shy to stare with someone. I saw that his mustache wanted dye, its gray roots showed bright on his pink face. Strangely, this made my hate for him less, because it showed him to be sad and ridiculous. But then I saw the face of the girl on the back of his donkey, and from the way she looked at me I thought she might be simple, and I hated Gatán again.

"Of course!" I heard my oldest brother say. "Of course you brought them here, Galvica."

Galvica is a "small name" like Galvicha, but it is not so affectionate. A *merdicha* is a little shit, said of a beloved dog getting underfoot, or a clever child who got the better of you. A *merdica* is actual shit on the bottom of your shoe. He was calling me "Small Galva," not "Little Galva."

Not so small a difference.

When a member of the family first begins to hurt you, they may choose from many weapons, all sharp, all sure to draw blood. The first cuts are the worst, though every cut will hurt, no matter how well you learn to hide it. I wanted to protest that I did not bring my lanza here, that I did not know he would be here, that I would rather we had come across any other group of armored officers robbing peasants. But I did not speak because in truth the quartermaster swatting the ox had put me in mind of Migaéd laying hands on me in Espalle, which had made me think of how fat dom Gatán was, and how it could be that he stayed fat out here. Some part of me must have known that, sooner or later, we would find exactly these men doing exactly this . . .

Now dom Gatán had, with some effort, turned his donkey around to the fifty or so soldiers who were actually under Migaéd's command. These were mostly discipline cases like the officers who commanded them, but without the benefit of birth. These were hard men and dams, with spears and flails, and one could see they felt lucky to be in a unit that fought so little and ate so well.

One could see they would do much to keep things as they were.

Dom Gatán did not say anything that could get him hanged for insubordination—discipline in this time of goblin wars was no joke if it actually fell upon you—but he did use his eyes in such a way as to suggest to Migaéd's soldiers that some great outrage was taking place. Migaéd's soldiers did not attack us, but they did move themselves between us and the cart that some of them were still loading. These last were not loading food, but bolts of fabric, and a small harp, and a money-chest covered in dirt. It had been buried. I later wondered what rough means had been used to convince the owner of the chest to say where it had been hidden.

One could see that the birds made these looters nervous, but they were just as angry as scared, and more of these were men than in other units.

Many men do not like to be told what to do by a woman and will act against their own interests to defy her.

Migaéd walked up to us now, with Grandfather's shield slung on his back, and with the Galtish Coldfoot and six rich bravos a few steps behind him. He seemed sober, which told me they were out of wine. Little wonder, as quickly as they drank, and as rarely as new barrels turned up. There was little wine-making in the most of Gallardia now, and this had been so for two years.

"You are really going to do this, Galva?" he said, perhaps thinking better of calling me Galvica again. "You are really going to use a writ of our brother to take all of my fucking food?"

"With respect, Sixt-General, it is not Daguera dom Braga who gives the orders here . . ."

"Oh, is it not, Lanzamachur? And why exactly is that, given the fact that our father is Duke Roderigu dom Braga and yours is one whose name escapes me?"

I opened my mouth to speak, then realized it was not my place. I felt Inocenta at my left side now, noticed she had her axe off her back.

Nouva said, "It was not my father but myself who fought in the Threshers' War, under Count Marevan Codoreç dom Nadan, though my father did fight in the Knights' War and had more scars on him than all of your officers together can show. If you have any problems with my rank, I suggest you take it up with your superiors, of whom there is no shortage."

The corvids were agitated, sensing violence, which did not make them unhappy, though they were confused at the absence of goblins. These birds had been well trained not to harm kynd, but it had taken better with some than others.

Richu was trying to steal closer to the line of soldiers who had put themselves in front of us, but Inocenta edged him back.

"Control your animals, Lanzamachur," Migaéd said.

"They are agitated by your men, Sixt-General. Perhaps you should call them back so we can . . ."

"Take all of our food?"

"Only half. But if the birds grow further agitated, they may need more."

Migaéd's nostrils flared so wide I thought dom Gatán could ride his pony and his concubine into one and out the other.

I bit my cheek not to laugh, or cry.

He was about to order his men to step back, I think, which he did in a moment anyway, but something happened now.

One of his line fighters, a huge fellow in rusted scale armor and with a pot helmet that had probably belonged to his grandfather, and in which his brains were surely baking in this heat, cheated forward, his war mace not exactly raised, but not exactly lowered.

Dalgatha did not like this.

All of the corvids are trained to pluck weapons, they are quite skilled at this. But none more so than my Skinny, who can snatch thrown coins out of the air, or steal a card from the table before you react. She grabbed the mace away from this man as though it were a toy in a naughty child's hand, and put it behind her.

The man was a brawler, the kind who acted before he thought. He now punched Dalgatha in the beak with his leather-gloved fist.

Dalgatha hesitated because she knew she was not to attack kynd, had seen what happened to birds who did. She scolded him, saying, "Bad." It might have been funny and broken the tension, but Bellu was already in motion.

My beautiful boy kicked the man in the breadbasket.

He did not use the blade at his heel to slash, but he pushed so hard with the pad of his foot that the man had the wind knocked from him and went to his knees.

Several in the Scarlet Company raised weapons, and the hard-looking spearman who stood behind Migaéd now stepped in front of him. Migaéd and his bravos, of course, did not move forward. Rather, the men and a few dams of the line who did their work for them would do any fighting. I had my shield off my back and on my arm, my *spadín* to hand, in horse pose, which is powerful but not aggressive. I could not believe this was happening, but the part of me that felt that was small and I would not let it distract me. I was in Calar mind, where the body becomes the mind. Strangely, I was less scared of these, though they were many and hard, because they were kynd, and I had trained against kynd.

My sisters were also ready. If the bravos hated us because we were here to halve their plunder, the dams of my lanza hated them for their wealth. Not just the wealth of the officers, which was clearly great, but for the rarer wealth of such a gathering of fighting-age men. All of these dams had lost fathers, uncles, grandfathers, or husbands to the biters. All of their hearths had been robbed of low voices and heavy treads. Whatever these scavenging, bearded boys had done to keep their skins, it did not speak of honor.

Perhaps my brother saw this hate in my sisters' eyes, because now he spoke.

"Weapons down! Step back!"

His troops obeyed.

I relaxed my guard, pulled Bellu back, caressed his feathers to calm him.

He rubbed his beak on me in pure affection, and I looked him in the eye. Only for an instant, but it was clear that I loved him.

My brother saw that I loved my birds.

We took the food we needed from the Scarlet Company of Sword and Horse.

Nothing else was said—sober, Migaéd could hold his tongue.

All the same, I knew this was a beginning, not an ending.

A week later, the army would fight a large battle to lift the siege of Carrasque, which lay close to Goltay and guarded its southern approach, and we would all see action of the worst kind.

But Migaéd forgot nothing.

———— • ————

22

A siege by goblins is worse than a siege by kynd, or so I have read, and so I believe. While we are better at building siege engines of wood, such as trebuchets and rolling towers, there exist no sappers in our armies who are the equal of goblins. The biters are hived underground, they need little space in their tunnels, and they dig fast. They dig well without tools, for the ends of their fingers and toes are sharp, and harder than bone—it is not for joking, a scratch from a goblin's hand—but with tools they are far quicker than us.

Every castle and fortress will set down pans of water to be watched for ripples that mean goblin miners are digging below, and if these ripples are seen, a countermine will have to be dug. Then our half-mad badgers will go down with war dogs, and a hellish underground fight will take place. The goblins often win, and then bring down walls and gatehouses by burning the wooden supports of the tunnels beneath.

The best possibility to resist the digging of the biters is to build your stronghold on the rockiest possible ground. North of us, in the mountains that divided the northwest slice of the country from the land below, there were a series of fortresses and walls called the Hounds of Mour, where they might be held, and there was much talk of falling back to this point. Though this would mean giving up most of Gallardia—and all of her vast farmlands and best cities—so this would not happen while the Western Army had strength.

Unfortunately, the stronghold of Carrasque, just outside of Gol-tay, was built on the sort of fertile soil that one finds in central Gallardia. The warm, drier hills near the coast are perfect for wine, and for hardy but bitter summercorn, but central Gallardia is for wheat and barley and sweetcorn, and root vegetables of every sort and color. Great, fat cows and sheep chew good grass from Carrasque to Goltay to the delta of Aperain. Central Gallardia is a land of beehives and wild deer and streams dammed by beaver. They export wheels of cheese that, turned on their edge, stand the height of your belt.

One could smell how fertile the soil was now, and it lay very black in the fields.

Of course, rain is needed to make black soil, and in this we were rich as we marched closer to Carrasque. No matter how well I oiled my boots, or how carefully I dried them and my stockings and other gear by campfires, there always came the moment when I stepped in one too many puddles and my toes and feet went wet. I found this more bothersome than blisters—though of course these were also unpleasant—because I dislike being dirty. The odor of wet feet and boots in summer is distinct, and these days of Highgrass rain stand out in my memory as smelling quite awfully. Though we would march harder and in worse rain later, we did not yet know this, so these days seemed a hell of endless trudging.

At night we would line up at cookpots for thin rations, then go to smaller fires, each one surrounded by a garden of branch-hung socks wept in by blisters. Bare feet were raised to these fires as dams wiped from between their toes mud, more mud, and a parting gift of mud. One in our camp had a hurdy-gurdy, and I had never liked them—I once heard a comedic poem about a man so angered to be mistaken for a hurdy-gurdy player that he harmed the genitals of the fellow who pestered him, causing him to make the sound of the instrument. But I was so starved for music here that I confess I enjoyed the playing.

In the rain it was necessary to oil every piece of metal, including the gear on the birds, and still small specks of rust like freckles would grow. Mushrooms in great variety grew in the fields and alongside the sides of roads, and many kynd would kick the caps off the stems of the larger ones out of sheer spite because it was known that mushrooms were friends to our great enemy. It was said mushrooms grew fatter near them, and indeed, it seemed that more and more were seen as we approached Carrasque, and more of the deadly sorts as well.

I heard that several Ispanthians had died while foraging. By the time the Pragmatist had forbidden mushroom hunting, except by quartermasters employing expert local guides, the rains had stopped, and the fires of Carrasque could be seen.

"All right, sops and fuckers," Nouva said, "put on your driest surcoats and shine the shit out of your gorgets—we approach the king of Gallardia, who is badly in need of rescue."

I will admit that I was excited by this. It had been some time since I had been near court, or seen a king. And any king must be more just and good than Ispanthia's own Kalith the Usurper.

It was later that day we drew over a hill and saw the goblin lines, and their hives in the shape of great mounds.

Many of us gasped.

As a breeze from the north hit us, the dogs in the camps of our sappers barked or howled and the birds became agitated.

I looked at Inocenta, and she at me.

Many of us shared the same thought, though none of us wanted to say it.

They are too many.

Past the goblin Horde, girded round by siegeworks, standing tall despite a breach in the west outer wall and two burning turrets, was the famed fortress town of Carrasque, southern gateway to the old capital city of Goltay. I saw the blue banner of Gallardia, with a golden lion standing before the white tree of wisdom, with two golden swords on the edges, one up for war, one down for peace. I saw also the personal banner of the king, the one he had made after his coronation, a green toad beneath a crown of gold on a white field.

Carrasque was indeed the gateway to Goltay for any army that needed roads, but the goblins had just gone around it and, now that Goltay was theirs, had come back to clean up. Happily for the future of Manreach, they had failed to break the walls before our arrival. It was a near thing—they had gambled that they would be inside the walls before we showed up, and, thanks to the many tunnels they were weaving under the walls of Carrasque, they were perhaps two days from achieving this.

But we had come in time, and, for as much as their host looked uncountable, we were more.

Worse for them, we were not the only army coming.

The goblins knew this, they always knew at least roughly where we were, and this army would withdraw and lift the siege before they could be pinched between us and the armies of Holt and the Far Banners.

But first we would test them with attack.

Our lanza was not ordered to be part of this.

But we went anyway.

23

The battle of Carrasque is remembered as a minor victory for the Ispanthian army, though it was less a battle and more an orderly goblin retreat, with skirmishes. Yes, the goblins left us in control of the field, and yes, the siege was lifted, but the biters were saving their strength. There is a toast in Braga—"Loyal friends, wise kings, stupid enemies." We were not so blessed with goblins. They are at least as smart as we are, and, worse, more unified. No goblin commanders refuse to retreat for the sake of honor and no units fail to understand their orders. It is said they communicate through scent, and this allows them to move as one with great speed and coordination, and I think this is true. It is also said their priests may send information many miles through the ground, though the means are mysterious. All I knew this day was that the main force of the goblins unrolled itself from the shadow of Carrasque's mighty towers with great precision.

Our heavy infantry was ordered forward under cover of archers to probe the southern line covering their retreat, but the biters had laid covered pits, and some of our vanguard fell into these attempting to close with them. I saw that one unit of goblins overwhelmed and surrounded, but these were only a few dozen, maybe a hundred. Meanwhile, they were hitting us with such a weight of crossbow fire that the poisoned bolts were striking the quick here and there.

Nouva swept the battlefield with her farglass and showed something to Inocenta.

"There," she said.

Inocenta looked, and then showed me.

A patch of forest stood near their lines. Forest near us swept down and joined with it—it might be possible for a small unit to make contact with their army moving unseen through the trees.

"You dams feel like hunting?"

The distance was more than it seemed.

It took no small amount of time to get through these trees, even though we were moving fast. We wore less armor than knights of the line. We were classified as medium armor, with brigandines and light chain rather than plate and heavy chain. Our brigandines were of varying qualities, some little more than studded leather, but mine was of good cloth with small steel plates sewn within. I wore a good bascinet helmet, which covered my ears, though this had no visor—our birds needed to see our faces, much was said between us with the eye. We had scarves about our necks that could be raised to cover our nose and mouth if the spores of the nightmare cap were used against us to cause terror and visions—but usually we would see the long wooden pipes they used to blow it in time to mask against it. Most of this lanza were knights-communal, of ordinary birth but having been recognized and titled by a knight-martial—no small matter, as the knight giving the title bound up their reputation with those he or she named. So we ran with our light chain-mail coats, our brigandines and gorgets, our greaves so tightly fixed to our shins we barely felt their weight, our boots of good Bragaene leather thumping the ground. We ran through pretty tree-shadows so at first it seemed like some fable, with our fantastical birds running alongside us, but reality hit us as we neared their army.

The first thing we heard was the noise of ravens.

We came to a clearing with many of these, gathering on a long, thick branch, perfect for hangings.

This branch had been strung with butchered kynd.

The meat of the thighs and calves were goblins' favorite cut, and this meat had been taken, so that what we saw were villagers and soldiers hanging dead with scraped, skeletal legs.

My work with Bellu and Dalgatha had made me love ravens, but this was my first time seeing so many of them eating kynd flesh, and I did not love them so much after.

More of these branches came into sight, and more again, and the butchery soon overwhelmed us. Here were Gallard soldiers, mostly dams and a very few men, strung up scraped, gutted, and half-eaten like suckling pigs. The biters had stripped their pants from them to get at their legs, so many of these swung with their nakedness displayed above the raw bone and hanging tendons of their legs. I felt rage and fear struggling in my breast. I wanted both to avenge these grossly insulted kynd, and to run away before some goblin used its cook-knife to lay bare my knees and shin-bones. But those around me became furious, and my anger, fed by theirs, was soon greater than my fear. It was when our outrage was at its peak that we first saw the goblins, both soldiers and mess-goblins, and, past them, a trio of huge cage-carts pulled by boars.

The faces of kynd looked out from those enclosures.

Nouva did not have to tell us to get our shields on our arms and our weapons in hand.

We all did this as one.

They had seen us now.

Their soldiers turned and formed lines before their carts, and readied crossbows.

Most of those before us were proper soldiers, perhaps a hundred. This would not be a matter of castaway goblin sailors.

We were forty-eight dams and eighty-seven birds.

This was my first real battle.

That I went into this fight more angry than scared helped me through it.

This makes a difference, and I would later learn to shape these feelings before a fight.

Fuck goblins, and fuck whatever wretched god made them.
They are only for killing.

The crossbow bolts were more than in the skirmish with the sailors, and heavier.

They hit much harder.

Several hammered my shield; one scored my helmet, and this
hurt.

Three of my lanza were struck to the quick before we closed,
despite the shivering of the corvids' wings, and these dams died
of poison, their bodies racked with spasms. When we did close,
the goblins rose up with their hooked spears, or gisarmes, and
made a good defense against the birds. They fight in wedges of
three, as I have mentioned, and we trained for this. But no kynd
moves wholly like a goblin, and no amount of sparring with
dams playing their part can prepare anyone for them.

The clash was madness, a thrashing, bloody storm of hooks
and points, and feathers, and screams, and rasps, and their
strange and doglike whooping. I remember facing one of these
wedges, how they hooked my shield, how I was nearly killed or
blinded when a point licked just in front of my eyes without an
inch to spare. But I was too angry to worry about my own hide—I
wanted theirs. I struck at their small limbs, felt the Calar mind
take over—right move, right time. I began to anticipate their
stabs, the off-rhythm with which they stabbed at my legs then
jerked back with those bladed hooks trying to cut my heel tendon or at least tangle up my feet. I hopped and stepped on one of
these gisarmes with my back foot, stomping the forefoot down
to slap the shaft flat against the ground, wrenching it from the
biter's hands. I split the creature neck to crown with my upswing,
knocked another spear down with my shield, then chopped down
at that one's arm. I would have had it off, too, but for the armor
many of them wore, which we call mesh. We have nothing like

it. Think of cloth armor, not so thick, but woven somehow with strands of metal, like wire only more supple. We do not know how this is made. It is lighter than chain mail, though, and very good against a blade. Luckily, the *spadín* has some weight. My blow ruined its arm, which flopped bonelessly in its sleeve while it gave a raspy scream. Its eyes went white with pain.

Now Bellu grabbed the third one from that wedge by the head and flung it into a tree, breaking its neck.

From the other side, warm liquid hit my eyes and I shut them.

One goblin had stabbed a dam to my left—her name was Perla Barescu—driving its spear under her chin. It flicked her blood into my eyes, which is a favorite tactic of theirs, before it leapt to stab me as well. My shield went up by reflex, and I stepped into its attack, shoved it back, and blinked the blood out of my eye. I moved to stab it, but it had already moved back. They were regrouping fast. I saw a dying corvid thrashing, its feet kicking to drive it in an awful circle as its cut throat washed its life into the dirt.

We had killed many, perhaps two dozen, but more were coming, and they had formed a defensive hedge of spears it would cost us to break. I believed these birds could do it, but then there would be another line.

We were perhaps facing 150 or 170 goblins now.

We should retreat, but still we saw the cart of kynd who would end up like the others, hanging with bones for legs. Closer now, I could see children among them. Anger and fear struggled in me.

I cut my eyes to Inocenta, expecting to see a face as desperate as mine must look, but, and I will never forget this, she was smiling.

"Today might be the day," she said, as one might speak of taking a long-anticipated lover, and I knew that she meant her death. She was saying that she might die now and she felt glad about it. I did not understand, but I took strength from this.

"Die with me, sister," she said to me.

"I would be honored," I said, though my voice shook.

Nouva formed us up—our charge had stalled, and she would send us forward again when we were in formation. We crouched behind our shields, our heads down so only our eyes showed between helmet and shield-rim, our birds finishing off goblins at our feet, then moving in front of us, wings shivering.

Crossbows clacked and quarrels hummed and whistled.

Some injured dam moaned behind us.

Another yelped not twenty feet from me as a quarrel's point sank into her flesh—she would die of poison.

Nouva jabbed the thumb.

I took off at a sprint.

Bellu and Dalgatha saw me in their sideways eyes and leapt ahead on either side. Inocenta, running to my left, screamed a war cry worthy of devils.

Inocenta's scream did something else as well.

It made her bird Richu scream, imitating her, wanting to please her.

Bellu, good boy, the best of corvids, sweet sweet Bellu, also screamed.

I had never heard a corvid make that sound before, and I had not known they could.

It hurt my ears, it was the voice of the goddess of death herself.

I screamed, too.

It felt right in my throat, it gave me strength.

Now Gannet took it up, and Dalgatha, and Boxer. Soon all of our huge birds were shrieking to shake the pillars holding up the sky as we ran at the line of goblins, ran to our likely deaths.

But the line of goblins was barely a line anymore.

The crossbows had stopped.

The biters were running.

First in ones and twos, and then in clumps.

Those that were not running, perhaps one in three, stood frozen, their membranes white over their eyes, blinding them as they swayed and shivered.

What was this?

We had not known the birds had this scream, or that it would affect the biters so. The potential in this would be for thinking about, but this was not a time for thinking. I stepped up to one and stabbed it in the face, knocked its helmet off as my point went out the back of its skull.

Our line advanced now. We no longer ran, but walked like children finding a field of gifts. Our birds pulled the heads off frozen goblins without resistance. We pulled their helmets off and crushed their heads with shields, we beheaded them with carefully aimed blows, we kicked them over and stomped their heads to jelly.

I saw a great many of their helmets on the ground, and noticed for the first time how each was different. Some had crests of bronze or bone, or sharp horns in twos or threes, or even blades of metal. Some were ornamented with bits of coral or amber, both of which they admire greatly. Some had trim of goblin silver, with its greenish way of giving light back. These helmets were often beautiful, but confusing. Their irregularity both caught and hurt the eye. It was possible to stare at them too long.

Inocenta elbowed me to bring me back to myself.

Nouva signaled for us to stop near the cage-carts, and we caught our breath and watched the goblins run. Would they come back? This would be a good place to stand if they did.

"Free the kynd," someone yelled, and I moved to do this.

"Don't," Inocenta said, and I was unsure why at the time. It sounded less like an order than like some kind of misunderstanding, so I kept on. Someone had to help these people, and I could not understand why I was the only one who seemed interested in doing so.

I went to the first cart, and I cut the thick ropes securing the door.

The kynd inside moved back from the door.

These were mostly women and children, all nude and bruised and starving.

The smell from the cart was nearly as bad as the goblin-scent.

"Don't worry, I won't hurt you," I said.

They were looking at me with mad, white eyes.

I could not begin to imagine what they had been through, though if you know much of goblins, you will know their stupor was more than just an effect of trauma.

"Galva," Inocenta said, almost gently.

I got the door open, but they had all crowded against the far end of the cage, as though I were the worst of all goblins.

I saw that a few of them looked like they might be able to fight.

"Can we get them weapons?" I said.

One or two of the girls who were new like me began to pick up spears or swords, but Nouva and others who had fought before stopped them.

I looked back at the people in the cart.

"What's the matter?" I said. "You are free."

I moved out of the doorway, gestured with an arm that they should come out.

"Galva, come away," Inocenta said, grabbing my hand, but I shook her off, saying, "No, we have to get them out of there."

Now one of the few and healthiest-looking men in that cart looked at me with his mad eyes and made a sound.

It was not exactly a moan, or a cry.

It was more like the lowing of a cow.

A woman next to him started to low as well, and soon the kynd in the other carts took it up. It was an awful, hopeless sound, and I began to understand that the goblins had destroyed their minds and made livestock out of them. It is called "dumbing," and it is accomplished with a kind of mushroom that has since been forbidden outside the Hordelands by treaty.

"No," I said, when I understood what had happened to these people. They bleated and lowed and I just kept saying "no" like a child, while others who had not known about this sobbed or stared into the distance.

Nouva ordered the doors of the other carts opened just in case any had kept their wits, but they were all dumbed.

They did not leave their cages.

We unhooked the huge dray boars that had been pulling the carts and herded them along with us, tying our six dead to their backs. I saw that Vega Charnat, the bare-knuckle fighter from Galimbur, was among the fallen. A poisoned quarrel had pierced her chain mail and found the meat of her shoulder. She would not be punching me with those big, scarred fists as she had wished to do. I would not be carving her with my *spadín*, as I feared she would force me to. Her fists were blue-white claws. Her face was also a bad color, her mouth was locked in a frown. I was sorry she had hated me. I had not felt the same way about her, and now I only hoped she was at rest, though it did not look that way.

Her remaining corvid, Hammer, followed her body on the boars, plucking at her foot now and again, hoping she was playing a game with him. The corvids of the other fallen dams were equally distraught. They allowed themselves to be led, though one—that of Perla, who was slain beside me—started to pluck its chest feathers.

This bird would not eat again, and would join her mistress by the end of the week.

I looked over my shoulder one last time as we marched back to the column through the trees, though I should not have.

I saw the kynd still in their cages. They had stopped lowing. Now it seemed they were waiting patiently, even hopefully, for their owners to reclaim them.

I think now that we should have killed them.

24

I had little time to think on the events of that day in the woods near Carrasque. I would have liked nothing better than to be left alone with my sisters in arms to drink away the sights of the afternoon, but a rich name is expensive in obligation.

The invitation came by runner, as they always did, and the young dam found me as I bathed my hurts in a stream, with others of the lanza, trying to ignore the dead in it. She presented me a letter, and a crown of flowers I was to wear, as well as new clothes. I winced taking the flowers from her hand, knowing they could only embarrass me—I am not made for delicate things.

I read the letter.

It was brief.

Sister,
We dine with the king.
Unmarried youths are asked to wear garlands of the sort
I have provided you.
There shall be . . . interesting news.

Pol d. B.

Youths, I thought, trying and failing to smooth the scowl I felt bending my mouth, and I considered tossing the garland in the stream and declaring it lost. But even a small lie is a lie. To my horror, the other women in the stream and dressing on its bank started chanting, "Put it on! Put it on!," so there was no way out of it. I sat the merry thing on my head slanted, and made a vicious face, snarling at any who came near as I dressed.

The actions near Carrasque were fought on the twenty-eighth day of Highgrass, a half-moon Lūnday, but the battle is not why I remember the date.

This was to be the night I first saw the woman I would devote my life to.

Queen Mireya and King Luvain threw a ball to thank the army of Ispanthia, which had saved him and what remained of his army. Migaéd was also there, though we did not directly speak. I stood with Pol as his honor guard in my plain armor and the fresh, new shirt he had sent for me. My crown of flowers felt like thorns and nettles, and I was one of the only dams wearing one and not a dress. Oh, there were soldier dams, of course, but those of lower station who merely executed their office were not expected to be festive. I noticed some young, beautiful men wearing such crowns, but I quickly realized they were whores, so I felt no better.

Pol had no flowers, though he did wear a circlet of silver to show his noble birth.

I thought I should have the same, but I shut my mouth and wore my fucked-silly flowers. Honestly, it was just a trick to keep my mind busy, thinking of the flowers and the circlet rather than remembering what I had seen at the battle of Carrasque. Even now Nouva would be telling our immediate commander of the screaming corvids and their effect on the biters. She had directed me to tell Terce-General dom Braga, which I had done when I met him outside the castle, and he had told the Pragmatist. It seemed there was some appetite to see if the experiment could be repeated. For my part, I would do whatever was required of me, but I never wanted to live such a day again.

I still dream of dead meat-dams dancing on legs of bone, when I am not dreaming of the juggernaut, and of other things from Gallardia, which, alas, you will hear of soon.

Pol and I stood in the great hall of the castle of Carrasque, the stone of which moaned and creaked ominously from the tunnels that biters had been making beneath it, and from the counter-tunnels Gallard sappers had dug. This whole place had only been a day or two from being taken, and I supposed that it could still collapse. It would be an amusing end to be crushed by stones while wearing a crown of flowers, surrounded by boy-whores, listening to music.

It was fine music, at least.

Gallards are known to be the best musicians with instruments, though I think Ispanthians are better singers. Perhaps everyone thinks this of their own country.

Dancers came after the singers, and these were all dams, and greatly talented. Though of course they were also soldiers; several bore the scars of cuts or bites, and one had an eye out, and one had no hands. This made their dance more beautiful, and with music to unlace my heart, I began to weep, though I quickly made myself stop. I saw that I was not the only one so affected.

Now trumpets sounded a fanfare, and royal guards with hal-berds and feathered helmets entered around a pair of empty thrones. These guards had also clearly seen action, but not in this armor, which was beautiful but ridiculous, not the sort of thing to get blood on.

I remembered the sensation of warm blood in my eye and blinked and gasped.

"Are you well, Galvicha?" Pol asked.

I nodded.

The royal court of King Luvain the First of Gallardia, called the Toad King by some, began their entrance now, following behind an Allgod priest holding Sath's golden sunburst high. Several children followed with stars and a moon. One barefoot priestess with good balance bore a staff topped with a vessel of seawater for Mithrenor, and a very beautiful priestess of Nerêne held up a *ferula* with stained-glass eyes in lavender. These clerics went to right and left, and Luvain's children from his late wife came in and stood on either side of the thrones. Now several courtiers walked in, and, to my great surprise, my brother Migaéd walked among them.

I wanted to ask Pol why he was there, but this was not a time for speaking.

A hush had come over the great hall.

King Luvain of Gallardia entered, and also the queen consort.

Someone clapped, I think someone whose job it was to clap, and soon the entire room broke into applause, and cheers. The king had survived. The king would prevail. And the Ispanthian officers commanding the ninety thousand soldiers who had saved him clapped for him, as if he had done anything more than last long enough to be rescued.

Though I suppose this was not nothing.

I took a good look at the court of Gallardia, and I admit I was affected.

It is fine to see a king, but it is an even better thing to see a queen.

Luvain looked very much the monarch, dressed in ceremonial armor of rose gold and steel, and he wore the rose-gold crown with its hundred emeralds.

But he is not the one who drew the eye.

Nor was he supposed to be.

A king may appear in whatever state of dress he cares to, so long as the crown tops his head. He may command armies while dirty from battle, or make jokes open-shirted after a round of rackets on a court. He may address his council robed from a bath and shave. Even in these days of warrior dams and dams at blacksmiths' forges and dams who box bare-knuckled for money on the streets, a queen is still measured by her appearance and must strike at the heart of those who see her. She must enchant, and she must awe. This is even more true for a queen consort, who rules only by her husband's let, and does not inherit the crown should he die.

And so it was for Queen Consort Mireya of Gallardia.

She was the Infanta Mireya of my country. She was the daughter of the poisoned king, and so, by blood the true queen of Ispanthia. Her throne had been usurped by her uncle Kalith, may his mustache be dipped in the fiery shit of devils.

Mireya stood in a dark gray dress worked with silver, but above her chest she wore a sort of mantle, made of silver chain mail, though only ornamental—it was too fine and light for armor. It rose into a collar of chain mail at her neck, and it had silver scales at her shoulders that put one in mind of a dragon. Her thick, black hair she wore in twin braids, one of which was being held and chewed on by the small monkey sitting on her shoulder. This monkey, Peppercorn, was famous in my country, as it was rumored she could speak to him, and that he had saved her from poison. Now he just looked like an ordinary *jilnaedu* hair-chewing monkey.

I surprised myself by thinking that I would also like to chew on that braid.

Mireya's face had been made up white, with copper accents, including copper leaves at the eyes. I do not know the words to describe the style of her makeup, except that it was done and made her look half a goddess. Then, out of nowhere, I imagined her in profile, her hair down, her eyes closed. I imagined yellow light behind her, like dawn. In my waking dream, her hair was as beautiful as a garden, or a river, or the night itself.

Then I blinked my eyes and came back to myself.

My eyes went from the queen to my eldest brother.

No, in all seriousness, what by all the gods gathered was Migaéd doing on that dais?

King Luvain spoke.

He said a few words in Gallard, but the address he had come to make was delivered in perfect Ispanthian, which he spoke with barely an accent. This Toad King was an impressive man.

"Friends of Ispanthia. Many years ago, when your land was beset by Our Great Foe, knights and soldiers of Gallardia answered your call for help, and together we trampled those first goblin Hordes under hoof and drove them out of your country with fire and steel. You have now repaid us tenfold, a hundredfold, with the blood of your men, and now of your dams."

That warmth in my eye.

The biter's rasp as its spear hit the shield I raised blind to save my life.

I blinked again, hard, though this time I did not gasp.

"It is a debt we must admit that we can never repay, and a gift we shall always strive to be worthy of, through friendship, and through gratitude, and through continued trial of arms until the scourge is once again repelled. As they were repelled yesterday from Carrasque!"

I would think on the king's words later, and how the biters were not repelled, but left on their own terms and for their own reasons. Speeches are woven from feelings, not facts, however, and these words of the king of Gallardia moved me.

"As they shall be driven from Goltay tomorrow!"

Cheering.

"As they shall soon be scourged, burned, and beaten out of all the Crownlands!"

More cheering.

"And, the good gods willing, as we shall one day chase them back to their Hordelands and archipelagoes and exterminate them entirely, like the wretched plague they are! *Vivat Ispante!*"

"*Vivat Ispante*" all the Gallards repeated, in a high and grate-ful roar, and I felt my heart swell. I was proud of my country, and of my fellow Spanths, who would never make the art or music the Gallards did—but we had our own music, and it was martial, and we were generous with our blood if the cause was right.

"*Vivat li roy!*" a woman yelled in Gallard, and it was yelled again, and soon we were all wishing long life to this charming, doomed king.

"But we are not only here to talk of war, which is death's

handmaiden. We are here to talk of life, and of the friendship of our great nations, the two greatest in all of Manreach."

Oh shit, I thought. *It cannot be.*

But it was.

"And in that spirit, I would like to announce that our daughter, the princess Seraphine, is today betrothed to Migaéd dom Braga of Ispanthia, son of the Illustrious Duke Roderigu, our distant cousin and friend."

Migaéd now stepped forward, smiling like a dog that ate a cake.

He took the hand of a blond girl of twelve, who looked both stunned at the speed of events and also charmed that she should be given to a man so handsome. Ispanthian law would not allow a girl so young to go to the marriage bed for several years, and I assumed Gallardia was the same, but one could see the poor thing was smitten with the dashing libertine. I gritted my teeth, hating this. Princess Seraphine had hard lessons about her future husband to learn, and perhaps the contract would not survive these lessons.

I hoped this.

While the rest of the room clapped and cheered, I looked at Pol, and though his face showed nothing, I think he was also surprised by the king's announcement. How had Migaéd managed this? Had Father arranged it?

My head spun with questions, but these were soon quieted.

The queen was looking at me.

She was not so close that I should have been able to say for sure, but I felt that she was looking at me.

And later, she told me that she was.

At the dinner that followed, I sat near Pol and he sat not so far from the Pragmatist, who had been placed near the king and the queen consort of Gallardia. The meat served to us was swan, and

I later learned that these had been tamed and once lived in the moat. I say tamed, but what swan is really tame? I had known one in Seveda, kept in the garden of a great lord, and I was afraid of it, with reason. It bit me, and chased me. It was a bastard. I am sure that these swans had also been bastards, and, though I refused to eat them, it was not because I felt badly for the swans. I noticed that the Pragmatist also ate no meat that night, but only the soup, which was of peas and the ends of bread that were left, and I think now her reasons were similar to mine. I believe she would not enjoy privileges while her army suffered. For my part, I would not dine on swan and gravy while Inocenta and the other dams of my lanza ate pottage. When Pol raised an eyebrow at my nearly bare plate, I simply shrugged. It is not always necessary to explain reasons. I saw the Pragmatist notice my scant dinner as well; she met my eyes for a second, and I thought I saw her nod, as if I were her sister in hunger, but now I am not sure.

The king's fool, Hanz, now told a funny story in Gallard though with an Unthern accent. I assume it was funny, because all who spoke the Gallard tongue laughed. He was a dwarf, which is not an unusual quality in fools, and I like fools better than clowns. This king also had clowns, and they were crass, relying on bodily noises and pratfalls. The fool had sad, smart eyes, though, and I liked him. Perhaps people who heard his funny words missed this sadness, and I only noticed because I could not understand him.

You can imagine my surprise when the man proved to have mastered three tongues—he came up to Pol and said, in good but heavily accented Ispanthian, "Terce-General, you are invited to meet Luvain the King, if that seems the appropriate thing, and if you are quite done nibbling. Please bring your lovely sibbling!"

From the main keep in Carrasque one long, skinny tower goes into the sky. It is the highest point of many miles, and it has no roof. It was here that Pol and I joined the king, his queen consort, the fool, and several stewards and musicians. The queen consort had changed. When had she even left? She now wore black silk pantaloons and slippers, and a robe of rose gold, and a net of rose gold and emeralds over her hair, which was still in braids.

I could not help noting how well-made she was, and I thought that she must swim, or run, or tumble, for hers was not a sop's body.

"Welcome to the Tower of the Gift of Stars, which you can see is well named," the king said to us, showing the many stars with his hand as if they were indeed within his gift. "I would be pleased if you drank some good wine and listened to a few merry songs with us here, beneath the stars that remind us not to take ourselves and our troubles too seriously. They wink over birth and death with equal beauty, after all. They will nicely ornament our conversation, I think. We have some few things to discuss."

"Thank you, Your Grace," Pol said. "May I ask, will our brother be joining us?"

Now the queen consort spoke.

"He is with his bride-to-be, under chaperone of course. The king and I thought it better to let the children play together while the grown-ups speak."

"Ha!" Luvain said. "You see why I love her. A rare and lucky thing in a state marriage."

Now the monkey, Peppercorn, flung a grape at the king's face and it struck him on the forehead with a tiny sound that made us all laugh.

I heard again the strange groaning of the weakened castle, and thought how like a song it was. If Carrasque collapsed, this tower would fall first. I surprised myself by feeling not unease, but a thrill at the thought of such a rare and beautiful death. It is with such thoughts the Bride becomes dear to us.

Luvain now addressed my brother.

"So. What do you think of our plans to wed our daughter to the House of dom Braga? Please, Terce-General, speak freely."

I had been drinking this night, enough so it seemed to me that the stream of wine a steward now poured into Pol's cup was full of starlight. Pol pursed his lips, drank, and ordered his thoughts.

"I am proud to see our houses draw nearer, Your Grace."

"Thank you," the king said. "I am glad of it as well, though I should be gladder to marry the girl to you, were you the heir. Your brother is . . . Well, he just is."

"That he is, Your Grace," Pol agreed.

"Enough of this 'Your Grace' business. I am Luvain to you, if you will indulge me. May I call you Pol?"

"Of course," Pol said, "though I may have to spend a few more Your Graces before I reach Luvain."

"And I am Miri to those who love me," the queen consort said, looking at me in a way that I felt in my skin. You will not believe this, but now the *jilnaedu* monkey came down from Mireya's shoulder, took up a small, round bottle, and filled my glass with sweet port wine. My mouth fell open. I had heard that this Mireya was mad, and a witch. She did not seem mad to me, but I had no doubt that she was a witch of some power. The monkey touched one finger to his head, as though to say *and now you know*, then went back to her shoulder and his dull-eyed chewing of the queen's braid.

"Miri," I said, and the smile that lit her lips to hear her name on mine was candlelight made flesh.

I saw now the twin violet stars that were the Eyes of Nerêne seated just behind the queen's shoulder, near the constellation of the Crab and Pitcher. To notice the Eyes of Nerêne behind someone was said to mean you will be their lover. I felt my face color, and I was glad it was night. Then all at once I was taken angry, thinking she was bewitching me, and that it was unfair because she was a queen and I had only twenty years. Then I thought myself foolish because twenty was not so young, and if I knew nothing but the sword and shield, that was my own fault for hiding on the training yard while others danced and coupled.

I wanted both to leave and to wait and see what happened.

One heard rumors about the Gallardian court.

Mireya pulled her bare feet out of her slippers and tucked them beneath her legs.

A ring of rose gold on one of her long toes caught my eye.

She noticed this and smiled again, then looked away so not to press too hard.

I looked down at the cushion I sat on, a purple or dark blue fabric I think, and very fine. Gold embroidery of elephants reflected the light of the lamps. I sometimes felt as though I ran from fine things only to have them find me anyway. Inocenta would not be sleeping on a silk pillow tonight, with a belly full of port and good soup.

I felt the night breeze, which was still warm, and which smelled faintly of goblins and death and fires despite the height of the tower and the incense pots at the corners of this pretty roof. I knew that we had been brought here only because the night's darkness hid the carnage on the fields below us.

"You have not told us what to call you, sister of two generals," Mireya said.

"I am . . . only Galva."

"Only Galva," the queen said, "I cannot help feeling that you are discomfited. I know that you saw hard action, and that all of this must seem frivolous to you. But it is the Gallard way to seek pleasure even in extremity. As a born Spanth, this took some getting used to. Tell me what I may do to help you be at ease."

I looked into her eyes, which were of a very pleasing shape, and said, "Let me go."

She held up a closed hand, palm up, and then opened it as if releasing a bird.

Her smile had waned, though not from anger, as it might have been with a man.

She was merely sad to see me leave.

———————

Hanz, the Fool, walked me out. "Daguera," he said as we made our way down the snail staircase of the Tower of the Gift of Stars, laboring at the steep stairs, "I wonder if I might tell you a story as I walk you home."

"I would be honored to hear it," I said.

"Yah," he said in that Unthern way, "goot. Years ago, during this war they call the Threshers' War, I was back in Unther, and I had been a mummer. Of course this is some of the only work open to one of my . . . gifts. Happily, I enjoyed it and I was good at it. I fell in with a company of other little people, four of us, and we played goblins in muster-plays. You know the sort, I think. We go around in wagons and make our faces gray, act out the worst abominations, shame people who look capable of being soldiers. I had the jawbones of a pig, and I would nip and bite at people, saying, *Look at your long, strong legs, they should be marching! Aren't you ashamed to be home, with goblins in Gallardia and Istrea? They will come here if you don't go kick them into the sea, long-legs!* But people do not like to be shamed, and it will not surprise you to learn that sometimes we were beaten. Oh, sometimes we were fed and given money, and even taken into beds for the novelty of it or because there were so few men. There is a fable in Unther that says that to sleep with a dwarf is good for the crops, and I am thankful to whichever dwarf started this rumor, I will be his friend and buy him beer forever. But the worst thing that happened to us was an accident. We got very good at playing goblins, you see. We had the makeup, and real goblin armor and their real weapons that people brought home from the war. Those who had fought them would tell us how they moved and we learned to imitate this, and how they sounded. Listen, I will speak some goblin for you . . . *Haskx-ath-ththatl, rzzzsp a-thaxat*. You see? I told you that you look good enough to eat. Soldiers taught me that, and I worked very hard to get it right. I will even say, without arrogance, that I was the best mummer at imitating goblins in all of Unther. So, you will guess where this is going. As we got farther into the country, villages got smaller, more isolated, more fearful of the broader world. After a visit to one such village, word began to spread that real goblins had taken the place of the mummers and were stealing children. So, we were attacked by men with flails and clubs, men who had in fact fought goblins and knew how they moved, and knew that the hooked spears and moth-axes we carried were real. My three companions were killed, and I survived by hiding in the woods, up a tree. I am not so bad at climbing. You are thinking, why am I telling you this tragic story? I am supposed to make people laugh, not cry, yah? And so. I was taken to begging now, and juggling; I wanted no part of dressing like a goblin. A Gallard saw me in our capital city, and said he was a lord, just over the border, and would I like to come home and entertain his children? What other prospect did I have in these times? I did this. I made his children laugh with games and jokes, and he was the envy of his town. He also abused me in ways you can imagine. Perhaps it was for his crops. Happily for me, I was seen by the Toad Earl, Luvain, when he came to visit on progress on summer, and he loved me because I was clever. He said something to the cruel border lord that made him let me go. He made a gift of me to Luvain and his court, as if I were a pony, or a greyhound; but Luvain took me to Mouray and gave me monies and told me I could go my ways. It was enough that I would not have to work as a mummer for a very long time. But do you know what happened? Of course you do. I stayed with the Toad Earl. Before he was anointed, and after. Because he is that rarest of things, a decent man beneath a crown. And his queen is well matched to him. I will always stay with them. And now, here we are at your cold stables, where you may sleep in straw or mud to be loyal to your fellow soldiers. I admire this. But please know, daughter of the duke, that there is nothing romantic about being hunted or beaten, or starving, or abused. These are just the things we can expect here, in this world. Most of us. And those of us in the shit like to know that somewhere, someone isn't in the shit. And every time I drink a good glass of wine or eat a pastry or bed a whore, or a priestess of Nerêne, I do it not with hardness in my heart toward those who suffer. I do it in gratitude that there *is* something besides suffering."

He looked me deeply in the eyes and said, "Now, Galva dom Braga, before you go to your stable-bed . . . would you like to be my lover? For the sake of the crops?"

I do not know what expression I wore when I said, "What??? No!," but he smiled a devil's smile and said, "No? That is your answer?"

"Yes!" I said, and before I could correct this, he said, "Well, which is it, is it yes or no?"

"It is no!" I said, and I think I was half crying and half smiling at the same time.

"So . . ." he said, looking very sad. "You mean I made up that horrible fucking story for nothing?"

25

As Hanz left the stables, I heard the birds click and stir. They were still agitated from the events of the day. I also found that Inocenta was not in her bedroll, but she had left a note for me.

Galva,
Come to where we fought the biters, and then go east. You will find a low stone wall, mostly hidden by brush. It is the boundary to an old Keshite temple to My Serene Lady, which you will find one hundred twenty paces farther on, tangled up in young trees. We were marching and raiding your brother for food during the New Moon, and could not gather in her name, so we sing for her tonight. I have always wanted you to see one of our services, but at an ancient temple? Built when she was first worshipped? There will never be another such chance. Come and see! You will be safe, you are my invited one. We begin at midnight.

'Centa

I wanted very badly to sleep, but I knew this was of great importance to my *irmana apracera*—she had invited me to her church, and much of her heart was in her belief. I will also confess that I was jealous of her calm before battle. This gift alone seemed greater than anything Sath and his all-seeing sun offered. Come to think of it, I was not aware of much good he had done anyone, except to make some less pale and encourage them to make their bodies fit, which I suppose has value. But a good training regimen does the same. And this matter of not fearing death? My fear was great, and it shamed me. I wanted to know more of

Dal-Gaata. So I spurred my weary limbs and, by the light of the waxing moon, made my way back through the woods alone.

When I came to the temple, it was not yet midnight.

Inocenta took my hand from the darkness, as though she had anticipated my steps exactly, and I was glad to see her face.

"*Irmana*," she said, and I said it back. It was just so, with our hands clasped, and our warm feelings of amity, that I walked with her into the closeness of the old temple. "You wore a garland for her," she said, and I realized I was so tired I had forgotten the *chodadu* crown of flowers.

"Well, I wore it," I said, "I do not know for whom."

Other soldiers greeted us in hushed tones. The worship of Dal-Gaata was not forbidden exactly—the Pantheistic Creed had been upheld in the Charter of Olives—but many felt that our King Kalith, who had made himself head of the church of Sath, would soon begin to purge other gods. This would not be from any true religious feeling, but because he wanted power above all things. Dal-Gaata would make an easy first target for him since many were fearful of her worshippers. It was said we began as opium addicts and ended as assassins.

I would like to state that I have never been either of these things, as you well know.

Several banners of the Lady's worship had been brought and displayed in this place, and at the time they made no sense to me.

Here was a finely dressed western man, perhaps from old Kesh, holding a jeweled and feathered turban over the empty space where his head should be.

The second showed a skeleton's hand grasping a heart.

The third was an hourglass on its side, with the sand evenly divided between the two chambers, and one grain stuck in the middle, as on a bridge.

The last banner I saw was of the Lady herself, in her terrible aspect, which is how she appears to those who have not yet learned her mysteries: a woman's skeleton with a full head of hair, and crowned with thorns. From her back spread the wings of the carrion eagle. She holds aloft a sword with a black blade, and a black moon is seen behind her.

How out of place this fearsome banner seemed next to the warm welcomes I received.

These worshippers were mostly, but not all, dams.

They went with their faces uncovered, all but the very highest of priests.

There were three of these priests, an old man and two dams.

These wore a mask made of hand bones, as if death herself had come up behind them and covered their eyes, saying, "Guess who!"

Before the service began, Inocenta showed me a true marvel—a statue of the goddess from before the Knock. The statue was smaller than life-sized, maybe four feet tall, and standing on a pedestal overgrown with lichen. The stone she was carved from was black, and her figure was not terrifying, as on the banner. Yes, she had carrion-eagle wings, or one wing, the other having been lost to time. But her face, though smoothed by centuries and by the hands of her worshippers, was clearly beautiful. This is the aspect she shows to those who know her. Once you see her true nature, and invite her to come whenever she wishes, she is no longer an intruder, but rather a welcome guest. I know you do not wish to be converted, you have your own ideas about these things, so I will simply tell you what was said that night.

I remember it exactly.

These were the words of the high priestess, one of the Blessed Dead, for whom a funeral has already been held. We were not to see her face or hear her voice. Her words were spoken into the ears of her second priestess and third priest, who spoke in unison, which was strange but beautiful.

Listen.

Welcome, friends, new and old. There are more of you here than on the last new moon, though of course we gather in greater numbers to face Our Friends. I will start, as always, by reading from the Book of Welcome.

Whether you are newly courted by the Bride or long wedded to her, welcome.

Whether you are fated to stoop over a cane three score years from now or die brightly on the morrow, welcome.

Ours is a sisterhood, and a brotherhood, that, like Our Serene Mistress, welcomes all, come they soon or late, from near or far. Time and place mean nothing to her, and even less the coin in your purse. All she asks is that you look upon her with love, not fear; know that this is for your sake, and not hers, a gift she gladly offers. When you know the meaning of the Hourglass Reclined, when you delight in the Song of the Tongueless Mouth, when you understand the mystery of the Union on the Shore, you will at last reject the temporal promises of the great eye who is blind to his own blindness, you will know a peace that is not fragile.

A strength that is tireless.

A love that cannot be disappointed.

And yours will be the Paradise of the Last Grain.

I will confess that what I thought now was *Donkeyshit. This is donkeyshit,* for so are we trained by our old prejudices to reject and ridicule what is new.

The priests went on, the Dead One retiring, handing the others a book. They took turns reading from this in their separate voices.

And now, as always, a reading from the Likely Tales.
The Parable of the King of Wounds.

"Tell it!" everyone said but me. I whispered into Inocenta's ear, "Poke me next time so I can say it too." She smiled and put a finger across her lips to silence me.

Once and long ago, there was a king who ruled by the strength of his arm, and so fearsome was he and quick to harm, that he was known as the King of Wounds. He took to wife the third daughter of a third daughter, and, though time has forgotten her name, we know he coveted her for her long black hair and long, brown limbs. Though her face showed no joy of it, he took her to wife. They were given a child, just after whose naming the king went off to war, and to victory. Yet so brutal were the rumors of his command, so many the orphans, so many the violated, so many the towns needlessly burned, that the wife was moved to smother their babe beneath a soft pillow, saying

> *As thou hast made so many mothers*
> *Of their sons bereft*
> *So art thou freshly quit of heirs*
> *Not one to thee is left.*

Inocenta poked me now.
I said, "Tell it!," half a beat behind the others.

Of course, the cruelty of the gods toward infants being well-known, the queen was not suspected. The king and court grieved, and soon the queen's belly quickened once again. So too did rumors of war to another compass point, and no sooner had the King of Wounds greeted his second son than he rode off to subdue another kingdom. His cruelty was redoubled against this other nation, and many were the lamentations. The queen, hearing of her husband's bloody hand, took their second babe to the waters, and turned their small boat over, saying

As thou hast bedded cruelty
And made rapine thy bride
Better should thy seed be sown
Upon the heartless tide.

"Tell it!"

The cruelty of seas being well-known, the queen was little suspected, at least by the king, and the palace entered into even deeper grief. It was some time before the king made another child upon his wife, and just so long before another realm dared defy the King of Wounds. Now was the queen a daughter given, and no sooner had the king scowled down into her crib than he took the sword and rode away again, his black deeds outstripping even those he did before. The queen hearing this, she held a knife to her girl-babe's soft neck, and cried, saying

Thy father's crimes are not thine own,
Nor was his fault thy brothers'
And yet I cannot part thy skin,
And so must take thy mother's.

"Tell it!" we said.

So saying, she took a curved knife from her belt and cut both belt and dress from herself, laying these in a neat pile. Then she cut the skin from her bones, all but the scalp with its long black hair, and laid this in a second pile beside her. She took the heart from her body and, grasping it in her bony hand, laid this on the bed beside her daughter. She turned the hourglass on its side. The knife she had used to flay herself grew into a great sword, and from her back grew the wings of the carrion eagle. And she flew to that place that none living has seen, but each knows how to find. Her husband, the king, grieved her loss, and most especially that she had left him only a daughter to heir. He swiftly made plans to marry anew, and had his daughter put away in a temple.

While the king and his wedding party were ahorse on their way to the wedding, a seer approached and spake unto him, saying, "Marry not in such haste, Your Majesty, lest you offend she of the great wings and swift sword; for your late wife is become the queen of the dead, and the bride of all living who must die."

The king said, "If she has so many bridegrooms as that, what use has she of me?" And he rode to the wedding, where his bride was young and beautiful, and bore no joy in her eyes to see her husband, but only esteemed the royal turban upon his head. At the feast, where many herons and peacocks, many lambs and good fish, were served, and all the hottest spices, the king stood with a glass of honey wine and said, "I offer a toast to my new bride, whose beauty outshines all those living; and to my old bride, whose beauty now awes the dead. For I am husband to two queens, one of the earth, and one of the world below."

And then, much in his cups, the king said things unworthy of a monarch.

At that moment, his new bride beside him screamed, and the flesh fell from her arm, leaving only bone. This arm now lurched across the king's body, pulling the new queen behind it, grabbing his sword from its scabbard on his belt. The bride wailed and tried to fight the dead arm, but it mastered her, and before the king could escape, or his guard intervene, the sword struck his head from his neck. So swift was the blow that the turban remained aloft, spinning like a child's top; also did the king's body remain

seated, his blood corrupting the feast before him. Now the
bride, her eyes glassed as a sleepwalker's, said, in the first
wife's voice,

> *As thou from thine own head*
> *Am I now divorced from thee*
> *Neither mother nor thy bride*
> *Henceforth shall I be*
> *Thou art no more friend to me*
> *Than sparrow to a cat*
> *And I have no more need of thee*
> *Than thou hast of a hat.*

"Tell it," I said, but I was the only one. This was not to be said
here. Some laughed, but in fellowship, and Inocenta pinched me
as an older sister might.

The second priestess finished.

> *And now the king's arms, for decency's sake, pulled the*
> *spinning turban down from the air, and his body fell dead*
> *to the floor. And whatever he thought in his last moment*
> *became his paradise, or his hell, though the look on his*
> *face suggested hell.*
>
> *And so it was.*

"And so it was," we said. Not half an hour into my first service,
and here were infanticide, flaying, and vengeance after death. At
the very least, Dal-Gaata was not boring. The same could not be
said for the church of the sun.

> *Remember the Bride in your darkest moments, and she*
> *will give you strength. Anticipate your union with her on*
> *the Strand, her glad kisses, her true, living face. Believe*
> *it; or, as your learning in the faith advances, find your*

own incarnation. She can be a prince on a horse. Or an
old woman with hot soup. She will come to you where you
summon her, in a forest, on a mountain, in your childhood
home. But if you are new, hold to the thought of Our Serene
Mistress in the flower of her beauty on the beach at night.
This is her strongest avatar, and the face she most often
shows those who love her. Those who fear her will ever see
the skeleton, the sword, the wings that blot the sun.

    And so shall it be.

"And so shall it be."
And now the priests said the words most sacred to warriors in
Dal-Gaata's worship.

    Short life, bloody hand.

To say this is to pray for skill and strength in combat, and to
acknowledge and celebrate that one's death will come sooner in
return for this.
I said it with the others.
"Short life, bloody hand!"
I still say it every day.

26

The armies of Holt and of the other Far Banners arrived at the liberated fortress of Carrasque the next day. We had exercised the birds and drilled, and had eaten our skinny rations at a cookpot with long lines. We had fed the birds well, as the quartermaster's cart delivered much more for them after their success against the goblin butchers, and in hope that their scream could prove effective against greater numbers of Our Foe.

Now, from atop a small hill, Inocenta, Alisenne, and I watched the arrival of these new soldiers into the shadow of the castle of Carrasque. There was much dust, and the beating of drums, and, from the Holtish host, the droning of Galtish cornemuse and Norholt tallpipes, which annoyed me. Try not to be offended, the Ispanthian goatpipes are no better, but all these instruments sound to me like a rape of cats. Yet every country has some version of it, as though the gods command that nowhere should people be able to rest and have peace.

"Whose banner is that?" Alisenne asked, pointing at a white flag with a black serpent around a sword.

"Some lady of Unther," I said.

"You know your flags and heraldry, then?"

"No," I said, "but we were taught to fight against different types of armor. That plump-looking armor is cloth, thick and bulky, but very hard to cut someone through."

"They look like pillows."

"Yes. I have heard them called pillow knights. I imagine it is very good at keeping crossbow bolts off them."

"I bet they look like hedgehogs after a few get stuck in there. Anyway, it looks hot."

"And what we wear is so cool and light?"

"That bit looks worse. I would never want to wear it in High-grass."

"We are nearly at Ashers."

"Highgrass or Ashers. Both are summer months."

"It is fucked-hot today," I said.

"Yes," Alisenne agreed.

This talk got me looking around for a water-butt, but I did not see one.

I became aware of locust-song in the fields.

"Who do you think the best troops down there are? 'Centa?"

Inocenta chewed a blade of grass and sharpened her axe. She said, "The best troops aren't down there, Ali," and winked.

I loved her in that moment.

"Besides us, then, if you are going to be like that," Alisenne went on.

"Besides us? Hard to say. Not much can stand against Brayçish greatbows. A hundred pounds' draw at the average, though some of those fuckers can bend a hundred and fifty."

"Gods gathered, put a bodkin on that and it would go right through you."

"Right through you, and your fattest uncle."

"If he had a belly full of my aunt's hard bread, that would stop it," Alisenne said, and we laughed. It was good to laugh. I stood up, straightened my legs, bent over and hugged my knees to my face.

Inocenta said, "I have seen Galtish Coldfoots and they are brave as hell. Not much armor on them, but they can drive a spear through a gap in armor faster than a snake strikes. Best sworders, besides us, might be Unthern two-handers, or maybe Gunnish thanes."

Alisenne said, "I hear Brayçish swordgrooms are the best. They fight naked wearing magic paint. Though I do not know if I believe in magic paint."

Inocenta said, "Maybe only they have to believe in it for it to work. Anyway, they are nearly all dead. I hear there are not half a thousand of them."

"Or half a hundred of us," Alisenne said, and then she noticed me crouched on one heel, folding myself straight against the other leg where I had it flat to the ground.

"Galva, why are you stretching when I am trying to relax?"

"So I do not fall asleep."

"Gods, take a nap, we've done for today. You make me tired," said Inocenta.

Alisenne said, "You made us both tired with your late-night . . ."

"Hush, woman."

"Anyway, I do not want to miss this," I said, and it was true. I had never seen so many armies and flags. Holtish, Brayçish, Unthern, Sadunthern, Istreans, Beltians, Wostrans, Gunns. Even a few volunteers from Oustrim, Axa, and Molrova, who were not officially part of this league.

Alisenne said, "There are so many! How can we . . ."

"Careful!" Inocenta said. "If you say 'how can we lose,' I will punch you in your teeth."

"I was going to say how can we feed them."

"Ah. Good question. But look there," Inocenta said, handing her farglass to Alisenne, who looked, and then passed it to me. "We don't have to."

I saw that the Unthern host had with it great caravans of ox-drawn carts, a mile of them at least.

"Is that all . . ." I started.

"Sausages and flour and barley. Cheese of all denominations, and beets, and peas, and hens just rattling with eggs. Nobody brings more food to a feast than an Unthern, and it looks like they have emptied their larders for us. Oh. Oh, and look there."

She directed the farglass for Alisenne.

"Is it . . . ?"

"Yes. That ram's head on the barrel means the Rammsgelt

estate, the king's household, and that means beer. Dark, barley-brown Unthern beer."

"Gods bless them," Alisenne said.

"Yes. Gods bless them and their fat-packed hearts, and the mustard in their veins."

The thought of beer gave me thirst, and I drank from my waterskin, which I had filled at the nearby stream.

"Their larders are not all they have emptied," I said. "Look how many holding pikes are women. Lots of grayhairs, too. I bet there's not a healthy young man or dam left in all of Unthern."

"Why should there be? There are none left in Ispanthia."

"Or Gallardia," Alisenne said. "This is it, isn't it?"

Inocenta's tone, which had been quite light before, now darkened.

"Yes. I should think this is it. Or very nearly so."

We were to march for Goltay two days later.

But first we had a visitor.

I woke with a fever in the night, and my bedroll was soaked with sweat. My hair was pasted to my head, and Inocenta was sitting up, watching me, just a shadow, but I knew her well enough to know there would be a furrow in her brow.

"You are sick," she said.

I felt cramps in my belly, and I went with haste to the ditches that served us as a latrine. I will spare you further description, except to say that I was very sick, and that I would spend the next days either on my back or at a squat. At one point I was so weak that I needed to have my arms held as I took relief, because my legs shook so badly I was afraid I would fall into the middens.

A fourth of the army fell ill all at once, and it seemed the whole camp was groaning, and everything smelled of human waste.

The Holtish and Far Banners had brought this scourge with them, and, since we did not know how it was spread, we had only to hope for the best. Fortunately the barber-surgeons were stretched so thin taking care of kings and courtiers that only wise-women were left to us, and I will take one of these with her herbs and her gentle touch over a bleeder and his pans and leeches and burning salves. The woman who saw to me and the others of the lanza was a black-tongued Galt, and, though I was at pains to understand her Ispanthian through that accent, she prepared for us a tea that made us feel better by the second day. We were well within a week. A Coscabraisian dam of our lanza had turned blue, and had come quite near death, but she did not die, and it was only because of this woman's help.

So, you see, Galts are good for something, sometimes.

The rest of the army was not so lucky as my lanza, to have someone who knew what she was doing. The barber-surgeons caused more harm than healing.

We had six hundred dead of the Western Army of Ispanthia, and I have heard a thousand died of the Gallards and the Far Banners. I will never forget those days of sweating in the summer heat, of thirst and of throwing up water as soon as it had been drunk. Inocenta did not get ill, and she nursed me and wiped my head with a cool cloth. She even cleaned my backside while holding me at the ditch.

A thousand flatterers are not worth one person who is willing to wipe your ass.

The dreams I had in camp were many and vivid, mostly unpleasant, and having to do with things I had seen in recent weeks. A few were of the "I cannot find something I need" or "Why am I doing this task naked?" sort. But one dream helped me a great deal. It was when I was sickest, but it was the one that told me I would not die of this flux.

I walk toward a brown hill in a land of brown hills. It is spring, probably the month of Flora, for empress trees are flowering

purple, and the wild plums have gone pink. This is the Braga estate, and I am a little girl. I know this because I see my small
hands and feet, and because when our governess, Nunu, calls me,
it is with her happier, younger voice, not yet piping and crisp, as
it would become.

Damicha! she says, or "little lady." She knows where I am going, and I do, too. I know from the sharp way she calls for me a
second time that I am just about to be in trouble. My little feet
move faster.

I have a carrot in my hand, and someone is waiting for it.

The hill is larger than it is in life, but this is the way we dream
things from childhood. It seems a small mountain rather than
merely a rise, and the posts of the enclosure seem like pillars. We
call this hill the Little Girl. I am going to see my best friend in the
world, besides Amiel.

Idala! I yell.

Her name, as I have said, means "star."

She whinnies and looks up from the grass she was plucking at,
her tail swishing against the flies it has only just become warm
enough for. I smell her in the dream. The smell of horses is not
for forgetting, even after so many years. You are thinking, this
was not so long ago, and you are right. My father had so many
horses before the Stumbles came that he had several mares with
foal when it struck. Why horses in this state had a chance when
it killed every other, no one knows, but so it was. Two of these
mares survived, though of course their foals were born dead.
One mare died the next year.

But the other? That was Idala. Horses cannot know such things,
but she would one day be the oldest horse in all of Braga, perhaps
the oldest in Ispanthia if one does not count the mare of King
Kalith kept alive by magic, and suffering at every step when she
bears him in state parades, which is a disgrace, and another reason to hate him. Idala was still alive when I left for war, standing on her hill, under guard, for her old bones living were worth

more than a horse of solid gold. But like many precious, kept things, she was lonely.

In the dream she sees me, and brightens.

Amiel is too young to care about her yet, and Pol and Migaéd are rarely home. I am the one she looks toward the house for, the one she is glad to see. The governess is still yelling for me to come back, but I climb the fence.

Idala's guards, a sword-and-buckler man and two archers, yell *damicha!* at me, too, but this word cannot call me away from the fence as Idala moves against it. She wants to feel me on her back, she wants my little hands in her coarse mane.

Most of all, she wants that carrot.

I feed it to her—there is nothing like a horse taking food from your hand—and I climb on her back.

I look back at the soldiers' faces. One is laughing, two are afraid they will be disciplined. I am not supposed to ride alone, but, in my defense, nobody bothers to take me to ride anymore. I know the guards, of course; Guram, Santu, and the Calar Bajat swordsman, Feru, who would be the first to tell Father I was made for fighting. They will all go to the Threshers' War next year, and only Feru will come back, blind and crippled. He will learn to carve wood, and will carve my first wooden sword for me.

He still lives on the estate.

Father sees to his needs.

The duke is not all bad, however I make him sound, and I would like to say that no one is all bad.

But some are.

Some very few are.

I ride Idala. I laugh hard and I smile so wide I think my face might split. I just want to ride once around the pen, and so far this has been just as it was in life. Me stealing away, riding with the fresh breeze in my hair, Nunu saying she is going to get punished on my behalf, though we both know this is not true.

But in this dream, Idala kicks up and her hooves leave the ground.

I clutch her hide, terrified at first, but then I understand what a gift it is to be so high up. We are flying.

I look at the house, with its turrets and narrow windows; I see our river, the Abrez, and the olive grove with its silver-green leaves that always look dusty. I see the haystacks of the archery range, and the old stables, now used to kennel Father's hunting dogs. I see the other hill, called the Old Man, terraced in hundred-year-old humiya vines, and the little wetlands near the river where I used to catch frogs.

How the frogs sang on that estate.

I look up and see the light of the clouds, and feel the cool air, and everything is as it should be. I understand that I can stay here if I wish, flying.

But then I think of Nunu, and of Guram, Santu, and Feru. I think of Amiel, and how sad he would be to learn that I am not coming back. He is only four or so in this dream, and he loves me, and makes up little stories for me. So I turn Idala's mane around and steer us back for the ground.

Then we land hard, so hard that I snap my teeth together and I shit myself, because of course I was just in my camp bed with the flux. But I knew that if I was going to die of it, it would have been then. I thought of the hourglass on its side.

The last grain poised forever.

I thought I understood, and in truth I was beginning to.

That dream, and that choice, were a gift from the Bride.

But there I was covered in shit with poor Inocenta putting cool water on my head.

"Sorry," I said, nodding down at the soil.

But Inocenta only kissed my burning forehead and smiled.

"You almost left us," she said.

"I think so."

"I am glad you stayed. But that is because I am selfish."

—— • ——

27

Of course, while I flirted with the Serene One, or she with me, Amiel was making his way north as well.

Here is what he says of his journey.

Fulvir has been working on a potion for going unseen. He can make himself unseen, the stronger magickers can, and this power can be granted through an object such as a ring or a torque, but these are rare and highly prized. A potion with temporary effect would obviously have great benefit to the army; he has perfected an ointment to flatten our scent and a sort of reed that, when sucked on, drinks up sound, both potentially useful for small actions against biters, who rely more on these two senses. But though their eyesight is not as sharp as ours, they do see better in the dark than we, and a company of troops, though silent and scentless, would not escape a sentry's notice.

I have been spared the usual rigors of a long march by means of Fulvir's art. Once the household in Espalle was packed and loaded into carts, these to be borne by mixlings of both taurine and canine extraction, we went north by means of a spell process called "tree binding." To the best of my understanding, it involves convincing a tree of a certain species to act as a gate and convey us through it to a willing tree of the same species some miles away. This may be done with most any kind of tree by an individual, but only a mature oak has the bones to convey some thirty kynd and mixlings, all their possessions, giant corvids, and a rabbit with hands. The most important thing is that no one should have any wood possession of the species of tree so importuned, so I was required to leave behind one oaken trunk, and to put my clothes in a sack instead. It is also important not to panic in close spaces, for, as each of us enters the tree, we feel ourselves to be pressed all about by wood, and to be smothering in sap. Emerging from the tree on the other side is not unlike a rough birth. The wizard came through last, coughing so badly I thought he might die.

"I love oak trees," he said, when he caught his breath at last, "they agree most pleasantly with the chemistry of my body. Also, we must find another one, as this asshole does not wish to send us further. He is very fond of briar trees, and objects to my pipe. Fuck him, we will ask that fat one, with the lightning scar, which I may be able to fix for her, I sense that she is vain."

To my horror, we had to do that seven more times, requiring rest after each birthing, and one of the dog-men suffered a broken arm when a tree ejected him violently because it did not care for mastiffs. This took us nearly a week, and at the end of it I felt sick, tumbled, weary, and abused. Worse, I itched all over, both from the rough embrace of the wood and from insects who had found homes in parts of myself I had never thought worthy to entertain guests. And yet, we had come to the outskirts of the fortress of Carrasque, well ahead of the army, having saved a week of slogging.

"We will not be going to the castle," Fulvir said. "Carrasque is under a siege I do not have the strength to lift, and moreover it is on the verge of collapse. The presence of a wizard of my renown near it might tempt it into some dramatic display, so that its name would always be mentioned with mine. No building wants fame so much as a castle."

I readily confess that I do not know what percentage of what he says is true, and what is the ravings of a half-mad genius misanthrope for whom lying is a sacrament. Do buildings want things? Before meeting Fulvir, I would have said no, as I would have assured you that humans cannot under any circumstances pass through trees, and that rabbits have no hands.

What I do know is that we walked the rest of the way from Carrasque, word having spread through the entire tree population of *western Gallardia that an abrasive Molrovan was exploiting and insulting the oaks. This pleased the pines, if Fulvir is to be believed. I can only report what he says.*

We did not go all the way to Goltay, as the goblins were still there, but Fulvir believed they would be leaving. We found a deserted estate—to the southwest of the city, in a vast forest called Arlasque Woods—in which some local refugees were squatting. Fulvir animated a trio of dead bodies to frighten them out. One of these bodies had no head and spoke through a cut in its hand. I had mixed feelings about such dark magic being used to terrify starving and displaced Gallards, but, on the other hand, he secured us needed lodgings without hurting anyone. I mean, he could have sent the mixlings and corvids, but things have a way of getting out of hand with them.

Once settled into the estate, he began to send me and Vlano foraging for ingredients to perfect his potion. He would be angry if he caught me writing down the entire spell, so I will omit most of what I gathered. One item I had difficulty acquiring was a mantid that disguises itself as a leaf or a stick. One can sort out for oneself why it might be challenging to find and capture a creature whose chief talent is hiding. It took two days before I located one and popped it in its jar. Lightning bugs were easier, as any child allowed outdoors in early summer has had some practice catching these, and I was no exception. The spell required a great many of the wonderful bugs, however, so more than one evening was spent in this pursuit.

That I was not mauled by the mother bear whose cubs I practically tripped over while frolicking after fireflies is probably due to a greater understanding between mammals in the wake of the goblin incursion. She snuffed at me and led her two cubs on, as if to say, "Yes, he is rude and stupid, but at least he is not one of those."

As the days progressed, Fulvir let us know that the goblins had left Goltay, and that the kynd armies were approaching. They arrived on Ashers Eve, and by the second of Ashers we were meeting with the prince of Widmarch, heir to the crown of Holt, and selling him bull-men.

Fulvir's mood was much improved in these first days in Goltay, for he had heard of the success of his other mixlings, the war corvids.

I saw him fill a horn with strong honey mead, a larger drink than he normally allowed himself. I had not meant to gape at this, but he was unoffended by my gaze.

"What, you have never seen a man celebrate before?"

"What do you celebrate, Master Fulvir?"

"Music."

"Forgive me, I do not understand."

"It seems the goblins are much enchanted with the singing of my birds."

28

The city of Goltay had been abandoned.

We arrived there seven days after our evening with the king and queen, on the thirty-sixth of Highgrass, Ashers Eve. We camped outside the walls, which were mostly still intact, save for two places where goblin tunnels had collapsed them, and where earthworks had been quickly raised, and rubble piled up to repair the breaches. The walls were a thing of great beauty, built of darker stone near the bottom and lighter stone up top. The crenellations had stone figures peeking around them that would be hard to distinguish from true soldiers in the heat of battle. Spouts for pouring hot oil were carved in the shapes of deer's heads, and reliefs of animals, the hunt, or nudes bathing in streams decorated the stone in unexpected places. It seemed that Goltay had been so rich it tried to make even war pretty.

But war cannot be made so.

The fighting at the earthworks where the walls were breached had been intense. The dead were so many that the goblins had not harvested all of them for food, as they normally would have. Here and there, a thigh had been cut to the bone for meat, but mostly the soldiers and citizens lay where they had fallen, half-buried in collapsed stonework, shot with poisoned quarrels, or stabbed, or bitten, or cut. Dead for weeks, the kynd were much given to rot. The flies were many. The smell turned my knees to water, especially as I was still weak from the fevers that had nearly killed me at Carrasque. Goblins lay among our dead as well, beaten to pulp with flails and clubs, hacked in quarters by axes and swords, burned by defender's firepots. Since they do not rot and flies will not have them, it looked like they had fallen yesterday—like two battles had happened at different times.

I had never seen so many dead, except perhaps after the sea battle and flood in Espalle, and those had been in water, among wreckage. The dead outside Goltay lay in the open, under the sky, in their uncountable numbers. It is hard to find words for how small I felt to see this. How is one to make a difference in such a calamity? I looked at one dam near my feet with her spear and her good but very old scale armor; some of the bronze scales had been replaced with deer bone, and horn, and even one piece of springwood. There was not another suit of armor exactly like this in all the world, nor would there be again; and yet the armor could be salvaged, while the dam who wore it, and who was no less unique, could not.

She was too long dead for me to tell her age, but her hair was chestnut, though matted with blood, and some of the spoiling skin of her arm bore a tattoo of oak leaves. A silver pledge ring on her left hand spoke of some lover waiting at home, or also under arms. Long would they wait.

Who was she?

Her shirt looked Bragaene, with its double seam, and olive-wood buttons. Did her father pay taxes to mine? Did we know the same songs? Was she grim, or given to laughter? Did she have children in a grandfather's care, or at an *ucal*?

Her death seemed to have been a quick one.

The goblin near her with its white eyes and mouth of wicked teeth had probably not been the one to stave in her temple—I saw no axe or club nearby. Only one of their gisarmes, a weapon for stabbing.

Still, I stepped on the dead creature and pressed its head into the soft earth.

As we arrived near dark and had to make camp quickly, I did not get to see the city proper until the next day.

The moon, which would be full tomorrow on the first of Ashers, was bright. From my bedroll, I could make out a few goblin dead, and a wrecked siege engine for throwing stones. A forest of arrows stuck out of the ground, and these came in and out of view as cloud shadows raced across the ground.

It would be interesting to see if my troubled mind kept me awake or if my weary body dragged me quickly into sleep. My limbs were heavy from marching, my feet had many blisters that burned like touching coals. I wondered where Amiel was. I thought of Inocenta nursing me through my illness as a mother would a child. I thought of the eyes of the queen, so warm and beautiful, and the Eyes of Nerêne behind her. I thought of Migaéd, and the child-bride princess he had been promised, as unsuitable a gift as our grandfather's shield on his back. And, like everyone else in the army, I wondered where the goblins had gone, and why they had left us such a prize without a fight.

"Rest well," Nouva had said. "The generals will send us into the city tomorrow to see what's what. We will need our wits about us."

Goltay sat divided by the river Arve, which flowed down from the fortress city of Arvise, half again as far north as Espalle had been west and south.

Our lanza patrolled the university quarter, a maze off the east bank where close buildings darkened streets of cobblestones, which were smooth and shiny from many centuries of feet and hooves. Goltay was a center of art for all the Crownlands, and the statues were many and fine. Here a mermaid rose from a fountain, holding up a spear as if daring the sky to fight her. There the famous wonder called the Swinging Man; a niche three stories high in the College of Arts held a boyish titan hanging upside down, his feet flexed to hook him to a branch. The Swinging Man creaked gently as it swung, the fingers of his extended hands disappearing into twin ruts in the stone, touching nothing.

How had the Goltayn done that?

And how had the biters gotten out of town so quickly?

"Why have the goblins not wrecked everything here?" I whispered.

Inocenta said, "I heard some poleaxe dams saying they left to try to take Carrasque and seize the king. They did not have time to shit on the drapes and knock the corners down here."

"Good thing," said Alisenne, "I have never seen such a beautiful city."

"So, if they left Carrasque, and they are not here, where did the biters get to?" I said. "Did they dig down?"

"Not that quickly," Inocenta said. "And if they had, there would be dirt and broken stone to show it, or so the engineers say. That is some of what we are looking for. If we find big piles of soil and rubble, that means a tunnel, and badgers will go down after them. But even the biters will not be able to get their whole army underground. No, they moved off north and they will swing back down at us and pinch us against the third army. Rather than sit here and let them do it, we will head north to fortresses built on stone too hard to undermine."

"The third army is a myth," I said, for so I had heard around cookfires.

"That there is no third army is the myth," she said, for so she had heard around cookfires.

Whether you believed this goblin army existed or not was a mirror, showing whether you were an optimist or a pessimist. Of course, it existed or it did not, regardless of belief. But it was better to think it did not. Now that we had linked with Holt and the Far Banners, there was no third army of kynd, at least not until the next wave came from Ispanthia and Unther in the fall, both older and younger than the last. We would have to win, or, at the very least, survive.

Many of the homes we cleared still had fine things in them. Our lanza did no looting, but we saw other groups of soldiers at it. The Unthern were bad for this, they are skilled metalworkers and know the value of jewels so that even their farmers are weak for fine things. I remember a group of blond and sandy-haired pillow knights, hung with necklaces, some of them wearing two hats, carrying off a bronze statue of a goat, and it was heavy enough that two were burdened to walk with it.

I raised an eyebrow at Inocenta as if to ask what they could possibly want with the goat, but of course she made a vulgar gesture. It was not just the Untherns, though; I did see Ispanthian units bearing carts with furnishings, tapestries, fine clothes, and other prizes. I felt anger and outrage, but then realized that was because I had lived in a fine house, and did not like the thought of foreign soldiers who were supposed to be our defenders despoiling the Braga estate. Carrying off Mother's bridal dress of silver thread and ivory, or the statue of the Harvest Queen, or the tapestries of her daughters with hair of wheat, and rye, and grape leaves, and barley. How would I see rough men and dams with cartfuls of looted treasure if I had been raised in a charcoal burner's hut, with a doll made of sticks for a toy, and the sound of an uncle coughing himself to sleep for a lullaby? I felt Amiel's influence in these thoughts—these were questions he had taught me to ask. And I asked them. But then I thought that I would still like to see these thieves whipped, whatever banner they came here under, and whatever sort of house they grew up in.

Some things are just wrong.

The looting was somehow worse in a city of such rare angles and beauty, a city of bridges and libraries and everywhere a statue looking at you, or so caught up in pleasure or grief it paid you no mind.

I speak of treasures, of course—none can be faulted for seeking food or wine.

I would have you know more of the wonders of Goltay, but I

am not so skilled in description as Amiel, who had just arrived in town with the wizard Fulvir, attached to the Holtish camp.

Here is what Amiel wrote of those days, and of that city:

Goltay, even ruined, is the most beautiful place I have seen. I mean no offense to the Ispanthian capital, Seveda, with her white stone and strong towers; or to Galimbur, squat and brown and impregnable, guarding the river approach to Seveda. And I have never seen Mouray, which became the capital of Gallardia thirty years before, and which they also call the City of Candles for all its public lamps, and its firelit canals. Mouray may be as beautiful as Goltay, but, if it is, it will be this city's only rival.

First, the river Arve is so slow and mild that its waters seem still, and reflect the sky. It cuts the city into east and west, and the east is the greater portion, though the west is newer, richer, and more carefully planned. Both banks have been planted with flowering trees, and it has been written that to see the river in the spring is to fall in love with Goltay forever. I am half in love with this river, even choked with dead and with wrecked boats and overturned machines of war.

Two of the six bridges are Winter Bridge (Pondaverre) and Gloaming Bridge (Ponglaôme), and there used to be one for each season, but Spring, Summer, and Fall were made of wood and did not last. The new bridges are all stone. My favorite is the Bridge of Hands because it has great carved hands clasping in a knotwork from one side to the other, but I must admit that the Bridge of Wrecks is impressive, with its prows from enemy vessels along the base, all covered in greening bronze. Gallardia was never a great naval power, but they did capture enough ships to ornament a bridge.

The center of town is a huge open area called the Field of Flowers, and it is not really a field so much as a cobbled plaza with many fine fountains, but I have heard that there was a flower market there each spring. The stalls have been moved to make way for bright banners and massive royal pavilions, another sort of flower, I suppose. The stalls have been moved to side streets and smaller plazas, and farmers are returning from the country even now to take them over and sell food to the army, though at ruinous prices.

It is hard to imagine the luxury of a royal tent.

Even the Gallard king, Luvain, in whose country the worst of the fighting rages, has a tent woven with cloth-of-gold and painted with scenes from the godfables. Though I suppose Gallardia poor is still as wealthy as most countries rich. The kings of Wostra, Unther, and Istrea are here, as well as Barwyn, prince of Widmarch, heir to Conmarr of Holt. His is the second-largest army, with Holtish knights and pikedams, and with Coldfoot guards and archers from Galtia.

Our king, Kalith, did not come, as he is head of the church of Sath, but his army is the largest and strongest, so none will speak against him, or against the Pragmatist, who commands our army in his name. Tales of her victories in the east touch all lips.

On the river side of the Field of Flowers lie the ruins of the Castle of Eights, so named for its gorgeous octagonal towers, all laid low now. This was the one act of destruction the goblins had time to carry out—they could not leave that mighty central keep standing for us to merely reclaim. It is said they had a devil's time taking it, that thousands on both sides died in hellish fights underground, with spade and knife, and with war dogs and spore and fire. So once they had it, they underdug its walls and towers until these fell. A great shame, too; much has been written about its beauty and strength.

On the other side of the massive square, directly across from the ruins of the Castle of Eights, the temple of Sath stands, with its glasshouse attached to the main cathedral, and its massive Vault of Mysteries to one side. The priests were allowed to reclaim the

Vault, as in Espalle, so its mysteries, whatever the biters left of them, remain safe; and the holies have already opened the temple to worshippers. Though I am not much given to religious feeling, I have been to services, and heard the helion, and I think it is a great salve to hear this. I think the priests, for all their vanity, give hope to many who would not find it otherwise, and all of us love the smell of incense, recalling each season in turn through the powerful medium of scent.

For all the light and wonder said to wait within the massive Vault, I could not help noticing what a deep shadow it cast.

29

I met with Pol on the third of Ashers, my third full day in Goltay.

It was two nights past the full moon, and the town had been carefully searched. No sign of living goblins had been found. The entire army had been made to search house by house for sign of a "dive," but the piles of dirt and rock that such digging would have left behind were simply not found.

Pol and I sat in a rooftop garden late that night, after his meetings with the Pragmatist and with Segunth-General Samera dom Vinescu. This garden was in the house she had taken over. Her husband, the captain of her personal guard, stayed outside, by the door at street level. This seemed to me a large abuse of his trust if my suspicions about her and Pol were correct, but I know that I am unusual in my sensitivity to deceit and betrayal. Most people have made peace with the realities of human nature, and this makes their daily lives more comfortable. I am still trying to learn to do this. I try to remember that I am not responsible for what others do, nor should I hold them in judgment. But this is very hard for me, especially when they are being bastards.

In Pol's defense, the segunth-general is a woman of courage and intelligence, besides being tall and well-knit and easy to look at, so, if he were doing something unwise and unkind, I supposed he could have had worse taste about it.

"You summoned me, Terce-General?" I said, once Solmón had shown me to the rooftop.

Pol stood, and the segunth-general did the same.

"I invited you, Galvicha. There's nothing official about this, please be at ease."

"And be welcome," the segunth-general said. "I am Samera tonight."

There was good wine, and food, as there always was for generals and their guests.

I ate what was offered to me, this being a matter between family, though I did put in my pouch an Istrean sausage for Inocenta.

The just-past-full moon shone hard and high over the beautiful city, which we could see to great advantage from this rooftop on a hill. The month of Ashers had begun, high summer was upon us.

We spoke briefly of small things, and then Pol said, "I wanted to let you know that your lanza will be ordered forward tomorrow. A small force of biters has been attacking farmers trying to bring food to the city. As you can imagine, it will not take much of this before the farmers stop coming altogether, even if we are buying eggs at a copper apiece and paying gold for skinny goats. We think the goblin raiders are few enough for you to dispatch; your lanza moves fast, and you will have opportunity to see if the birds terrify Our Friends again. You will be told all this officially tomorrow."

"So, why . . . ?"

"May a brother not wish to see his sister?" he said, holding out his hand to me.

Before she dies, I thought.

Our mission would be no barefoot walk in soft grass.

But I saw the necessity of it.

I nodded, and put my hand in his.

We spoke much that night, and he told me of the challenges facing the army.

Now that Goltay had been retaken, for example, the people of the town who had hidden in the countryside were making their way back. Some were going back to their old homes, and even reopening such businesses as would serve an army, although this proved to be a nightmare of bureaucracy. How to prove who owned what before? I had expected war to look like death and weapons and marching soldiers, and it did; but I had not thought to see battalions of clerks sitting at outside tables, being pled with or shouted at as they searched tax documents, hurrying to cover papers with oilcloths when a summer rain came. I had not considered seeing men and dams hanged for fraud, of all things, while monsters were butchering us. But a scaffold had been built, and seven bodies already swung near the clerks' desks and the very long lines of Gallards before them. Two of the executed wore signs that said DESERTION; one each of murderers, rapers, and takers of godsmilk; and two who had committed fraud.

But many of those coming into Goltay those first days of Ashers had no claims to make. They were simply refugees, hoping to be sheltered and fed. The refugees were making a sort of second city outside the gates, exposed to sun and rain. The Pragmatist was faced with a terrible dilemma—deplete the food stores of our massive army, or turn these starving hordes away.

She found a middle ground.

She would put them to work.

These would help to fortify Goltay enough to satisfy His Majesty, but only those who worked would be fed.

And so, over the next days, refugees who were fit for hard labor would go into Arlasque Woods and cut lumber for hoardings, temporary walls, and stakes for the moat.

Of course, this plan depended on the remaining farmers feeling safe enough to bring their food to us.

It was not lost on me that our lanza had to destroy these raiders before they cut off the already small supply of farmed goods we relied on.

We were going to take the fight to goblins to keep this city fed.

There were worse reasons to die.

30

I saw the queen of Gallardia for the second time as I marched out with the lanza and our birds. It was Ringday, fourth of Ashers. She had personally invited the refugees into the city in their many thousands, and she oversaw their rehousing. Military tents were put up in the old Keshite Hippodrome, and also on the banks of the river, in the shade of the trees on the south side of town near the tanners and dyers quarter, where their soil and washing would be carried off. I later heard that Mireya had argued with the high priest of Sath because he would not let her use the huge Vault of Mysteries for housing. He had said, "Forgive me, Queen Consort, but I cannot violate the sanctity of Sath's temple for any reason. As it is said you first serve the Gallardian goddess Nerêne, perhaps the Covenant of Keeping between Sath and his children is unknown to you, so you may be forgiven for suggesting we breach the trust the King of Light has placed in us, to set our hand over his physical mysteries. If you knew what his servants know, you would take comfort, for the powers of the mightiest god are great, and the love he bears mankind evident within. I cannot open the Vault to any but fellow priests of Sath. If this displeases the king, he may command me to step down." Mireya said, "Perhaps your god so loves his children that he cannot bear to think of them sheltered away from his burning sight, which saps their water and life from them without the benefit of shade. We are not all so used to lying in the sun as you men of the priesthood, may your hands remain uncallused. But I am no theologian, and will leave this matter to your conscience."

At the present moment Queen Mireya stood away from her guards and ladies at a huge cookpot near the north side of town. She let her monkey roam among a group of Gallard children waiting in line to be fed soup. The monkey climbed the children, perched on their heads, gifted them rocks then stole these back again. I heard them laugh that laughter of children who have forgotten their troubles, if only for a moment. I smiled despite myself, and despite where I knew my feet were carrying me.

Then, and I was not sure this really happened, the monkey pointed at us.

"He pointed at you," Mireya would tell me later.

The queen smiled at me, and nodded her head slowly, in a way that was more than a sovereign acknowledging a knight. I returned this, dreading what Inocenta must think. But Inocenta has ever been a good friend and she knew everything that was in my heart. No one has ever known how to put me at ease better than her.

"Did you see that queen?" she said.

"Yes," I said, feeling my cheeks color.

"I think she likes me."

My laugh was girlish and grateful.

Inocenta took off my helmet, messed my hair, then put the helmet back on backward.

No more needed to be said.

I had three brothers in this war.

And one close, good sister.

We left Goltay by the northern gate, called Houndsgate because the road led to Arvise and the other fortress cities in the north of Gallardia that I have already mentioned, called the Hounds of Mour. The white road laid by the Kesh roughly followed the Arve River here. Nobody knows how they moved the stones for this road, they are larger than anything we build with today. I looked at the road and thought how elephants had once walked these same stones, and I remembered that one of the main streets in Goltay is called Elephant's March. I was deeply charmed by this city. I wished I could have seen Goltay in its prime, before the wars. I thought about how natural Mireya looked here, though she was born a Spanth. There was something about her that was more artful than others of my country, and more graceful. Her strength was soft, in an old way that I think this world is losing. To see a man or a dam helping others as she did with the feeding, and with letting her wicked monkey pinch and amuse the children, is every bit as strong as to stand with a sword and shield, just different. It is something to inspire. I wanted to help her. I did not know how to cook food or tend wounds, but I did know the use of the *spadín,* and I wanted to stand near her and see that she was safe while doing these softer but good and necessary things.

But then it occurred to me again that she was bewitching me, and I let myself feel angry, because that was easier than to think that I might be . . .

"Cuntstruck."

"What?"

"Exactly," Inocenta said. "Get out of your head, however pleasant it is there, and stay sharp. We are looking for goblin fast-raiders, and they are masters of ambush."

"Sorry," I said, embarrassed and knowing she was right.

She gave me a playful nudge, then put her business face on. Playtime was over.

We were coming up on a farm, and a dam and a young boy approached us.

They took us to a path between farms where they had seen biters.

To look at the tracks the boy showed us, there were fifty or more of Our Foe, plus at least six boars. We had been told about war boars, but I had never seen one—those we captured at Carrasque were dray animals, used the way we use oxen.

These were something else.

And we were not the only ones to look for them, or to find them.

Here was an example of the difficulties of commanding armies of many lands in one cause—an Unthern general of the Far Banners had sent forces looking for the raiders, too.

We found the Unthern by the banks of the river, and they were in a bad state. I thought at first of the flux, the way they were all lying about, covered in sweat, and some with their clothes and armor off. Then I saw that some of them were injured. Some of them were also dead. One had died with her head in the river, and the others were too weak to pull her out.

Inocenta understood before I did.

"Sath's kiss," she said.

These northerners in their bunched and quilted armor had succumbed to heat. Their skin was shiny pink, or red, or dangerously white. None of them spoke much Ispanthian, and none of us spoke Unthern, but a few spoke decent Gallard, and these told Alisenne what happened.

They had been ambushed.

They started with a full company of one hundred, mostly flails, a score of crossbow dams.

The biters loosed bolts at them from the trees, and the crossbow dams sheltered in a rut by the side of the path to return fire, a rut that provided good cover. Then they heard a creak and before they could run, a tree the biters had staged fell right into the groove where the crossbows were gathered, killing eight or nine. The company ran and lost the rest of the crossbow dams to the biters' poisoned bolts, though the flail men and dams were well protected. That is when the boars and their spear-wielding riders struck.

"The flail is good to smash the goblin, but it is not the weapon for the fucking pigs," Alisenne translated for us.

These eleven pillow knights were all that was left.

"And we only got away because they took time to capture the others alive."

I remembered the lowing of the kynd prisoners in the meat cart.

To this day I wish we had cut their throats.

I thought about doing it for these.

I wished I had some of Pol's bittermead, I could give it to the Unthern to ease their passage and keep them from the goblins' bellies.

They were too weak to make it back to Goltay.

Nouva put a knife in the lap of the strongest-looking woman, and told Alisenne what to say.

"We cannot stay with you. Don't let them take you alive."

The Untherdam clutched the knife in one pink fist, and said, in Ispanthian, "Kill them, please."

Nouva said, "We will."

I think of this next action as the Battle of the Pigs.

I was different after this.

We followed their tracks for an hour, perhaps two. The day had become hard to bear, as the beginning of Ashers is exactly the middle of summer and the worst time for heat. The sun was strong, and violent, and there was much dust. As before, the birds became agitated first, and then we had the smell of goblin in our noses. We were lucky the hot breeze was in our faces and not at our backs, or they would have known of us first. We crouched low and moved forward, toward a group of farm buildings. Alisenne is the most quiet, she is a great hunter, so she went ahead, on knees and elbows, and came back soon nodding and pointing. She made the signs for *fifty,* and *six boars,* and, with a disgusted look, *eating.*

We couched our shields as quietly as we could, drew our weapons, staged our birds just ahead of us. As we rounded the corner of a stone barn, I saw a sight I cannot forget. Yes, many of them ate, but others, maybe six, were standing in two groups, playing a game where one pitched a human head at the other side, hard, and the others rushed to catch it on a spear.

Once it was caught, they used the spear to pitch the head back.

If the head was pitched high, or at great speed, it might land with such force as to break the skull and spill the brains, ruining the "ball."

I think the goblin team who failed to spear the head and prevent this lost something, perhaps a point, or some gambled-for item. I have heard that they gamble.

There were several such ruined heads in a pile, one I remember looking almost at me, its jaw in the wrong place, sagging as if deeply disappointed.

Can you believe this, friend Spanth? The way they have treated me here, and left my busted head in the sun for the flies?

I was not sure if it was a dam or a young boy.

Nearby, another goblin used a long, jagged knife to saw at the neck of an old man, whose crossed legs jiggled with the biters' efforts.

I wanted to vomit, from the heat, and the smell of the goblins, and the fact that I was truly seeing this scene with my eyes, that it did not go away when I blinked.

I felt my teeth bare, half in anger, half in terror.

My head could be a ball for goblin sport this very day. I thought of my head flung, a goblin spear catching it, piercing the thin bone of my temple, some of my brain spilling out as my tongue flopped out of my mouth like a cow's tongue. The thought embarrassed me, but then I thought that I would not be there to be embarrassed, or to even see that scene. And this disturbed me.

Where would I be, then?

Just gone, it seemed, like the flame of a blown-out candle.

And so what?

Was that so bad?

Who was I but a soldier?

I had orders to follow.

But it is not so easy to act when your body knows its own doom lies steps away.

I had fought well before, but this sight of the heads and spears undid me.

I went forward on weak legs with the others, but my shield and sword seemed to weigh fifty pounds each.

Now they smelled us.

They barked their whoops and they rasped and they hissed.

It is a sound to father bad dreams.

Crossbows cracked, and no less than three bolts hit my shield and rang my helm. The biters fell back, leaving an awful mess of human parts where they had been eating, dropping bags of mushrooms they had been passing around. One biter shot his crossbow while holding a head by its long blond hair, its cheeks and ears eaten off, one eye staring.

Goblins like the taste of our cheeks nearly as much as thighs.

Nouva screamed and ran at this one.

He had stayed too long, and her bird Gannet took him. No more damcheeks for him. Fuck him, and fuck the rest of them.

I need a moment, it makes me angry to remember.

Part of what makes me so angry is that I was terrified.

I do not know what happened for the next instants.

I do not know if we closed with them, or they with us.

I know that I struck, and was struck at.

My head.

Something had hit my head, hard, hurting me despite my helmet and arming cap.

Someone called my name.

I heard the snort and whuffs of their boars, I saw one kicking and thrashing at the birds.

Our birds were not screaming as before.

I was dizzy with heat, there was dust.

One struck at my head and I spun away.

A dam was down, her jaw torn off, her teeth near her in puddled blood. She was a city girl, from Seveda, she had small dogs she talked much of.

Her dogs would have no more meat from her plate; their mistress would make thigh steaks for hivelings.

I swung at something and stumbled.

I wanted to say *help*. I was crying. I tasted my own blood in my mouth, I had bitten my own lip, had I been struck?

Yes, on the head.

I felt confused and terrified.

Someone was saying my name.

I looked up.

The lanza was in formation, but I was out of it. This still comes to me in dreams, this feeling of everyone else but me being where they are supposed to be as danger comes on.

It was the greatest fear I had ever felt, or ever would again.

I was alone on the field, and I saw my death coming. I saw Dal-Gaata. She stood on the back of a boar the size of a small cow, riding at me. The boar's tusks were lowered, its barrel body armored in leather with spikes, blood trickling down its limbs because its armor had prickers on the inside, too, to make it mean.

But it was she who drew the eye.

"Galva!"

Her carrion-eagle wings were spread to their full span, wider than the span of the corvid I had jokingly named "Skinny" because the word sounded like her name, oh gods I had offended her with that and now she would take me personally, in her hand, she had spared me for Inocenta's sake, for Inocenta was her handmaiden but I was unworthy, I had been tested and I was breaking now, in this moment, I was dying now, the sun behind her, Sath behind her, powerless over her, the shadow of her wings black and moving over the dry soil slowed down somehow but coming.

"Galva! Say the words! Now!"

Inocenta.

What words?

Oh.

Those words.

"Short life," I said with a tremble in my voice.

"Say them and mean it!"

Coming, coming, her black sword leveled at me, her skeletal face, her black hair, black as the queen's, riding out behind her impossibly long on the hot breath of the wind like a draft from a bread oven, her hair a wedding train her eyes just holes with nothing in them this was my forever this fear this failure this how the duke his daughter a smear in Gallardia a nothing, the nothing in Dal-Gaata's eyes.

"NOW, YOU SOP BITCH! SHORT LIFE!"

Inocenta.

She had broken formation for me, was running at me.

She would die, too, if I did nothing.

I screamed the words, hot tears in my eyes.

"SHORT LIFE, BLOODY HAND!"

Dal-Gaata was gone.

A goblin stood on the charging boar's back, stuck there, wearing boots of downward-pointing nails.

Holding the boar's reins in one hand, a spear in the other, coming at me.

It blurred in my teared-up eyes and in the heat, but I was as still as still water inside now.

I fell back from the point driving at my heart. It would have pierced through chain, through my breastbone. But I was too fast for it. I fell back in a move I had practiced a hundred times, slapping down with my shield arm to break my fall while making a hard rising cut almost parallel to the ground, under the boar's armor.

One of the boar's legs hit my face as I sheared it off.

The boar and the goblin wrecked with much dust and squealing.

My cut had also gutted the boar.

It thrashed now and tusked its rider, and trampled him in a mess of its own viscera.

Then it died on him.

I stood up, blinking the boar's blood out of my eyes, and heard one of my lanza screaming. Then the birds screamed, too, in that way that brings terror to Our Foe.

Some of the goblins ran, a few fought, but most of them stood still for their killing, staring, as terrified and frozen as I had been.

I understood now.

When you say the words and dedicate yourself to her, you no longer see her in her death aspect.

You become her.

Your enemies see her.

I cut down eleven.

I was calm.

I was where I belonged.

And then everything went black.

31

The Great Lady did not take me, of course.

I would now spend some days recovering from my hurts, which were not small, and since there is nothing interesting in a dam lying in bed trying not to move her head very much, I will share more from my Amiel.

Mark every word, he has not many more to write.

Fulvir declared his potion of invisibility a failure, but he did it in that Molrovan way that meant it was a success. "I have now three bottles of a substance that will in no way render one who drinks a cup of it invisible for six to eight hours. I have given it to a goat, and I would show him to you to prove it works, but I cannot find this goat. The thing to do now is to try it on a person."

The dog people who did Fulvir's most menial tasks began to whimper, suffering with their warring desire to please their master and dislike of taking medicine. I raised my hand.

"You, Amiel dom Braga?"

"Yes, Master Fulvir."

"And what shall I tell your father should you die?"

"You would not give it to me if you thought I might die. But you might give it to others, which is not fair to them."

He tried not to smile, which made him look like he had gas, but I knew that I had pleased him.

"Come and drink then, my little Egalitarian."

"I will, sir, if I will be permitted to leave the house and venture into Goltay while so affected."

"What? Why? You do not need to peep at women in the bath, you can afford a whore."

"I do not want a whore, sir."

"Please yourself. But see that you finish your creeping and peeping by the first hour of the morning, and return here so I can watch what happens to you. Or, at least, hear what happens to you."

And so I drank a cup he prepared for me, which I expected to be vulgar, as he had been in his workshop using the wretched things I brought him to produce horrible smells all week. I was pleasantly surprised that it tasted of mint and honey, though the taste that followed the first impression was gamy and thick.

"How is it?" he asked, raising one eyebrow.

I heard a snorting or snuffing sound behind a door.

"Not so very bad," I said, though I could feel that I was making a face.

"Interesting," he said. "Would you say that it tastes familiar?"

"Notes of it do. The mint and honey. But overall, no."

"Good."

"Does that affect its efficacy?"

"No."

"Molrovan no, or real no?"

"A real and truthful no. Its efficacy is wholly unaffected by your reaction to its taste. In fact, it is starting to work already."

I held up my hand, thrilling to think it might be half-transparent. It was not.

"I see no difference."

"I should have told you, you will not be able to. The spell acts on the perception of others, on their expectations."

"But it is working?"

He considered me, rubbing his beard, and then he nodded.

"Congratulations, you are now fully invisible."

To test this, I walked across the room. His eyes followed me.

"You can still see me," I said.

"I can see your clothes."

"But if it affects others, why do the clothes matter?"

"Did your shirt drink the fucking potion?"

More animal sounds behind the door.

"Well?" he said.

I stripped off.

I walked around in a circle, going on tiptoes so not to be heard.

His eyes did not follow.

And this is how I ended up walking the path through Arlasque Woods to Goltay as an invisible creature, naked but for my shoes and stockings. I tried to go without them, but walking outside barefoot is painful without practice, and I soon returned to find Fulvir had anticipated this and left my shoes by the front door for me. Soon after I left, I realized I would get blisters on such a long walk if I did not also wear stockings. So I returned, and knocked so I would not surprise anyone by opening the door.

"Yes," he said from inside, but without opening the door.

"My stockings. I must fetch them."

"Of course," he said. His voice sounded tight and choked, and it only just occurred to me that magic costs its maker something, and that he might be in pain.

He did not invite me in.

Instead, after a moment, the door opened a crack and my most comfortable stockings, made of wool from Montabrecola, appeared, pinched in his fingers. I took them, and put them on, wishing he had given me a cotton pair, with the day being so hot, but then I supposed I would be a great deal more comfortable as I had no need for clothes on the rest of me.

"Are you well, Master Fulvir?" I said.

"Yes," he said again in that tight voice.

I left.

It was not long before I saw a pair of Gallard dams walking, both carrying bundles of bound sticks for kindling on their backs. They looked right at me, to my surprise, then made horrified faces.

But then I figured it out.

I might also be frightened watching a pair of ownerless shoes and dark orange wool stockings walk down the road. I kicked the shoes off and tried to peel off the stockings, but they were damp from sweat and I had to sit down, getting dirt in the most uncomfortable place. But it was too late. The women dropped their bundles of sticks and ran off the way they had come, one of them squealing. I hung the stockings up and determined to tough out the blisters.

If I saw anyone else, I would hide my feet.

Only a few moments later, a very old man came walking up the path with a hoe over his shoulder. I kicked my shoes off and stood still. He started pointing at me and saying unkind things in Gallard, so it occurred to me he must have seen the shoes.

I crossed the road, slowly so as not to kick up dust.

He was looking right at me as I did it.

Worse, he was looking right at my parts.

I believe they felt as inconvenienced as I did, because they now seemed to be aware of all the sunlight and attention and were making some effort to withdraw into my body.

You will have guessed this already, but I was not invisible at all, to anyone, and never had been.

"Godsdamn it!" I yelled, and then said, "Fuck! Fuck! Fuck!"

I must have looked even more out of my mind at that moment, because the old man now held the hoe in a more businesslike fashion, and spoke even more angrily than he had been. I was particularly unsettled by the occasional gestures at my cock.

I crossed to my shoes, but the old man wasn't going to let me put them on.

"Fuck you, Fulvir!" I said, and started running.

Imagine my surprise when I slammed headlong into something unseen, knocked it over, and also fell.

Fulvir himself now appeared on the road, quite naked, scream-laughing and holding his sides.

An actual invisible person and a mad rapist being perhaps more than the old man felt himself capable of hoeing, he took to his heels. Quite quickly for a man of his years, I'd say. It was a wonder he hadn't been mustered; they were taking anything that was capable of marching a few steps without stopping for breath.

As furious as I was, I had to laugh as well.

But then my face pinched up in horror and disgust.

"What did I drink?"

He laughed even harder, and this turned into coughing.

"No," I said. "Please, no."

"What are you so angry about?" he said between dangerous-sounding coughs. "You are not the one who had to jack off the rabbits."

If it is possible to laugh and to dry-heave at the same time, that is what I did.

"All right," he said, finally catching his breath. "Let us go home."

He started walking.

"Wait, don't you have a spell or something?"

"I could turn invisible again if you prefer to be alone."

"No, I meant to transport us."

"For what? Is less than one mile."

I collected my shoes and walked after him.

Soon I found my stockings. I put one over my nakedness and offered him the other.

He thanked me, and wore it as a hat.

When we came to the dropped bundles of sticks, he picked up one bundle, and, using the ropes that bound them, slung it over his back, then directed me to do the same with the other.

"Why waste them?" he said.

I would like to say that was the last noteworthy thing that happened on this adventure, but it wasn't. Not far from our borrowed house, he stopped, and sniffed the air. He then looked at a fallow field choked with weeds.

Fulvir flicked his left hand at it three times, like you might before you dry after washing.

I heard an unearthly rasping and clicking, and then a rush of hot wind, and sizzling. Columns of smoke rose into the air. I counted nine. One goblin managed to rise from his ambush spot, burning hard with a blue-white flame, but then collapsed.

"Congratulations," he told the burning goblins, "you have found me. May you have much joy of it."

The smell hit us then, and I stumbled from it, but Fulvir took my elbow and led me home.

As we returned to the house we were making our home in near Goltay, Fulvir was moving more slowly. The burning of the goblins, though beyond the skill of most who call themselves mages, was not one of his greater magicks, but it did not come free. Once through the door, he dressed, solemnly removed a tooth and placed it in the pocket of his robe, then rinsed his mouth with cold tea to flush the blood out.

"It is nothing, I can grow it back."

"And what will that cost you?" I said, putting my pants on.

"Ah, you are learning. Probably some pain in the bowels, but I can ease it."

"And what will that cost?" I said, enjoying the game.

"I will be gifted an assistant who asks too many questions, though at least I can amuse myself by abusing his trust, which is too easily given."

"So, magic is borrowing from one thing to pay another," I said, clumsily dressing yet another question as a statement.

He seemed to remember the rust-colored stocking on his head, plucked it off, and tossed it at me.

"Constantly. Sometimes the cost of magic seems too great, but a magicker can no more stop using it than a gambler can walk by a dicing table. Now will you continue to dress, or do you truly wish to go invisibly into Goltay tonight?"

32

I woke to the sound of a woman's voice.

She was not speaking. She just made a pleasant sound. My head hurt so much I did not want to open my eyes, though I knew it was daytime by the redness of my closed eyelids.

The sound went on for some time, and it was so comforting I fell back into sleep.

When I woke again, the sound continued.

I pried an eye open, and the light was not so bad as I feared, dimmed by curtains that blew in through a tall, narrow window. That the breeze was merely warm, not hot, told me it was morning.

I saw wildflowers in bunches on a small table.

I saw a woman's legs pointed straight up against the wall, her feet bare, her toes pointed. Now the feet flexed, the heels pointed up. The owner of these legs was quite limber.

I mumbled something, but my mouth was not yet working well.

The chant stopped.

"Again, please?" a young voice said.

"Is. That. The. Helion?"

She laughed.

The legs fell gracefully from the wall and a young woman of perhaps sixteen years rose swiftly in their place.

"Am I a man, to sing the helion? Have I burnt my skin like pie crust?"

Her blond-brown hair was cut in a bob, bound off her forehead by a linen band of off-white with the faded green emblem of a sprig of leaves on the front. Was this a nun? I looked around for some symbol or banner, found, on the wall to my left, a wooden hand pinching a sprig of leaves in copper wire-bound colored green glass.

"What?" I said. Her accent was Gallard, but light. Her Ispanthian was perfect.

"Sorry, I was challenging you to see if your brain was ready to work yet. It had quite a knock. I am a sister of the Green Path, and I was singing health into you, through the grace of the lady of wood and garden. We do not serve Sath in this place. You find yourself in the Hospital of Esselve the Giver, in Goltay. They call her Selveya in Ispanthia, though her only abbey there is in Cestia, on the Cassene Sea. Rather far from Braga. But beautiful, with unparalleled gardens of healing herbs, but also flowers just for the eye-song they make. Cestia is your most beautiful city, I think, but I am partial to the water, and to fountains. Do you know your western coast?"

"Once."

"If you mean you have been there one time, hold up your left hand. If you mean you knew it once, hold up your right hand."

My left hand went up.

"Name," I said.

"If you mean your name, hold up your left hand."

I thought for a moment, then held up my right hand.

"My name doesn't matter. I am an unworthy vessel for Esselve. But if it pleases you to call me something . . ."

I did not learn her name then because I fell asleep while she spoke.

When I woke again, it was night, and another girl was intoning pleasant sounds upside down.

"What day is it? What happened?" I said, my mouth working better now.

This one stood, said, in a thick accent, "I look for Punch."

In my addled brain, I thought she met Punchel, my grandfather's horse.

The blond returned in a moment, wiping sleep from her eyes. She carried a lantern with three candles in it. She set this on the table, edging aside one jar of wildflowers.

"Punchel?" I said.

"No, just Punch, that is me."

"What happened?"

"You slept for three days, and there was some fear that you might not awaken. You were struck quite hard in the head, says your red-haired friend, with an axe. I mean you were struck with an axe, but also that your friend had an axe. I am not helping you very much with this gibble-gabble, am I? Anyway, your helmet saved your life. We think your skull had been cracked, but it seems to be whole now, and, now that you are awake, we will see how much of you is left in there. If your brains are not scrambled, you should knit quickly. I am personally hopeful, as I have treated a great many head wounds and your eyes are already brighter and smarter than they were yesterday. There may be lingering effects from such an injury, but I believe you will be able to continue your dark work for your dark goddess. You are one of hers, right? The Skinny Woman?"

I said, "Yes," and it came out louder than I meant it to.

"Well, her purposes and those of my lady are aligned, so long as you practice your injuries on goblinkind, which have managed a great feat by actually being worse to humans than we are to one another. Please destroy them all so you can get back to chopping up people, as your god intends. It sounds like you are off to a good start, though. There is talking of you and your birds in the city. Several farmers bore witness to your deeds from hiding. Nobody ever saw goblins run away like that."

She gestured at the many wildflowers on the table.

"These came from those who saw what you did, and also some who merely heard. We have turned away others so that we would not lose you in the foliage. There was one we dared not turn away, though, however discreetly she came to us and however she avoided making her request sound like command."

She pointed now at a single rose of lavender color. On its stem was a small carving in wood.

It was a monkey.

I laughed, but my head at that time was not for laughing.

"Now your sort do not complain, which is a mixed virtue, but your head hurts you quite badly, no?"

I shrugged.

"I thought so. The pain will likely stop."

"What can I do?"

"To get better? That depends on how much better you would like to be. First, move slowly for a while, do not lift anything heavy, do not fight. No shocks or jars. Are you understanding me?"

I nodded.

"Next, if you are serious, stop drinking wine. You drink more than you should, like most soldiers. It shows in the eyes. Everything shows in the eyes. Also, eat fish and shellfish, but stop eating the flesh of animals. Esselve loves them also, and blesses with health those who spare them."

"This will not happen."

"I know. But you asked."

"What about fish?"

"Excuse me?"

"She loves sheep and cattle, but fish can get fucked? What are they, carrots that swim?"

"Our warm blood binds us to sheep and cattle. And before you say 'What about cook-hens?' she loves them, as she loves fish, but the eating of them is less harmful to us than our fellows who calve and kid and make milk."

"Perhaps I should listen to one so intelligent. Your Ispanthian is better than mine. Were you raised in my country?"

"No. But I spent fifteen years at the hospital-abbey in Cestia, where those with lingering injuries from the Threshers' War were brought."

"So . . . you *were* raised there."

She smiled brightly and said, "No."

"But you . . ." I started, but the words escaped me, and I gestured at her girlish face.

"Your god has her mysteries, mine has her own. She appears as a crone, but she is always pictured with children. She loves youth, for in youth is health, and some of those who serve her well have their winter years shortened and their spring years lengthened. If we shouted a creed before we began our day, it might be 'Long life, gentle hand.'"

33

———— • ————

I am happy to report that when one is actually invisible, one cannot see oneself, so one who has been abused by deceit may feel reassured.

I downed the truly insalubrious-tasting brew Fulvir now supplied me with, asking me first if I knew my weight. I offered my best guess. He eyed me sole to crown, then told me I was wrong, and adjusted my dose by adding to my goblet a few drops of something aromatic that seemed to glow with the coals of the fireflies I had nabbed.

It took nearly half an hour for the effects to begin. First, my skin tingled unpleasantly, and then it seemed to sink into my bones. I did not fade, as I thought I might—rather, I went transparent in patches. First my trunk, and then my extremities. The last thing to vanish was my fingertips.

"I think I shall be sick," I said.

"Do not dare to throw my brew up, Amiel Chickpea dom Braga," he said, but I could tell he was looking in the direction of my voice, not at me.

I fought and kept the brew down.

Who told him about my family nickname?

He took notes while I stood there not knowing what to do.

At length, he said, "Are you still here?"

"Yes," I said.

"Why? Never mind, it is good that you lingered awkwardly when I clearly had no more need of you. I nearly forgot I have something else to help you accomplish whatever villainy you have in mind. Do you want it?"

"Do I, Master Fulvir?"

"You want it."

He now held up for me a sort of reed.

I accepted it, with some difficulty, because I could not see my hands—this would take getting used to.

"If you breathe in through this, you suck in any sounds you might cause to be made. If you walk while drawing breath and stand still while exhaling, you should go quite unnoticed. Will you be encountering dogs? Or goblins?"

"I . . . do not think so?"

"Then I will not waste my ointment of olfactory ambiguity, it is quite unpleasant to make."

To test the breathing straw, I drew in a long breath, in the middle of which I dropped a small brass pan onto the floor. I saw it fall, even felt the vibration through my bare feet. But it made no sound whatever.

"Good," he said.

He waited a moment before saying, "Now begone!"

I did not give him the pleasure of answering, just let him wonder if he had addressed an empty room. I breathed through the straw as I fetched my shoes out of his sight, then opened and closed the door as soundlessly as if I were underwater.

Six to eight hours, he had said.

It took me nearly forty minutes to walk to the walls of Goltay, by which time, as I feared, I had blistered my feet quite badly wearing shoes with no stockings. I hid the shoes behind a stone and approached the gate. I hesitated for a moment, gathering my courage, finally annoyed into action by a pack of probably bewildered flies that began to swarm about me. Once I ventured forth, it was an easy matter getting past the gate guards, two mean-looking but bored grandmothers wearing ill-fitting, sweat-soaked brigandines probably taken from the dead. It took me less than a quarter hour to navigate through sparse groups of Goltayn and foreign soldiers going about their business, and to find the city center; the broken fortress, the Field of Flowers, the temple of Sath and his Vault of Mysteries. I went near the cluster of royal tents, and the guards were many here, and more alert. I did not believe I could be caught while making no sound and stopping no light, but, if I were, would they think me an assassin? The city was quiet. I could hear the gentle gurgle of the Arve beyond the wreck of the Castle of Eights. On the other side of the great square I saw the priests at the Vault of Mysteries swinging their censers and urging us all to look as the sun sat over the river, their god going to his nightly rest. I walked about, identifying which tents belonged to which kings or princes; I was pretty good with flags and heraldry. Of course the tent that most effectively drew the eye was that of His Majesty of Gallardia, itself the size of a manor house, and shimmering with cloth-of-gold and beautiful paintings. I heard music and laughter from inside, and decided to get the lay of the land before circling back here. This was where I thought my brother might be, but it would be a difficult place to move undetected.

I would try my luck elsewhere first.

What did I want here, among the tents of the great and mighty? I wanted to see Grandfather's shield.

I wanted this even though I understood that there was something about magicked things that made one think overmuch about them, and that I might be under such a spell.

I did not want to own it.

I was no soldier.

But my sister was, and it belonged with her.

What was I truly doing here, though, in my invisible hide?

Did I hope to reason with my stubborn, spoiled drunk of a brother, and talk him into honoring Father's wish by giving it to Galva?

Or was I actually going to take it?

No.

Though the thought made the hairs on my neck and arms stand up with thrill, I did not have the courage for that.

I only wanted to see the Mouth of the Storm, and to make sure Migi still had it.

At least, that is what I told myself.

I had a bad moment when a group of Unthern knights on some errand trotted toward me in a narrow passage between tents, forcing me to climb a tent pole, which rocked, and someone in the tent cried "Ai," though once the knights had gone I melted back a discreet distance before a pair of Brayçish archers came out of the tent. I had the wild fear that they might start flinging arrows, but calmed myself by reasoning that, with the tents in such proximity, they would be reluctant to use those heavy-looking war bows without a clear target lest they pierce some royal buttcheek and so deflate the alliance.

Another scare involved an Istrean knight wearing armor only on her legs for some reason, taking her racing dogs for a sunset stroll by the river. Maybe the dogs had demanded their walk while she was dressing? A serving lad trotted behind her. One of the dogs caught wind of me and looked straight at me, issuing a couple of half-hearted woofs as his eyes and nose gave conflicting reports. His mistress, eager to see the sunset's glory on the mirrored Arve, pulled his leash until he was dragged into compliance. The servant boy looked at me for longer than I liked, but then he went along as well.

I realized I was going to have to start peeking into tents if I wanted to rule out Migaéd's presence outside the crowded royal pavilion, so I steeled myself, feeling dirty but resolved. I thought the constellation of smaller but still opulent tents in the Gallard neighborhood near that of the king would be a good starting point. I peeked into several, and at first saw only older Gallard nobles going about their evenings; taking food, talking quietly, supervising servants who polished or cleaned; when I stumbled across an older woman performing an act of oral affection on a man in elaborate

*stage makeup, the truly invasive nature of my actions sank in. I
closed the flap as quickly as I dared. I was so ashamed that I was
on the point of giving up for the evening, when I saw three richly
dressed young men stumble to a patch of clear cobblestones with
a drain leading to the sewers. At the count of three in Gallard (ai,
du, troy), they all began to piss. One stream failed, and that man
sighed, threw down two gold coins, and relaced his breeches. The
other two started to falter. One man swore and strained, but finally
dried up, just before the other fellow did the same. The second-place
man threw down one gold coin, though it took him a moment to
pay and relace because he had only one arm. The third man picked
all three coins up, laughing, and also plucked a small flower that
had been growing through the cracks.*

*He shook this, then tossed it aside, wiped his hands on his pants,
nearly tripping on the scabbard of his slakesword.*

Migaéd.

In all his splendor.

The shield was not with him, and he was unarmored.

I followed them.

The three of them made for the tent of the king.

*Just around the corner from the door, and just out of the sight of
the four finely dressed but capable-looking royal guards who stood
near it, Migaéd and his new Gallard friends smoothed their hair,
brushed themselves off, and tried to stop giggling as if they were
all thirteen, not thirtyish. Happily, the door to this tent was wide,
and open to allow in a breeze. I was able to slip in at the heels of
the libertines, smelling their brew of wine, brandy, sweat, piss, hair
ointments, and expensive perfumes. The first hall of this tent—for
one could not call it less than a hall—was lit with more oil lamps
and good candles than I had ever seen in one room. The walls of
the tent were hung with tapestries showing wine harvests, knights
doing battle with giants, and various gods enjoying the sport of
love, Nerêne most prominent, sitting lavender-eyed atop a reclined
woman's face while ecstatically holding two disembodied members.*

The king of Gallardia, Luvain, sat at the head of a large table piled with money and cards and copper coin-goblets. Men and dams at the highest level of society were playing what looked like two separate, intense games of Towers. Migaéd and his friends took their seats and got dealt in. A dwarf wearing the king's crown sat astride a tipped-over wine barrel as if it were an elephant, and it sounded as if he might be narrating the card game. Despite the open door and other open tent flaps, the air was hot and thick.

I sucked air through my reed and walked, stopped, sucked and walked again, until I was quite near my brother. His Towers hand was awful, four Soldiers, only one Bee, almost a starveling hand. He did not seem to care. He was having a grand time. I looked around his seat for Grandfather's shield, but did not see it.

Should I try to find his tent and see the shield?

Or should I stay here, in this den of opulence, wine, and wit?

Happily, Migaéd's poor luck and worse playing solved the problem for me, because, over the half hour I lingered in the royal tent, his pile of money dwindled quickly.

The king, seeing this, said, in Ispanthian, "Our future son-in-law, perhaps you should close the evening? Your luck seems dry."

"Only part of me that is, Your Majesty," he said.

Now the dwarf on the barrel said, also in Ispanthian though with an Unthern accent, "If you leave the Braga fortune on this table, there'll be no need for anyone to marry you."

"Happily, my little friend," he slurred, "the Braga fortune will not fit on this or any table."

The dwarf said, "Sixt-General, we will build a bigger table, you will find that we are able. But if luck keeps shitting more in your basket, soon your coins won't fill my casket."

The room erupted in laughter and I actually felt bad for Migaéd. The king would never marry his daughter to such a buffoon—what was he doing? Dangling the bait to keep Ispanthian armies bearing the brunt of the war?

"Ease off, Hanz," the king said. "We like this man well. Take yourself home, dom Braga."

"Yes, and come straight back with more money," said the one-armed Gallard he had pissed with, perhaps some cousin of Luvain, as he had overlarge eyes of a similar shape.

Migaéd stuck a finger in the air as if to say *That is just the thing to do,* and headed for the door.

"Go to sleep!" the likable king said, laughing, knowing that he would not.

What was his game here?

Why did he not marry the daughter to Pol, if he wanted a dom Braga in the kennel? He is brave, moderate in his vices, successful.

But, of course. Of course. Pol is not the heir, not any more than I am.

It matters not at all if you are ten years or twelve months younger, the oldest son is the god-king of an Ispanthian father's eye, whatever his qualities. Would that Imelda had pushed Pol out a year before Migaéd instead of the reverse; then Migaéd could whore and gamble his allowance away and when that is done, go begging. But, as the eldest, he can leverage the promised key to Father's vaults, and, with the Braga fortune in play, no door will be shut to him.

I slipped out of the tent to follow Migaéd, and soon he weaved through the labyrinth of pavilions and found the door to his tent. His servant, Pedru, greeted him, offering him water. He did not take the water, but he went in, and I drew breath in the straw and followed as quietly as a dream.

It was a fine tent, probably a loan from King Luvain; red in color to honor Ispanthia, and the size of a cottage. I regarded Pedru with some affection. He was not much younger than me, a clever, well-organized boy with a poor father who was only too happy to see him somewhere besides holding a spear. Pedru wore a variety of pouches and had a talent for producing items and making them disappear without fumbling, or even seeming to look for anything. He demonstrated that talent now, handing his master the key to his money-chest, but not without asking "Are you sure, Sixt-General?" first.

Migaéd was sure.

He scooped out a fistful of silver and gold coins it would take Pedru's father a year to earn, agonized over these, and put about a third of them back, swaying as he knelt. He put his reduced fistful of gambling-fodder in the money-pouch at his belt and now looked intently at something on the other side of his bed.

Leaning against the tent wall.

The Mouth of the Storm.

Too magnificent even for this fine tent.

Far too good for its current owner.

Migaéd approached it, licking his lips.

No, I thought, don't do it, Migi.

I thought this at him as hard as I have ever thought anything, I thought it like a shout.

But he swayed over to the glorious shield.

He picked it up.

And he started carrying the Mouth of the Storm toward the card game raging in the tent of King Luvain.

34

The same night Amiel crept in the tent of the Gallardian king, and then that of our eldest brother, I was answering a summons from the queen. Perhaps *summons* is the wrong word. There had been a note attached to the rose left for me at the hospital by Mireya, written on nearly clear paper rolled around the stem and clutched by the carved wooden monkey.

> *Has ever any soldier in her lance*
> *Displayed a suchlike gift for thievery*
> *To make off with her sovereign lady's glance*
> *While clad in drab and martial livery?*
>
> *By what permission, or by what decree*
> *Wouldst thou upon serenity intrude*
> *Insisting that I bend mine eye to thee*
> *And all thy beauty, natural and rude*
>
> *(Thus by thy warlike natal stars imbued)*
> *And which I have no shield or mail to stop*
> *To save my poor heart's treasury of blood,*
> *Of which I doubt thou meanst to leave a drop?*
>
> *Thus wounded by thine eye, I fear to know*
> *What injury thy sword might do a foe*

Even with my limited schooling at letters, thanks to Amiel I knew how to recognize a sonnet. But I had never had one written to me before, and certainly not an amorous one. This was amorous, right? Was there any other possible way to read this?

No.

No other possibility.

Especially with the words written on the bottom of the beautiful little paper.

> *Statue of Nerêne*
> *Elephant's March*
> *Eighth Hour*
> *The day of your release*
> *All is permitted, nothing expected*

Still not a summons, not a command.

An offer.

My heart beat faster.

My breath grew shallow.

I felt a very pleasant anticipation, remembering Mireya's face and her eye, the little copper leaves in the makeup around her eye, her bare feet sliding from her slippers to be tucked up under her legs. Her hair, black as the most fertile soil.

Was the paper magicked?

Because that would be grossly unfair.

I grew angry there in my hospital room, and hissed my breath out of my mouth.

Punch looked in on me.

"Such a hiss! Are we safe to let you go today? I mean, your bed is needed, but not if you are going to turn into a dragon."

"No. I mean, yes. Wait, today? I am to be released today?"

"Yes. Within the hour. Your skull has knitted. You have no trouble speaking or using your limbs. Our magicks have made you sturdier than you would have been without them, though every day you refrain from taking a knock or a spill will be one day closer to knowing you are fully healed. There may be other troubles, as I have said, but we do not have the space to keep you while you sort those out."

That struck me.

"On that subject," I said, "why did I get a room here instead of camp treatment?"

"You are a duke's daughter, are you not? And a general's sister. Your treatment was well paid for."

This bothered me. Of course I was glad to be getting well so quickly, but having exceptions made for me seemed weak. And besides, I had been unconscious, and had no say in where I was brought or whether a fortune would be spent on my treatment.

"So your healing goddess is a mercenary?"

"The world is mercenary. Esselve does what she can in it. When a wealthy patient is admitted to benefit from our art, we include service for two poor patients in the reckoning. We cannot help everyone, but we do not let that stop us from helping those we can. Especially those of talent in war, for such people are needed with an urgency words can barely embrace. You would have lain for weeks in camp to achieve what we did for you in days. Now get out of here, dragon, and feed more biters to the fire. It was good to know you."

I was not required to report to my lanza until the morning, so I was free to meet the queen.

Or not.

Either way, I would want a bath.

I missed Inocenta and the others of my lanza, and especially my birds. But I was also going to miss the privacy and peace of that room. It cannot be overstated what a luxury a clean bed and a room of one's own is to a soldier on campaign. Walking around the city of Goltay, which was coming back to life after being violated and emptied, I felt like one of those crabs that steals its shell, but now without a shell.

A bathhouse would be just right.

There was only one open in the city, so you can imagine how crowded it was.

I did not care.

I waited two hours in the block-long line.

While I waited, I heard the archers and speardams and knights who waited as I did, and their talk had a new quality, one that I had not heard before. They spoke of trying to find wine, or of boys or girls they fancied, or of the beauty of the city. They made jokes about Our Foe. These were soldiers who, for the first time in a very long while, held death a bit further off.

It was good to hear.

After I paid my admittance at the baths, I left my clothes and armor, which the hospital had been good enough to clean, at the wardrobe service up front. I went with soap and a towel and a coin purse around my neck to the crowded cells in which soldiers rested, washed, even knew each other carnally. The fires could barely keep up with the bodies crowding in, so the water was only warm, not hot. I was bumped often, and my ears were bothered with loud boasting and bad singing. I was stared at by a haunted-looking woman whose lower lip was missing, giving her the look of a dog. Next, I was wept on by a boy who had just been in combat for the first time and could not stop shaking. I held him, believing his emotion to be sincere, but I was ready to four-knuckle-punch him in the throat if he moved his parts near me or tried to touch mine. He did not. I told him he was brave, and I kissed the top of his head, but then I moved off to try to find a place to be more alone.

There was one very hot room of steam, and I sat in this for a time, wrapped in my towel, pleased by the colorful tiles showing birds and flowers.

A girl with one leg of wood came around playing the flute for tips, and I gave her copper. I paid copper again to a girl selling stopper-dabs of various perfumed oils. One that smelled of cedar and black pepper was quite dear, but it pleased me, so after I paid her she smeared that on the killing spots of my underjaw and underarms.

I was very much enjoying this room until two large dams and one larger man with no fingers at all on his paddle of a hand came and got right against me, saying pardon so there was no reason to take offense, but still being too close and fleshy and smelling too much of beer. They were all quite hairy as well, probably from the mid-southern provinces of Dorau or Lagusa where it is said that the beards meet the hair of the chest, and that the men are even worse. The fellow rubbing against my left side left a thick, black shoulder hair on my arm and I willed my face not to react. The woman just next to him said, too loudly for the echoing room, "What scent are you wearing, coz?"

Calling everyone cousin was very Dorauan.

"Black pepper and cedar, I think. Ask the girl. I have to go."

Back on the street, I thought about returning to camp. I knew my birds were in good hands, and I was not required to return, but I hoped there might be wine. There might also be singing. I did not turn that way, though. I was passing the pleasure quarter, not far from Elephant's March. The color of love in Goltay is light purple, and the love houses wore that color in various shades. Here lavender, like the rose I carried, there a smoky purple-gray. The roofs were tiled with the roundish tiles popular in mid-Gallardia, in potter's brown or green like old copper. The narrow and graceful chimneys here were particular to Goltay. This was indeed a lovely city. The names of the love houses, when I could translate them, were perfect. It is easier for a Spanth to read Gallard than to speak it because these tongues are written similarly and share some words. But Gallards speak as though they have no bones in their faces.

I looked at the elegant buildings named by their pretty-lettered signs.

NERÊNE'S SISTERS AND ONE BROTHER

THE HIPPOGRIFF AND STAR

THE ORCHARD

THE BEEHIVE

THE HOUSE OF SIGHING WALLS

This last might have been the House of Moaning Walls, but I hope it was Sighing, this is more pleasing.

A pale, lovely woman looked at me from a window of this last house of courtesans. When she saw that I was looking, she let her very long auburn hair spill out, along with a shower of pink flower petals that delighted the eye against the dark purple stucco of the building.

I gasped and said "*Sala*" at her.

"Hello yourself, soldier. Would you like to try your pretty feet on our staircase? I promise I am worth the climb."

So saying, she rose up a bit so I could see that her breasts were naked.

She was lovely, though her ribs were for counting.

I colored and waved.

"Thank you," I said, turning to walk past the many petals on the cobbles, most of them mashed to paste by the soles of boots. I was excited. I smelled my own fresh sweat, which had cedar and peppercorn.

I found it not unpleasant.

I stopped lying to myself that I might be going back to camp.

The statue of Nerêne was one of the most fine and lovely parts of the street she stood on, and there is much to compete for the eye on the Març d'Elefanne. Twelve feet tall and carved of cream-colored stone, she stood on the balls of her feet with one hand on a bared breast and the other reaching high as if to seize a star or a moon in crescent. As with many of the statues in this city, it did not look possible for an object of stone to balance as she did, but such was the art of the Gallards. Her body was at once feminine and athletic. It was a body that would not tire at carnal sport, yet looked soft to hold. Her face seemed to say *However bad things may be, yet we have this, so let us take it gladly.* The artist was clearly in love with whatever model stood for this piece. And yet her beauty was such that it was possible to see many women in it—there was some little bit of Mireya in this divine face, but also of other lovely women I have met.

I have not seen a statue of greater artistry.

I do not know what happened to it, but I am sure it is no more.

The first time the goblins left Goltay, they did not spoil it. This gift of the city was a dream, and a lie—when they took it back, they spoiled it, as is their way, ruining the angles of buildings, wrecking statues, burning. When, later, they would be forced out of Goltay again, they would sink its bridges, and salt its farm-lands. I hear Goltay is now a grave and a ruin, that trees grow wild through shops, and that its churches and brothels alike are homes to wild dogs.

But for those of us who marched into Goltay under arms, and stayed there in those hot dreamlike days of Ashers, some part of that city goes with us until we die.

I looked about the statue of Nerêne, and saw three women, quite young, one of them a brown-skinned dam of Axaene or Keshite blood, and none of them Queen Mireya. It seemed as if these women were bound to linger near the statue—it was a popular meeting place—but were inconvenienced by having to avoid the attentions of a young man. He had the sort of mustache one might see in a whorehouse, but never under a helmet. He was behaving most rudely, staring openly at these dams as if he were a cat trying to decide which bird to pounce on. None of them had a soldier's look about them, which was unfortunate, as it would have been pleasant to see him punched.

Perhaps I would do it.

He was leaning against the trunk of a small tree quite near the statue, and I took it in mind to stand near him, and give him enough eye to let him know his rudeness was flirting with consequence.

An old woman with skin like leather in need of oil arrived, making her way with a cane, helped along by a young woman with the look of her granddaughter. The rude fellow now stared at this girl, even as she turned her face away from him. It was not her face he was interested in. The older woman stared at the scoundrel, but he stared back. I will confess that I had thought the man might be Mireya in some magical disguise, but this behavior was so far beneath her, or at least what I imagined of her, that I could not credit it.

I now walked up behind him, meaning to kick his leg out from under him so his tail hit the street, but he sensed my approach and crossed Elephant's March away from me. I stared at him to let him know it would take little to make me cross the street after him. He was a strange fellow, and he never met my eyes, though he continued to stare at the remaining girls.

"Ay," I said to him.

He looked around, everywhere but at me.

He was clowning me.

I do not enjoy clowns.

"Ay," I said again, "you want to stare at something like an animal, stare at me."

The girls were walking farther away from him, but one of them said without voice what I believe to have been Gallard for "thank you" at me. They were on my side of the street. He, on his side, walked down to be across from them. That was enough for me, this *jilnaedu* needed more than talking to. I set down my rose at the feet of the statue of Nerêne and crossed Elephant's March at him, walking with purpose. He waited until I was almost to him, and then, with surprising speed, he leapt away from me onto a wall, then down, and he sprinted at the statue of Nerêne. I thought he was going to make for the young dams, who had begun to half run away from him, so I ran.

But the bastard took my flower from the ground, and ran down the street, in the direction of the river.

"*Merdica,*" I said, and ran fast after him.

He now had the flower in his teeth, turning his head to grin back at me as he dodged others with no effort. He jumped over a cart and ran along another length of wall with great ability. Was he a Guild man? I had heard that thieves of the Takers could run up the sides of buildings and defy death in all manner of ways to escape pursuit.

I was falling behind, not only because I was in armor and he wore only light summer clothes, but simply because he was faster. To be clear, I was not slow, but there was no keeping up with this man.

Now he approached a quay by the river, and turned in to it.

I saw a small, covered wherry with a hired man at the oars and a section allowing privacy for passengers. You know the sort of thing I mean, like carriages people once used with horses, but for traveling by water. Such vessels were popular on mild rivers like the Arve.

I did not now see the *jilnaedu* who had stolen my rose, but I did see a beautiful arm come from the darkness of the wherry's cabin and gesture me forward.

I smiled.

I was charmed down to my bones.

I no longer even cared if magic was being used on me.

I went into the close, warm little space, and there I saw Mireya, infanta of Ispanthia, queen of Gallardia, lying back on cushions of lavender. She wore only a sage-green robe that might have been made of cobwebs, and a golden torque with two amethysts set like eyes.

She put something in my hand.

A goblet of cool honey mead.

I saw a small chest with a large piece of ice and a small spade in it, and a bottle rested in this.

Where had she gotten ice in this baking city?

"I made it. Water is mine to command, and I am strongest on a river, or in it," she said, as if I had asked the question with my mouth rather than just my mind.

Now I saw the monkey chewing on my flower's stem, making a mess of it.

I opened my mouth and then closed it again.

The queen said, "Are you going to get in and watch the sun set on the Arve with me, or would you rather pick fights on the Març d'Elefanne?"

I said, "I will get in, Infanta. But the monkey must go outside."

I am sorry not to have the words for what happened in the river carriage, with the sun setting so beautifully on the Arve. However, even if I did know how to phrase these things, it is not in my nature to speak of intimacies. I will say only that the queen is as tender as she is strong, and more beautiful without a thread upon her than in the most cleverly made dress in Seveda. Despite her greater experience, she never made me feel dull or ignorant. She never made me feel coarse, even when her soft fingers touched the calluses on mine. Whether I left with my virginity is a matter of little interest to me, but if pressed I would say no.

I took great pleasure.

This is owing both to the queen's art in amorous play, and also to the deep feeling I had for her, for even an unskilled lover—if they are the object of great affection—can bring one to that small but intense paradise we kynd enjoy in close spaces. But when this affection is given to one who possesses great art, such as this woman schooled in the mysteries of the goddess Nerêne and practiced with the love-masques and unmarriages of the Gallardian court?

No, Mireya left very little of me to be initiated.

When I stumbled drunkenly from that boat, smelling of our joined sweat and perfumes, I found my world much altered. Later, I would lie with men, for reasons that are my own, but not many, and each encounter further showed me that I am not made for men. Their tongues are too thick in their heads, and their smell is like something from a barn. Worse, that buffoon between their legs demands too much attention, and for as much as it can grant pleasure, it does so in a way that feels anonymous. To be loved by a man is to be issued a decree he has written in advance, and has presented to others; to receive a woman's love is to have a very personal letter written on one's body.

I stepped from the wherry onto the bank of the Arve with weak knees. The queen—*Miri, I am Miri in here, to you, like this*—gave me one last look from the shadow of the cabin and then pulled its door shut with one bare foot. The oarsman did not look at me, but the monkey did. He sat on the roof of the cabin looking philosophical, if this can be said of a monkey's face. It was easy to imagine he was thinking *Congratulations, woman. Now what?* But then he opened his mouth in a smile of mischief and threw flower petals on me. I laughed, and he let me scratch the crown of his small head and his eyes gratefully, and even pulled my hand back the first time I tried to withdraw it. I finally parted from him and followed my feet I knew not where.

I felt confined in my armor, my skin now too sensitive for all this weight and pinching and tightness.

I saw a pretty dam walking and, now that I knew what a mouth was capable of, I stared at hers. Her lips were thinner than Mireya's, and her eyes a bit smaller in her face, but they were bright and put me in mind of a sparrow. I would say that she was

nearly as unlike Mireya as it was possible for another attractive
dam to be—very short where Mireya was a bit tall. Fair-haired
where Mireya's mane was dark as the sea on a moonless night.
From her makeup she appeared to be a pleasure-house woman,
but I was not sure. Did she know any of what the queen knew?
Was her love given to women, or did she bear the weight of
men? How would she hold me, if I were hers for the night?
When she met my eye, I almost looked away, but then I did not.
I had a right to look strangers in the eye with something besides
violence in my heart.

This was new for me.

"Sister," she said to me in Ispanthian, but with a Gallard accent, and something in her voice spoke to the center of me, something in my hips and in my womanhood. Her voice smoked, like
paper about to burn.

What had happened to me?

This was not me.

"Sister," she said again, and took my hand in hers, which was
small and soft and warm, but also strong. "I was just returning
to the Beehive, in Nerêne's quarter. Would you like to come with
me?"

These women of the Goltayn pleasure houses were courtesans,
not common whores.

They were their own masters.

My skin tingled.

I thought of the queen's note saying *all is permitted, nothing
expected*.

Her use of the word *irmana*, sister, made me think of Inocenta. Strangely, taking a second lover would seem to make the
offense to Inocenta, if there were any, something less.

I have given myself to the goddess of death, not Nerêne.

*But Dal-Gaata does not mind if we use our bodies for pleasure,
so long as we do not bind ourselves too much to this world.*

"Yes," I said.

Little did I know that the queen also walked the city after our lovemaking, and that she, too, met someone on her way.

Though this was a very different matter.

I leave you once again with Amiel.

35

If I did not act, the shield would be lost.

Despite Father's power, the Mouth of the Storm would not find its way home from a gambling table a second time.

I followed Migaéd through the lavish tents, got in front of him, then stood fish-mouthed as he passed me by, too scared to act.

I did this twice.

But the third time my brother loomed near, I knocked the Mouth of the Storm from his hands with a harder blow than I thought myself capable of.

The magnificent thing rolled away on its edge.

Migaéd stared stupidly at his hands, then stumbled after the rolling shield. Now I had a dilemma; if I picked it up, I could easily outrun him, but then he would be treated to the sight of it flying through the air and it would be clear that spellwork had been employed. Magic was not so common in the army that Fulvir would not be suspected, and he knew very well that Galva's closer brother worked for the old wizard. So I did not fetch up the shield. Rather, I rolled it farther on.

"Ay," Migaéd cried. The prospect of losing the shield in such a ridiculous fashion seemed to have sobered him a bit, as he began to gain on me. I rolled the shield harder. Still he gained.

"Come back here!" he said, and I had the idea that he was speaking to the shield, which, to be fair, we all suspected had been magicked. I couldn't resist having a bit of fun. I stopped the shield briefly as if it had heeded his call, then even rolled it back in his direction. He stopped running, and I saw that he was winded.

"That is better," he said to it. "What were you thinking?"

He plodded heavily toward me.

I started it rolling away from him again.

"Please!" he said. And stopped, holding his palms open as if to say Let us be reasonable.

I stopped the shield.

He nodded his head and took a slow step toward it.

I rolled the shield a step's worth away.

"All right, all right," he said. "What do you want? You want me not to gamble you?"

I rolled it just a little closer to him at that, biting the inside of my cheek to keep from braying laughter at this poor, credulous drunk. But then I remembered that this creature was my eldest brother, whom I had once revered, and I did not feel so amused.

"I know that I do bad things," he said, his face grown suddenly sorrowful.

I swiveled the shield so that the storm's-face boss was toward him, then waggled it up and down as if the puff-cheeked little steel face were nodding in agreement.

"I know that I should not bet you at cards."

I waggled it side to side, a headshake no.

"But I will not lose this time. I will not. You shall help me with your magicks, here made manifest. And I shall restore my reputation with the Gallards, for now they laugh at me. I know they laugh at me. And I cannot blame them."

Gods, this was hard. I had never seen him self-reflective. This was not the time to mock and punish him, was it? I wondered if I might make myself visible and speak to him, reason with him. Perhaps he might soften his heart and let me take the shield to Galva.

But no, such weathervane turns are not to be trusted.

A drunk's sorrow is more fragile than his wrath.

I took a half step as I shifted my weight, wondering whether to take the shield and run, roll it farther, or just stand and hear if Migaéd felt like examining his deeds further. My heel sank into something, some foul mixture of mud and vomit, I think. I looked down, and though I could not see my foot, I saw the impression it made in the foulness.

Migaéd saw it, too.

Faster than I would have given him credit for, he whipped his slakesword out of its scabbard.

"Ay!" he said, and stabbed at me.

It is worth remembering that training gets into the limbs, so that even when the brain is impaired, the body might repeat familiar motions with some skill. Migaéd was not one-tenth, not one-twentieth the swordsman my sister was, but he had some of the best training money could buy, and he was still young enough that the drink had not yet unmanned him.

His lunge very nearly killed me where I stood.

It would have done, in fact, had I not been so startled by his sudden motion that I put my weight on the heel in the vomit, and felt it slip from under me.

I went "eeeep" or made some similarly rodentish cry, falling back and watching his sword and arm punch through the air my torso had only just vacated.

I will interrupt here to note how similarly both he and I evaded death just days apart. I imagine Amiel falling accidentally backward away from Migaéd's lunge in much the same way I intentionally flattened myself under the thrusting spear of the goblin raider standing on his pig. I do not know what, if anything, this means, except to say that I have noticed the gods are fond of echoes.

I nearly grabbed the shield, but instead rolled away from it, for the shield would have given away my position. I stayed low, too, more by base instinct than training, for I had been given little enough of that once it was clear my lessons were wasted on me. Migaéd's sword now carved pretty arcs in the air above me, and I kept rolling.

Migaéd sheathed his sword, then bent and grabbed the shield, meaning to strap it on his back. Well, that would not do. I stole close to him and plucked the slakesword from his belt, tossing it far away from him. Sober, he might have carried on securing the shield before going after the sword, but he was not sober. He held the shield in one hand and ran after the sword, saying, "Thief! Devils! Help!"

People began to stir from pavilions, though half-heartedly. If the cry "Thief" had made them more alert, "Devils" sounded like ravings, especially coming from a drunk nobleman who had just been executing swordplay sans partner, and may earlier have been observed playing the game of the long piss.

Migaéd grabbed the sword even as I once again plucked the shield from his grip, this time not rolling it, but sprinting with it, devils be damned.

I am a very fast runner, and I can run longer than most.

Had I been born to a lower station and matured in peacetime, I would have almost surely found my way to the Runners Guild, who pay decently for young men and dams who can run without easily tiring.

Let us just say that on one warm high-summer night soon after full darkness at last came to the city of Goltay, a shield of great beauty was seen by some to fly of its own volition down this or that alley. It settled against a wall while a blanket was stolen from a bed past a window open to let the river breeze in.

While this dark, shield-shaped blanket floated near the river-walk, a woman in a hooded cloak stopped and drew the hood back from her head.

I looked at her and stopped as well.

She was looking right at me, as though she could see me.

I now noticed a monkey on her shoulder. It was the monkey who had pointed me out to her. It now sniffed the air and chittered something in her ear that made her laugh with delight.

Only one highborn woman was known to walk the streets of Goltay with a monkey. I was in the presence of no less a personage

than the queen of all Gallardia and, many said, the true queen of
Ispanthia.

Gods, she cut a fine figure, at once regal and friendly, powerful
and benevolent.

And I do not know when I had seen a finer-looking kynd of any
gender or rank.

"Amiel dom Braga," she said, "I do not know what knavery you
are about this fine Ashers night, but, for reasons you will probably
not guess, you have found an accomplice."

36

"Should I go?" Inocenta asked me as I woke up in my own camp bedroll. I had, for the first time in a long while, gone to sleep on my own, as it had seemed in poor taste to crawl in with my *irmana* smelling of other women. And yet, she had joined me, lying curled with her belly to my back, as I slept.

"Not if you . . . are not offended," I said. "I have . . ."

"Yes, I know," she said, kissing the back of my head and holding my arms in a hug that felt strong, but not as though I were her captive. "I confess, I was hoping for that honor. But to be jealous over you feels foolish, considering my own experiences, which are many, and that I have two brats in an *ucal*. And yet I am jealous. Though not so much as to be bitter."

"I would not blame you if you did feel bitter."

"Was it . . . ?" she said, handcanting the gesture for *crown* before my eyes.

"Yes," I said, "and not only her."

I felt her fill her lungs with a long, slow breath in and a long, slow breath out.

"I have taken lovers as well, waiting for you. But that was scratching an itch. This is more than that, I think."

"Yes," I said.

That breath again.

"Do you know, I prayed to Sornia," I told her. "About you."

"Yes?" she said, her voice brightening.

"I asked her to be patient with me while I tried to discover what I wanted. Not to hate me for hesitating before such a gift."

"I am no fucking gift," she said, in a way to make laughter.

"Be serious with me," I said, "just for a moment. This is important."

"Is it?" she said, using her freer arm to indicate the birds, our weapons, the camp.

"As important as anything else is. I have been thinking about this. If we say that nothing matters, then what is there to fight for? Why not just be eaten by them, watch them burn everything down?"

She breathed out long, into my hair, last night's wine on her breath.

"Yes, I have thought that as well. In my better moments," she said. "And I prayed to Sornia about you too."

"Your love *is* a gift," I said. "A greater one than carnal love, I think, because it feels as if it is not breakable, at least not in this form. I would not be your lover not because I do not see you in that way. I do. You are beautiful, and you have stirred want in me. But I could not bear it if the beautiful, irreplaceable thing between us turned sour over a want of the flesh. I pray that it has not."

"And to whom do you pray that prayer?" she said.

"To you."

She breathed easier, squeezed me hard and then released, so that her arms lay upon me lightly.

"I think some part of me hoped the Bride, if not Sornia, would deliver you to me as I delivered you to her. Of course I recognize how awful that is. I did not deliver you to Our Serene Mistress."

"Oh, but you did," I said.

"Even so, it was done for its own sake, for your sake, and for hers. I should not expect reward. Her peace is the reward."

"Yes. It is . . ." I started, but I realized I had no word for the new feeling in me, that my own death was welcome, and not to be feared.

"She was here," Inocenta said. "The queen. Not long before you arrived."

My own breath caught in my throat. Inocenta noticed that.

"With your little brother, the poet. He had something for you, but said he wanted to give it to you himself. No, let me rephrase that—he said he *must* give it to you himself, that it was too important to be left with, how did he put this? 'Even such a capable guardian and loyal friend as you appear to be, lovely and formidable lady.' 'Lady,' can you imagine? I wanted to slap him and kiss him at once. Also, he was all wrapped up in a cloth, as if he were a nomad of the Axaene desert."

At the time, I did not know what to make of how she said he dressed. I wanted to ask her if the item he had for me was a shield, but some instinct told me that the less I said to her of this, the better.

"He will return tonight, after his duties," Inocenta said.

"To speak of duties," I said, nodding where Nouva had taken up her baton of command.

She struck a fence three times, then sang out in her clear, martial voice, "On your feet, dams. It is a new day."

Would that I might have lived the previous day again instead.

I will tell you of these events, but first, enjoy this entry from Amiel dom Braga.

It was the last one he had the time to write.

37

I am besotted with the queen of Gallardia, and she is besotted with my sister.

There is nothing unusual in falling under the spell of Mireya of Ispanthia, countless men and dams have done so. But how strange and thrilling and powerful to have been gifted with the queen's confession that Galva is, how did she put it? "The most sad and beautiful kynd I have met in all my days; I fear ever to see her made sadder, for I will not be able to think of anything but trying to cheer her."

You are thinking, why would a woman and a queen open her heart to a boy of barely eighteen years? You will be happy to know that I asked her exactly that question somewhere in the middle of the long, strange night in which she hid me from my brother, gave me opium to smoke in a pipe, and toured me around the beautiful fever dream that is Goltay. All the while I was invisible, at least until nearly morning. All the while, her eyes glittered for Galva, and I was at once proud and jealous.

As I write this, I am still not fully and wholly myself.

I have looked in a glass, and for some reason, I am returning to the world inside-out. Which is to say that some of my skin is not visible while the workings below are. It is quite gruesome, to be honest. On the other hand, not all of us have the gift of seeing our own skull, but I have seen mine, and I thought it a handsome one before the muscles and veins started asserting themselves.

But I was writing of the queen, and of her confidences.

Toward the middle of that night, we sat by the Arve, listening to its pleasant gurgle.

"Why does a woman and a queen open her heart to a boy?" I asked Mireya.

"That is not a boy's question," she said. "So there is some of your answer. I think you of that house are something quite particular. At least, three of you are. You are not a boy, so much as you are 'this' boy. This quizzical, well-read, well-spoken young man, so much keener than many the king sees fit to surround himself with. Of course, you are still quite young, for all your books and insight. I confess, I feel quickened by youth, perhaps because I did not get to be young in any real sense myself."

"How old are you?"

"Twenty and eight."

I know this is not old, she is younger by two years than Pol, and by three than Migaéd. But she has half again as many years as I do, and no one may call her girl. I was of a sudden conscious of my nakedness, transparent though it was, and asked her for her cloak, which she had laid aside for the warmth of the night. She gave it over, her eyes twinkling with mirth. I first wrapped it about me wholly, as I would when I began to reappear. But then I thought this looked strange, and only placed it about my waist where I sat. But that was no less ridiculous. So I put it aside, but ready in case I should materialize—I had a horror that the first parts of me to appear might be the ones I least wanted to display.

She had watched my awkward struggles, trying not to laugh.

That was when she produced a thin-stemmed, delicate clay pipe and let me try the gift of the poppy. She marveled at the sight of the smoke going into my lungs, disappearing, then reappearing on my outbreath.

Then she took back the pipe, and I watched it in her hand lest she put it away.

I fear I will never know such pleasure again.

"That is enough," she said, when I asked for the pipe again. "This lady will chase all other pleasures from your life if you kiss her too often. Only godsmilk sets a deeper hook, and that is not to be tried, for it will drag you straight into service of Our Foe. God-smilk comes from underground, from darkness. The poppy is ours, *a flower of light and rain; it gifts a glorious view, as from a cliff that may be balanced on, and then retreated from. You are not to taste this again for at least a year. Promise me."*

"Has it been a year since your last taste?" I asked.

She smiled like a child caught at mischief.

"I am different," she said.

When Mireya and I went to seek Galva at her camp, first light hung in the east, and I kept myself well wrapped in a cloak, thinking little of the stares I was getting. Upon entering the camp of the lanza of corvids, my sister's friend, the sturdy redhead, greeted the queen axe in hand before she recognized her and made obeisance. I was sorry to learn Galva was not there, for I wanted very badly to present her with the Mouth of the Storm.

It is too heavy and too valuable for me to be at ease with it.

But I must keep it until I can give it into her hand. Corlu dom Braga was my grandfather as well, and it must stay with someone of our blood, someone who respects it as it deserves.

I explained this to Mireya as we walked away, and she nodded.

"There is something great in your sister, as there is in you. This shield is for her hand, and it is right that you should give it to her. I think I will know her for a long time, if we survive this place. I hope to know you just so long."

I do not think it was just the poppy which made me see this woman as wise and clever and kind.

Queen Mireya is the flower of two countries.

I will write a poem for her.

I have tried several times already, but I am too tired, and she is too much for ink to capture.

I am only staining paper.

The page before this is missing.

I would pay any price to read what he wrote of her, even if he did not think it worth keeping. This last page of his journal is like a door that separates the time before and the time after, a door I will be happy to step through again when I am freed from my body, which is the manacle that chains us to time.

Those warm days of false peace in Goltay were coming to an end.

The next day brought horror.

38

It was afternoon when Migaéd and the chainsmen came to our encampment. Like many kynd with the habit of hard drink, the sixt-general was not given to early rising, but I think that on this day, like me, he had not slept, but for less pleasant reasons.

He looked like a corpse stood up in boots.

But he led a formidable group of soldiers. Not his own line soldiers, this time; he had used his floating authority to commandeer a group of royal chainsmen, those who are charged with enforcing discipline in the army. They were not many, perhaps a hundred in all, but he had some twenty of them with him. They were armored half in plate, and armed with heavy truncheons for beating, and with hand-and-a-half swords for killing.

They carried the authority of the king.

I was exercising Bellu and Dalgatha for the second time that day, just before their last feeding. We were near a breakthrough—Dalgatha had just begun executing a brilliant move in sparring, where she pecked at my face, making me raise my shield, then, while I could not see, she would leap over my head and get behind me, turning as she did it so her beak was at my back. She was trying to teach Bellu to stay where he was so that I would be surrounded, but he was so eager to join in the game that he leapt, too. If he would stay put, a single enemy caught between these two monsters would have no chance.

But Bellu did not learn this.

Migaéd and the chainsmen made right for me.

The lanzamachur intercepted them.

"May I be of service to you, Sixt-General?" she said.

"Yes, Lanzamachur," he said, looking and sounding like he

wanted to lie down but was kept standing by anger. His voice was thin and choked, but his words had consequence. "You may stand aside while I question the daguera, over there, who is under suspicion of possessing a stolen item of some worth."

He made to move past her but she placed herself in his way again.

"Yes, Sixt-General, I hear and obey, but I must ask you for your own safety not to approach the corvids with hostile intent."

I had a very bad feeling.

I handed the tethers of my beautiful birds to Inocenta and said, "Get them away from me."

I walked forward.

Migaéd had already pushed past Nouva, saying, "Those birds are your responsibility, Lanzamachur. I suggest you control them. I will speak with Daguera dom Braga."

It is still hard for me to understand how this man I had once thought half a god had so quickly become half a devil. It is not just drink, although this is to bad character as fat to a fire.

He got very close to me before he spoke.

"Daguera dom Braga, where is my shield?"

"I do not know, Sixt-General."

"Don't you lie to me, by the gods. Don't you do it."

"I did not lie, Sixt-General. I do not know the whereabouts of the shield."

"*Whereabouts* indeed. Do not hide behind language. Does your pup of a brother have it? It was stolen with the use of magicks, and he works for that bone-mixing, word-twisting Molrovan."

Your brother.

That stung.

If Amiel was only a half brother to Migaéd, then so was I half a sister.

"Sixt-General, I know nothing about it."

He looked at me long, little beads of sweat on his forehead and cheeks. The sun was already strong in the sky. Goltay was farther north than Espalle, but it did not benefit from the breeze off the sea.

"We will see about that," he said. Then, to the chainsmen, "Search the camp. A quarter trounce to the man who finds it."

He had perhaps not noticed that more than half those he commanded were women.

That is when it happened.

"Please, brother, do not provoke the birds," I said, then knew I had only made things worse.

"Fuck your birds," he said. "Get her away from me."

A chainsman and a chainsdam now took me by the arms and moved me back.

They did not harm me, but they moved quickly, like soldiers, and did as they were told.

I looked to see how far Inocenta had gotten my birds away from me.

It was not far enough.

They had both been watching, even as they let themselves be led away.

As soon as I was touched, Dalgatha cawed loudly in distress, a sound to raise henflesh, but Bellu made no sound.

He simply bit through the tether fixing him to his sister.

And leapt.

"Bellu, no!" I yelled.

The chainsman at my left arm screamed as the huge corvid pecked him. It is to be remembered that a corvid's peck is like the hard swing of a pickaxe. It stove in his breastplate, which did not kill him, but I believe his ribs were cracked. Bellu now used his head to push the dam away from me, then bit her arm hard enough to cause hurt without breaking bone. I tried to step in front of Bellu to protect him, but he batted me back with his wing and stepped in front of me.

He thought he was just correcting and warning these errant kynd.

Everyone stood still for a moment.

"Dams, get your birds in, now!" Nouva yelled, and most in the lanza were able to.

Inocenta got Dalgatha away in time.

"Kill that thing," Migaéd said, pointing at my handsome boy.

Bellu would not let me step in front of him, and soon I was grabbed from behind again, and held.

The chainsmen with their huge, sharp swords killed my Bellu, I will not describe it.

He was too good to strike at them, even as they took his life. He did not see me get grabbed the second time, or he may have struck at those. But he would not defend himself against humans.

These humans knew their work.

It was one of the worst things I have ever seen, which is something to say.

I fell to my knees, but I did not sob.

I hated.

I stared at Migaéd dom Braga, and I trembled and I hated.

Once the other birds were secured, the chainsmen searched.

The shield was not found, of course.

Migaéd said nothing when he left.

He had said he meant to question me, but this was not done.

He did not even dare to look at me.

His hand made a gesture at me, a reflexive farewell or a dismissal, or something in between.

And then he was gone.

I walked to Bellu with weak steps.

It seemed he was already smaller, that he might simply shrink away to nothing before my eyes, and I was desperate to touch him and stop that from happening.

I grabbed handfuls of his feathers and shook him to stop the shrinking. I tucked in his tongue, and closed his great beak for the last time.

It did not close smoothly.

The chainsmen had busted its hinge. He would not croak my name with that beak again. I closed his black eyes with my hand; I would not see myself, or the sky, or the moon in them again. One of my sisters walked up to me, I could not tell which of them through my wet eyes, but I know it was Inocenta who steered her away.

I laid my cheek against Bellu's beautiful, perfect head.

His blood was on my face now, and that was good. I wanted to be covered in it, I wanted to wear his skin and feathers and become Bellu.

I started to make noises from low in my belly, noises that were not words, and would not fit in words. Noises like birthing, but when something good leaves the world. How was he gone? I had raised him from a chick. I could still see his mouth pink and gaping; I had fed him mush, and then green grasshoppers that wriggled and spat black liquid in my palm, and then hens' legs and the flesh of goats. My bitch-coward of a brother had robbed me of this noble, this powerful, this deadly-to-our-foe, sweet, loving thing whose beak was so deep in my liver and heart that I would curl around the injury of his loss for the rest of my days.

And then he just walked away with that stupid sop gesture, whatever it meant.

I backed away from the anger because I was scared of it, and where it would take me.

I later wondered if my sorrow for Bellu was blasphemous to my new Lady, but I do not think it was. The death of kith, as you call close animals, is not the same as the death of kynd.

I do not know if My Serene Mistress takes beasts into her hand.

Animals have no gospel.

And why not?

Are they less than us, those who speak with beaks, or make questions with sideways heads, or give comfort with paw or tongue?

I do not think so.

I will tell you I prefer them.

I like their silence better than our flattery.

I like their honest wants better than our lies.

I do not know how long I lay there with my cheek against him, and my hands in his feathers and blood. But I had stopped him shrinking, and I could go in to Dalgatha now.

She would need comforting.

I thought that if Dalgatha had died, Bellu would be waiting to give comfort, not receive it, and then I pushed that thought away.

I love Dalgatha exactly as she is.

But she is not Bellu.

I took a small feather from his chest before I rose.

I carry it in my pouch still.

See it?

If you are the one that finds me dead, put it in my hand.

39

The calamity we call the Kingsdoom started at the temple of Sath, not long before sundown.

The high priest, the one who had refused to let Queen Mireya use the huge Vault of Mysteries to shelter refugees, was seen to walk through the pavilions of the kings with his censer-boys swinging smoke-pots. I was not there, but I am told the smoke was of myrrh, which is burned at royal funerals. The priest was urging the crowned heads and their retinues to repent their worship of other gods. He was saying Sath would chase them all before him even unto vanishing, as the morning sun destroys the night-proud stars who thought their light so great.

He was laughing and crying at the same time.

The *censerichus* looked terrified.

It was then that runners came to the generals from the engineers and sappers stationed at the walls.

Their little pots of water had begun to ripple.

There was digging in the earth.

Bells began to ring then.

I was sitting in a stable with Dalgatha, stroking her feathers as she trembled.

Her head lay in my lap, her eye unfocused.

My reflection in it.

Three of my lanza-sisters had given me what little was left in their wineskins.

I was not drunk, but neither was I sober.

I heard horns blowing, and drums.

I heard cries that a goblin army had been sighted, moving fast at the city. It was the feared third army, not a myth after all, its ranks endless.

Nouva came and said we were to go to the south wall, but then a runner came and Nouva told us it would now be the east wall. I could not get Dalgatha to move. Nouva told me to keep trying with her, to bring her if I could, but to come without her if I must.

Nobody seemed to know what was happening.

It was beginning to get dark.

I heard the cracks of onagers and ballistas firing.

I heard shouting, now from this direction, now from another.

"Come on, sweet skinny girl. I know, I know, but we have work to do," I said to her, standing, and I coaxed her and stroked her beak. She rose as well, and she moved jerkily once so that I nearly pulled my hand away by reflex because I thought she might bite it off.

But I did not let myself fear her.

"If you want to kill me, I understand," I said. I laid my face against her beak and she suffered me to do this, great trembles still running through her.

"Bellu," she said in her raspy voice.

"Yes, Bellu," I said in mothering tones.

"Bellu bad?"

"No," I said, squinting against tears. "Bellu was not bad." I could see part of his wing in the yard, and his blood. I would have to walk her out past that. "Kynd were bad."

I gave her tether a gentle tug, and she moved in the direction I pulled.

"Are you ready to go? Is 'Gatha ready to go?"

"Go," she said.

And I led her to the east wall.

Of course, that is not where they came in.

The army that had raced up to our walls, getting a head start through a massive tunnel, was the greater part of their force.

But the first blow would be struck from a far deadlier location.

The captain of King Luvain's guard, on orders from the king, brought a dozen soldiers over to the Vault of Mysteries, from which odd noises had been heard. He pounded on the door, demanding entry. The high priest cracked the man-sized door in the middle of a much larger one, and his sun-spectacles were off him.

He was laughing madly.

"What goes on in there, and what is so funny?" the captain demanded.

"Everything is funny," the priest said. "Especially this—it turns out their god is actually stronger than Sath. Sath is a weak cunt. He certainly let me fall from his hand, did he not?"

That is when the guard noticed that the priest's eyes were yellow.

Godsmilk is hard on the liver, as I have said.

The priest and several of his order had been enslaved by the goblin drug.

They opened the great doors now, to show where the goblin host stood gathered, the great piles of rubble from their dive under the city reaching all the way to the vaulted ceilings. The sacred Mystery this temple held was that the city of Goltay was already breached and that we were all fucked.

So very badly fucked.

You are thinking, how do we know this business of the door?

Who that lived was close enough to see the eyes of the priest, or to hear his words to the unfortunate captain of poor Luvain's guard?

I will confess that I do not know.

I know only that this is what is said, and that it sounds true, and that is enough for me.

It really does not matter how it happened, does it?

But something in us needs a "how" to explain the worst events, and this is the only one I have to give you.

Some few survived the massacre in the royal pavilions, though, and their accounts agree on what I tell you next.

First the ghalls came.

Eight feet tall, nearly a quarter ton each, wielding hammers and greatswords strong kynd could barely lift. Wearing great pot helms with airholes giving some vision, but no slits through which a stiletto or arrow could pierce. Rattling in long coats of scaled armor that went almost to their feet. Not quite as big as giants, but better armored and better led than any giants that had ever crossed the Thralls.

It is not for joking, a charge of ghalls.

They came like a wall of muscle and fat and iron, mad for the blood of their small, fragile ancestors. They were mad to die in service of the biters, who rationed them the godsmilk that made them dream worlds they believed they would inhabit forever if they died pleasing the God of Smoke.

The ghalls charged straight through the square known as the Field of Flowers, butchering.

The guards of some of the kings and princes in their pavilions had already formed up when the outer host had been spotted; preparations were in place to get the crowned heads moved to Highseat, the strongest tower that remained, but we were out of time. The royal guards of Unther and Gallardia were smashed like teeth before a hammer, just that painfully and bloodily. Perhaps forty ghalls wrecked two hundred men and dams before running out of strength—they do not have much endurance. But they do not need it. They break lines quickly and well.

As the ghalls died or fell to their knees panting in the fields of gore they had created, the goblin skirmishers came, and these shot poisoned bolts and threw javelins. They circled the remaining pockets of resistance, harassing. A second wave of them circled the pavilions so nobody could run. A third wave then ran through the streets of Goltay as night came on to light fires and cause panic.

But still the royal tents stood.

Now an eerie sound rose up, a sound like horns but lower, unlike anything I had heard. It was the carnyx, a tall horn that curves up and then down like the head of a dragon. Something like these had been used by ancient kynd armies before the Keshite empire spread, so the word had been ready when the biters brought their version of the instrument—much as the word *goblin* had been ready in our fables when these things showed up after the Knock to claim it. I would see these carnyxes later, stuck through human heads, the jaws opened and the teeth removed so the bell and tongue of the thing became the heads' mouths.

Like my brother Pol, I would often hear the sound in dreams, as I would see the line of wailing, rotting heads held above the battle.

This is what the defenders of the royal pavilions saw and heard as the Kingsdoom struck.

The honor of killing the kings of Manreach would fall to the Moth Knights, as the most elite biter warriors were known. They marched before the carnyx players, under the banner of a moth, which was a holy animal to them. The images on these banners were made from sewn bones. Some of these biters had axes in the shape of moth wings, and, at nearly five feet tall, the Moth Knights were strong enough to wield them to great effect against us. They wore dried human faces as masks, and wore cowls made of our hair. As they drew their weapons, goblin priests in wooden armor shingled with mushrooms shook wooden rattles filled with human teeth, and, as they closed, blew the spores of the nightmare cap through long pipes.

Prince Barwyn of Widmarch, and heir to the crown of Holt, mounted the only effective counterattack. This was due not just to mixling bull-men he got from Fulvir, but also because he was the exception to what I have said before about soldiers of Holt. He was strong, courageous, and he had more than a hundred heavily armored knights with poleaxes with him, their noses and mouths covered with scarfs against the nightmare-cap spores. They finished off many exhausted ghalls, then clashed with the fast-moving Moth Knights. They stopped these long enough for a few very fast or very strong survivors to break through the ring of skirmishers surrounding the huge plaza.

None of these survivors were kings or princes, however.

One was a bull-man, who ran from the fight and only survived because of the heavy magical runes Fulvir had tattooed on him. After leaving the prince and his fellow mixlings to die, he opened a hole in the ring of goblin skirmishers by killing a great many of them, perhaps twelve.

He survived the war.

But you already know what happened to him.

It did not occur to me until later that this was almost certainly Marrus.

One kynd survivor claimed to have seen King Luvain in his sleeping robes emerge from a huge rip in the royal tent, trying to fight with a sword in one hand and a wooden phallus in the other, laughing because what else was there to do? I do not know if this is true, but there would be no more Gallardian way to die. But die he did, along with King-Elect Yanusz of Wostra, King Augan of Unther, Queen Elga of Sadunther, Queen Laera of Brayce, six minor Gunnish kings and queens and their thanes, two princes and one doge of the Istrean cities, and Prince Barwyn of Holt.

It is said Barwyn's knights drank something before they charged.

I am willing to bet it was bittermead, meant to bring death and to poison their flesh.

I hope some of those little *jilnaedus* tried to eat them and choked.

40

I lived because I was sent to the west side of the river.

The mouth of the tunnel in the Vault of Mysteries never stopped bleeding goblins, and these quickly seized the two main bridges across the Arve, trapping the bulk of the Ispanthian army on the city's east side. Most of the regular army had been camped outside the east wall in a series of fields called Onion Market—though it was no more a market now than Field of Flowers was a field—but these were quickly summoned inside at the approach of goblin forces from the east. Goblins do not usually knock gates in—they prefer to tunnel under walls and collapse them. Just as they had dug under the city center, they had dug under the walls to the east, near the university quarter, in such a way that they would fall at the biters' command. The walls collapsed from Marshgate to Scholars Gate, with a great rumble we heard all the way from near the tower called Highseat, on a hill in the middle of the city's western half. We were at the bottom of this hill, but we heard those higher up, who could see what happened in the summer day's last, late light, cry out with a great gasp as people will when they see disaster. Dust and powder went up, white in contrast to the many columns of darker smoke from fires, and the cries of many thousands rose up to the sky. Many to the east had rushed to man the walls against climbers, or stayed ready in their shadows, so there is no counting those who died in that one stroke.

But this was just the beginning.

As the goblins poured into the university quarter, we all heard their whooping and barking. I had never heard so many of them, and I never would again. The corvids, so recently injured by seeing my Bellu killed by strangers, were angry and agitated and ready to fight. I feared they might start with the soldiers crowding in near us. Nouva arranged us in a perimeter around a dry fountain in a square, and we armed with sword and shield. As the whole of the army and the refugees flooded west, we were required to use our shields to keep from getting pressed in, and I am sorry to say I bloodied a few heads and broke an arm or two.

"We need to fight!" Inocenta said to Nouva.

"The Pragmatist ordered us here expressly. She has a use for us. We must wait for her command."

A runner came down from Highseat soon after, and thank the gods she was not for us. I do not know if I could have carried out the orders she bore.

A company of archers soon formed up, along with thirty chainsmen, of the sort who had killed my boy. Behind these came what looked like several hundred spears. Now the chainsmen, some of them holding lanterns, started crying in Ispanthian and Gallard, "Clear these streets by order of the king!" The massed people saw no easy way to make the streets clear, however, and just screamed and wailed. Some were saying "Let us out!" or what sounded like "Porplay," which was Gallard for the Gate of Pleas. But their pleas were answered with brutality. The archers feathered a half dozen, and then the royal chainsmen cut them to pieces with their huge swords. The butchers then cried "One. Two," and on two, they took a step forward and cut down more. At the third "One! Two!" the mob began to clear, pushing in the other direction, or pressing against the buildings, or climbing up. Many were pressed to death against the houses, which were of brick or stone here, for this was a merchant quarter.

The spearmen and dams now came. They fanned out along the sides of the street to keep the road clear and they stabbed any who tested them. In this way, a path was cut between Highseat and the Bridge of Promises, the southernmost bridge in Goltay, and one of the only ones still open to us. I will never forget the face of a girl in light armor, her helmet too big for her, crying as she jabbed her spear into the leg of a panicked old man who tried to rush onto the road. He howled, and fell, and she kept crying and stabbing him, I think because the noise he made was breaking what remained of her sanity.

I hid my face in Dalgatha's feathers, which were less black than what I saw on that street.

A quarut-general now ran with his close-guards, saying to all of us, "Be ready to move. Gods be with us," then saying it again farther down the line. We heard battle, and whooping, many streets away. We heard their rattles and horns. Behind us, our birds rasped and cawed. Animals screamed somewhere, at least I hoped they were animals. A woman in a high window across from us yelled in Gallard again and again, and from her tone I think she was saying, "What is happening? Tell me what is happening?" I think she was blind, but it was hard to tell in the darkness. I could see that she was holding a cat harder than it liked, and I feared it would free itself from her grip and fall to the street. But she would not let it go, even when it clawed her. I think she was so afraid that she did not feel it.

I still think about her. Was she some soldier's mother? A merchant who unwisely came back to her home, after arguing with the clerks at their tables, who at last found her name on a tax roll and doomed her by confirming her ownership? Someone was caring for her, I suppose, and I hoped they were not on the east side of the city. But then I did not know what could be done for her now in any case.

Or for us, for that matter.

The city was going to fall, you could feel it.

Soldiers began to come from the east now, some ghostly white with dust from the wall's collapse, sometimes also spattered with blood. Some were dark from soot where buildings had burned. Some were clutching hands where fingers had been bitten off, or limping from leg wounds. One dam quite near me screamed, say-ing, "They are eating us! They are eating us right on the street!," and her ear was hanging by a small string of flesh and her eyes were so wide and white that I did not know if she had a whiff of nightmare cap, or if she was just reacting as any person might to what she had seen.

Many still looked like they had fight in them, though.

Spanths are not so cultured as the Gallards or Istreans, but we are brave.

We fight.

"We fight, we fight," I said to myself like a prayer.

The Pragmatist would get us somewhere to regroup.

Would we counterattack?

Would we run?

There is nothing so confusing or dangerous as the fall of a city.

Especially when it falls to *them*.

What the earless dam said was true.

They *were* eating us.

They had been so long in the tunnel waiting to spring their trap that they needed feeding, and fallen kynd were butchered in the streets.

I saw a boy with long dark hair being carried by two dams, his leg off.

"Amiel?" I said, but it was not him.

Where were my brothers?

Then I thought of Migaéd and felt so many things at once that I put him out of my mind.

The city shook.

It shook again.

People yelped and screamed, or prayed.

A chunk of stonework fell from a tall house and killed one of the poor Goltayn pressed up against the wall.

Now the quarut-general returned and said, "Lanzamachur Monçera?"

Nouva saluted, said, "Yes, Quarut-General."

"Follow me."

We followed in single file, each dam's birds behind her. We marched at a quick pace past the faces pressed behind the spear-line to make room for us. Some of these refugees were angry at having been stopped in their flight, but more were just terrified. The worst were those who just stared at nothing, or shut their eyes and shook, waiting for it to be over. Of course we could only see the closest ones—there were few lanterns, and the smoke hid the moon.

At one point when the crowd was very close to us, a bird—I am not sure which one—bit the hand from a woman, who screamed and fell.

The bird spit the hand out and shook his head, spattering blood on several of us.

But nobody cared now.

The streets got narrower as we quit the merchant quarter, and then entered the Snares, which was an older, not-so-rich part of town with leaning wooden buildings, many of them wineshops, some of these on fire. The smoke was getting thicker. There was no crowd anymore, and this seemed bad.

We went into a square with empty market stalls and a statue of three rearing horses, and, at Nouva's command, we formed up.

There were many dead here.

I looked for my brothers as well as I could while staying in formation.

I did not see them.

It occurred to me that I might never see any of them again.

Amiel was staying out of town, with a clever and powerful wizard.

He had the best chance of all of us to get away, I thought.

I quietly said "Take me, save Amiel" again and again. I did not even know who I was praying to.

Not Dal-Gaata.

She would not like me asking for someone to be spared her embrace.

So I stopped praying.

I kept making small sounds in my throat. This was not from fear of my own death, or at least I do not think it was. It was excitement, horror, awe, and a sort of chill. Many things at once. I cannot explain it. It just felt better to make a noise than not to.

"They have taken the Bridge of Promises, two streets up," the quarut-general said. "The Pragmatist thinks that you and your birds can get it back. We still have soldiers on the other side of that river, a lot of soldiers, and we must save as many as we can. Open that bridge, wait to be relieved, then come back to Highseat." Then he said, "Do not fail," but the way he said it made it clear that he only expected us to die there.

The quarut-general and his close-guard left, in something just more dignified than a run.

I squinted my eyes against sparks from the window of a smoking building, and I drew my scarf over my nose and mouth.

I leaned my head against Dalgatha's beak and rubbed my face against it.

I looked in her strange, dark eye.

She cocked her head at me.

"I think this is it, girl," I said. "Good Dalgatha. So good."

"Ready yourselves! Masks up," Nouva said. "We are going to turn the Arve green with their blood!"

The Arve.

Had I really made love to a queen on these waters?

Surely this was not the same river.

It was not the same city—that other city was already dead.

The smell of goblins hit, stronger than the smoke.

I put my scarf over my nose and mouth.

I heard a dam behind me throw up, and by the way it was muffled I thought she had done so in her scarf.

I heard someone crying and moaning, and I heard Nouva saying, "Shut up with that, I need you killing, not dying."

A crash sounded and sparks rose as a burning building fell one block over.

Screams and clashes of steel in the distance had become so normal I barely noticed them.

Through the open door of a wineshop, I saw a soldier from the Far Banners, perhaps a Wostran by his floppy, bright red hat. An old man of sixty. He was rolling his eyes crazily, twitching and moaning, trying to use a chair to get up, but unable to. Poisoned, but at a lower dose. Panicked with spore as well, I thought. How long had he been like that?

I wanted to end it for him.

I wished I had a bow.

I am not good with a bow.

"Forward!" Nouva cried.

We raised our shields and charged.

The birds went before us and shivered their wings, making smoke swirl.

We came to a pile of kynd bodies, stuck with many bolts. A burning beam had fallen on the far end of it. I saw and smelled one woman's hair on fire, smoking greasily.

"They've massed their crossbowmen," Nouva said. "They will hit us hard when we clear this heap! Heads down, shields high!"

The birds were first, and at the sight of them, a great barking rose up, and rasping. It was for making one deaf. It seemed like they knew about our birds now.

The crossbows hammered, so many of them.

A bird was stuck through the eye and fell.

Many were pierced through the wings, or had their beaks grooved, or their breast armor dented, but they are not easily killed by arrow or quarrel. They are made for this exactly.

Now I had reached the pile of bodies, and we fell behind our birds because we could not leap so well as they. I felt the head I stepped on, then someone's back. I put my hand down on a cold face to steady myself, but stumbled anyway and came up bloody. I saw an open eye, very green, looking at me from under an arm in a wrong position, the head above that eye gone. I wanted to vomit. I felt the fear leak in, that I would end up rotting in a pile like this, thrown in a pit, unknown and forgotten in a tangle of parts. My death was close, and it would be just this nasty and impersonal. My palms went tingly and slick and I felt my heart beating much too fast. I was losing control of my breath. Was it possible to die of terror? I had heard that it was, and perhaps it was happening to me. Perhaps just thinking that it could happen was enough to make it so.

"Galva! Come on!" Nouva said, fear in her voice as well.

I wanted to tell her I thought I was dying, that I could not make myself move.

But then *she* spoke to me.

Perhaps I spoke to myself in my head, in her voice.

But it helped.

Galva, if you fall I will find you. I declare you mine, but also I am yours. You cannot ever be lost. I know your face and your name and I love you. Yes, your death may be today, but come gladly, beloved Galvicha, and be welcome!

"Short life, bloody hand," I muttered, and found strength.

Up and go, *go.*

Thanks to the many fires here, I saw the outlines of goblins through the smoke, formed up before the bridge, so many, too many. The heads of the front line bobbed down, hitching the crossbows' cords to claws on their belts, then up, drawing the heavy bows by standing, their feet in stirrups at the bow's end.

These crossbows were two hundred, two hundred and fifty pounds.

So many *clicks* as the front line reached full draw and locked.

The crossbows of the second line fired, and my helmet was struck, my shield, so many times, the force slowing my run. The bolts stung, I had felt a hard blow to my chest. Was my brigandine pierced? I would find out if I started to twitch and spasm.

Two more birds down, one thrashing in agony, but the rest were almost at them.

I screamed.

The others of the lanza did as well, all of us.

The birds understood what was wanted and opened their beaks, screaming their great, terrible scream.

The first line of biters had raised their bows, but only a few fired, and not well.

They were screamstruck.

Most of the second line broke and ran toward the bridge, which we could just make out now.

Our beautiful birds tore into the first line, and picked them apart like bugs, but did not stop. Those they did not behead—or kick the arms from with their bladed spurs, which hit hard enough to sever even their mesh armor—they batted back at us with their great wings, stunning them. We cut them with such fury I saw goblin pieces in the air.

One bit at my sword hand so fast it almost cost me fingers, I felt the air of its closing teeth. I rang its helmet with my pommel, posted it back with my shield, then cut its leg hard. The mesh-cloth stopped the edge from severing, but the bone broke and it bared its teeth in pain. I punched the point of my *spadín* through its teeth and out the back of its neck, ripping its head fully in half and sending its helmet aloft as I withdrew the weapon and ran on.

We followed our birds onto the Bridge of Promises, which was narrow and made of prettily carved wood. This bridge was only for pedestrians, nothing with wheels.

The narrowness and delicate shape of the bridge made them look even bigger.

The ghalls, I mean.

Our birds ran into ghalls now.

Maybe thirty.

Only two of them abreast could fit on the bridge.

Our birds could go in threes.

The birds did not know what these things were, they had never seen a ghall.

I had only seen them dead and pale, the rowers from the juggernaut in the waters off Espalle.

The first corvid tried to bite at one's ankles under its great coat of scale armor, and the ghall's massive axe fell and killed it instantly.

"*No!*" someone screamed.

The bird's name was Breaker, I have forgotten the name of his dam, she was newer.

I think we all felt the same thing—that *this* was how and when we died. The heavy crossbows had only been the juggler before the joust.

These monsters were too well armored and just too fucking big for our *spadíns*.

The birds were smart, though, gathered gods bless them.

Gannet, Nouva's bird, was next to fight, and he saw a way to kill them.

He leapt high and at an angle, dodging the huge hammer that broke a piece of wood off the bridge when it struck. Gannet pecked the ghall right in the middle of his pot helm, as hard I have ever seen one strike. He stove the metal in, and with it, the ghall's eyes and nose. That one stopped, then staggered and fell, tripping the one behind him. The other corvids saw what to do, and soon they were crowding into each other for the honor of staving in those fuckers' helms and faceplates. Ghalls are so big they are not used to defending their heads.

Hells, they are not used to defending anything.

They usually just crush everything before them until they tire and then die or fall back.

But now the bridge was stopped up with seven, eight of the

dead brutes, lying in a heap the others were not agile enough to run over, as we had over our dead.

And then something marvelous happened.

The ones behind the dead, so crazed with drug and so mad to get at us, pushed at their fallen comrades with such anger and effort that they began to tire. One fell over, its heart burst, and tumbled into the river. And then others fell or slumped down.

And still the birds went at them.

Nouva ordered us to stay back and let our children work.

One ghall grabbed a leaping bird's leg and broke it. But the next bird, my Dalgatha, leapt up and pecked the back of the man-thing's neck as it turned its body to pitch the first corvid off the bridge. Her beak struck at a just-opened space between its pot helm and its coat of scale. This is a perfect killing spot, and the ghall fell so fast it was like it had never been there.

The first corvid fell into the Arve. I do not know how many dead men and women were in the river, islands of them, lying together in impossible knots of limbs and heads. There was no counting them.

Another score of birds came behind Dalgatha, easily leaping the dead ghalls. They slashed and screamed and kicked in a great fury.

And now we saw something that no one had yet seen.

The rest of the ghalls *ran.*

They ran.

And so did the goblins behind them.

I smiled at a dam near me, Olicat, who had lost one of her birds on the march to Goltay and who had been friends with Vega Charnat. She smiled back. But then something changed. The smile went wrong somehow, then froze.

She began to suffer tics in her face.

She fell and twitched, and I saw the orange-red fletching of a goblin quarrel tangled up in her boot. I do not think she had even known she was struck.

She fell, still jerking.

A few bolts clattered on cobblestones.

The goblins on the other side were trying to regroup.

"Shields up!" Nouva yelled.

We all raised our shields and crouched.

I readied myself to charge again, but then I heard the sound of heavy boots on the cobbles behind us.

I turned to see a wave of Ispanthian poleaxe knights coming to hold the bridge we had won.

These were serious men and dams. The Pragmatist wanted this bridge open, and she was going to get it.

The crossbows stopped now.

There was fighting across the bridge—more soldiers from the east side were linking up with us.

"Corvid lanza, back! Fall back!" Nouva ordered.

I did not want to leave Olicat dying, but her other bird, Boxer, stayed near her in distress, and I did not think he would let me give her peace. I reached for the top of his breastplate, meaning to take him away with me, but he snapped at my hand and would not come.

Now Nouva picked up Olicat and carried her.

The bird followed.

On the way back to Highseat, I looked down a tight, firelit alley and thought I saw a goblin taking a wheel of cheese from the pack of a dead refugee.

I did not know they ate cheese.

Dalgatha leapt at it, but then did not attack, because its startled, high scream was human.

I went over, sword in hand.

What I saw cowering against the wall, clutching a small wheel of Gallard sheep's cheese, seemed very much to be a goblin, but wasn't.

It was a small man in expertly done goblin makeup.

"Hanz," I said.

The fool of King Luvain.

"Oh yes," he said, "I remember you."

"Come with us," I said.

He shook his head, smiled at me, and said, "I have a better chance to get out of the city like this. The sweet king is dead. They are all dead, I think."

"The queen, too?" I said.

"I do not know. She was not with the king when it happened. Though, before, she spoke of you to me. I hope you find her."

I did not mean to sob with hope and gratitude when I heard that, but I did.

He smiled at me, touched my cheek.

I leaned in to kiss his forehead, came up with the taste of greasepaint on my lips.

"That is it, you have smeared my disguise and killed me," he said, and I could not help but laugh.

"Daguera, get moving," Nouva said, panting as Inocenta took up Olicat from her now.

"Good luck, Hanz," I said.

"More to you, pretty Spanth. Kill a lot of them," he said, and, clutching his wheel of cheese, rasped a convincing goblin rasp at me, then moved off, imitating their strange gait so well I hoped one of our archers would not feather him.

41

I have heard it said that perhaps six thousand Ispanthian soldiers got across the Bridge of Promises, and also the Owlet Bridge outside the walls and farther south, and one of these was my brother Pol. We would meet later, and he would tell me how Segunth-General dom Vinescu assumed command of many knights and archers of the Far Banners, which she added to her own survivors, and led a brutal counterattack east against the first wave, which drove them over the rubble of the fallen walls and out of the city. The Pragmatist ordered her, by means of lamp-signals from the tower at Highseat, to fall back; but a quarut-general named Portescat ordered his two thousand heavily armored knights—an elite veteran force we could not spare, some of which had cleared the Bridge of Promises—to pursue the biters into the farms of Onion Market. This was south of the city but still east of that bend in the Arve. Portescat hoped to drive them against the river. When the segunth-general saw that they were going, against her orders, she sent her forces forward, too, though Pol all but begged her to let Portescat go.

"His plan is sound," Samera dom Vinescu told Pol, who was in fact her lover, as I had suspected. He did not learn until later that Portescat was as well.

"The Pragmatist is ordering us back and she has the high ground—she sees things we cannot," Pol said.

"How can she see anything? It is too dark out here. We cannot lose Portescat's armor!" the segunth-general said. "Gods of water willing, we can press them against the river and make it a killing field."

That is what it became, though not as Samera dom Vinescu hoped.

The large kynd force went out, with heavy infantry in front, massed archers behind and center, and spears on the wings. The goblins they chased were mixed units, crossbows, gisarme wedges, axe-men. Goblins are at a disadvantage in field actions because they are not as big or heavy as we are, they may be pushed about. You will see that the ghalls and the dreaded chariots are both remedies for human shield walls.

Earlier, while still in the city, Portescat's knights had used shield, polearm, greatsword, and mace to push and bludgeon a much larger goblin force back through the streets of the university quarter. Pol described a moment where he saw the knights begin to falter because they were fighting uphill and the cobbles were so slick with goblin gore and brains that they could barely get traction—this would later be known as the Battle of the Painted Stair. But still they pressed, the green-spattered statues of Gallard poets and courtesans smiling down at the carnage.

But now, in the fields of Onion Market, the segunth-general's forces, with the mutinous Portescat at the van, had a mob of several thousand goblins with their backs to the river.

"Push!" the quarut-general screamed, and his wall of knights closed ranks and pushed.

Something to know about goblins: the more of them that gather, the harder they are to fight. It is not known how or why, but they communicate without words. Some think it is with sounds too fine for our ears, and this is why they do not stop their ears against birdscream. Others say it is with smells, or even shared thoughts. However they do it, when enough goblins are together, they *swarm*. They abandon their individual wants and become more willing to sacrifice, more able to move as one.

There are certain maneuvers they can only use en masse, and they used one such on the banks of the Arve.

As Portescat's shock troops hacked through, knocked down, and pushed back their smaller foes, at once the first line of them fell to the ground. These were stomped and stabbed, but a second and third line threw themselves quickly on top of their fellows. A fourth line, a fifth piled on, such that the knights were stopped, watching a wall of prone biters build up before them, now knee-high, now waist-high, now up to the tits. And as they piled on stomach-to-back, still they stabbed and raked and bit. The knights hacked and chopped at the wall of faces, teeth, and spears, but were unable to stop it growing taller. At last the wall was high enough for the next waves of biters to leap down upon our heads. This tactic we call *stacking,* and it costs the goblins many lives. But it is worth it when they outnumber us, as they did here, and when there is a dangerous charge to be stopped.

Portescat was stopped.

When dom Vinescu ordered him back this time, he saw fit to obey. Our archers feathered the stack as it unpiled, and the wings of spears killed a great many as well, but our force had lost momentum, and the goblins had avoided a slaughter. The survivors retreated in good order along the flanks. As the segunth-general prepared her forces to wheel and pursue, a great rumble rose up.

Pol knew the sound.

The goblins had brought up a reserve force from east of Onion Market.

The Pragmatist's farglass had seen the dust of it even in the weak moonlight, and that was why she had signaled for her forces to pull back.

When the cry "Palisades!" went up, Pol saw that now the kynd army was at risk to get pushed against the river and butchered. At the disaster of Orfay, he had seen what these palisade-chariots, armed with shin-high blades and pushed from behind by war boars, could do to us. They were useless in the confines of a city, but, on an open battlefield, they are deadly. The greatest danger is not from the blades—these may be stopped by posts, or by heaps of dead—but simply from the fact that they make mobile platforms for spears and crossbows. The fronts of the palisades are effectively pavises, or man-high shields, which the biters reload behind.

"Form up, form up!" the segunth-general screamed, while the tower at Highseat, just visible through the dust, started winking *bridge south bridge south.*

"Owlet Bridge, to the south!" Pol yelled.

"Yes," Samera dom Vinescu said. "Light troops, follow the river south, take them, Terce-General, move! Heavy infantry, hold until they are away!"

So Terce-General dom Braga and his archers and spears ran for the small market bridge near Arlasque Woods, past which Fulvir and Amiel had lodged. Segunth-General dom Vinescu stood with Portescat and his remaining knights. But they could not outrun the palisades. They could only keep them from mowing down the faster and more numerous archers and spears.

"Stand and hold!" she said.

Now something very awful happened, on a day of awful things. As the wheels of a hundred palisades squeaked, and as the goblins barked, and the boars chuffed, the bull-men sold to Ispanthia panicked and broke to run. The general cried "Stop them!" without thinking that she really did not have much that *could* stop them, the archers having fled.

Several knights tried to lay hands on the enormous mixlings or to block them with shields, but these men and dams were broken like dolls. It is possible that the monsters had gotten a whiff of nightmare-cap spore, but, whatever panicked and angered them, two of the taurines became so enraged at General dom Vinescu that they busted through her close-guards and assaulted her. One, though disarmed by a close-guard, managed to grab the general's neck and twist her head almost off before being cut down by her husband. I tell you in honesty, though, that she was one of the lucky ones who took arms in the flowered fields of Onion Market that day.

The entire force broke then, and most were massacred, or taken.

Not everyone in these ranks had bittermead, so much in demand was the flesh-spoiling poison, and though many thought they might escape, few did.

It is a sad fact that while heavily armored knights are harder for the goblins to kill, they are easier for them to take alive, as they must only be exhausted or knocked down. And, unlike in previous wars between humans, knights captured by goblins are not ransomed, no matter how many vineyards, servants, or coffers full of gold await them back home.

It is said Onion Market is now called Butcher's Bank, and that nothing sprouts there but tears.

I have one more thing to tell you of Goltay before we leave it forever.

If you have whiskey or strong brandy somewhere, I would say, drink it now.

This is too much for wine or water.

First though, here is my favorite story from the Likely Tales, the gospel of My Mistress. It is worthy to remember, and it has helped me more than I can say.

42

Now once and long ago, there was a man
who feared to die. This is quite commonplace.
But this man was particular in that
he was a wizard and had thus prolonged
his years to keep him out of any grave,
and unburned on the pyres of the dead.
This Durgash, as they called him, had his home
in northern Kesh where poppies multiply.
And in the town he traveled to betimes,
the essence of the poppy would be smoked
in parlors where its subjects dreamed awake.
To Durgash would the man, Marbaja, cry,
who mongered both the poppy and the pipe,
"Come, magicker, and taste a paradise
no summoner aspires to surpass.
I wonder, is today the hoped-for day
you'll bless yourself to tell Marbaja yes?"
"That day will never come," Durgash would say,
"for you are full the tenth to beckon me
to enter in that door your shadow haunts,
for I have lived two hundred years and five,
preserved by arcane regimens quite strict
whose dictates I must follow to the dot;
I may not taste the poppy, or I rot."
And on he walked, until he passed before
the pleasure house where women and men
are rented for an hour or a night.
To Durgash would the fair Amala cry,
for so was named the mistress of that place,

"Why, Magicker, you walk your ways alone!
Will you not try these stairs, and have a bath?
And after this, some morsel haply choose
between the legs of woman or of man?
All you see is offered for your use.
I wonder, is today the hoped-for day
you bless yourself and tell Amala yes?"
"That day will never come, and nor shall I,"
Durgash would answer her most bawdily,
"for you are full the tenth to beckon me
to enter in that door which sweetly frames
the silhouette you seek to tempt me with,
now I have lived two hundred years and five,
preserved by rites the gods themselves have writ.
Alas, I know that I would surely die
were I to spend upon your lovely thigh."
And on he walked, until a certain day
he passed the House of Ease, where those who wished
to part themselves from life were given rest.
The mistress of that house said, "Magicker,
your step is heavy and your visage drawn,
too long you've kept yourself from death and age,
and now your spirit groans beneath the weight
it's carried for two hundred years and eight.
I can help it lay its burden down.
I wonder, is today the hoped-for day
you'll bless yourself to tell Dal-Gaata yes?"
So arrogant was Durgash that he failed
to mark the name the mistress offered him
and started to reply to her in haste
"That day will . . ." but his tongue seized in his mouth
as if a fist had grabbed it where it wagged
before he could say "never," as he wished.
The Empress of the Night sloughed off her skin

as if it were a robe, although her hair
remained where it had been; and from her back
now spread the mighty wings of black and white
which bear aloft the eagle of the plains
who makes her dinner on the bones of men;
and in her fleshless hand she held a sword
more ebon than the cloth behind the stars
and finer than the line dividing hate
from love, its gentle sibling, and its mate.
"Durgash the magicker, before you say
'never' and condemn your clever mind
forever to the prison of your flesh,
I bid you follow me and so observe
the wonders that I hold within my gift."
So saying, did she grab his fragile wrist
and fly him to the pillars of the sky
to look down on the city's highest roofs,
which not even the emperor had seen.
"Respectfully, dread lady," Durgash said,
"by certain spells I often go aloft
and nap upon the summered backs of clouds.
You may bewitch the minds of artless men
and trick them from their bodies for the gift
of lifting their dull feet above the earth;
but though I thank you for the kindly loan
of your great wings, in candor I must say
I find small wonder in the vaulted sky."
She said, "Your thanklessness can have no peer;
be still you fool, we do but travel here."
And now the sky about them boxed them in
so that they walked within a vault of stone
its rugless floor piled up with coins of gold
and stacks of ivory instead of chairs;
and tigers' skins were hung from every wall

and from a spigot like a dragon's head
did emeralds like fountain-water spill.
"Respectfully, dread lady," Durgash said,
"o'er elements have I such sure command
and have befriended every mineral,
that gold falls willingly into my cup
as rain into a laden aquifer;
I sing such pretty songs to elephants
they gift me both their tusks of ivory.
Though for this reverie I give you thanks
I find small wonder in a treasury."
She said, "Your gratitude is scant, I fear.
Be still, you fool; we do but travel here."
Now with a whinny and a spray of stones,
a knight in armor rare burst through the wall
and no more were they standing in a vault,
but stooping on a furious battlefield;
with arrows was the leaden sky adorned,
and fires burned, and maces sang on shields.
"Respectfully, dread lady," Durgash said,
"I hope you do not seek to give me fright,
so that I might go willing to your arms
if only you will spare my flesh from hurt.
I have such cunning that from these low clouds
I can weave down a coat of mail so stout
that there is not an axe in all of Kesh
can cleave it through to find my vital font.
Before these archers I am just as brave,
and turn their merry-whistling mortal flights
to flocks of tender-hearted garden doves."
And now Dal-Gaata told him with that smile
forever on her lipless grinning face,
"I hold each living heart within my grasp,
my bony fingers telling every beat.

Yours would not skip like dancers' feet unless
you feared your fellow men to die so close,
lest you might share a blade with some of these,
your several bloods commingled on one edge.
But I am not intent to frighten you;
come, see what those who find my gift enjoy."
Now with her gloveless hand she seemed to seize
some fruit from empty air, and with a squeeze
she stopped the warring soldiers all around.
They all stood wooden as a gallery
of dolls held up for childish martial sport.
The din of butchery alike grew still
in such a way that Durgash only heard
the beating of his heart and nothing else.
Now did the wizard spy a soldier lad
unhelmeted and cleaved from crown to ear,
but freshly so, the sword still in the air
amid a spray of garnet stones,
his legs yet in this instant holding him
above the earth he would soon wear for clothes.
"Pray, come," Dal-Gaata said, and now she made
astonished Durgash small enough that he
might follow his divine companion 'neath
the soldier's ghastly wound, into his ear,
which in an instant changed its aspect so
it was an ear no more, instead a hall
that led up to a door they both went through.
This portal opened up onto a view
as beautiful as erst was so obscene;
the lad stood barefoot on a starlit beach,
a woman of great beauty coming forth
to welcome him into her glad embrace.
These lovers kissed without a sprig of shame
and seemed no more aware to be observed

than did the beach itself, or yet the sea.
When Durgash turned his gaping mouth to speak
and ask Dal-Gaata what he witnessed here,
he found her gone, and understood that she
put on her skin again, that it was she
with whom the soldier was entangled there;
and never had the wizard seen a soul
more happy than that boy who lost his life
but found a bliss that, parted thus from time,
expressed itself in fair Dal-Gaata's kiss.
Now Durgash felt a tug upon his sleeve
and turned to see a boy of so few years
they might be counted off on either hand.
Between his tiny fingers did the boy
now pinch from off the strand beneath his feet
one grain of sand, and this he offered up
into the palm of Durgash, who perceived
the riddle of the hourglass laid down;
that while we wear our flesh we are enslaved
to time, and so the running of the sand
first strengthens us, then steals our strength away;
but when we breathe our last the chain is burst,
and we are everything we ever were;
no more imprisoned within ruined flesh,
but all at once a babe, a groom, a bride,
or whenever we lived our finest day;
or even whatsoever we have dreamed
and wished to stay asleep and not dispel
the wonders in the palace of our skull.
So Durgash found himself back in the town
before the House of Ease, as had he stood
before Dal-Gaata stole him far away
but also never moved him half an inch.
The door was closed and locked before his gaze;

he thought to knock, but then he stopped his hand,
turned on his heel and went back to his home
where stood the philters and the magic toys
that kept him counting off so many years
amused by magic wonders but without
the pleasures common folk know every day;
these trappings that had bound him to his bones
he smashed, and burned, and threw them all away.
So Durgash lived another twenty years
of drink and smoke and pleasures of the bed,
and when at last the Lady Most Serene
took in her grasp the soft meat of his heart
and stopped it in her hand so smooth and white
she laid his hourglass upon its side
its final grain of sand now infinite,
and wide enough to hold ten worlds and more,
and there he dwells with her, and should he tire
to be with her he might go off and see
his mother holding him unto her breast,
or go back to a beach where, when he had
no more years than a single hand could count,
he bent down to pinch up a grain of sand
and gifted this to that old man with whom
he shared a name, and also shared a tomb.

43

It was outside the walls of Goltay, in the last hours before we began our long flight north, that I saw my grandfather's shield.

There would soon be another battle, but I tire of telling you about these. We would meet palisades, our birds would scream the biters tame, then leap up on the cars to pick the drivers and crossbowmen and spearmen apart. We would get the leavings of the corvids, and guard their rear, and sometimes we would butcher the boars, for which work I wished we had spears. But these boars of the palisades were lashed to the vehicles they pushed, and so could do us little harm.

I stopped counting those biters I slew by my hand, but I have heard that we thirty-seven who remained, and our sixty birds, killed nearly two hundred fifty of them, and destroyed some fifteen of their wicked chariots.

I do not think there was another force so effective in all the army, pound for pound, but we were few, and fewer every time we fought. By the end of that battle, we were thirty, and our birds were fifty-one. The others started calling me Lady Hate, because of the look on my face and the viciousness of my attacks, though the name did not stay with me because all those who called me this are now dead.

At this time I was new in the mysteries of the Bride—I was still prey to anger, and let it shape me rather than the reverse.

And my anger going into that fight was great, because fury was easier to keep in my hand than sadness. The sadness within me was so black and monstrous that, had I given it any leash, it would have taken my legs from under me. It would have driven me from the world into some dark place, like my mother, though it would be more in my nature to starve than to smother myself with food.

I will tell you the root of this despair, though you may have already guessed at it.

Perhaps an hour before, I saw a group of Holtish knights. These were burly, dirty men and dams with rough manners. They came from the western gate, which was well lit with torches, and where a quarut-general stood, doing her best to sort soldiers into their proper units. When one of the Holters, a bearded, bearish fellow with a taback pipe and a sallet helm, turned to make a joke to an axe-dam behind him, I saw upon his back that so-familiar blush of springwood and wink of polished, sculpted steel.

My heart hammered and tripped.

Amiel.

He had been trying to find me.

My mouth formed *no no no,* though I had no voice to make the words.

"Daguera dom Braga, where are you going?" Nouva called.

"A moment, Lanzamachur!" I said in a weak croak, and I ran up to the Holters; these were part of a long chain of soldiers heading west to help us stand against the palisades, who were said to be making their way through the city and had crossed the Arve over Crownsbridge. We would be part of the same holding action—our job was to give what remained of the army time to quit the city.

I took a breath in hope of finding voice.

"Pray, knight," I said in Holtish to the man who had the shield, "a word."

"It's nae for sale, Spanth," he said. "Ye'll be the third who asked, and it's mine."

From his accent, I could tell that he was a Norholter, not from Holt proper but from one of its conquered holdings.

"May I ask where came you by it?"

"By a pile of dead."

No, no, not him.

"Was there a boy?"

"There were fair many boys."

Not my Chichún.

Please.

"Was there a boy with long hair, and my color? Finely dressed, perhaps in a doublet of gray and silver?"

I saw that this struck him.

And that of course struck me.

I could also see that he struggled with his virtue, for it was in his interest to lie. His virtue lost the fight.

"I have nae seen such a boy. Away with ye."

He started to move on, but I got in front of him.

"Will you swear it, sir knight?" I said.

"What?"

"Will you swear, on your honor, that you did not have this shield from a boy, alive or dead, of eighteen years, with hair and face like mine?"

"Who are ye to demand oaths of me, woman? Are ye callin' me liar?"

"I am Galva dom Braga, daughter of the Duke of Braga. The boy I described to you is my brother, Amiel. The shield on your back is the Mouth of the Storm, and precious to the House of dom Braga, whose honor I am bound to even unto my life. You will see that I cannot see the front of the shield from where I stand, but perhaps the dam behind you will say whether the boss is of a man with curly locks and puffed cheeks blowing, as if at the end of a map. And if the working of that face is so detailed that one can see the lids of his eyes, and his lips, and that he faintly smiles as he blows?"

The dam behind him whistled now.

"Before you speak," I said to him, "please know that I have not called you a liar. It is possible my brother had already lost the shield. It is also possible it was with my other siblings, Sixt-General or Terce-General dom Braga. But in your heart you know my claim to the shield is just. And if you are looking in my eyes with honest sight, you will see that this road we walk splits into two very different paths, and that much rides on the next words said between us."

At that, I raised the mail of my sleeve so the Calar Bajat tattoo was visible. It was only fair for me to do so. This man was not yet my enemy.

At the sight of it, the dam behind him whistled again.

"Stop that, ye fuckin' shrike," he said to her.

"Umbert, ye know what that is? And who she is?" she said.

He sighed a deep sigh and removed the shield from his wide back.

I took off my lanza shield as well, offering this to him. He took it and nodded.

"I saw a lad like ye told," Umbert said. "Nae dressed in a fine doublet. But with a gay pair of orange stockings on him. Cut down by spear and axe. With many others. We killed the biters what done him, if it matters, and dumped the lot in the river. He was not meat for their table."

I nodded.

It mattered.

I said, with what little voice I could muster, "My thanks to you, Sir . . ."

"Umbert of Swatlingmoor."

"Sir Umbert of Swatlingmoor. The House of dom Braga is in your debt. My thanks to you. If you name yourself as he who returned to us the shield of Corlu dom Braga, my brother Pol or my father Roderigu will give you . . . whatever you ask. I will not insult you by offering the humble coin in my purse, though I would gladly give it if you have need of it."

"Daguera dom Braga! Now!" Nouva called.

"Lass," he said, "if this day goes as I think, we'll nae be needin' coins but for our eyes."

I nodded at him, and took his great hand in mine.

I turned from him before he could see my tears.

In that moment I told myself the lie that it was not Amiel he saw, with his stockings from Montabrecola. And his dark hair just of my color. Lying slain near this shield. Now feeding river-fish in the Arve, whose hearts are warmer than those of Our Foe.

I would like to tell you that I found the body of my little brother.

That I kissed his cool cheek to set him on his path.

That I took a lock of his hair, and that I keep it in my pouch.

But such goodbyes are rare in calamities.

I see the generosity of the gods to give me word from this man, and I am thankful. Many who were lost in that city simply disappeared, and so it might have been with Amiel. Of course, Sir Umbert could have seen a different body. But even if he did, I know that Amiel was lost at Goltay. I could feel his absence in the world. A gentle boy who should have gone to Seveda in a scholar's cap and robes was stabbed or poisoned or cut down in a foreign city, surrounded by strangers and monsters, and all because he was trying to give our grandfather's shield into my hand.

My Chickpea.

I had no joy of the shield on my back that day.

If Migaéd had given me the Mouth of the Storm, as Father commanded, or if I had challenged him for it, or if Pol as terce-general had ordered it from his care to mine that evening, Chichún would not have felt he had to steal it. He would have been with the wizard, who would have kept him safe when the hammer fell.

I have no words to describe these seas of rage and grief and make myself understood, except by those unlucky enough to have survived one without whom the world loses color.

The only things I could do to ease the pain of it were to study the ways of the Bride.

And to drink.

And to kill.

I did all of those things.

I do them still.

3

The Butchered Man

44

The Pragmatist stood before us on flat ground near standing stones, and these were more elegant than those of the tribes. These were of the sort some said elves had left. I used to think those who spoke of elves were not serious people, but what would those who raised these stones think if I described goblins? Maybe elves did leave these oddly curved pillars that drew the eye with their shape, and with their placement. Maybe we warred with elves and killed them all, and if so, it could be said that goblins serve us as we deserve.

As we gathered to hear our prima-general, it seemed clear to all the survivors of Goltay that goblins would prevail in our great struggle.

I was numb.

I looked to the Bride for comfort, but found little.

She had gentled my fear of death as an individual, but against the thought that all kynd might perish, she seemed to me that day no more than a toy. What is so special about a skeletal goddess when no flesh remains on any bone? What power does a mere animal's skeleton hold? We dread human bones as reminders of our mortality, but to goblins, our bones are merely what must be cleaned up after a meal, of no greater import to them than the ribs of beef cows to us.

Our commander spoke.

"Soldiers of Ispanthia, the Far Banners, and Gallardia," she said, letting her voice echo. Of the Ispanthians and Far Banners, it could be said the two together still made something like an army. For her to speak of Gallardia was a courtesy—so few remained, and they were in such low morale since the fall of Goltay and the murder of their king, that they were little more than armed refugees. Perhaps that was true of all of us, but it was easier to pity the Gallards than ourselves.

She continued.

"You have borne a terrible burden, and paid a high price for the errors of your commanders. We are not yet done paying. We are pursued by a great host of Our Foe, of such size that we must not stand against them on open ground. We make north, for the chain of fortresses called the Hounds of Mour, which are stood on such rocky ground that they may not be dug under. What we will do from there is not yet your concern. But let your hearts hope—we have a plan, and though it will cost us, I believe it will cost us less than any other. I have never been one to make speeches that stir the blood. I am a bringer of fact and truth, even when these are ugly. But by facing ugly truths, we limit their power to harm us. You do not need me to tell you the blow we suffered at Goltay was worse even than the defeat at Orfay. You do not need me to tell you the importance of keeping the goblin armies from crossing the Blue Mountains into Ispanthia before the snows come. What you need to hear from me is that I have a plan, and that is what I have come here to tell you. I need each and every one of you to trust in that plan, and to act for the good of this army, which is the good of both Gallardia and the Crownlands. I will be asking hard things from you. I know you will deliver them. Although I may not speak of this in detail, a new wave of soldiers is being readied in Ispanthia, and in the spring, these soldiers will carry the fight to our enemy in ways that will astonish you. I want you to live to see that. I cannot save all of you, but I can save enough of you to matter. What happens in the next weeks will matter. You will write the history of humankind with your blood and your swords, and if each of you is ready to die today, you will make it so that most of you, and those depending on you back home, may live tomorrow. It is obvious to the simplest of you that staying in Goltay was a mistake. This mistake allowed our enemy to encircle us, and even to rise up at us from below. I was given an express command to hold the city. I did not agree with that command, but I carried it out, as was my duty. But I now recognize a higher duty. I promise you here today that, until I get us out of the teeth of our pursuers, I will obey no order that does not correspond with the best interests of this bloodied but unbroken army. A beast is never so dangerous as when it is injured, and cornered. We will show the biters the truth of this, to their great misfortune.

"To that end, I have promoted Terce-General Pol dom Braga to the position of segunth-general. He is an able tactician, a courageous and skilled fighter, and I know he is the second-in-command this army needs. A full list of field promotions will be posted by the mess tents. I have marched you hard and will continue to do so. But your hard marching has bought you a night of rest. Honor your dead. Fill your bellies. Tomorrow we run with long legs."

Pol and I met late that night, at his tent, a far humbler dwelling than he was used to.

On the way in, I heard someone say, "Good evening, duke's daughter."

I looked and saw the mighty and beautiful Carlota from Veista Pulcanta standing guard in her armor. I was so glad to see someone I had felt a spark of warmth for living that I embraced her hard. She returned it, the strength in her arm almost painful.

"Carlota, you . . . It is good to see you," I stammered.

She smiled.

"And you. It is good to see you, and better that you remembered my name."

"Neither your name nor your face is for forgetting."

I patted her arm as I passed her, and smiled an awkward smile.

I wished to say more, but it was not the time.

Pol dismissed his servants, and Carlota, and I told him of Amiel.

He embraced me tightly, and for a very long time. I could feel that his body wanted to sob, but he could not. Instead, he blew hard out of both nostrils several times in a way that reminded me of a horse. Then he ended our embrace and went to a chest, from which he pulled out a bottle half-full of brandy.

"You would be ashamed of what I had to pay for this," he said, falsely rallying, "but we find ourselves in a sellers' market." He opened it. Even on this sad and dire night, the sound of a bottle uncorking cheered me. We drank gratefully, speaking of Amiel. I had more recent stories of him, being closer in age, but he told me about things I was too young to recall.

"I taught you both to swim, you know," he said. "Separately, when each of you was three."

"What?"

"Yes, summers, when I visited from school."

"I thought Nunu taught me."

"She was there, but she could only wade, and that no farther than her knees. Holters are so proud of their ships they account it cowardice to learn swimming. You loved it. But Chichún, he cried most of the time. Pulled my hair like a bastard that first lesson, yelled at me for backing up when I told him to swim to me."

"Were you backing up?"

"Of course! How else to push you?"

"Start further off! No, in seriousness, that was you? I have a memory of Nunu deceiving me by backing up."

"She was further in, by shore, gesturing. But it was me you swam to. Servants get blamed for everything."

"Yes," I said, turning sad. I did remember something about Pol being at those swimming lessons. Maybe Migaéd as well, but I did not ask about him. I did not want to see him, even in my mind, or hear his voice, even in memory. *Your brother*, he had said, of Amiel. Such things cannot be unsaid. And then there was his murder of Bellu, for which I hated him so much I was afraid of the ideas that came to me. I resented that he had dared to enter my thoughts, and I shut my eyes very hard for a moment to drive him out. A tear leaked out and I thumbed it away before it could bring others.

Pol put his hand on my shoulder, thinking I mourned Amiel, and now I felt ashamed that my anger was closer than my grief.

"I am glad you have the shield," he said, pointing at it with his chin. "It suits you. Grandfather was about your height, built small for those well-fed days." It was an acknowledged fact in Ispanthia that babies had gotten smaller, and that kynd grew shorter since the wars started. "I wonder if you could wear his armor. It was too small for Father."

"I like the armor I have," I said.

"It is a handsome brigandine," he agreed, leaning closer to look at it. "Needs repairing, as it should on a soldier. White with the salt of sweat from your hard marching. I am very proud of you, you know. The actions with the birds have been inspiring. Your lanzamachur is like to be promoted. Would you like command of the lanza?"

"Gods no. One called Inocenta is next in line."

"I cannot say I blame you. I never wanted . . . *this*," he said, indicating himself, "and certainly not in this way." It was then that he told me of his affair with Samera dom Vinescu, and how he had just learned of her liaisons with the rash, disobedient Portescat.

"And her husband, poor bastard, I do not think he ever knew about any of it."

"Good thing. He was known at my academy. With respect, I fear I would be mourning two brothers now had he learned of your indiscretion."

"Very likely, yes. I have a strong sword arm, but I have always been more beater than dancer. You who earned the Calar Bajat tattoo could always best me. No, the whole affair with Samera was stupid, but I felt powerless against it. The pull of it was like a great tide. If her face was near mine, our mouths just came together. Perhaps I say too much to you, the years between us are many and I suppose I seem foolish to take on so."

"No, brother. I am beginning to understand something of love. It is . . . strong. And it can be painful, even when fulfilled. I cannot call you foolish for heeding its commands. Besides, I have always wished to know you better."

"You are no half sister to me, Galvicha," he said, his eyes fixed on mine so I knew he spoke in earnest.

"Nor you half a brother, Pol," I said, though quietly. I am unused to such declarations, even when they need to be made.

But now he turned his speech back to his heart's greatest mistress.

"You know, you really would have liked her. Samera, I mean. She was a magnificent woman, but for the falseness."

"To me that sounds like 'It was a fine house, except that it collapsed.'"

He laughed bitterly at that.

"No, Galvicha, you could never abide a liar. You take it personally."

"It is personal, to abuse someone's ear with a lie."

"There is where we disagree," he said. "Dishonesty is rarely personal. Liars by habit lie to everyone, but they get reputations quickly. One can see them coming. Liars by necessity lie when circumstances warrant, but, again, this is about context. As admirable as your honesty may be, thinking someone else owes you theirs is a bad habit. One that leads to disappointment."

"I hear your words and understand their wisdom, but still I hate a liar. Please never deceive me, brother."

He raised his glass to me in lieu of making promises, which was, I suppose, a very honest thing to do.

We decided he would be the one to write to Father about Amiel. It would be easy to think a hard man like the duke would scorn a weak boychild, that a martial man who had loved falcons and the open sky would think little of a son who grew pale over books, but this was not true.

Here was a letter Father wrote to him:

Chichún,

It is with great pride that I send you what I think may be your first letter received at a military posting. I have made sure to put a smudge of ash from the last of the ylang-ylang incense at the bottom of the page, so you may be reminded of this house in summer. I should imagine your nose will be grateful for something besides beer, sword oil, leather, the sweat of soldiers, and whatever it is that Molrovan magickers smell like.

One shudders to imagine it.

I have arranged to have you posted with Fulvir not only so you will have some access to books—he has assured me he will make parts of his infamous library available to you—but so that you may forge some ties of friendship with him, if such is possible. While many men of the sword—as I accounted myself before my injury made me a man not of one sword but of two canes—disdain the wizards among us as mere illusionists, they do so at their peril. I have seen magickers of consequence at their work, and they are indeed fearsome. In battle, I should rather one magus of Fulvir's power by my side than a hundred armored horse. And in other affairs, they prove themselves useful in subtle ways that can assure success in business or protect against the machinations of those who work against you politically. I daresay this allegiance I prod you toward is more for your sake than mine, for I have not so many years left, and yet such are the most powerful mages' arts that even though you are just now ten and eight, you are like to know him all your life.

Please me in this and I shall indulge your wish to study poetic arts, though I believe this will result only in lengthening *your letters, and your hair, if either may be made longer.*

In seriousness, keep yourself as safe as you may in such a place.

Do not seek to impress hard men with false martiality, for they know their own. Let soldiers scorn or admire you for what you are in truth.

Do not be coaxed into rudeness when in the company of the rude. It is better to be thought dull by the vulgar than to be thought vulgar by those of consequence.

Observe the people local to a region and learn from them. Avoid the places they avoid, and endeavor to take your food and drink where they do.

When first you see grave injuries or death, you may cast up your bread and meat. This is normal, and no sign of weakness. Expect it and recover as quickly as you can. Do not be seen to linger in indignity.

Do not indulge in duels, these are for idiots; yet suffer neither yourself nor our name to be insulted. If any seeks to dishonor you, tell him to repeat what he has said. If he persists in trying to humiliate you before others, bid him a good evening and leave, saying no more to him. Then have him beaten if he is smart enough to take a lesson, or killed if he is not.

Do not gamble.

Drink the grape and barley in moderation. If you cannot stop with your third cup, for many cannot, and your eldest brother is one of these, drink only small beer, and water your wine. A drunkard wants nothing but to fight or copulate, and has no talent for either. Drunkards give away too much in blood, treasure, and especially in words. Blood might be replenished, treasure rewon. Words can never be recalled.

You are of an age to think of carnal matters. Give yourself to this in moderation, and beware any woman or girl who attaches herself too quickly to you. Either she is a fool or seeks to make one out of you, or wants money. It is no crime to spend money in this arena, but be wise about it. A whore is far cheaper than a lover in poverty, and a lover in poverty far cheaper than one from a noble house, for these are always in debt. For pleasure, find a merchant girl, one of middling wealth—she will appreciate your gifts, but will also be too proud to be kept. If your nature draws you to men or fellow boys, indulge this discreetly, but learn to take some pleasure from women, if you can, for one day you shall marry one of these and create dom Bragas.

Beyond that, your business is your own.

Come home alive to us.

Your presence here is missed.

I would be the one to find the wizard and ask for Amiel's possessions, if any were saved. Of course they were, which is how I am able to show you these words. As you will guess, that of Fulvir outliving Amiel is hard to bear. Such is the Braga curse, to be right, but in all the wrong ways. Before the Stumbles, Father once boasted that soon no one in Ispanthia would own more horses than he.

It will not surprise you to learn that it would be some time before I saw Fulvir again after my meeting with Pol.

We were running for our lives.

45

The next week was hard.

We were starving, and we had no time to forage.

Our rear was harassed by raiders with war boars.

Water was not a problem—it rained more days than not. Some said the widowed Queen of Gallardia had done this, for she was rumored to be with the army, and her magic was strongest in the element of water.

But I had not seen her.

Some said Fulvir had brought the rain, which might have been an easy matter for one who had dragged a summer hurricane into Espalle, though I did not see him either.

Also, sometimes it just rains.

The mud was the sort that will pull a loose boot off or spill you on your backside, but it slowed the goblins more than us, and bogged their chariots down so that they barely got them out of Goltay.

Sickness visited us again, though this was a cough, not the hell of squatting that struck us near Carrasque. It mostly took the older ones, and I feared for a new friend I had made.

Simón was an old man and a Petoneru, serving with Ispanthian medium infantry, veterans of ordinary birth who fought with spear, shield, and arming sword, and wore vests of scale armor in steel or leather. His shield was painted with a beautiful scene of a naked goddess in water, though this had been beaten to hell in the fight in Goltay and needed repainting. His helmet was a conical cap of boiled leather, though this was harder than one would think, and not so hot as steel. On this he had painted a big eye for good luck. Simón had seven fingers left, though these were strong as claws. He had only started beating me thumb-wrestling when we began to bet. He and I shared many campfires, and though the booze had run out, we spoke longingly of the wine we did not have, and argued the merits of Petonese wine and Bragaene. Petón and Braga are neighboring provinces, his on the coast. Petón is known for its poetry, and for handsome men who tend to be rakes, but also for its humor, which can be quite biting. It is said that if a man says he slept with your mother, you should fight him, unless he is a Petoneru, in which case he is either trying to make you laugh or he is merely stating a fact.

"Your wine of Braga is not bad," he would say, in that croaking, slow way of old men who have few words left to utter and wish to make a gift of each one. I would wait, smiling a little, because I knew he had loaded the crossbow, and would now loose. "Not bad, I say, if you need something to stand a candle up in. It is not bad if you wish to stain a white shirt the color of grease. It is a greasy wine, I say, wrung from the greasy beards of your women. The men's beards are too thick for wringing, they are for hurting hands. They are for scrubbing barnacles off ships."

"What!" I would say. "Your mouth is full of lies. It is a pot for night soil. And I know this from both your breath and your vulgarities."

"Yes!" he would say. "I have filled my mouth with shit." I would wait, trying to make my smile a frown. "Because shit is the only flavor that will cleanse it of the Bragaene wine I just drank. But let us have another, since night soil is drunk for pleasure, not intoxication."

"You old goat," I would say, and pour and pass him a pretend cup of wine, which he would pretend to drink. "Now let us speak of the wine of Petón," I would say. He would nod graciously, and stroke his wiry, white beard, his merry blue eyes twinkling.

"The wine of Petón is like the beards of Petón. Barely there. If our men of Braga grow thick beards and our vintners make thick wine, this is better than the boyish nothing on the chins of you fainting . . ." and here I might grasp for a word. Always gallant Simón would say, "What? What are we in Petón? Don't stop now, my heavy-eyebrowed boy of Braga, you were doing so well I thought your voice might at last be about to crack and your stones drop."

Here I would laugh, "You are fuckers. *Jilnaedu* fuckers with wine that casts no shadow."

"Go on, I will correct you when you are wrong. Speak more of the wine of Petón."

"I will, whenever you make some. This that you put in barrels and sell to fools is only a rumor of wine. A neighbor of wine. It is water that has stood so near Bragasc that it has grown pretentious. I could drink two helmets full of Petonasc without drunkenness, and the piss I made after would not be wet."

"Ahhhh," he would sigh, as if he had just settled into a hot tub. "Now here is good vintage."

He was not always for japes.

He would also speak to me in seriousness.

"This is my third war," he said to me once.

I thought he was about to yank my trouser legs some more, so I said, "Well, I assumed you were in the Threshers' because we lost."

"It was a draw."

"A draw? How, when they occupied a quarter of Gallardia?"

"Not the best quarter. Just the bits by the coast. Also, we kept them the fuck out of Ispanthia, did not we?"

"I concede the point. But how did you manage not to scuttle our victory in the Knights' War?"

"I stayed out of the way."

"Very wise."

"I kept my fingers until the second war."

I waited, the corners of my lips coming up. He squinted at me.

"What?" he said. "You think I am going to say something funny, do you, you long-faced cow? I am trying to tell you the hilarious joke of having my fucking fingers bitten off."

I cleared my throat.

"Go on."

"Thank you. As I said, I had all my fingers between the first two wars, and I moved to Mouray, where all serious painters go. I was not able to make much living at it, but I did not starve quite to death, and I slept with a lot of women. Gallardian city women like artists in the way that they like cats. As long as we shit where we are told and do not fight with the other cats, we get petted. If we do not wake them up too much in the night, we can stay 'til morning. They even feed us if we *rao* plaintively enough and let them feel our ribs and cluck. But then of course the Threshers' War came, and the long party was over. I was no longer a young man. Nor was I ever a rich man. But the king of Ispanthia called me home, and that war was not for joking. So many of us had been mustered, the forges could not keep up with the need for arms. Luckily, I kept the sword I had, still have it. Most of those in the ranks with me had flails, *wooden* fucking flails. This shitfuckery we just suffered in Goltay was the biggest bloodbath I have seen, and right on the heels of Orfay. But eleven years ago? We were having one of those a week, and not just us. Goltay and Orfay may turn out to be the worst, but what about Tremay? Cortain? Monseverne? Porlasque? One of their armies got as far as Unther before the snows chased them back south. There were massacres in Bittburk, Heimsvaller, Kulne. I wager you never heard of any of those, because they were coming too fast to write down. And most of the fuckers who knew how to write came out of their castles and died first. Turns out we were not such mighty things without horses under us. Do you know, we actually outnumbered them in most of those battles we lost? They got so good at killing us that after just a year we had nothing to throw at them but bodies. We learned, though. By the time that one ended, half the soldiers were women, but those of us that lived knew a few things about fighting them on foot. Making shield walls, marching in good formations. Everyone built forges, whole forests were cut to make charcoal, so there was more armor. The Practice Laws were in place, so the boys and girls came to the army already knowing how to use a bow, lock up shields, knew handcanting and drumtalk and horntalk. We managed to make our remaining numbers matter, to use our size against them. We killed enough of them toward the end they sued for peace. We were too depleted not to give it to them. But they only gave us five years, did not they? And here we are again. They breed faster. Their hivelings are ready to fight in ten years, not fifteen. I tell you in seriousness, if some of us do not stay home and fuck, they will breed us right out of Manreach one day."

"Seems like they are well on their way."

"Aye. But we are not in the worming vaults yet. I think we will get one more truce out of them. But after that? Gods help us. I like your birds. First thing I have seen that gives me hope. If old Kalith hatches up a fuck-pile of those monsters and sends them over, I might even forgive him for being a usurping cunt."

"Keep your voice down!" I hissed at him through a smile, astonished at his cheek.

"Yes, yes, I will keep my voice down," he said in that freighted way. He made me wait five heartbeats for it, during which I tried not to smile. "Otherwise they might send me to Gallardia to fight goblins and starve in the mud with only Sornian finger-fuckers for company."

I laughed as hard as I had since Bellu and Amiel.

I hugged him to me then, fiercely.

It cannot be stated enough how emotional one can become to make a friend in war. I loved that old man. I only told you about him to let you know that, as bad as it was, there were still moments I hold dear. This is part of the Bride's gift. She tells you the hard truth that she will not spare you, makes you look at it until it isn't fearful, and until you learn to value the treasury of small things she gifts you with each day. This was the riddle of the treasury in the gospel I shared with you.

I tell you about Simón also because he lived.

I have had to tell you so much of death, I wanted to gift you the knowledge of someone I loved who is still on this side with us.

I loved him, though I only knew him for weeks.

I had a letter from him after the war, with a painting of birds.

Inocenta and I still shared a tent, though we were not intimate in the same ways we had been. We remained very close, though, and I will always admire the grace she showed in loosening her grasp on one she so loved. We held each other when it was less hot, but there was no more love-play. Not that there could have been in that crowded space—there were not enough tents, and Alisenne had moved in with us. Even packed in as we were, we were grateful not to be among those who made do with a bedroll or blanket or nothing at all in a field or ditch. There were many of these.

One small kindness was that we slept hard, even in the warmth. Even with the sound of coughing and rain, and the smell of our boots at the entrance, boots we had scraped as much mud as possible from before crawling in.

It was not only the goblins and their palisades that struggled in the summer rains. We lost many carts in the mud, which worsened our shortage of food, and slowed our lines. The engineers became the most valuable part of the army. They freed what carts they could, repairing wheels and axles. At a place where the river Arve was fast and swollen from rain, these engineers strengthened one weak bridge, then, after the long crossing, they pulled it down behind us. I looked among these carpenters and metalworkers for Larmette, Sambard's sister, who had made dinner for us so long ago in the clever tree house she had built. I had not seen her or the boy since Espalle, and I feared for them. They had survived goblins once before, though. Maybe the biters had sent all the force they had to crush us at Goltay and could not double back to Espalle.

"Is it wrong, in the Bride's eyes, to wish for one to be spared?" I said as we marched one day.

"She understands love," Inocenta said, in a freighted way.

She thought I meant the queen.

"I was thinking of the children who fed us in their tree house long ago."

"Was it so long ago?"

"Not on a calendar, perhaps, but yes. These days are like weeks."

"Aye, they are. And here is evidence of time being nonsense, which is at the heart of our creed."

"Yes," I said, scratching my fingernails on understanding.

Now Dalgatha bickered with Gannet, and I had to see to her.

The birds were hungry, too.

There would be consequences.

But first, there was the lottery of the Butchered Man.

We came to a marsh through which a road raised by the old empire was the only path. We could not destroy this path behind us, as we could a smaller wooden bridge, but it was a choke point, the first of several we would encounter, and this was where we learned of the strategy the Pragmatist called the Butchered Man, after an old Ispanthian fable.

In this fable, a man and his family are riding in a cart, pursued by wolves. There is the father, the mother, and three children, one almost a man, one in the middle, and one a babe. The wolves are too fast to be outrun by the horse, burdened with the cart, and they are too many to fight, as the kynd have neither bow nor spear, nor any sword. The wife says, "Husband, let the children take the horse. The oldest will watch these two when we are gone, and raise them in our memory."

The father says, "You are too much to lose, but I have no need of this ornament."

So saying, he cuts his hand off, and casts it to the wolves, who stop to fight over it.

But a hand is not much, and soon the wolves catch up with the cart again.

The middle child, who is overcome with fright, says, "Father, cast the babe behind us! You can make another, and this one is too young to know her peril."

"She is too much to lose," the father says, "but what is a stem without its flower?"

So saying, he cuts his arm off, and throws this to the wolves, who fight over it, even longer, but then they come again.

The eldest son says, "Father, you murder yourself. Give me that knife and I will fight them, and give them good account while you escape."

"You are too much to lose," the father says, "but with a son so brave, I fear not to use a crutch."

And there goes his foot.

And then his leg.

His other foot and leg.

And just before he dies for want of blood, the gods are moved by his sacrifices, and make him whole again. The wolves they turn into sheep, and the family take them home, and never want again.

So now each unit of the army was assigned a body part. Ten fingers, ten toes, two hands, two feet, two arms, two calves, two thighs. No one was excepted, not even the prima-general herself, who was grouped in with others and became the right arm. Our lanza was assigned to a group of our engineers, Istrean crossbow-men, and Ispanthian irregulars, which just meant odds and ends that did not fit neatly into other units. These were mostly medium infantry, and contained Simón's lanza, about which I was glad. He would be a good man to die with. We had the honor of being the right second toe.

These parts were written on wooden tokens, and, in the near presence of the concerned commanders, and in sight of much of the army, Pol mixed these up and blindly drew. He handed this to the prima-general.

We all leaned forward.

You could have heard a mouse crawl on soft cheese.

"Left ring finger," she said.

Some gasped, one sobbed.

The terce-general who had replaced Pol stepped up, accepted the lot, then saluted, for she was assigned to command and die with this patched-together battalion.

She said, "Give me that knife and I will fight them, and give them good account while you escape."

This reference to the fable earned a cheer, and I saw few dry eyes around me.

And so we cut from the body of our fleeing army the left ring finger, which included Brayçish greatbows, Untherian pillow knights, and four hundred Ispanthian sword and shield, several of whom had studied at my school. I embraced these, and saluted them, and they saluted back. One had been trembling so hard she made little hitching noises in her throat. But still she did as she was told.

Enough provisions were left with these fierce souls that they might wait the goblins with strength in their arms. Some musicians had been arranged in every group, and these had a group of horns, including a sackbut, and a drummer, who played a sad but defiant martial song. It was an Unthern song, and I did not know the words, but the Unthern both in the left ring finger and the rest of the army did, and they all sang. These were mostly women, and the song was sweet and high and haunting, especially as the larger group of voices drew away from the smaller.

Inocenta was crying as she said, "The Pragmatist is not stingy. She gives of our best. The Bride will favor us for this gift."

Her eyes were bright and mad as she said it, but even as I thought that, I wondered what my eyes looked like.

You will be wondering what became of Migaéd.

One night, just after we made camp following a twenty-mile march, I wandered on my exhausted legs and blistered feet, looking for the latrine ditch.

I went the wrong way, but soon after I was given proper directions, I saw my eldest brother.

He and his useless fellow officers, and his misused line soldiers, were sitting around a large fire, looking dour for want of wine, and food, and women to make toys of. I noted that they tended the fire themselves, a task that should have fallen to Pedru, and I knew that the clever boy with the many pouches had been lost in Goltay, with so many others. This struck a pang in me, but I had no time to savor it.

Migaéd met my eyes, and I met his.

His face seemed to look several ways at once, now furious, now regretful, now bewildered at how we came to this place. If he had, in that moment, and in sober penitence, said, 'Come and sit by our fire, Galvicha,' I might have. Warily, and without the possibility of restoring fraternal warmth. But I might have made a kind of peace with him. This is not what happened. He knew that I had not truly wronged him by taking the shield; it was mine by right, as Father had commanded it.

He knew it was an obscenity for him to kill Bellu.

He knew he had wronged me, so he redoubled his anger at me, because this is easier for men of his stature than to admit fault or to try to make amends.

No one is so furious as a small man caught in a misdeed.

Still looking at me, hatefully now, he dug something from behind his teeth and threw it in the fire. It might have been one of his teeth, I do not know. That sounds like something from a dream, but this march had the strange feel of a nightmare, where things are too big, or too small, or too vivid. And we were all so tired. I might think my mind had invented my friend Simón to keep me from going mad, had I not received the letter from him.

So I did not know if Migaéd was losing teeth.

But I hoped so.

Especially when he handcanted these words at me.

You.

Are.

Not.

My.

Sister.

You.

Bitch.

I did not respond.

I turned from him quickly. I did not want him to see my eyes, which teared.

I am surprised at how much that had hurt me, even now.

But it did. It felt as if my guts had caught on a nail and had unspooled with every step I took away from him.

It was the next day that our birds revolted.

46

We marched by the provisions wagons to receive our rations and, as usual, several of the dams stayed near the birds at what we thought was a safe distance. The corvids are very smart, as you know, and I think it was the sight of how little we were carrying back to them that sparked the catastrophe.

It was not all of the birds, thank the gods, and Dalgatha was not one of them.

But two of them started it, crying *Food, food* and *food now FOOD NOW NOW.*

A third rasped *kynd bad.*

Most of the birds said *NO.*

One said *goblin bad.*

I had never seen this before, but they were having a fucked-serious debate.

And they were getting hot about it.

Those of us who had been in line for rations now went back and helped try to calm them down, but now fully six of them were facing about fifteen, the rest still deciding whether to pick a side. The dams trying to hold the rebels were tossed about, and one was nipped hard enough to draw blood, though the bird could have taken that arm off had it wanted. The other soldiers watching this will not have recognized this chaos as restraint, though I knew that it was, for the moment. I saw Simón watching the fight worsen, coming closer to see how he might help, the rest of his lanza following him. They were forming a human wall of sorts to help contain the event. This was a useful thing to do.

The birds started to peck at each other now, feathers flying, though they had not yet worked themselves up to killing.

I ran to Dalgatha, who was standing with the largest group of birds, who were agitated but impartial. The noise of this, as you imagine, was not for forgetting.

Now two of those *chodadu* chainsdams came up, meaning to restore order.

At the sight of these big dams, wearing the armor and surcoats of those who had killed my Bellu, three more corvids joined the uprising and stood with the *upstarts*. I use this word intentionally, so you will know how much these corvids were done with us. But the rest were no less passionate that the upstarts should get back in line.

Dalgatha moved to join the rebels, but I grabbed her full around the beak, making soothing sounds, and soon she calmed, allowed me to take her to the ground. Others were doing the same, but some still had two birds, and these had difficulty. In the end, the chainsdams were not attacked, but three of the upstarts escaped, and made for the quartermaster's wagons.

With the great screams they had only used on goblins, they came at those men and dams guarding the food, and I saw one piss himself. One ran. We weren't much better than biters when that scream was directed at us. Three, by the way, is the fewest birds I have ever seen use birdscream. It is a group behavior. They are a very social animal.

These three overleapt the guards, and started gorging themselves on the scant rations remaining—tough root vegetables, peas, some very dry sausages.

Archers formed up, a lot of archers.

Black-tongued Galts with medium bows.

"NO!" some of my lanza shouted, but what choice was there?

The corvids were so mad with hunger they did not shiver their wings, and soon they had been badly stuck through, mostly in the head and beak, as it was clear their trunks were protected by steel.

They cried out in pain, falling from the cart, and thrashed in the mud, using their claws trying to get the arrows out of their beaks and heads. Now knights with poleaxes came up and finished them.

Among the main body of corvids, things were no better.

One of Simón's lanza had been pecked, hard, so her kettle helm was staved in; she staggered with her crushed skull, looking for a place to lie down and die.

She found it.

Those birds who loved their masters were tearing apart those who wished to kill us.

The one who pecked the dam was killed first, her wings torn off by Gannet and Boxer.

The other three were next.

One of the loyal birds was so badly injured Nouva gave him over to the sword.

I just held Dalgatha's beak in a tight hold, using the weight of my body to anchor her. She struggled a few times, but finally lay still and moaned.

"Shhhhh, 'Gatha. 'Gatha's a good girl."

I remember seeing Simón's face, the tears wetting his cheeks.

I remembered what he said.

These birds were his one great hope.

He was watching the death sentence of humanity.

At that moment, I agreed with him.

I remembered I had said to Dalgatha that kynd were bad.

I hoped she had not spread that heresy to them, or this would be on my account.

Or maybe they were just mad with hunger.

Or maybe we were just all fucked and the gods were done with us.

Whatever the reason, the result was consequential.

Nouva was summoned to the Pragmatist's tent.

She reported her words back to us verbatim.

My first instinct of course is to put such volatile beasts to the sword. However, I am sharply aware that these corvids have proven the most effective remedy yet against Our Friends, and I am loath to discard them. And yet, discipline is the most important thing in this army, and without it we are all lost. I cannot be fully clement in what was effectively a food riot, or soon we will see the same behavior in our own ranks. I am aware that our shortage of food provoked these creatures, and that our retreat has meant they may not be properly contained. Ultimately, however, the fault for not controlling these creatures must lie with you. As such, the offending animals having been dispatched, there will be no further cost imposed solely on them. Rather, your lanza will now be attached not only to your battalion of the right second toe, but also to Sixt-General dom Braga's of the left foot, and to mine of the right arm—selfishly, I should like the chance to see these creatures in action personally before I die. Also, I have decided a promotion is in order for your earlier successes. Congratulations, Campamachur—you have risen. Also, the legitimate need of these birds to be better fed has been ably demonstrated, and their rations will be quietly trebled.

That is all.

After Nouva recounted this decree to us, someone's stomach growled loudly, and with the timing of a master comedian.

There was nothing to do but laugh.

Three more battalions were sacrificed over the next weeks. One fought and died in a pass through rocky hills and thorn scrub that was made by the gods for ambush. One in the town of Trochette, which was blessed with a stone bridge over the Arve. And one again at a bridgeless bend in the same river, where our scouts indicated there was only one place for many miles shallow enough to ford.

The army learned to hate rivers.

You will be thinking that with Pol in one battalion, Migaéd in another, and me in seemingly all of them, there was little chance the dom Braga family would escape the lottery.

You would be correct.

There was some good fortune first.

As we drew north, we were ever farther from the areas the biters had ravaged. This meant more people still occupying their farms.

Which meant more food.

Though it also meant sorrow, as we had the sad task of telling villagers they should evacuate, as a host of goblins was only days behind us.

One walled town, Verday, begged us to make a stand in their city, bragging of the wide walls, the great round turrets and hoardings, and the city's wide moat. The Pragmatist told the mayor, after we were all billeted around town for one night off the ground, "I am sorry, you Verdayn are kind, and your beds are quite soft. Unfortunately, so is your soil, and Our Foe will dig under these walls faster than terriers under a fence."

We then took as much of their food as we could carry, every animal that could be herded away, and every man or dam who could cook, tend a wound, sew cloth, or, and these were rare, use a weapon.

A small part of the town elected to follow behind us, though they were warned not to expect help if they could not keep up.

Most of them could not keep up, though they had not been under Hordelaw and had not suffered the cut. We were just marching hard, and most kynd are not built for this.

But the Pragmatist did not forbid them, because she knew that, while feeding the goblins would strengthen them, it would also slow them down.

We came to the great bridge known as Li Cornēct d'Haros, or the Horn of Haros, toward the end of our march for the rocky fortress of Arvise, the first of the Hounds. We had reached a higher altitude, and as we were at the end of the month of Ashers, the air had become lukewarm during the day and cool at night. The air was thin up here, as well, and this pushed already exhausted men and dams to their limits.

Deaths from exertion were not unheard of.

We slowed.

The goblins did not.

We could see the wink of weak sunlight on their weapons and armor in the rocky hills behind us.

Our scouts guessed their number at one hundred twenty thousand.

The Pragmatist announced that though we were within a few days' march of Arvise, the proximity of Our Foe required one last lottery.

The groan that rose up was for breaking hearts.

I knew our lanza would be called this time.

Life resolves in poetic ways more often than not.

When people tell us of these things, we doubt because they seem so unlikely, and also too neat somehow.

And yet, think back on your own life.

Has it truly been random?

I cannot speak for you, but mine has not.

I mouthed the words with the Pragmatist even as she read the token.

"Left foot."

I was to fight and die with my beloved lanza, my Dalgatha, two hundred elite Galtish Coldfoot spearmen, three hundred Ispanthian heavy infantry, and two hundred archers, Wostran light archers, a few drummers, a cornemuse player, three cooks, twenty Ispanthian badgers, and, of course, the soldiers—and those wearing the kit of soldiers—under command of my half brother, Sixt-General Migaéd dom Braga.

47

What I will tell you now is the version of events my family tells to this day. I am forbidden by my father to contradict it. The battle of the Horn of Haros was a closer thing than one would think, given the numbers involved. We lost, of course, and I survived. These things are known. As it is known and agreed that the badly outnumbered forces of Manreach gave the biters hell, and inflicted on them fearsome casualties. That it is spoken of as a battle rather than a massacre speaks to the bravery of the Galts, and of the heavy infantry, and to the skill of the commander. This commander, my father will say, was Sixt-General Migaéd dom Braga, who in no way froze up when asked for his orders. My father will tell you that any rumors that Campamachur Nouva Livias Monçera assumed command of the entire force despite her lower rank and birth are lies told by those who wish to harm the name of dom Braga. Hateful are the lying tongues of those who claim to have seen the eldest dom Braga take the Scarlet Company and depart the main force just as the goblins approached, when they were too far away to do him harm and too close for any of those who remained to give chase. No, I am to say, the glory is to him and he died a hero, with all his men. Though, you will be happy to learn, not one horse of the Scarlet Company of Sword and Horse was lost this day.

The bridge itself was a wonder.

The early tribes in Gallardia were three; those of the north were the Mour, stoneworkers of great knowledge and talent, and their descendants in these regions share this gift. Even the Kesh had not dared to raise a bridge over the ravine here. The stone faces rising on either side of the small but fast-running river Coufre, which I have since learned means "copper," were high and treacherous, and this area prone to earthquake. But the Gallards had made a bridge of stone higher than any of its length, and so connected the fortress city of Arvise to Goltay and the south by a route that shortened the journey by many miles.

To look over the sides of this bridge was to grow dizzy.

The river below was swift and full of rocks.

The ground on the defending side of the bridge was terraced, allowing archers many places and angles from which to rain death upon the narrow span.

It was a perfect place to try to hold.

My father will say that the Pragmatist was disgraced because she blundered here—that she should have stood the whole of the army at this mighty bridge instead of sacrificing the Ispanthian knights who perished, many of whom were from families nearly as distinguished as the dom Braga. He would remind you that our family lost its heir here, never mind that the willful younger sister very nearly died as well. If the former prima-general's few defenders pointed out the lack of resources nearby to support an army, or the fact that losing too many in this place would have meant the even stronger walls of Arvise and the other Hounds could not be properly defended, they did not say these things in front of my father.

Whatever the wisdom of the decision, we prepared.

We stood back from the bridge, out of sight, and let them come.

Our lanza would be held in reserve, spent only when we might most delay our defeat, or when we might extract the highest price for it.

The birds grew restless as the now familiar stink of goblins filled our noses.

We heard their soft chuffing and rasps, snatches of their odd speech.

We heard the shuffle of their feet, bare at the bottoms, and the click of their sharp, hard toes. The wind was with us, they did not smell us yet. The commander who devised our plan—my fa-

ther will tell you this was not Nouva, even though I can still hear
her clear voice ring the word in my ears—shouted "Attack" and
a drum beat its sharp, coded tattoo. At that, sixty of our heavy
knights, in their breast and shoulder plate, and in their new
articulated leg plate, and in their chain hauberks, rushed from
the hiding places among the rocks on the goblins' side. They
cut the bridge off at just the moment enough of the goblins were
across that Nouva felt we could easily kill. Now, on our side, more
armored knights and kynd-at-arms fell on these, and made short
work of them. Goblin crossbows began to rain down now, but not
enough to stop them—our knights were so well armored that the
quarrels did not easily find the quick.

The goblins had no ghalls this time to break our line.

Several hundred of Our Foe were smashed and hacked to bits
in moments as the rear knights waded through them to meet the
knights in front; at the same time, these retreated to the halfway
point of the bridge. I remember seeing them against the gray sky,
their armor bloodied and spattered dark green, not red. The biters
rushed at them, but these powerful men and dams, some of the
largest and strongest in our army, cut and stabbed them down
with great force and in great numbers. When the goblins began
to stack, hurling themselves down front-to-back to make a living
wall over which others might leap down, the knights laid their
swords, axes, and polearms aside, and simply began to *unstack*
them, using their mailed arms and hands to throw the fuckers
over the bridge, like they were loading sacks of grain. The goblins retreated, and the crossbows began again, but with greater
intensity—they had positioned a great many more of them among
the rocks on their side.

But now a roar went up, and the Galtish Coldfoot guard came
from where they, too, had been concealed on the wrong side of
the ravine. Fifty of them rushed from each flank. These men and
dams were the finest in Galtia. Too poor for heavy armor, they
had trained until their bodies were their armor, and used their

leaf-bladed ash spears and javelins to great effect. Likewise their swords. They fought and marched barefoot, except in winter, and painted their faces with woad, as the old Galtish tribes had. Their armor was boiled leather with iron rings, little protection against crossbows, but they were fast as devils, and though they lost several in the first rush, once they fell among their foe, they speared them like apples from a tub as the biters tried to squat to cock their bows. The Galts howled wolflike, never stopping, and slew many dozens before retreating barefoot along the narrow sides of the bridge, above the knights who stood its middle, and who cheered them on their way back across.

The crossbows kept firing, but at this moment they were fewer.

Inocenta and I looked at each other, both raising our eyebrows.

Can we win this one?

"Short life," she said.

"Bloody hand," I answered, and we removed our helmets for a moment to kiss cheeks.

Of course, the numbers of the biters were too great.

More goblins with crossbows were brought forward, and more again.

Our knights were worn down by sheer weight of envenomed bolts, which only had to pierce skin to kill. No matter how closely our fighters held shields, no matter how strong their helms and faceplates, there were still places where chain mail was the only armor, and a war bolt from a heavy crossbow will pierce chain. Shields were falling apart from having been struck so many times, and some of us were killed while trying to clear bolts from these shields, which grew heavy with them. The crossbows shot and shot as the day wore on, and when our archers tried to pick them off, the archers often fell. I heard one dam with a bolt through the joint of her shoulder sobbing for her father as she started to jerk. One Wostran near me fell into twitching fits of agony after a bolt passed through her open mouth and out one cheek. Inocenta gave her rest with the knife. After a quarter hour it was clear that we were losing this long-range duel, and our archers were ordered to stand down and take cover.

Our knights were ordered back and behind cover. The green-washed and red-spattered bridge stood still and strangely quiet for a moment before the biters charged again. Again our knights met them, and pushed them back across, and even raided onto their side, only falling back when the biters retreated to the rocks, raining quarrels and stones on them.

And so it went, all that day and all that night.

The knights were rested in thirds, fresh groups of fifty or so going for each charge.

It was a thing to be remembered, the valor of these knights.

I knew that I could not stand against one so armored for long, not without a corvid.

Here was the future of our war against them—more armor, more birds.

Whether we survived would come down to the hammer, the anvil, and the hatchery.

Watching this stand, I dared to hope.

It was near morning when they got the siege weapons to the front.

We first heard the rumble of wheels, and the squealing of their dray boars, around the fifth hour of the morning. Inocenta prodded me awake where I had dozed, said, "Listen." I risked a peek over the rocks, and at first it was too dark. I could barely make out the shapes of the dead on the bridge as the fattening moon shone through tears in the clouds. But then the biters barked and whooped and charged. Our heavy infantry rushed out to meet them, as before. But then all the biters fell flat to the ground, and several great cracks rang out. The sound of metal and bone smashing rose up, and the shouts of men and dams. A half dozen of ours fell, others stumbled back. At first I could not tell what had happened, then the crack came again, and more smashing, along with a great *splang*. Movement high up caught my eye, and against the waxing moon and the lit clouds I saw the silhouette of a ballista bolt, four feet long if an inch. It had pierced one of us, then struck something which deflected it upwards. It sprayed blood and other matter behind it as it rose, and then tumbled away.

More of us had fallen, we had lost perhaps ten in these few moments.

The drums called for the knights to fall back.

The goblins pressed close behind them, flattening themselves against the stones of the bridge each time the ballistas fired, and these killed many of us.

"Fuck," I said.

"Looks like today is the day we meet her after all," Inocenta said.

Inocenta's words were well-timed.

"Corvid lanza, forward and kill those ballistas!" Nouva yelled.

I wiped the last sleep from my eyes and stood.

"Short-life-bloody-hand-short-life-bloody-hand," I said as the birds got into position.

The Coldfoot guards had just met the new wave of biters on our side of the bridge, and the fighting was brutal. Now the drums sounded and the Galts parted, showing the goblins.

I stole a look at Inocenta.

I saw her axe weakly reflecting moonlight.

I saw one stray lick of red hair coming from under it, and this blew in the wind, which was picking up.

I saw her blue eye in shadow beneath her helm and knew it would be the last time our eyes met.

"Sister," I said, and she said it back.

We charged.

We screamed.

The birds screamed.

We were ordered to halt so heavy infantry could smash into the screamstruck biters.

The knights moved forward at the goblins, who were too shaken to obey whatever signal told them to hit the floor. We followed behind the knights. The cracks sounded again, but this time only one bolt struck kynd, the others having hit the goblins who failed to duck, and these were impaled like meat on a spit. They skidded in streaks of green gore and came to rest at our feet as we crossed. The knights threw and swatted goblins over in great numbers, clearing the bridge as they went. We all pushed to the opposite side of the gorge, meeting a fresh line of goblins. Most of these were frozen by the screams of our birds, but not all.

What followed was the most intense killing I have yet seen, and I was in the thick.

I could not begin to describe it in any way that will make sense—it was madness.

I was bitten on the leg, hard, and it hurt like burning.

This one fell back before I could kill it, I do not know what happened to it.

I was spattered with blood of both colors.

I saw corvids killed by ballista bolts.

The noise of this fight was deafening, shouts and cracks and the scream of the birds echoing off the rock faces.

Now an unpleasant surprise greeted us.

They had moved ghalls up from the rear.

Not many.

Perhaps a dozen.

But this was on wider ground than a bridge, and the big monsters could move. Yes, the birds remembered what to do, driving at their faces, but also the biters fought beside the ghalls. Many had frozen or fled, enough to let us survive as long as we did, but the strongest-minded of them can resist birdscream, perhaps one in five, and the more goblins are gathered, the greater their swarm-mind, which is less fearful.

And they were so, so many.

Their vicious spear-hooks reached up and yanked our corvids

down as they leapt at ghalls' faceplates, and ghalls grabbed the birds by wing or leg.

I do not know how many goblins I killed, perhaps twenty.

I blinked their blood out of my eyes, wiped at it with my sleeve until I was just smearing it around.

A ghall was among our lanza, laying about with an iron ball on a chain.

Killing us like puppies.

I heard someone madly laughing and that laugh was cut short.

In the distance, the eerie wail of carnyxes sounded.

The Moth Knights were coming with their masks of human skin, ready to clean up whatever the ghalls left.

I ducked the iron ball on the chain, heard a great bang next to me.

I stood again to see Nouva looking at me, her helmet off, her head staved in, one eye out and hanging.

"Is it bad?" she asked me, touching her face, already falling.

A blow from another direction, perhaps a thrown rock, struck my helmet and knocked my head back so I saw the moon for an instant. Then I crashed into a goblin with my shield, knocking it into the ravine, and stabbed another in the face. I dove between the feet of the ghall with the chain and stabbed up into its soft loins. I barely got clear before it fell.

A goblin grabbed my leg, sank its hook into my chain mail.

I cut that arm off, crawled forward.

I saw a goblin lying atop a dead woman, her face in its mouth. It was dead, too, it had been cut in half at the waist, but still its jaws worked and it chewed her.

I stumbled to my feet, dry-heaved.

Saw the goblin's arm hanging by its hook from my mail coat, pulled the arm off, but the hook stayed.

Swatted at something flying by my head, missed it, but it missed anyway.

Just as I realized I was near the ravine, I heard a crack.

A ballista had fired at me.

I saw the bolt and its huge, lethal point grow larger impossibly fast.

And then something happened which I am not sure of, and will not swear to you is true.

But the wind blew hard, very hard, only for an instant, the sort of gust that makes banners snap on their poles.

That bolt flew up and to the left.

Its rough fletching scratched my cheek and eye, grazed my helmet.

The bolt struck a ghall that had been coming up behind me, impaling it.

Perhaps the bolt was badly aimed.

But in my gut, I think the shield of my grandfather blew the ten-pound missile away from me and into the monster that was about to crush me.

It knocked the ghall violently off its feet and toward the ravine.

I got my last glimpse of that battle then, etched into my memory like a mural, or a mosaic.

More of us were down than not.

The ground was covered with dead goblins and ghalls.

One of the ballistas had been overwhelmed by corvids and our dams.

I saw Alisenne, our half-Gallardian translator and archer, with her throat cut, trying to stand while also trying to hold her blood in with her hand.

She fell.

The First Lanza of His Majesty's Corvid Knights died at the Haros Horn bridge, as we had been ordered to.

I lived because the ghall who had been about to grab me instead grabbed my belt as he fell down the ravine, spitted like a quail by his slavemasters.

I lost my *spadín,* clutching the Mouth of the Storm with both hands.

The ghall's hand released my belt, but I was already over the edge.

I hit rocks hard, so hard, and tumbled.

Dust.

Yelling and the moon above me.

The moon's reflection broken on the rushing water below.

Something sharp and hard grabbed my arm.

Now I was falling, away from the rocks, not so fast.

Water.

Cold.

A rock under the water, breaking my ribs.

Maybe my back.

I gasped a breath and went under.

48

I woke under a rock overhang on the banks of the Coufre, in great pain.

The Haros Horn bridge was nowhere in sight.

It was day, threatening rain.

So cold, and I was wet, but I had something like blankets about me.

A torn banner.

A bit of oilskin.

I looked up, could only see out of one eye, saw Dalgatha coming toward me with some poor wretch's bloody cloak. She let this fall from her beak over my legs, then poked with her beak to tuck the edges under me.

"Cold," she rasped.

I could not speak.

I nodded.

"Cold," she said again, and limped to a pile of sticks and branches, nosed at them with her beak.

She had gathered firewood.

She was such a smart bird, the smartest of the whole lanza.

I felt a sob well up at how good she was to me, but I had no tears.

Had she always been so good, and had my adoration of her brother blinded me to it?

Remembering the fall, I realized it was she who grabbed my arm, steered me away from the rock face, spread her wings to slow our descent into the water.

She had been my savior, and now she was my nursemaid.

I tried to say "Good Dalgatha," but my mouth was a mess of blood and my jaw hurt too much. I tried a second time and said the words, but they were sloppy and wrong. I had meant to praise her but I think I just made her more worried.

I was missing teeth.

I had bitten my tongue, and badly.

The pain had only just started.

Of all the injuries I suffered, the goblin bite on my leg was most dangerous. Its nasty little teeth had gone deep into the meat of my thigh, above my knee and the steel greave protecting the lower leg, which was one of the vulnerable places. I had meant to get a longer mail coat, as mine stopped mid-thigh, but I liked how light my coat was, and I delayed.

This time I paid for it.

The wound had filled up with river water before Dalgatha could pull me out, and the flesh around the bite was already puffed and red.

The first time I stood, I was grateful the bones of my legs seemed to be whole, though I had pulled or twisted an ankle so that my limp was worse than my bird's. I looked at her leg, and found an ugly gash cut in it, probably caused by the side-blow of an axe. It looked like it would heal, though, and they are much more resistant to wounds going sour than we are.

Fulvir had made the corvids sturdy, I will give the old bastard that. He had made them clever, as well. They always surprised me with how much they understood.

I tried to say "Fetch" to Dalgatha, making some awful sound, and then "*Spadín,*" though it sounded more like "Thpadee."

She cocked her head at me.

"Sword," I said, or "*Thort,*" and showed her my scabbard, mimed pulling a sword, stabbing, cutting. The cutting hurt my shoulder.

I slept again.

When I next woke, I heard a snuffling, and here came a large, brown bear, wet from fishing the Coufre.

It walked with its head down, wagging this back and forth, trying to look indifferent to me. I have heard that a hunting bear tries to get as close to you as possible before showing its intent. Black bears may be found all over Ispanthia, but the brown ones are only in Montabrecola and Portres, north of Braga, and are much more dangerous. I would not want to face a brown bear on a good day, but now I had no sword, and I was badly hurt.

I started to laugh.

I had survived a killing flux, the battle of Carrasque, the fall of Goltay, the battle of the Horn of Haros, and a fall into a river down a rocky cliff.

And now a fucking bear was going to eat me.

No, I decided.

No it fucked-wasn't.

I got to my feet and limped toward it, holding my shield and a small belt knife. I did not approach the bear cautiously. I hobbled at it as fast as I could, banging the shield's rim against the rocks and yelling like a madwoman, which at that point I might have been. And in my mind, I was not simply frightening the bear. I actually meant to kill it with my knife. Of course, I never would have been able to, I doubt I would have scratched it before it bit my head off my body, but if I had thought that way, it would have known. As far as it could tell, I believed I could kill it, and it decided I must know something it did not. The bear moved off somewhat faster than it had approached.

I roared once at it, to close the matter, then went back to my nest of dead people's clothes and some banner.

The banner showed an animal I could not identify.

I decided it was a bear.

Dalgatha returned perhaps an hour later with not one but three swords gripped in her beak.

"You are late," I tried to say for a joke, but she made no effort to understand. She knows when someone is making mouthwind. She put the swords down in front of me, and I scratched her head feathers.

Gods bless her, one of the three blades was a *spadín,* and it was only a little longer than mine had been. It fit in my scabbard but for the breadth of a finger, though the fit was tight. I would have to work the blade around so it would not stick when I needed to draw it.

One of the other swords had belonged to someone of high birth, and was chased with gold, but this I left in the shelter.

I am no looter of the dead for wealth.

It was too much to hope that Dalgatha might be sent for a healer in this desolate place, and I doubted I would find anyone in the wake of the goblins. Our army had warned everyone we came across what was behind us, so anyone who could travel would be far away from the only road I knew to take. Besides, this country was rough going. I was not sure I could make it back up to that road, and did not know how far past the bridge I might have floated.

Also, and this was strange to say, I was embarrassed to have lived. I did not know how I could rejoin the army now. My mission, under the order of the Butchered Man, was to die, was it not? If the man in the cart fed his fingers to the wolves, what was he supposed to make of a finger that showed up on his door again?

But no, I thought. Nobody said I had to die; I just had to fight the biters' fucked-huge army and kill as many as I could before they killed me. And they had tried very hard to kill me. It was not my fault they failed.

Or so I told myself, but the faces of my comrades haunted me.

That last glimpse of Inocenta's blue eye.

Nouva, already dead and asking me how bad her wound was.

I felt the deepest guilt of my life.

But to die of guilt was stupid, and I decided not to do this.

I took my flint and steel out of my pouch.

I felt strong enough to build a fire, and needed one. I could only hope that all the goblins were on their way to be killed at the walls of Arvise and would not see the smoke of it. I shaved bark off the branches to make kindling, then opened the sealed tin with the dry cotton and resin fireplugs.

Soon I had a good fire.

I held my knife in the flames until it was very hot, and, gripping a stick between my back teeth, which were still whole, put the knife's point in each of the wounds the goblin's bite had made in my leg.

Dalgatha cocked her head at my grunting and hard breathing, then shook herself out and puffed her feathers.

I was doing mysterious kynd things, and this bird wanted no part of it.

I passed out from the pain.

It turned out to be a great blessing that I had risked the fire, and that the smoke from it had risen within sight of the bridge.

It caught the attention of a very welcome party, who had been looking for me.

When I came to, the fire was still going, and Dalgatha had brought me a fair-sized salmon from the Coufre. Her beak shone with scales, and a bit of meat hung in her breast feathers, so I knew she had already taken her supper. I cleaned the fish, then ran a stick through a few pink fillets and cooked them as well as I could.

Then I ate them as best as I could.

My jaw was not broken, and I had enough back teeth to chew the soft flesh.

I still remember the grease of them, the good taste of them, despite the pain.

A hot meal in the cold is one of the most fine things I know.

I dared to hope I might get to Arvise, and fight again.

I dared to think the Bride did not want me yet, and that the other gods would find more use for me in my skin.

I nodded as I ate the last piece of fish.

I pulled my new *spadín* and looked at its blade in the firelight.

I tested it against my thumbnail and it bit. It had a keen edge, and had been well cared for.

I do not know whose you were, but you are mine now, I thought. *And we will do good work together.*

And so it went.

Dalgatha foraged for food, and brought me other needful things.

It was two days later that the lecherous man with the thin mustache poked his head around the rocks.

He grinned at me, then withdrew his head and was gone.

I recognized him, of course.

It was the bastard-man who stole my rose on Elephant's March in Goltay.

The man who was not a man at all, but a monkey.

The queen came at nightfall.

49

"I traveled by means of the river and cannot bear you back," Mireya said, her eyes wet. "I expected only to find your body. I thought only to take a lock of your hair."

It was the first thing she said to me.

"Oh, your poor mouth," she also said.

It is strange to think that at such a time I might be concerned for my appearance, but if you have felt your heart fully in someone's grasp, perhaps you will understand. I knew my eye was swollen shut, and I imagined my face was a mask of rude, bruised meat. A rock had dashed four teeth from my mouth. I hid my mouth behind my hand and tried to smile. Mireya took my hand in hers and gently lowered it, kissed the air just in front of my ruined lips.

"The army made it to Arvise," she said. "*You* did that. *You*, Galva dom Braga. And your sisters. And those who fought them in the marsh, and at the other bridge."

Now my eyes found their well of tears.

"The goblins are laying siege. Another army has joined them." Then, she said again, "I thought to find you dead."

Her tears came hard now.

She held me, and this hurt my ribs, though I tried to hide my wince.

Then I coughed, and she let go.

"First thing," she said. "Let's get you well. I will not stand by while my lover suffers such pain. Is it as much as it looks?"

I shrugged.

"You forget I am from Ispanthia like you, and I know you just said it hurts like hell."

I laughed, and this hurt so badly I staggered.

She did not let me fall, and her holding me also hurt.

This second healing by magical means was very different from the first. In the first instance, I had a crack in my skull, which would have knit by itself. The sisters of the goddess of healing merely quickened this. Mireya would now have to heal ribs, re-grow teeth, heal a tongue, unsprain an ankle, open an eye that may or may not see. By herself. She was not such a powerful thing as Fulvir; but her gifts had to do with water, and animals, and near a river, in the wilderness, she was strong.

She sent the monkey, Peppercorn, to gather herbs for her, and with these, and using my helmet as a witch's pot, she made a brew, which I drank when it cooled enough. She undressed me, and she rubbed me crown to ankle with an oil.

"That was just so you will not feel this as much. Now the hard part."

She helped me to the river, and laid me back in the cold, snow-melt water. I felt something in the water with us, something of the river. I think now that it was an elemental, or some spirit of the river, though I understand little of these things. It embraced me, and the hurt of its touch was great. I was glad not to bear it with-out the oil for pain. It kissed me, and filled my mouth with cold water. I felt new teeth push themselves up from my ruined jaw. I bled. I felt my badly split lip and my cut tongue sewn and with all the itch and pain of healing long weeks happening in perhaps two hundred heartbeats. My eye burned, and opened, and saw. Where it hugged me, the ribs ached like ice in my side, and when it slith-ered its tail around my ankle, it hurt so much I would have agreed to have my leg severed at the knee not to feel it. Then, and I think I may have dreamed this, the river-thing wanted something from me that Mireya was unwilling for it to have; she had to dismiss it with a song in a language I did not know. It seemed to me that if she stumbled in her singing of this song, it might have taken us both into the river and been nourished by our drowning, and by its own tears for the sadness of our fate.

I know that after it had gone, I was carried back in, and laid by the fire.

"Should you not. Be helping. At the siege," I managed to say.

"I am not for war," she said. She struggled to stay awake, for the spell had taken much from her.

She held me from behind, and we both slept long.

As my consciousness sank, I knew I would not wake soon, and in my dimming mind I worried she might be harmed while we slept. But then I thought of what I had seen from her monkey, and what I knew Dalgatha could do, and I felt safe enough to let go and give in to the waters of nothingness pulling me under.

But the place I went to was not exactly sleep; at least, not sleep as I have known it. I walked up stone steps to a lovely stone tower on a hill that looked over a valley in fruit and flower. The tower was Keshite, and the reliefs on its stone were of leaves, and of trees, and deer at play. It was not a ruin, but it shone new and white against a sky at sunset, or sunrise, I did not know where west was here, or if there was such a thing as west.

The door, wooden and braced with copper in patina, bore writing I could not read, and the knob by which it opened was a copper dragonfly, which buzzed gently in my hand when I reached to it.

The door opened of its own accord.

This first floor was tiled in travertine, and a great, eight-sided pool of hot water steamed. A statue of a woman on one side of it held in the palms of her joined hands a bar of soap and a brush. A second statue held a towel of white cotton. The scents of flowers I could not name drifted in the open windows. I thought to disrobe, but I had not a stitch of thread on me, nor any sense of shame to go naked.

I stepped into the pool, and bathed. I thought the water would go murky, or bloody, but I brought no stain to it. I became aware that the light outside was failing, and that candles flickered in sconces. I listened to hear what sounds I might, and heard crickets, as on a lazy summer night in the countryside. But when I thought, *I wonder what music would play in such a place,* I heard such a sweet chorus of flutes, soon joined by viol, that I had a troubling thought. For want of anything else to do with my mouth, I spoke my thought.

"I have died!"

Now girlish laughter came from upstairs. I had not noticed the stairs, but a greater, flickering light, as from many candles and lamps, shone down.

A voice I had not yet heard my fill of words from said, "One need not die to make a paradise. Bathe as long as you care to, my beautiful Bragaene. And come up to me when you are ready."

I was ready.

I climbed out of the warm tub, and dried, and wrapped the towel about myself. I turned toward the stairs, but felt a tug on the towel. I looked to see that the statue, whose hands had been joined at their blades, palms up, in offering, now clutched the towel. These hands were still of stone, but the woman's face now smiled in play, her eyes closed. I stepped away, and the towel came off in her grasp.

I looked back at the staircase and saw that a doe was standing on them, her white tail flicking, her ears perked at me.

She took two steps, still looking at me.

She twitched her tail.

She waited.

I walked after her, and up the stairs.

The deer was gone when I reached the top.

I stood now at the top of the tower, though I did not remember passing other doors.

A bed stood in the middle of the tower's floor, and at the crenellations and in many sconces, candles of beeswax burned with a mild light. Silver carafes of cool wine sweated on nearby tables, reflecting the candles.

The stars overhead were more than I had ever seen, though none of these burned so bright as two the color of amethyst.

I might have expected Nerêne herself to appear now, and I hope it is not an affront to her to say that I was glad it was merely the queen of Gallardia.

As you will imagine—and do not even think about interrupting me to tell me this was just a fever dream, I have thought the same thing—Mireya waited for me in the same state of undress as I, under the sky, on that bed with sheets the color of lavender.

"Where are we?" I asked.

"I will tell you after," she said.

"Should . . . should you not mourn the king?"

"This is how he would mourn me. And I would not want it to be otherwise. Nor would he. He was a rare and good man."

And now she rose and drew me to her. I will say that the pleasure she brought me on that tower made our afternoon in the wherry in Goltay, which had been the best hour of my life, seem a crude and hurried business.

As much as you would like me to tell you more of this, I will not.

Simply imagine it for yourself, and know that your imaginings do not touch its shadow.

Later, I lay surprised to find this dream had not ended. The night breeze felt fine and cool, and an owl hooted somewhere in the valley below. I said, "But in seriousness, where are we, Mireya?"

"Miri."

"Miri, where am I?"

"In a place of my creation."

"Is it a real place?"

"Are you experiencing it?"

"With great pleasure."

"Well, then."

"But is it real?"

She made a growl of exasperation then that she learned in Gallardia. In fact, besides the eight sighs of carnal pleasure, this is the most Gallard sound one can make. At the end of this growl she mounted me, bent to put her lips to my neck, and then sucked with great force to mark me, and to reprove me for talking too much.

We did not speak any more for a while.

Later, as I caught my breath and drank cold white wine, she spoke.

"A good magicker can build a place in the mind. A very good one can bring others to it in dreams that are more than dreams. A great one can bring this place into the world, so that every brick and tile of it has weight and matter. I hope to learn to do this last thing one day. So, is this tower I have fashioned in honor of Nerêne a place that strangers might stumble upon, or which might be invaded by goblins, or subjected to taxation, or a place in which anyone might observe me at play with you and think to instruct me in a more properly Ispanthian expression of grief? No. But is it a place where you and I might, in dreaming together, find ourselves alone, in our actual bodies, outside of the myth of time, and make shared memories which will, in fact, last longer than memories made under time's crushing weight? I am happy. To tell. You. Yes."

And at each of these she touched my nose with a finger.

"I loved Luvain, you know," she said.

"Yes. I think you did. I loved my *irmana,* Inocenta, though I think it was not the same."

"No two loves are the same. But they are all loves."

I sighed, and said, "The only bad thing about this place you have made is that I do not wish to leave."

"You do not have to. Not forever, at least."

"I am not sure I understand."

"Magic is not for understanding. It is for imagining and accepting."

I opened my mouth to speak, but she stopped it with a kiss.

"Do not say *how*."

And now she lay directly atop me, so my eyes stared into hers of almond and hazel.

"I can visit you here, in dreams that are more than dreams, for as long as you wish. It is not easy, but I am happy to do it, sweet Galva."

"Call me Galvicha," I said.

And she play-bit me in a way that did not make me think of goblins.

50

---•---

When I woke, she was gone.

My body was whole.

Weak, exhausted, too skinny.

But whole.

I took my wire scour from my pouch and scrubbed at my bascinet until a part of it shone. I looked in this and made square-lips, saw that my teeth were as they were before they were dashed out by the rocks of the gorge. I also saw something that made me blush, wonder, and gasp all at once.

A purplish love-bite on my neck.

It was no fever dream, *jilnaedu*.

A magicker can summon you in your own skin to a world they have built somewhere not in this world. I do not understand it. And that is good, because if I did, I would not be sane.

Outside the shelter, I saw something that made my heart soar.

With pebbles, and with flowers, and with white twigs, a word had been spelled on the stony ground.

ARVISE

Dalgatha and I crossed the Haros Horn bridge again, with a great cawing of ravens, who were making much of the bounty. Many of them fell silent or stopped their pecking at the sight of my corvid, who affected her smaller cousins wherever she saw them. Human scavengers had already been at their work, stripping boots and belts, weapons and shields from dead kynd, though they were well into rot. If any watched us from hiding as we passed, I was not aware of them.

The dead biters still had most of their gear, for kynd do not like to touch them. Once the last of the usables from our dead were gone, those who came late would wrinkle their noses and take the gisarmes and crossbows of the biters, though not their reeking clothes, even the mysterious mesh armor, which would be a useful material if one could stand to work with it. What coins and amber and greenish silver had been taken from goblin pouches would be boiled, if the takers had the leisure of a fire.

So, with the ravens awed and no human pickers at work, we crossed the bridge with quiet, hearing only the wind, in that sad way that wind sounds in high places.

I did not look for my friends.

I had no beliefs about whether a body should be burned or buried, and no means to do either. I could do nothing for Inocenta or Alisenne or Nouva but sorrow, and I would rather not have seen the dark, beak-scraped faces of those I loved, their teeth and bones white in the ruin they had become.

But I did find one lanza-sister that day, and see her in death.

Bernuz, our cook, had died on all fours, up against a rock. I only knew it was her by the smell of sea-buckthorn soap in her pack, which made me think of bathing in the sea by Espalle when we first arrived. I did not like the pose she had died in, and I settled her down in a more restful-looking way, though this was awkward because her limbs had stiffened. I did look in her face, from which the eyes had been stolen by beaks.

I saw the face of death, and I tried not to be troubled, because this was the face of my new mistress. And yet I remembered Bernuz, who was always chewing something, and how she would smile with only half of her mouth, which made her dear to me, and I cannot say I was not bothered. The way of the Bride is the study of a lifetime. It is a worthy pursuit.

I left Bernuz, and reminded myself that this was only what she was now, and that the dead have grown larger than now.

They are of all time, and none.

It mostly worked.

I saw dead corvids as well, their great black wings here and there, usually near a great number of biters in many pieces. Dalgatha led me to one or two of these, and she stood for a moment, turning her head sideways as she considered them.

"You and your brothers and sisters did good work here, 'Gatha."

"Good," she rasped, cocking an eye at me.

"So good."

We followed in the wake of the two armies, north and west, until we came to a crossroads.

"Let us go east for a while, girl," I said, thinking we were pressing our luck to stay in the biters' footsteps any longer, besides there being no villages with any remaining in them. We had to find food, and another way to Arvise.

A sign pointing east bore what I took to be the name of some mountain hamlet.

"*Roncenay* sounds like a place where they feed strangers."

She crarked at me.

"No, perhaps not," I said, "but that is the only place I know here. It is both the best and worst choice."

And so we went toward Roncenay.

But our way there would not be clear—Dalgatha became agitated, and I thought it was a good time to get off the path. We went up into the rocky hills and made our way carefully forward, parallel with the road to Roncenay. It was in a fallow field that we saw them: a large force of biters, perhaps two hundred, with a few dumbed kynd in a boar-drawn cart. Other empty carts rolled nearby. Foragers, harvesting manflesh for their table. If there was anyone in Roncenay, they would need to be warned.

I led Dalgatha up, and around a hillock out of sight, and we raced as quietly but as quickly as we could, coming to the town in less than an hour.

It was a pretty little hamlet, one of the sort you find in the high

places of the world, where summer is as sweet as it is short, and
sheep and goats and the cheese of both are used as coin.

Walls of pine logs circled the place. The houses were of stone,
and the roofs of thatch.

Haros was well worshipped here, as he often was in places
made for hooves, and I saw his tower, with its stag antlers, and
its iron bell. This was the highest point in the village, and if look-
outs had been posted, they would be here.

Could the biters already have spoiled this place?

The gate stood closed.

And I saw no dead, no smoke.

We kept off the road, and watched the tower, the top of which
was open.

I saw no one near the bell.

Had there been a lookout of any worth, we would have already
been marked, but I thought now there was none.

I heard male laughter.

Then I heard a fiddle, and a woman singing.

"They are still here," I told Dalgatha. "They must be told what's
coming."

We were about to walk straight into the main gate when, in a
near field, I saw two Ispanthian dams of my years or fewer gathering wildflowers, but in such a grim way I thought it might be
for the dead.

Why might one gather flowers? Was there a festival?

Then I remembered the fat moon on the night of the battle.

The month of Ashers would be ending, perhaps tonight.

Tomorrow could be the first of Lammas.

Or even today.

Summer's end.

The dams in the field were not soldiers. They had the look of
workers, or farmers, well tanned, but their ribs were for counting, like mine. Like everyone's.

Each had a basket into which the flowers went.

"Sisters," I said, walking up to them.

They stared to see Dalgatha, and I thought they might run from her.

Instead, they looked behind them toward Roncenay, then ran toward us.

"Help us," one said.

"What is wrong?" I said.

"You are a knight? And well trained in arms?" she said, speaking quickly. "And this is one of those murder-birds I have heard of, who fight like ten?"

"Yes. Are there biters in there?"

"No," one said. "Brigands. The worst of men. A group of us had fled north from Espalle, hearing that the castles known as the Hounds might be safe from them. It has been a long, hard road."

I said, "Go on."

"Eight of us, both Spanth and Gallard, and one Untherdam, none of us soldiers. We travel together. The soldiers we had journeyed with were killed by biters, but they had hidden us away before they fought, two villages back. We got away, but we were starving. We found this place nearly abandoned, and there was food, and wine, and some very old villagers remained, saying they would die here rather than run. They fed us, and were good to us. But then these men came, and at first we were glad of their swords, but now they have made servants, and worse, of us, and use us for their sport. We would run, but we will not leave our friends with them, and they know this, and there is no other food. So they sent us to gather flowers for a Lammas Day feast tomorrow. They mean to crown one of us Queen of the Harvest, and try to get a child on her."

I gritted my teeth at this.

"How many are they?"

"They are fifteen men, and two dams."

"Spanths?"

"Yes, to our shame."

"Are they armored?"

"Their armor is rarely worn."

I looked at the other dam, who was even younger and more afraid than the first.

"Are these things true? How they have served you, I mean?" She nodded.

"Whom do you worship in your home?"

The second dam said, "Mithrenor, we are fisher-folk," and I saw that she was of chestnut hair rather than black.

"Arvaresca?"

"Yes, from a village called Pecat."

To look at her now, with her sad eyes and sun-freckles, it was easy to picture her with a basket of fish on her head and a flat-topped Arvarescan bonnet with its starched brim behind to keep the drippings from her back.

"There will be consequence of what you told me. Will you swear the truth of your friend's words, by Mithrenor, who brings bounty and sorrow from the waters?"

"Yes," she managed. "I swear it."

"Stay up in these rocks, and do not come down. Biters are on the way."

At this they both grew terrified, and who can blame them?

"Do not worry. I will come for you, or I will die."

"All right, yes," the first one said, fighting tears now. "Thank you, dama. Will you bring our sisters out?"

"If I can, yes. I will not leave without them if they live. Is there another way into town besides the main gate?"

They told me of a place where the wall was lower, where a nimble man or dam might scale it.

"They will fight you."

"If so, I will make them sorry."

I turned from the dams then.

I spoke to Mireya in my head, begged her to forgive me if I

died here after all her work to heal me. I wanted nothing more than to meet her in Arvise, as she told me to do with her pebbles and twigs. A servant of Nerêne would have recognized that this was too much to face alone, prayed for the safety of these girls, and gone to her lover's bed.

Nerêne is not for war.

But the Skinny Woman is.

I could not ask Dal-Gaata to save these dams.

But I could ask her to make me terrible to those who faced me.

I knew this would cost me, if not today, then from the soft end of my life.

That is the trade with Dal-Gaata.

"Short life, bloody hand," I said. "So let it be."

A raven cawed.

And I went to the small hillside village of Roncenay to face a man who was not my brother.

———— • ————

51

It had not been a difficult matter to scale the log wall, which was not tall, with Dalgatha's help and with a broken cart we dragged over, and stood up on end.

When we got past several rows of stone houses, we saw that a feast for Lammas Day was being held in the square. The deserters were gathered there, waited on by a few elderly kynd of Roncenay.

Tables had been pulled out of houses, and on these stood modest platters of onions and cheese, garlic and parsnip, some salted pork. The carefully saved rations of villagers preparing for hard times were now spent for the pleasure of foreigners with weapons.

An old woman bore a platter with a roasted suckling pig, and the deserters watched its progress toward the feast like dogs.

I counted ten at table, including two women with a soldier's look, who must have joined with the others in their disgraceful flight from the bridge. The man who was not my brother sat there, next to his fleshy second-in-command, dom Gatán, whose mustache was still large but now not so trimmed or waxed, looking like a gray and brown brush of poor quality.

None of these men or dams were sober.

A small keg of wine or ale stood on the table, perhaps the last in the village.

I crept around the small dirt square where the brigands feasted, keeping to shadow, the Mouth of the Storm on my arm, and my new *spadín* at hand.

Sad singing came from the square now, and a fiddle.

I heard a man's laughter coming from a house with horn windows, and, using the sword, I tipped a window out and looked in. The house was shadowed, and what went on inside was not for light.

Mattresses of straw on the floor, upon which two dams. Also, two rough men. A third man watched, having finished, or about to begin, or perhaps just making sure the other four dams sitting against the wall with blank faces did not think to make trouble. One of these dams ate something, perhaps bread or cheese, but took no joy of it.

What I was seeing half froze me with outrage.

The one hurt the goblins did not inflict on us, the one scourge that was beneath even them, was here being visited upon us by our own kind.

That was when I saw the thing that broke my stupor and made me act.

One of the brigands taking his pleasure had his clothes in a pile near him. On his belt on the floor were a number of bright cloths, locks of hair, trinkets. Like tokens. Or favors. But I did not think these favors had been freely given.

One of these was a beautiful scrap of cloth in gold and blue, with images of birds.

I had last seen such a cloth around Larmette's waist, or so I thought in that moment.

I believed this was a piece of the scarf I had purchased at a fair before I shipped out, the one I gave Sami's sister to thank her for the dinner in the tree house. The truth is that I have since come to doubt it was the same one, though perhaps made by the same artisans, or in the same town.

But in this moment of recognition, false or not, my body moved without thought.

I rolled into the window, my chain rustling; this could not be done with stealth.

I would have to be fast.

I was.

As the idle man turned to look at the noise I had made, I bashed him in the forehead with the boss of my grandfather's shield so the back of his head banged hard against the stone wall, leaving blood. As he slid down, I stepped to the mattress, grabbed a hand-ful of hair and yanked the naked man with what I thought to be Larmette's cloth on his belt up. I did not want to kill him on the girl, so I threw him off the mattress and killed him on the rushes of the floor, and his blood was on my hand and on my face. The last man said "Hey! Wait" as he rolled off, but before he could do anything but stand, I lunged and flicked my *spadín*, cutting his cock, not off, but lengthwise, and badly. His hands went down to try to hold him-self together, his eyes wide with shock, and as he opened his mouth to scream, I stabbed my sword into it and up, as I had done to sev-eral goblins, flicking down as I withdrew to paint the floor rushes and my boot with blood. He fell toward me, his bloody hand print-ing my shield on the way down. One dam against the wall went to scream, as terrified by me as by her captors, but the dam next to her stuffed a hand over her mouth, saying, "Shhhh-shhh!"

I booted this last man aside and said, to the dams, "Listen. Be calm and quiet. Are you Spanths?"

Three of them nodded.

"Dress and wait. I will open the front gate. When I do, go to the tallest hill near town, where your friends wait for you. I will come if I can, but do not wait for me. Run fast and far, or hide well. There are trees, and much cover from rocks. Biters will be here soon, a lot of them. Nod if you understand."

Most nodded, and as the girl who had silenced her friend now spoke softly to the rest in Gallard, I took the cloth-of-gold and indigo from the brigand's belt, and put this in my pouch. Then I pulled his other trophies from his belt, and threw them on his dead face, which bore an expression of surprise.

"You are well paid," I told him on his way to hell, stabbing him again in the heart to be sure.

The Spanth dam who spoke Gallard had already gotten her shift on.

I told her to come with me, and to help me get the villagers away.

The gate was barred by means of a great beam, and we slid this aside.

I opened the gate.

It was not guarded.

None of the brigands had wanted to miss the amusement.

We walked the short distance back to the simple square, and the feast.

I motioned for the dam to wait in the shadow of a larger, very old stone building, I think it was the mill.

I walked into the square now, ready for killing, glad for the blood on my sword, and on my grandfather's shield, and on my face.

A motherly dam with village clothes on was singing, none too happily, while an old, old man scratched at a fiddle.

The brigands were greasy with suckling pig, and they looked at me, not knowing what was happening.

I walked toward them and whistled once, loudly.

Perhaps they thought I wanted their attention, but that was not why I did it.

The first to understand that I was not their friend despite my Ispanthian gear was the man who was not my brother. I saw doubt in his eye, to see me blooded and walking toward him with my naked sword. But he had enough kynd around him that he felt safe to make mouthwind.

"So," he said. "You have come to return the shield you stole."

Some people are for talking at moments like this, but I am not.

I leapt on the table, and dom Gatán reached for my leg, so I stomped his hand and kicked him in the face.

He fell.

Not-My-Brother was up now. His feet were quick to run from fighting.

He pulled his thin slakesword and backed up, speaking curses and threats that are not worthy to repeat.

A soldier dam grabbed up a war hammer, but her hands were

so slick with the grease of the pig that she dropped it. I moved faster than she expected and cut her under the line of her hair so that blood sheeted into her eyes. If she was blind to the wickedness of those she followed, let her be blind here, too.

She was a fighter, and grabbed for me anyway, but I leapt off the table and shaved the fingers from one hand as I passed her, then posted her with a heel-kick to her guts that doubled her over and made her kneel to vomit pig and wine. The commander, a sixt-general by rank before desertion stripped him of all rank and honor, had formed up with three others, and seemed ready to make a stand.

But now Dalgatha was in the square, her wings shivering, stalking forward as they do when they are coming for blood.

She was terrifying to behold.

I was, too.

I had become Her.

I saw fear in Not-My-Brother's eyes.

It was good.

From the corner of my vision, I saw the dam from the house running away with the serving woman, the singer, and the old fiddle player in tow.

Heading for the gate.

That was also good.

When a brigand-dam and another of their officers ran for the gate as well, meaning, I think, just to get away, I gestured for Dalgatha to turn from the commander's group and attack these two in case they meant harm to the fleeing villagers.

I had never ordered her to attack kynd before, which is forbidden them, but they are loyal first to their masters.

She did not hesitate, and killed both of these cowards spectacularly.

Dom Gatán was crawling away on all fours, so I kicked him again to roll him over, then stomped his face, breaking teeth, then again for the crime of his mustache.

He groaned in agony, but I did not finish him.

He did not deserve the sword.

It was now that the most serious man in this band came at me from the side, showing me his black tongue in a devil's smile, as the Coldfoot guards of Galtia are known to do. He wore better armor than most Coldfoots do, a fine suit of boiled leather and ring mail. He also carried one of their wicked-sharp leaf-bladed spears. A spear is not for joking when you have a sword, especially a shorter one, even if you also have a shield.

But I had trained long hours against many kinds of weapon.

Later I would realize that this of Roncenay was the easiest fighting I had done in Gallardia.

Not that all of the Scarlet Company were soft—this one with the spear knew his business well—but I had only trained for two years to fight goblins.

The ten years before that, I learned how to fight kynd.

The spear licked out at me twice, and twice I dodged and covered. But it is not good to be predictable, so the third time I ducked the spear and struck his bare foot with the edge of my shield. I do not think I broke the foot, but perhaps a toe.

He hopped.

But then he was at me again, trying for my lead foot in return. I changed stance, pulling the left back just in time. He now jabbed at my right, but instead of retreating again, I caught the spear with my sword and spun low, hitting the side of his leg with my shield and nearly spilling him on the ground.

More hopping, his face a scowl of pain and rage.

I came at him now, deflecting a thrust with my shield, catching the shaft across one of my greaves as he spun, then kicking him in the meat of his thigh with that greave.

I barely avoided a spear-flick at my face, caught another one painfully in the chain mail of my arm. This one hit quick, and I did not know how badly. I tried for his leg with my sword, but he hopped out of the way. His dodge was graceless, though. I had badly hurt his legs—and thus his mobility—and would have him soon.

And yet, playing this game had lured me from the battlefield back into the duels of the academy, and I was too focused on the Coldfoot guard.

If Not-My-Brother and his remaining deserters had attacked me now, with purpose, they might have overcome me.

But despite his limping, they hoped this one would finish me before they had to risk their skins.

That is not how it worked out.

I had shaped my opponent into the fighter I wanted him to be—one that was slower and scared for his legs.

I pressed him, feinting as though to bash his foot with my shield again. He hopped his lead foot back, shifting weight. My shield's true task was to clear his spear, and this it did, knocking the point up left. The real attack came now, a backhand upswing of the *spadín* through the channel my shield had cleared and at the exposed head he had left too close to me. He moved enough to spare the undershelf of his jaw, but my *spadín* shaved an ear from him and knocked his helmet into the air. He staggered back and I followed with him, flipping my blade and stamping him in the forehead with the pommel, then raising the sword.

I brought it down blade-first and split his head like a melon, all the way to his top teeth.

This was perhaps the truest single blow I ever struck.

I dream about it sometimes, and, unlike most of the war-dreams, this is not entirely a nightmare. Mixed with the horror of ending a human life so brutally and at such close range—smelling his breath, his sweaty leathers, his blood, the contents of his head—is a feeling of great accomplishment.

Which in waking brings shame and confusion.

And then I remember My Lady, and I am at peace.

Mostly.

Killing fellow kynd is very unlike killing goblins.

It is a complex thing.

With time and practice, it grows less so.

This final exchange with the Coldfoot mercenary took four heartbeats.

Now Dalgatha was coming.

At the sight of their best fighter down and bleeding his brains into the dirt, and a bloodied war corvid moving fast at them with high wings and low head, Not-My-Brother and his remaining band took to their heels. They ran fast, like children who had stolen a chicken. They made for a strong-house of some sort, perhaps a granary, with narrow windows and a good door, which they entered and shut.

I heard them bolt this.

I followed.

Now there was a familiar crack and a crossbow bolt flew out at me from one of the narrow windows. Though it missed, this was so like what goblins did that I was offended.

I would like to tell you that I confronted and fought this deserter and drunk and wastrel and abuser of dams, and that I killed him.

Or that I saw him die.

I did not.

I did not bother to accuse him, or explain myself, or demand that they come out.

They would just piss themselves and load the crossbow.

What I did do while Not-My-Brother cowered behind his strong door was to go to the tower of Haros with its antlers and its bell, and to climb the spiral stone steps within until I reached the top.

I looked for a moment at the streets of Roncenay, and saw no villagers. Only brigands.

The idle man I had bashed with the shield boss at the start had wandered out of the house now, dizzy, bleeding from the strangely flat back of his head, and unarmed.

He staggered and fell, fought to stand again.

His skull was broken and he had no harm left in him.

I looked back toward the square, saw the strong-house, and dom Gatán drooling blood, begging the others to open the door.

Dalgatha was coming for him, and they wanted no part of her.

They did not open the door for dom Gatán, whom Dalgatha welcomed into Dal-Gaata's embrace with great enthusiasm, his shrieks rising into the air.

I looked to the horizon, saw biters raising dust up the road, making their way here at a leisurely march.

I wanted them here sooner.

They had not heard dom Gatán screaming.

But I knew something they would hear.

I took the rope of Haros's iron bell in my hand.

Rang it.

Saw the not-so-distant goblins break into a run toward Roncenay, as they always did when a warning bell was rung, to try to catch their dinner before it got away.

I ran, too.

My beautiful Dalgatha followed after.

I have since imagined my brother's face in the butcher's cart. I know they probably dumbed him, and when I picture it as it likely was, I see his bland eyes understanding nothing. I hear him low like a cow when the cart hits a bump.

But I hope it was not so.

I hope these biters had used up their dumbing brew.

I hope Migaéd went in his cart knowing what awaited him, trying to make jokes, then begging, then falling into silence when he realized that his captors did not care who his father was any more than I care about the parentage of bacon.

52

There is not much left to tell.

You know of course that Arvise held.

I could not approach it straightaway, surrounded by the Horde as it was.

I made instead for another of the Hounds, Durain, a week's march east.

I kept the dams with me alive, though this was hard. One dam had come from Espalle, and could not run because the goblins had cut the outer tendon of her leg, as I have told you they do to those under Hordelaw. Long walking tires one with this injury, so we took turns letting her lean on us. By the time we came to the gates of Durain, we were the very images of Dal-Gaata, all bones and hair. If only we had been blessed with her wings. My feet were never the same after the march from Espalle to Goltay to the Hounds. Oh, they work fine, but they are knobby, beaten things to look at.

I fought at the walls of Durain when they came to test that stronghold, but the biters found the rocks of that land too many and too hard to dig under with any speed. They also found Durain to be rich in onagers and ballistas, and we hurt them, and held them, and bled them on the rocks.

I was visited in Durain by the Infanta Mireya, who was on her way north, and west. With the death of King Luvain, the throne passed to his teenaged son, and Mireya, no longer queen consort of Gallardia, was wed by her uncle Kalith to King Hagli of Oustrim. I believe the Usurper wanted her as far from Ispanthia as he could send her.

We were lovers again at Durain, both in this waking world and in that of her creation. I told her of events in Roncenay, and she cried, but I could not cry any more. She asked if she could use me in a spell, one of consequence, to send the goblins off.

There is little I can refuse her.

After much preparation, including bathing me in rosemary and warm wine, she stabbed painfully yet without blood into my chest with a small blade. She cut from the muscle of my heart what she called a thorn of ice. Many who see too much in youth bear such a thorn. She did not wholly cut the coldness from me, as you well know, but she took the worst of it, which would have left me with nothing but bitterness and anger. There was grief in this sliver of my heart, much grief, which is potent in magic. Mireya took up a copper-headed arrow made from willow wood, and fletched it with feathers from Dalgatha's stall. She took a thread from the cloth of blue and gold, and with that, and with one of Amiel's white natal-day ribbons, she bound this piece of my heart to the arrow and loosed it into the clouds.

She stood in water then, and sang a song to Aevri, a Gunnish goddess of rain.

But also of snow.

The snows came early that year to the Hounds of Mour, very early, and drove the goblins south.

I was called back to Seveda, and then to Galimbur, in Ispanthia, and there I helped to train the next waves of raven knights, who were five hundred, with eleven hundred birds, and then four thousand, with seven thousand birds.

I went with this last wave, and commanded them as campamachur.

This last wave broke the goblins, and drove them even from the lands they had put under Hordelaw in the Threshers' War.

We burned them from the mounds near what was left of Orfay.

We lifted the siege of Gaspe, and then freed the coast cities of Cheraune, Sabouille, and, once again, Espalle.

Gallardia rang with birdscream, and Our Friends sued for peace, which we gave them, and which still holds. I think they fear we will bring the birds to their lands. I think they will not attack again until they find some remedy for the corvids, as they did for horses. I do not think they will find it. These birds do not fall to poison, and they do not sicken.

What they do, however, is bond to each other rather than to us, over time.

And they grow smarter.

Toward the end of the war, a colony of seventy corvids of the second wave drove its mistresses off and went up to the mountains to live alone. Some were hunted, but some are still there. The nearby villages are abandoned now. There is talk of clearing them out for good, but I do not know if this can be done without great cost.

For this reason, King Kalith, once the goblins were fled from the Crownlands, declared that all but breeding pairs must be put down at the age of two, and that the remainder will be kept only at fortresses and behind walls. The problem of their rebelliousness might have been solved, I feel, but there is another reason Kalith had the birds destroyed.

Think on it for a moment.

I was the only dam of my lanza with a dom in her name.

The raven knights were knights-communal, not knights of the blood. They were the daughters of farmers and miners and fishwives and carders and sailors. Many were unlettered, and cared nothing for religion, or cared too much for it. Did those who set themselves over others, and I include my own father here, want thousands of these vulgar dams to come home, in peacetime, with these murder-birds by the thousand? Cruel kings always fear revolt, and what would stop a revolt of the working folk with five thousand battle-hardened corvids and their dams as the tip of the spear?

I understood it.

But I did not obey.

I took Dalgatha with me to Fulvir. This was just before he left Gallardia, as we cleaned out the last hives near the coast.

Fulvir Lightningbinder was clearly unwell.

He was thinner than I had ever seen him, and, while we spoke, he pulled out white tufts from his very thin beard. I noticed more of these on the dirt floor of the house he stayed in, and on the table where he sat surrounded by documents I could not read. The magic he had spent in this war had done him harm. He told me a crab had spawned in his guts, but he had tricked it out of him and into an old boot, which he sewed shut and burned.

"I am sorry about your many losses," he said to me.

Among these was my mother, Nera dom Braga, who had recently died in a bodily sense though, as I have said, it seemed to me that her true self had slipped away to the Bride long before. At this time of fast military campaigns, my letters chased me, and news from home was rarely timely. The duke threw her a dignified but private funeral, only a year after having done the same for Amiel.

Braga, like the rest of the world, was weary of funerals.

Fulvir gave me all of Amiel's effects, and asked if there was anything he might do for me.

I said no at first, not wishing to try his health further.

But he looked at me with intensity, and in that look he communicated to me, without words, that he knew I had a want of him, and that it was right that I should ask. That he would be hurt if I refused him this.

I asked him to give me the cut of Dal-Gaata under the eye of a priestess, consecrating me to blood rather than milk, and then to tattoo my birds on me. "This will cost me the last of my beard," he said, "but I can no longer grow black hairs in it, so . . ." And here he shrugged, and gave me a kind look.

Kind for him, at least.

He seemed too tired for the word games of his strange country, and I was glad of it. I was tired, too. He prepared his kraken inks and his needles carved from the bones of corvids, and he sent his boy, Vlano, to summon a priestess of the Bride.

He did what I asked of him.

Bellu's tattoo was made only of memory and of my great love for him, but Dalgatha herself, as you know, was woven into hers, beak and feather. And there she slumbers still, as she has since my twenty-second year.

Now I must tell you of the business of Pol, and of the Pragmatist, and it is a sad thing to hear. It was this that estranged me from my father.

Prima-General Peya Dolón Milat had saved enough of the Western Army of the Illuminated Kingdom of Ispanthia to defend the walls of the Hounds of Mour, and to stop the Horde from spilling into our lands from the north. But to do this, she sacrificed many noble sons and daughters, and she did this by the tyranny of chance. She did not, as the dukes and barons and earls say she should have, command the lower orders to die, and let the kynd of noble birth volunteer if so they wished. She made them equals, and this is as dangerous to people like my father as giving his farmers corvids to take home would have been.

Also, he still had one son.

Migaéd, the Duke of Braga says, died with honor at the Haros Horn bridge.

But Pol would have saved him, and many more, by standing the whole army at the Haros Horn bridge. My father says Pol went to the Pragmatist and demanded she stand the army there. Pol dom Braga, though he had done no such thing, agreed that this was what happened.

It had not helped Peya Dolón Milat's case that she was revealed as a high priestess of Dal-Gaata.

Of course.

The woman with the mask of skeletal hands had been our prima-general.

I had not recognized her voice at Carrasque because she had only spoken to the high priests beneath her, and they had echoed her words.

This magnificent woman was relieved of her command, and drummed from the army. I spoke with Pol of this the last time I saw him. He now drank as much as Migaéd had, which made him melancholy, though not angry or prone to abuse.

And though Pol dom Braga was now Prima-general of the Western Army, and, in matters military, took orders only from the king, he was a shell of himself.

The lie that Father had cowed him into telling had poisoned his heart.

He had been made to destroy a better commander—for I have never seen Peya Dolón Milat's equal—for his own gain.

And because he was a decent man at heart, this sat poorly in him, and would have made him sick had he lived to middle age.

He did not.

Both he and the Pragmatist died by their own hands.

She fell on her sword, in the tradition of Old Kesh, her life short, her hand very, very bloody. And she had no funeral, because, as she was one of the Blessed Dead, this ceremony had already been held.

But Pol?

He took his life in the manner of those of Arvaresca.

He walked into the sea and let his veins out into it.

This devastated Father, of course, not only because he had lost his last male heir, but because he loved Pol. Pol was good, and competent, and strong in all but standing up to his family.

But this suicide also bewildered the duke.

Why had he killed himself in such a way? He was a good son of Sath, not a fish-smacker, as those who sit safely inland call the followers of two-tailed Mithrenor.

What Father did not know, and what I did not bother to tell him, was that Segunth-General Samera dom Vinescu, the niece of the Duke of Arvaresca, had been Pol's lover. And, it seems, his greatest and only true love.

It was in Arvaresca that he waded nude into the night-black sea, on a moon-bright Lūnday, in the summer.

On a rocky beach she had described to him as her favorite.

I have been to this place.

It is beautiful.

Epilogue

———— • ————

I returned home to the estate in Braga after all of this.

My chest still hurt from the cut that took my breasts, and from the tattoo.

I saw her, and set my pack down.

I walked up to her brown hill, called the Little Girl, and to her enclosure.

She still had guards, for though she was near her last grain of sand, and could barely keep her feet, and had gone blind, there are those who would pay a high price just to say they watched the death of the last natural horse in Ispanthia.

"Who goes there?" a young sword-and-buckler girl called, and another stood ready with a strung bow. A third soldier in my father's livery watched from a tower. I did not know them.

"I am Galva dom Braga, and I have come to see my horse."

At the sound of my voice, Idala raised her dear old head and filled her nostrils with my scent. She gave a weak nicker, then stepped from one front hoof to the next, her tail swishing. The flies were many for it was the end of Ashers, and that is their favorite month for swarming.

The guards both looked astonished, for I had a name now, and not just on my land.

"Dama," they both said, and dropped to a knee.

"Please," I said wearily, "I do not require that. A nod will do, and I will nod back."

They both nodded so deeply I thought they might have hurt their necks.

"Leave us, please," I said, "I am guard enough for her."

They ran off with the energy of youth, one shouting, "The lady! The lady of the house is come back from war!"

Idala had now pressed the whole of her body against the fence, as she might have done when I was a girl, so I could disobey my governess and ride her. She was of course too old for riding now. I just laid my head against her and wet her coat with glad tears.

I took in her good scent, and stroked her.

She nickered as a cat purrs, or as a faithful old dog wags his tail.

I wondered, in her long empty days up here, did she wish something, anything, would happen, as I had so often wished I could just stand on exactly this hill and do nothing? Had she missed my hand on her flank, or full of apple for her? Was I in her dreams as often as she was in mine?

I do not know.

I do not need to be loved as deeply as I love, and I do not need to speak of it.

All I knew was that she remembered me in this moment.

And one moment is all there ever is.

Someone was coming, a castellan in bright scarlet and gold.

"Dama, a thousand welcomes," she said. "A bath is being prepared for you, but first your father the duke wishes to see his daughter."

I closed my eyes again, my head still lying on Idala's side, and listened to her breathe.

I would take no breath of hers for granted.

I could hear frogs singing near the river.

I opened my eyes to see where the sun was setting beautifully over the hills of Braga.

The Eyes of Nerêne would appear soon.

Now the castellan said, quietly, not wishing to give offense, "Dama. Your father."

Idala nickered again.

Swished her tail.

"My father will wait."

HONORS

———— • ————

My editor, Lindsey Hall, and my agent, Michelle Brower, are deities, and not minor ones. There is no praise I can give them here that I have not intoned while burning incense at their respective shrines in my garden.

For matters military in this book, I conferred with the brilliant author and historian Christian Cameron. He generously lent me his hard-won experience reenacting classical and medieval warfare as we enjoyed a discussion about how goblins might overcome their "crisis of size" in massed armored combat against humans.

And thanks to a raven named Hoogin, who is a bit of a bastard, but no less loved by his hooman for it.

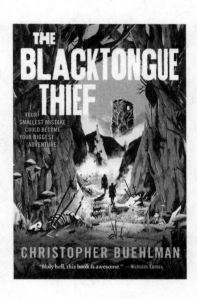

For more adventures in the world of

The Daughters' War

featuring Galva dom Braga,

check out

The Blacktongue Thief.

Now available from Tor.

1

The Forest of Orphans

I was about to die.

Worse, I was about to die with bastards.

Not that I was afraid to die, but maybe who you die with is important. It's important who's with you when you're born, after all. If everybody's wearing clean linen and silk and looking down at you squirming in your bassinet, you'll have a very different life than if the first thing you see when you open your eyes is a billy goat. I looked over at Pagran and decided he looked uncomfortably like a billy goat, what with his long head, long beard, and unlovely habit of chewing even when he had no food. Pagran used to be a farmer. Frella, just next to him in rusty ring mail, used to be his wife.

Now they were thieves, but not subtle thieves like me. I was trained in lock-picking, wall-scaling, fall-breaking, lie-weaving, voice-throwing, trap-making, trap-finding, and not a half-bad archer, fiddler, and knife-fighter besides. I also knew several dozen cantrips—small but useful magic. Alas, I owed the Takers Guild so much money for my training that I found myself squatting in the Forest of Orphans with these thick bastards, hoping to rob somebody the old-fashioned way. You know, threaten them with death.

It pays surprisingly well, being a highwayman. I was only a

month in with this group, and we had robbed wagons with too few guards, kidnapped stragglers off groups with too many, and even sold a merchant's boy to a group of crooked soldiers who were supposed to be chasing us. Killing never came easily to me, but I was willing to throw a few arrows to keep myself out of the shyte. It's the way the world was made. I had more than half what I needed for my Lammas payment to the Guild to keep them from making my tattoo worse. The tattoo was bad enough already, thank you very much.

So there I was, crouched in ambush, watching a figure walking alone down the White Road toward us. I had a bad feeling about our potential victim, and not just because she walked like nobody was going to hurt her, and not just because ravens were shouting in the trees. I had studied magic, you see, just a little, and this traveler had some. I wasn't sure what kind, but I felt it like a chill or that charge in the air before a storm that raises gooseflesh. Besides, what could one woman have on her that would be worth much split seven ways? And let's not forget our leader's double share, which would end up looking more like half.

I looked at Pagran and gave him a little shake of my head. He looked back at me, the whites of his eyes standing out because he'd mudded himself, all but his hands, which he left white to make handcanting easier. Pagran used a soldier's hand-cant he'd learned in the Goblin Wars, only half like the thieves' cant I learned at the Low School. His two missing fingers didn't help matters. When I shook my head at him, he canted at me. I thought he said to repair my purse, so I checked to see if money was falling out, but then I realized he was saying I should check to see if my balls were still attached. Right, he was impugning my courage.

I pointed at the stranger and made the sign for magicker, not confident they would know that one, and I'm not sure if Pagran did; he told me there was a magicker behind me, or at least that's what I thought at first, but he was actually telling me to put a

magicker in my arse. I looked away from the chief bastard I was
about to die with and back at the woman about to kill us.

Just a feeling I had.

To walk alone down the White Road through the Forest of Orphans, even on a pleasantly warm late-summer day in the month
of Ashers, you would have to be a magicker. If you weren't, you'd
have to be a drunk, a foreigner, a suicide, or some sloppy marriage of the three. This one had the look of a foreigner. She had
the olive tones and shaggy black hair-mop of a Spanth. With
good cheekbones, like they have there, a gift from the old empire,
and there was no telling her age. Youngish. Thirty? Built small
but hard. Those sleepy eyes could well be a killer's, and she was
dressed for fighting. She had a round shield on her back, a gorget
to save her throat a cutting, and if I didn't miss my guess, she
wore light chain mail under her shirt.

The blade on her belt was a bit shorter than most. Probably a
spadín, or bullnutter, which would definitely make her Ispanthian.
Their knights used to be the best horsemen in the world, back when
the world had horses. Now they relied on the sword-and-shield art
of Old Kesh, known as Calar Bajat, taught from the age of eight.
Spanths don't take threats well—I was all but sure if we moved, it
would be to kill, not intimidate. Would Pagran think it was worth
bothering? Money pouches hung on the stranger's belt, but would
Pagran order the attack just for that?

No.

He would be looking at the shield.

Now that the maybe-Spanth was closer, I could see the rosy
blush on the wood rim peeking over the stranger's shoulder
marking the shield as one of springwood. A tree we cut so fast
during the Goblin Wars it was damned-near extinct—the last
groves grew in Ispanthia, under the king's watchful eye, where
trespassing would get you a noose, and trespassing with a saw

would get you boiled. Thing about springwood is, if it's properly cured and cared for, it's known to stay living after it's been cut and heal itself. And as long as it's alive, it's hard to burn.

Pagran wanted that shield. As much as I hoped he'd move his cupped palm down like he was snuffing a candle, I knew he would jab his thumb forward and the attack would start. Three scarred brawlers stood beside Pagran, and I heard the other two archers shifting near me—one superstitious young squirt of piss named Naerfas, though we called him Nervous, kissing the grubby fox pendant carved from deer bone he wore on a cord around his neck; his pale, wall-eyed sister shifted in the leaves behind him. I never liked it that we worshipped the same god, they and I, but they were Galts like me, born with the black tongues that mark us all, and Galtish thieves fall in with the lord of foxes. We can't help ourselves.

I pulled an arrow with a bodkin point, good for slipping between links of chain mail, and nocked it on the string.

We watched our captain.

He watched the woman.

The ravens screamed.

Pagran jabbed the thumb.

What happened next happened fast.

I pulled and loosed first, feeling the good release of pressure in my fingers and the bite of the bowstring on my inner arm. I also had that warm-heart feeling when you know you've shot true—if you haven't handled a bow, I can't explain it. I heard the hiss of my fellows' arrows chasing mine. But the target was already moving——she crouched and turned so fast she seemed to disappear behind the shield. Never mind that it wasn't a large shield— she made herself small behind it.

Two arrows hit the springwood and bounced, and where my own arrow went I couldn't see. Then there went Pagran and his three brawlers, Pagran's big glaive up in the air like an oversized kitchen knife on a stick, Frella's broadsword behind her neck ready to chop, two others we'll just call Spear and Axe running behind. The Spanth would have to stand to meet their charge, and when she did, I would stick her through the knee.

Now things got confusing.

I saw motion in the trees across the road.

I thought three things at once:

A raven is breaking from the tree line.

The ravens have stopped shouting.

That raven is too big.

A raven the size of a stag rushed onto the road.

I made a little sound in my throat without meaning to.

It's an unforgettable thing, seeing your first war corvid.

Especially if it's not on your side.

It plucked Spear's foot out from under her, spilling her on her face, then began shredding her back with its hardened beak. I woke myself out of just watching it and thought I should probably nock another arrow, but the corvid was already moving at Axe, whose name was actually Jarril. I tell you this not because you'll know him long but because what happened to him was so awful I feel bad just calling him Axe.

Jarril sensed the bird coming up on his flank and stopped his run, wheeling to face it. He didn't have time to do more than raise his axe before the thing speared him with its beak where no man wants beak nor spear. His heavy chain mail hauberk measured to his knees, but those birds punch holes in skulls, so what was left of Jarril's parts under the chain mail didn't bear thinking about. He dropped, too badly hurt even to yell. Frella yelled, though. I glanced left and saw Pagran bent over, covered in blood, but I think it was Frella's—she was bleeding enough for both of them, spattering the ground from a vicious underarm cut that looked to run elbow to tit.

As the Spanth switched directions, I caught a glimpse of her naked sword, which was definitely a *spadín*. Sharp enough to stab, heavy enough to chop. A good sword, maybe the best short sword ever made. And she could use it. She moved like a blur now, stepping past Frella and booting her broadsword out of reach.

Spear, her back in tatters, was just getting up on all fours like a baby about to try walking. Beside me, Nervous cried out, "*Baith awayn*," Galtish for "death-bird," and dropped his bow and ran, his older sister turning tail with him, leaving me the only archer in the trees. I had no shot at the Spanth, who kept her shield raised toward me even as she lopped Spear's hand off below the wrist. Funny what the mind keeps close—I glimpsed the shield closer now and saw its central steel boss was wrought in the shape of a blowing storm cloud's face, like the kind on the edge of a map.

Pagran had taken up his dropped glaive and was trying to ward the corvid circling him. It bit at the glaive's head twice, easily avoiding Pagran's jab and not seeming to notice my missed arrow—these things don't move predictably, and at twenty paces, an arrow doesn't hit the instant it flies. Now the war bird grabbed the glaive-head and wrenched sideways so Pagran had to turn with it or lose the weapon. Pagran turned at just the instant the Spanth leapt fast and graceful as a panther and cut him deep just above the heel. Our leader dropped and curled up into a moaning ball. The fight on the road was over.

Shyte.

I nocked another arrow as Spanth and bird looked at me.

The bow wasn't going to be enough. I had a fine fighting knife on the front of my belt; in a tavern fight, it would turn a geezer inside out, but it was useless against chain. At my back, I had a nasty spike of a rondel dagger, good to punch through mail, but against *that* sword in *that* woman's hand, not to mention the fucking bird, it might as well have been a twig.

They moved closer.

I could outrun the Spanth, but not the bird.

I pissed myself a little, I'm not ashamed to tell you.

"Archer," she said in that *r*-tapping Ispanthian accent. "Come out and help your friends."

That they weren't really my friends wasn't a good enough reason to leave them maimed and wrecked on the White Road, nor was the fact that they deserved it. The Spanth had fished an arrow from the bloody tangle of shirt under her arm, matched its fletching to the arrows still in my side-quiver, and said, "Good shot."

She gave me the arrow back. She also gave me a mouthful of wine from her wineskin, good thick, black wine, probably from Ispanthia like she was. Pagran, grimacing and dragging himself to lean against a tree, got nothing. Frella, who seemed within two drops of bleeding herself unconscious, got nothing, even though she looked hopefully at the Spanth while I tied her arm off with one stocking and a stick. The wine was just for me, and only because I had shot true. That's a Spanth for you. The surest way to make one love you is to hurt them.

To speak of the injured, Jarril was still unconscious, which was good—let him sleep; no stander wants to wake up a squatter, especially one barely old enough to know the use of what he'd lost. Spear had picked up her lost hand and run into the forest like she knew a sewer-on of hands whose shop closed soon. I don't know where the bird went, or didn't at the time. It was like it disappeared. As for the Spanth, she was off down the road like nothing happened past a scratch and a bloody shirt, but something *had* happened.

Meeting that Ispanthian birder had just changed my fate.

ABOUT THE AUTHOR

CHRISTOPHER BUEHLMAN is an author, comedian, and screenwriter from St. Petersburg, Florida, whose previous works include *The Blacktongue Thief* and *Between Two Fires*. He spent his youth touring Renaissance festivals in the United States, performing his cult-favorite comedy act, *Christophe the Insultor*. As of this writing, he lives in Ohio with his aerialist wife, Jennifer; an ancient rescue dog named Duck; and two cats who just showed up, as they do.

christopherbuehlmanauthor.com
Twitter: @Buehlmeister
Instagram: @buehlmeister